A Dragon's Family Album II

Thea Harrison

A Dragon's Family Album II
Copyright © 2017 by Teddy Harrison LLC
ISBN-13: 978-1-947046-91-7
Print Edition

Cover design by Frauke Spanuth

Original publication in ebook and print format by Teddy Harrison, LLC

Dragos Goes to Washington, 2015
Pia Does Hollywood, 2015
Liam Takes Manhattan, 2015

This book contains _Dragos Goes to Washington_, _Pia Does Hollywood_, and _Liam Takes Manhattan_ (two novellas and a short story in the Elder Races series, previously published separately). All three stories focus on the Cuelebres, the First Family of the Wyr.

Dragos Goes to Washington

Dragos Cuelebre, Lord of the Wyr, needs to throw a party without maiming anyone.

That isn't exactly as easy as it might sound. After the destructive events of the last eighteen months, the Elder Races are heading to Washington D.C. to foster peace with humankind. Not known for his diplomacy skills, Dragos must rely on his mate Pia to help navigate a battlefield of words and polite smiles rather than claws. With Dragos's mating instinct riding close to the surface, his temper is more volatile than ever and the threat of violence hovers in the air.

Pia Does Hollywood

After making a diplomatic pact with humankind and the other leaders of the Elder Races, Pia Cuelebre, mate to Dragos Cuelebre, Lord of the Wyr, reluctantly heads to Hollywood to spend a week with the Light Fae Queen, Tatiana, before the busy Masque season hits New York in December. Dragos has never let the lack of an invitation stop him from doing anything he wanted. Unwilling to let his mate make the trip without him, he travels to southern California in secret to be with her. But when an ancient enemy launches a shattering assault against the Light Fae, Dragos and Pia must intercede. The destruction threatens to spread and strike a mortal blow against all of the magically gifted, both human and Elder Race alike.

Liam Takes Manhattan

Reeling from a deep loss, the magical prince of the Wyr, Dragos and Pia's son Liam Cuelebre, turns inward and withdrawn as he struggles to come to terms with who he is, along with the challenges that lie before him. Hoping to ease his heartache and offer comfort, a concerned Dragos and Pia offer him a gift, something he has desired for a long time. Liam's response has a ripple effect across all of New York. Soon miracles of all kinds start arriving just in time for Christmas, along with a visit from a mysterious person who gives Liam hope and a vision of his future.

Warning: This story contains a major spoiler from *Shadow's End* (book #9, released December 1st, 2015). If readers do not want to be spoiled, they should read the stories in order of their release dates.

Table of Contents

Dragos Goes to Washington

Thea Harrison

Chapter One

D RAGOS'S DENIM-CLAD, HARD thigh slid against Pia's as he sprawled back in his seat.

She wasn't wearing jeans. She wore shorts, and the small abrasive friction on her skin sent a frisson of sexual awareness thrumming through her body.

It was always that way between them. Heat shimmered whenever they were near each other, invisible yet intense. He burned up her world, until there was nothing else, nobody else but him.

The dragon would have been pleased to know it. Probably too pleased. He was demanding and possessive at the best of times, so she had no intention of telling him. He was in danger of becoming too complacent as it was.

The thought made her smile to herself. They must look very prosaic as they sat in the bleachers, just like the other parents, watching Liam practice on the football field with his teammates.

The kids were so adorable. Still in elementary school, their helmets were too big, their slim bodies undeveloped. Most were boys, but there were four intense girls on the field as well.

Other people were present and watching, several parents along with some of the other schoolchildren. Pia's heart constricted as her gaze lingered on one mother with two preschool children.

The mother handed a portable container of yogurt to the oldest, a delicate girl around three years old, who twirled to make the gauzy skirt of her sundress flare as she sucked on the mouthpiece of the container. She wore sparkly pink heart-shaped glasses. The smallest was a cheerful, fat baby in a stroller, wearing a floppy sunhat. Around six or seven months old, the baby gnawed busily on a teething biscuit.

The other parents were present to support the earnest players on the field, as they waited for football practice to end so they could take their children home.

She and Dragos were watching the practice to make sure they hadn't made a mistake in letting Liam join the team.

Since the school year had started, he'd had another growth spurt. It wasn't unusual for predator Wyr to grow at a faster rate than herbivores, but Liam's growth rate went far beyond that of a normal predator Wyr child. To minimize the strangeness of the situation for both Liam and his classmates, they had changed schools when they moved him up from first grade to fifth. The new elementary school was farther from home, but Pia didn't mind the extra driving time.

Sometimes she sent Eva ahead with the SUV, let

Liam shapeshift into his dragon form, and rode on his shoulders as he flew the route to school. It was exactly as they had once said to each other—as soon as Liam had grown too big to ride her Wyr form, she could ride his.

The morning flights were their little secret. She was certain Dragos wouldn't approve, but Liam was so nervous at having a passenger who couldn't fly on her own that he flew slowly and with extreme care. Also, between the two of them, they had serious cloaking skills, so she always felt quite safe.

Once they reached a prearranged spot where they met Eva, behind a sheltered copse of trees out of sight from the road, Liam landed and shifted back into a boy. Pia would take the wheel and drive sedately the rest of the route, just like a normal mom taking her normal child to a normal school. They often giggled about that together.

Liam appeared to have adjusted well to the change in schools, and was so excited about the thought of joining the football team, that Pia hadn't had the heart to say no, even though she knew, watching him, that he was much faster and more powerful than any other child on the field.

That didn't dim his transparent joy at playing the game. She noted with approval how carefully he paced himself to match the other children's abilities.

"I think he's going to be fine, don't you?" She turned to Dragos.

"He's fine, as long as he doesn't lose his temper. He could hurt one of those other kids all too easily."

Dragos's voice was logical and matter-of-fact. He sounded like he was discussing the relative strengths and weakness of one of his sentinels.

She frowned at him. He had stretched out his long frame so that he sprawled over three aisles, leaning his elbows on the row of bleachers behind them with his boots propped on the row below.

The afternoon was bright and hot for early autumn, but Dragos never wore sunglasses as protection from the sun. He only wore them when he wanted to put a barrier between him and other people. They sat some distance from everybody else, so he had folded his sunglasses and tucked them into the pocket of his shirt.

Dressed in a plain gray polo shirt and jeans, his silken black hair and dark bronze skin appeared more burnished than ever. His gold eyes gleamed thoughtfully under straight, lowered brows. The only part of him that did not tan was the pale, thin scar that slashed across one brow.

The dragon was a creature of fire, and Dragos never burned, no matter how long he stayed out in the sun, while Pia had to constantly wear sunscreen on her pale skin, along with a baseball cap and sunglasses.

Suppressing an envious sigh, she said, "I hear what you're saying, but I don't think it's fair to judge him on what-ifs. He's a good, careful boy. If he says he can handle it, I think we have to believe him. We can't give him the experience of a happy childhood, brief though it may be, if we're always limiting what he can have or do. He would only grow to resent us, and rightfully so."

Dragos remained silent for a long moment. As usual, it was impossible to tell what he was thinking by the impassive expression on his hard features. After a time, he said, "He's advancing faster than we thought he would."

Unsure of where he was going with that statement, she replied cautiously, "I know."

Her husband sucked a tooth, the set of his mouth slanting as if he tasted something sour. His gold gaze cut sideways to her. "He's not going to be a boy too much longer. Maybe we should let him have that dog he wanted."

"Let him…" Her voice trailed away as she stared at him. "But you've always been so adamant against getting a dog."

He lifted one massive shoulder, powerful muscles rippling underneath the smooth gray surface of his shirt. "Yeah, well, I've thought about it some more and changed my mind. It would have to be a puppy, from a breed that's known for being calm, so we can train it not to panic whenever it's around me, Liam, or any of the sentinels."

Dragos truly did not understand the desire to have a pet. It was, he said, like how he couldn't understand Liam's love for the toy bunny he'd had since he was a baby.

Now, Liam had declared he was much too old for the bunny, although he still insisted on keeping it in his closet. If Liam wasn't so adamant on keeping it close, Pia would have stolen it from him by now.

She loved that bunny, tattered ears and all. She loved remembering how Liam had chewed on those ears as he was teething.

"What about when Liam's old enough to leave home?" she asked, giving back to Dragos his strongest argument. "That's going to happen faster than we could have thought. What are we going do with the dog then?"

He shrugged again. "I don't know. We can cross that bridge when we come to it."

Dragos tried so hard. Parenting was new to them both, especially parenting such a magically gifted child. But somehow it was different for Dragos. Pia was younger. In a lot of ways, she was more adaptable.

Dragos was… Well, to be honest, she wasn't sure how old he was. She just knew he was very old.

But he worked hard at overcoming that obstacle. As frightening and ruthless as he could be, he was an amazing father.

Her gaze drifted back to the happy, fat little baby in the stroller, and her heart constricted again. A strange, unknown force built in her chest, until she couldn't contain it any longer.

"I want another one." The words burst out of her before she had time to consider them, spilling out of a deep well of need she had barely acknowledged in herself.

"You want another what?" Dragos asked.

This wasn't the time to talk about such an emotionally charged subject. She tried to bite the words back, but they tumbled out anyway. "A baby. I want another baby."

"You want…" He stopped and started again, speaking his words with care. "You want to talk about that here?"

The astonished look on his face was too much to take. The details of the sunny late afternoon blurred as tears filled her eyes. Quickly, before Dragos could see her expression, she whipped around to face forward.

"No, of course not." Her voice shook. "I shouldn't have said that. It just fell out of my mouth."

He straightened from his slouching position.

If he touched her or showed any sign of gentleness, she could feel the tears would turn into a geyser, and she really didn't want to burst into tears in public. She really didn't.

What the hell, self?

Bolting upright, she slid away from him as she stuttered, "F-football practice is almost over—why don't you wait here for Liam, and I'll meet you both at the car?"

"Pia," Dragos said, the gold of his eyes flaring to incandescence. Clearly he didn't like that suggestion in the slightest.

Telepathically, she said, *Dragos, it's all right. I'm having an emotional moment. I didn't expect it. It came out of nowhere, and I'm a little embarrassed by it. I'd like to take a few moments to compose myself. Please.*

After a moment, he growled, *We're still going to talk about this.*

Of course we will. Just not in public, okay? Backing farther away, she headed down the wide concrete steps.

As she walked away, she could feel his fierce energy boiling at her back. He hated it when she cried, and he would doubly hate the fact that she asked him to stay behind.

But he would do it, because she asked it of him. Because he loved her.

Aside from the small fact that he could be the most terrifying creature she'd ever laid eyes on, he was an excellent husband and mate as well as a father.

She reached the ground level. Just before she turned the corner, she looked back up at him.

No longer in a relaxed sprawl across the bleachers, he sat forward, bracing his elbows on his knees, his dark head angled toward her. He had put on his sunglasses, no doubt to hide the incandescence spilling from his gaze, and his jawline was tight. It made his hard, ruthless features look even fiercer.

Suddenly she noticed the incongruities in the scene.

It was a perfect suburban setting, on a perfect suburban day. Tame, emerald green fields rolled toward the town in the distance. The aged Adirondacks

Mountains provided a picturesque backdrop.

The coach's whistle sounded over shouts and calls from the children. They ran toward him and stood in the group looking up as he talked to them.

Pia had been wrong about nobody paying attention to them.

Nobody had been paying attention to her.

Everybody paid attention to Dragos. As she glanced around, she saw several other adults peek up at where he sat, some distance away from anyone else.

He was the anomaly in the perfect suburban setting. He was a lion sprawling in the midst of a flock of plump, clucking pigeons, a dark, brutally elegant Mephistopheles taking a silent stroll through a placid country church, and some instinctive part of them knew it. A couple of the women looked frankly covetous. One in particular looked covetous and a little afraid at the same time.

As that described to a *T* the beginning of her relationship with Dragos, she understood exactly how that woman felt.

Pia didn't like to think of the lonely days when she had been forced to steal from Dragos, leave her life behind and go on the run. Those early days before she and Dragos had developed feelings for each other were some of her most uncomfortable memories.

She had been so frightened of him. Then, when she had met him, she had been so frightened *and* attracted to him at the same time, she had been one confused cookie.

He had been just as confused—angry at the theft, mistrustful, and sexually drawn to her at the same time. When he had first found her and tackled her on the beach, he had fingered her hair while examining her with that laser-sharp focus of his, and his erection had pressed against her hip.

So, is that your long scaly reptilian tail, or are you just happy to see me?

It had been the first thing she had ever said to him.

How on earth did we find ourselves here, of all places? she wondered as she looked around.

All at once the humor in the perfect suburban scene struck her. As she walked toward their Cadillac Escalade, she found herself laughing and wiping her face at the same time.

ON THE TRIP home, Dragos remained silent.

Liam was full of excited chatter about his day, and the football practice, so he didn't notice anything odd.

However, Pia was excruciatingly aware of how quiet Dragos was. Nerves closed up her throat, and she responded to Liam just enough to keep the boy's momentum going, while she sneaked glances over at Dragos's hard, unrevealing profile.

He still wore his sunglasses. He wasn't hiding the expression in his eyes from her, was he? Biting her lip, she stared out her window at the passing scenery.

When they reached the house, they walked inside

through the kitchen. Dragos told Liam, "Get yourself a snack. Your mom and I have something we need to discuss, so we're going up to our suite. We'll see you at supper."

"Sure." Liam glanced from Dragos to her. "Can I go swimming in the lake?"

Even though they had an Olympic-sized, heated swimming pool, Liam preferred swimming in the lake because he liked to dive for fish. Clearing her throat, she said, "Go right ahead. Let Hugh know, so he can go with you."

"Okay!" He opened the door to the fridge and stuck his head inside.

Turning to leave, Pia walked through the ground floor and climbed the stairs on shaky legs. She knew exactly when Dragos left the kitchen to follow her, and not because she heard him. Even for such a big man, he could move in complete silence when he chose.

She could feel the heat of his Power when he came around the bottom of the stairs and drew closer. She picked up her pace until she was almost running down the hall. Leaving the suite door open, she looked around their untidy bedroom.

Clothes were strewn on the king-sized bed, suits for Dragos to wear, and her own outfits that she had laid along the edges of the bed and dropped various pieces of matching jewelry on top. None of her outfits were from Target, not for this trip.

She had forgotten that she was in the middle of

packing. Sighing, she walked into her closet and dragged her largest suitcase off the shelf. As she walked back into the bedroom, Dragos stood in the middle of the floor, his hands on his hips, watching her. He had finally taken his sunglasses off.

Not quite looking at his face, she asked, "How long are we going to be in D.C. again?"

"I'm waiting on confirmation now, but it might be eight days, depending on when the demesne leaders meet," he said. "You should count on at least a week."

Packing for a week's stay in D.C. wasn't like packing for a week on vacation. She did some quick mental calculations.

She wouldn't be attending any demesne meetings between the leaders, so she dismissed that as irrelevant. Seven days, with possibly three functions a day, meant she needed to think about taking as many as twenty-one outfits, and seven of those outfits needed to be evening wear. She might be able to get away with wearing the same outfit throughout the day, but she couldn't count on it.

One of those evening functions was a gathering she and Dragos were officially hosting at the Wyr residence in D.C., but other than designing and approving the menu with the Wyr event staff last week, thus far she hadn't had anything else to do except get ready for the trip.

Rubbing her eyes, she walked back into her closet, grabbed another suitcase and hauled it into the living room.

Other than his inky black eyebrows lowering in a frown, Dragos hadn't moved. He said, "Stop that."

"I can't, not if we're going to leave at eight in the morning." She dropped the second suitcase beside the first.

"It doesn't matter if we get a later start. Our first obligation isn't until tomorrow evening."

"The White House thing," she said. Sometimes her life boggled her mind. Once, never in a million years had she expected to attend anything at the White House as an invited guest.

"Yes, the White House thing. Come here." Quick as a cat, he snagged her arm and pulled her toward him.

She went over to him willingly enough, but somehow, as she got closer, her head grew heavier, until she was looking down at his feet.

Long, dark fingers curled underneath her chin and lifted her face gently.

At the same time, she lifted her gaze to meet his.

So many things had happened to them. Their relationship wasn't even two years old. Her pregnancy with Liam had happened as a result of their mating. Dragos didn't choose to become a father. He had adapted to it.

She told him, "Forget about my outburst of emotion at the school. I want you to know, whatever you say, it will be okay."

"Yes."

His response was so breathtakingly simple, at first it didn't register. When it did, her heart started to pound. She couldn't believe her ears.

"That's it—just yes?" she demanded, half laughing. "That's all you've got to say about it? I think I feel cheated out of a long, angsty conversation."

He raised one sleek eyebrow. "I didn't say that was all I had to say about it. I just thought I would cut to the chase." He studied her while he rubbed his thumb along the edge of her jaw. "You know as well as I do that the odds are against us. You also know that even if we do get pregnant, we would likely face many of the same challenges as we did the first time, and another baby isn't going to take Liam's place."

She shook her head. "Of course not. Liam is perfect just the way he is. Yes, it shook me at first to discover how fast he would mature, but I've dealt with that. Truly, that's okay."

"I believe you." He slid his hand away from her chin, his fingers caressing her neck. "And I believe that you want another baby for that baby's sake. Parenthood took us by surprise, and that's okay too. This time, though, I would like to make the choice."

"Exactly," she whispered. His touch began to drug her senses, soothing and arousing her at once, and she began to feel heavy for other reasons. Standing upright took more effort. Swaying forward, she spread her hands across the broad expanse of his chest.

He put his arms around her. "I think what we

should talk about is how we will deal with the disappointment if it doesn't happen. Because chances are, it won't."

"You never know," she told him. She peeked up at his face. "There's no real rhyme or reason to how difficult it is for the Elder Races to conceive and carry children to term. Some families end up having more than one child. Maybe your sperm is so mighty, you shoot magic bullets."

His intent expression splintered, and he burst out laughing. Almost as quickly, he sobered again and told her with a completely straight face, "Of course I do."

Then it was her turn to laugh. She threw her arms around him. "Yes, we might be disappointed, and we'll deal with that if it happens. At least you want to try."

"I do." His voice deepened. As he cupped the back of her neck in one hand, he cupped the curve of her ass with the other. "Trying to get pregnant is one of my very favorite things to do. We'll have to practice frequently, and with great enthusiasm."

She snickered, while happiness danced inside. Maybe they would have a small intense girl with Dragos's gold eyes. Maybe they might have another dragon. She adored her fierce, loveable dragons.

There was still so much she wanted to talk about, and so much they needed to consider. As Dragos had pointed out, another child might very well have the same capabilities as Liam and grow at the same accelerated pace.

And as they had just both said to each other, there was also a very real chance they might not be able to get pregnant again. Liam had come as a result of their original mating frenzy. They might not be so lucky this time.

If that were the case, she wanted to consider adopting a Wyr baby. She would actually be happy to adopt any kind of baby, but their household and lives were so predominantly Wyr, she didn't want any child of hers to feel like an outsider, as she had when growing up.

But that could be saved for a future conversation. For now, her thoughts fragmented as Dragos ran a light finger underneath the neckline of her tank top. The tiny friction of his callused skin against hers caused a shiver to run down her body.

They might have a lot to talk about, but she had a feeling that, for now, the time for serious talking was over.

"We have a while until supper," he murmured. His gaze had turned heavy-lidded and predatory. "Perhaps we should start practicing to get pregnant."

She licked her lips. For the Wyr, contraception was not something they needed to do externally, like taking birth control pills or using condoms. Instead, it was an internal, inborn trait. Once, she had needed to use an IUD before she had managed to change into her Wyr form and fully access her Wyr side. Now, trying to get pregnant was as simple and fundamental as telling their bodies to let go.

Just let go.

It was a heady experience, like releasing the throttle on a high-speed engine. The need she felt for him never eased. It was a driving, unrelenting force that drove the definition of her days and nights. She had never been so obsessed about anything or anyone before. It had marked her so indelibly, she couldn't imagine living without it, without him.

Attempting to sound nonchalant, she said, "Yeah, I think you could use some pointers on that."

His eyes narrowed, and he tightened a massive fist around the delicate shoulder strap of her tank top, a gesture at once both very gentle and unabashedly dominant. "I'll make you eat those words."

"You are very welcome to try," she whispered. Her attempt at cockiness had turned breathy and yearning. "Please, try very hard."

A smile lit his hard features. "Trust me, that will be entirely my pleasure."

Chapter Two

THERE WAS NOTHING new to their banter. It was a staple of their daily lives, and Dragos had come to rely on it like he relied on breathing.

He basked in the sparkle that lit her eyes as if it were sunlight. Her happiness warmed and sustained him. Her feminine scent fed a ferocity of hunger that never faded or mellowed, no matter how he tried to sate himself on her.

Even when he had forgotten her completely, he had still wanted her. The memory of his brief spell of amnesia tightened his mouth.

The construction accident that had caused his injury had happened a few months ago. It had only taken him a few days to recover almost all of his memory, but even when he could have flown away from everything in his life and never known the difference, he had been fascinated by her presence and ensnared by her perseverance.

Even then, when the dragon had been at his most feral and dangerous, he had mated with her. He still remembered the strange, possessive struggle he had felt—the odd jealousy toward himself, or at least the man he thought he had been, before his memories had come flooding back.

They were twice mated. Old as he was, he had never heard of such a thing before. Using his grip on her spaghetti strap, he pulled her closer and growled softly into her face, "You'll never be rid of me. Never, as long as either of us live."

The same miracle occurred, as it always did, yet it never failed to astonish him. An expression of peace softened her features. She gave him a soft smile as she whispered back, "Never."

She wanted him to hold on. She wanted him.

He took hold of her hips and pressed her against him, so she could feel his erection straining against his jeans. Her eyelids grew heavy, and her peaceful expression grew flushed. She licked her lips, moistening the plump, soft flesh so that he had to taste her.

Bending his head, he covered her mouth with his. She had taught him how to be gentle, a trait that did not come naturally to him, but he had savored learning it, because it brought out all the many, delicate facets to her pleasure that he loved to devour.

The catch of her breath. The way her violet eyes darkened. The trembling of her lips. She was cooler than he, but even so, when passion rose, it tinted her pale skin with a dusky rose, as if she was lit inside from an internal fire. He drank it all down, the evidence of what he did to her. He would have missed all of it if he had not learned the lessons that she had taught him.

He would always be a selfish man. The gentleness she had taught him brought him pleasure.

But despite himself and the enjoyment he took in her arousal, the combination of things that they had talked about—that he had thought about—were too potent a cocktail for him to resist.

The possibility of making her pregnant had him so hard, he almost spilled in his pants just considering it. And the memory of how recently he had mated with her—both times—put him in touch again with those earlier emotions.

There were so many times when he had almost lost her, and she had almost lost him. Back in the beginning, when he had such dominant, possessive feelings, she could have rejected him out of hand, and that would have been it. She'd had every reason to reject him. He had chased her, terrorized her, and yet she still ending up loving him. Mating with him.

The mating frenzy always lay in the back of his mind, rather like a place that he had left, just around a corner. All he had to do was turn back, step around the corner, and he was there again.

Crazy from wanting her.

Insanely jealous of everything that took her attention away from him.

And needing her so badly, it felt like a knife in the gut.

After passing his hand over her hair, he lifted his

head from the kiss. Tilting back her head, he pressed his lips against her vulnerable, beautiful neck.

He said against her fragile, petal soft skin, "You know how this goes, don't you?"

He had meant to take her back to the first time they had made love, when he had told her *I'm going to eat you until you scream.*

Instead, Pia grabbed his conversational gambit and skipped away with it.

"In a general sort of way," she whispered unsteadily. She ran her hands up his arms and dug her fingers into his shoulders. "You diddle here, I suck there. Or maybe you suck, and I diddle. Or both. Couple of pats, and ten or fifteen thrusts. 'Oh baby, you're so good, I can't take it,' *pow*, et cetera, 'let's go raid the fridge.'"

He felt his lips pull into a grin, and he made himself stop. Forcing some bite into his voice, he repeated, "*Ten* or *fifteen* thrusts?"

Her body shook as she started to giggle. "Well, you know, I never really counted them up. I'm usually too preoccupied with my own *pow* to keep track of what you're up to."

"Your *pow*," he growled. Her tank top was a pretty cherry red, one of his favorite colors. He eased the soft, thin material up her torso, and she lifted her arms so he could pull it over her head. "I think you're mistaken."

"About what?" Her laughing face emerged from underneath the top, hair disheveled and eyes sparkling.

She wasn't wearing a bra, and her breasts bounced free. Her beautiful, generously rounded breasts with the erect pink nipples. His mouth watered as he looked at them.

"That's *pows*. Plural," he told her. He cupped her breasts, massaging her nipples with his hands. His voice lowered into a growl. "You're too preoccupied with your multiple *pows* to keep track of what I'm doing. And I'm going to make you *pow* until you scream."

Her chuckle turned husky, and her eyes darkened with pleasure. She whispered, "Give it your best shot, big guy."

She hadn't called him that in months. A corner of his mouth lifted as he picked her up and dropped her on the bed.

Her eyes widened as she landed in a sprawl among suits and outfits. Her pale blond hair spilled over her face. Laughing, she started to roll away. "Clean clothes! Clean clothes!"

"Screw the clothes," he said. Bracing himself with one knee on the mattress of the bed, he picked handfuls of material up and tossed things aside.

Her laughter turned breathless. "I was going to pack all of that," she protested.

"Screw packing," he told her. As she tried to wiggle off the bed, he grabbed her by the hips and pulled her toward him.

"That's easy for you to say," she scolded, but there was no heat in her words. "You never pack your own stuff. Things just magically appear, clean and pressed, and ready whenever you need them."

She sat up, and her unsteady fingers caught the hem of his shirt and pulled it up his torso. He obliged her by pulling the shirt over his head and tossing it.

He picked up a handful of her hair, studying it. Pale gold strands gleamed in the late afternoon light. Obeying an impulse, he rubbed his face in the luxuriant mass. It felt like raw silk against his skin.

"Of course things magically appear when I need them," he told her. "That's why we have so much house staff."

She pulled back to glare at him. "Hey, I have news for you—all this prep work neatly laid out on the bed that you just threw on the floor? Your house staff had nothing to do with that. Your wife did."

His eyes narrowed on her. "We are both half naked on the bed, about to practice getting pregnant and giving each other multiple *pows*, and we're arguing about laundry?"

Her glare faded into uncertainty. After a pause, she said, "I guess so?"

Immensely satisfied, he nodded and pulled her up against his chest. They knelt there, skin against skin. Running his hands down the elegant curve of her back, he whispered against her mouth, "We are so married."

Her uncertainty vanished, to be replaced by happiness and heat, and a gleam of returning laughter. "Yes, we are, aren't we?"

"And twice mated," he whispered against her mouth. Her lips were plump and soft, and molded to his as he kissed her. "In case you were thinking about trying to get out of it."

"Well, technically, you're twice mated," she pointed out. "I didn't suffer amnesia, so I'm not."

His questing fingers found the fastening of her shorts. As he thumbed the fastening open and pulled the zipper down, he heard her breath catch.

"Don't give me semantics at a time like this, woman," he growled. "We're married, twice mated, and I'm about to get you barefoot and pregnant with my mighty sperm, so lie back and take your *pows*, will you?"

"*Ooh.*" Her sexy little murmur of anticipation shot straight to his crotch.

As he eased her back, she went willingly, and when she was prone, she lifted her hips for him to yank off her shorts and undies. He tossed them as well without looking where they landed.

All his attention was fixed on the gorgeous woman lying in front of him, spread out like a feast. She glowed gently in the late afternoon sunlight, and he realized she had stripped away her dampening glamour so that she lay utterly naked for his perusal. Because her Wyr form was so rare, and it would be so incredibly dangerous for her if it ever became public, she hid her true nature from everybody but him, Liam, and the most trusted of their associates.

Warmth spread through him, pleasure and some

kind of emotion he didn't know to put a name to. She gave him so much, before he ever thought to ask for it. She gave him everything.

He took off his jeans and lowered his body down over hers, watching her eyes darken as their nude bodies came flush against each other. When his rigid cock brushed against the graceful arc of her pelvic bone, he pulsed, and by the catch of her breath, he knew she had felt it too.

He reined in the impulse to cut loose. It was too soon, and she might not be ready for him. Growling under his breath from the buildup of internal pressure, he allowed himself to ravish her plump, inviting mouth, while with one hand, he roamed restlessly over the gentle curves of her body.

She twined her arms around him, kissing him with the same feverish need as he kissed her. The internal flames grew hotter, wilder. He cupped her breast, rolling her nipple between thumb and forefinger, while his tongue plunged deep into her mouth.

"You're burning up," she whispered against his lips.

"I'm on fire," he muttered.

Clear thinking disappeared in a haze of red. He bit down the soft skin of her slender throat, shifting his weight down so that he could suckle and tease her full breasts. Moaning, she moved restlessly under him. She held the back of his head with tense, shaking fingers, while the intoxicating scent of her arousal bloomed in the air.

His sucking bites brought the blood up under her glowing skin, so that the shadows of his touch clearly marked her.

He *loved* putting his mark on her. He *loved* that she fingered the places with evident enjoyment after they had made love. He knew her pleasure points, and he knew her limits, and the intimacy they had developed over the last eighteen months only enhanced their times together.

Moving farther down, he eased her long, slender legs over his shoulder so that she lay even more exposed to him. It was one of his favorite positions, and she shifted eagerly to accommodate him.

With the fingers from one hand, he parted the plump, pink petals of delicate flesh that surrounded her opening. Her earthy, rich scent filled his nostrils, and the sight of her was so exciting, his aching cock pulsed again.

Married. Twice mated.

Those human-inspired words were important, and immensely satisfying. They hinted at, but didn't touch the deepest essence of the truth between them.

But one word did. Finally, he put his mouth on her and growled against her most intimate flesh, "Mine."

DRAGOS'S GROWL VIBRATED through her lower body, and she started to shake in reaction. He was ferocity itself cloaked lightly in the guise of human flesh, but he had never once knowingly hurt her, and she knew he never would.

The sight of his dark head between her legs never failed to arouse her. Unerringly, his tongue found her clitoris, and he began to work her. The rhythm of his mouth pulsed throughout her body. It took over the beating of her heart and thudded in her veins.

Pleasure was a spiral, growing higher and tighter as he suckled her. When he worked two of his long, clever fingers into her tight passage, it blew through her like a supernova. He knew when the climax shook through her, and massaged her gently through it.

"My very first *pow* of the day," she whispered, stroking his hair.

His quick, gold gaze flashed to her. *Not your last one.* The sexy growl had taken over his mental voice. *Not by a long shot.*

Pure, languorous delight had her stretching in a luxurious, undulating roll. Thank the gods for a thorough, detail-oriented husband who was competitive even with himself.

All coherent thought blew out of her mind, as he suckled harder at her hypersensitive little nubbin of flesh. Having already peaked once, the pleasure came back stronger in a fierce wave of sensation. It cascaded along her nerve endings until the intensity became almost unbearable.

She couldn't keep her hips still. They rose up to meet his wise, relentless mouth. She tried to grab him by the hair, but he kept it too short, and the silken straight strands slipped through her fingers. The built-up tension was going to kill her if it didn't break soon. Her heart pounded like she was running, always running.

Always running toward him.

Her second climax slammed her back into the mattress. Flinging out her arms, she grabbed handfuls of the bedspread so that she could have something to hold on to in the maelstrom and coughed out a hoarse, breathless scream.

"Okay, okay," she panted, when she could formulate words. "Ease up now—Dragos, please…"

Not on your life, Mephistopheles purred in her head.

This time the peak of pleasure was immediate and savage, as if the dragon had taken her in his teeth and bodily shaken her.

Her legs clenched along his back, and another hoarse scream broke from her shaking lips. She swore at him, and her wicked lover laughed at her. Oh gods, everything inside of her was lit with fire, and he just wasn't… going… to… stop.

She tried to laugh too, but she had no breath. In desperation, she reached above her head for one of the pillows. She hit him over the head with it. "This isn't going to get me pregnant!"

At that, he rose up on his hands and knees and crawled up her body, at once so massive and liquid with power and grace, she lost what little breath she had.

From that angle, his chest looked immense, and his erection hung heavy and thick above his tight, round testicles. His gold eyes blazed with light and heat, and his expression had lost what little humanity it had.

"Oh, I'll get you pregnant," said the dragon in her face. "I'll fuck you until you can't walk."

"Promises," she tried to sneer. It came out more like a wheezing giggle. She hit him with the pillow again.

With a lightning fast move, he snatched it from her. Hooking an arm around her waist, he slid the pillow underneath her hips. She wiggled into place, tilting her pelvis up for him even as she reached for his cock with both greedy hands.

Together they positioned the broad, thick tip of his erection at her opening, and with one brutally efficient move, he thrust into her. He had lost his gentleness, and neither of them missed it. She was so slick and swollen, so sensitized, she came again as he ground himself against her. This time, she was past making any sound. She shook all over, and tears spilled out the corners of her eyes.

He destroyed her, completely. He tore away every barrier she had against the world, until he had conquered her at the core. Stripped and vulnerable, she did the only thing she could—she wound her arms around his neck and clung to him with everything she had.

He fucked her savagely, in short hard jabs, staring into her face with feral eyes. She was surrounded and filled with heat and pressure. He came in complete silence, thrust flush against her, his powerful body hard like iron. Her heavy eyelids drooped down as she felt him pulse inside of her.

As the pulsing slowed, she managed to unglue one of her shaking arms so that she could stroke his face, his hair. Gods, the love she felt for him was so intense sometimes it took her outside her own body.

Closing his incandescent eyes, he turned that feral, inhuman face into her caress and pressed his lips to her palm.

"How many thrusts was that?" His voice had gone guttural.

It took a moment for the meaning of his words to sink in. As wrecked she was, she burst out laughing weakly. "See? It's like I told you—I get so busy with my own *pows*, I don't pay any attention to what you're doing."

Breathing hard, he pulled out. Before she had a chance to make a disappointed face at his abrupt departure, he took her in a strong, unbreakable grip and flipped her so that she lay on her stomach, with the pillow still underneath her hips.

"Then don't mind me," he growled. "I'll carry on without you. Because I'm not done yet."

Not done yet.

The words ran down her spine in a liquid sizzle.

He had reached for the mating frenzy. Oh gods. It sent her muscles to shaking again, a deep, uncontrollable reaction.

Strength and energy flooded back into her limbs. She came up on her elbows. Tucking her knees in, she raised herself to him. It was one of the most primitive and enjoyable positions, and it satisfied something animalistic deep inside her.

Looking over her shoulder, she whispered, "I'm ready when you are, big guy. Let's go."

Like darkness eclipsing the moon, he came over her. It felt so right, so good as he penetrated her. It felt necessary. Closing her eyes, still shaking, she opened herself up and let her own mating frenzy come.

At one point, someone knocked on their door. When Dragos roared for them to go away, they did so, laughing. It was Eva.

Pia managed to pull herself together enough to say telepathically to the other woman, *Please feed Liam supper, and tell him Mommy and Daddy are very tired and will see him in the morning.*

Sure, I'll tell him, Eva said. *But you know he knows better, right?*

It's called polite fiction, Pia snapped. *That's what families tell each other, right?*

From down the hall, Eva laughed harder.

Pia was tempted to snap at her again, but just then Dragos did something to her to make her eyes roll back in her head, and the rest of the world faded away.

The rest of the evening and the night passed in a heated blaze, until finally exhaustion lay an inexorable claim on her and she fell asleep, draped bonelessly across Dragos's chest with his fists clenched in her hair.

Sometime later, much later, awareness brought her out of a deep sleep.

The first thing she noticed was that she was alone in bed, and every muscle ached. It was a good, deep ache that came from utter satiation.

Warm sunlight lay across one arm and shoulder.

Sunlight?

She managed to get one eye unglued. It revealed another bright, sunny day outside the nearby open balcony windows.

Sunlight never poured through those windows until late morning and early afternoon. They were so, so, so late, and she hadn't even packed yet.

"Oh, no," she muttered. It came out more like a croak.

"I've got to tell you, lover. That's not the most rousing thing you've ever said after a full night of lovemaking."

Dragos's voice came from across the room. With an immense effort, she turned her head and let it plop back down on the pillow.

Dragos lounged on a nearby chaise. He had showered although he hadn't shaved, and he had dressed in jeans while remaining shirtless and barefoot. Out of the corner of her eye, she saw that he had the bedroom TV turned to a news channel with the volume muted. He had his laptop on his lap, but as she watched, he set it aside.

"It's so late, and I haven't finished packing," she said. "What am I saying? I haven't even managed to sit upright yet."

One side of the bed dipped as he knelt on it to reach over to her. Pressing his mouth to her shoulder blade, he said against her skin, "I packed."

At the touch of his lips on her sensitive skin, heat coiled low in her body. She pushed it away, eyeing Dragos warily. "What do you mean, you packed?"

"I mean, I packed. Everything. My stuff, and your stuff." Running a flattened hand down her back, he nodded to the doorway.

She rose up on her elbows to look. All the suitcases were stacked by the door. "Makeup?"

"You had everything set on the counter."

She could hardly believe it. Dragos was the least domesticated person she knew. Scanning the floor, she found that it was bare of all the clothes he had tossed the previous night. "Toiletries?"

"Yes, your toiletries too. Don't look so skeptical. I watch what you do every day. I know what you use." His voice had deepened again as he kept stroking her back.

He loved to touch her, but late as it was, they couldn't afford to get lost in the mating frenzy again, or they would be two days late getting to D.C. and miss the White House thing altogether.

She reached for his hand, meaning to push him away, but somehow her fingers got tangled up with his instead.

Pulling his hand to her, she rested her cheek on it and mumbled, "Jewelry."

Even as she said it, she knew it was the most stupid of all her questions. Knowing him, he had probably packed the jewelry first, and only after he had gone through the case thoroughly in order to admire the jewels inside.

"You had your travel jewelry case out and ready to go," he said. "What do you think?"

The wide back of his strong hand had a sprinkle of black hair across the veins. She pressed a kiss to it. "I believe you."

"Everything is taken care of. All you need to do is shower and eat some breakfast, and then we can leave," he told her.

The thought of eating made her feel unexpectedly queasy. She pushed it aside as she sat up. "I'm not hungry, but I'd like a cup of coffee."

He nodded over to the chaise. When she looked in that direction again, she saw the tray sitting on the side table.

"You thought of everything." She smiled at him.

He didn't smile back. His gaze had dropped to her bare breasts, and his expression had turned sharp and predatory. Cupping a breast, he stroked his thumb along a darkened suck bruise.

He said in a low voice, "You know, we can always change our minds and go a day later."

The heat that shimmered between them felt volcanic and beat underneath her skin with a tribal tempo. Reaching hard for self-control, she covered his hand with hers. "And miss the kick off event for the summit at the White House tonight? Much as I would like to, you know we can't."

His black brows lowered. "We can."

The thing about the mating frenzy was, it had no sense. She smiled at him sidelong. "Or we can make love again on the plane."

His returning smile was quick and gleamed with anticipation. "Yes. Hurry up."

Chapter Three

P IA SHOWERED QUICKLY, and after wrapping the towel around her torso, she went into her closet to choose casual clothes for traveling—a comfortable pair of jeans, sandals, and a fitted, button-down shirt.

When she took the outfit to the bedroom, she found Dragos and their luggage already gone. While she had been in the shower, he had taken the news channel off mute and indulged in one of his bad habits by leaving the TV on.

It drove her crazy when he did that. She was congenitally incapable of leaving the room without turning off the TV first. As she shimmied into her jeans, she looked around the bedroom for the remote.

The news segment changed.

"Following on the heels of the terrible massacre in the Northern California Nightkind demesne this spring, Washingon DC is stepping up security for a week-long summit between the Elder Races demesne leaders and the human leaders of the U.S. government," the news caster said with a bright smile. "The recent upsurge in Elder Races violence over the last few years has made more than one human official pause, but the mass murder of ninety seven people—most of them human—by one of the Nightkind demesne's senior member of government has created a crisis for the Elder Races leaders that just won't go away. Federal lawmakers at the highest levels are calling for accountability for their actions, and all the Elder Races have responded…."

Which wasn't quite true.

Pia paused to glare at the image of the oblivious newscaster.

The truth was, federal lawmakers had called on the Nightkind demesne for an accounting of the multiple homicides, and the Nightkind regent Xavier del Torro had responded by suggesting the summit.

While the slaughter of so many people was quite horrible, over the last few months, her horror over what happened had turned to worried exasperation for how so many of the news channels insisted on making such a terrible crime sound like the Elder Races were murdering humans instead of reporting the more accurate story.

Which was that a dangerous, powerful, psychopathic Vampyre named Justine had killed all her attendants rather than risk letting any of them talk to her enemy, the Nightkind King Julian Regillus, and possibly leak valuable information about her whereabouts and activities. Or that Julian had personally seen that justice was done by hunting Justine down and killed both her and her co-conspirators.

But once the news had gotten skewed that way, other stories were highlighted—the damages in Chicago, when Dark Fae assassins attempted to kill Niniane, damages to various properties in San Francisco when Carling was a fugitive, and even the property damage in New York, caused by Dragos's roar when she had stolen his penny, were discussed over and over.

Skewed or not, they had a point.

They had a serious point.

And after watching the shit-storm that had hit the media in the aftermath of the Nightkind massacre, all the Elder Races leaders had agreed to the summit.

"But why does every newscast have to be an 'us against them' mentality?" she muttered. "Isn't it time to start talking about solutions instead of endlessly going over the problems?"

Finally locating the remote in the tousled bed covers, she clicked the off button forcefully, and peaceful silence flooded the room.

Yanking a hairbrush through her damp hair, she did a quick tour of the bathroom and their closets, but Dragos had been as good as his word and had packed everything.

In her closet, she paused at her jewelry cabinet. Then, after a few moment's thought, she opened it up.

What were the chances they might get pregnant? For the Elder Races in general, the chances were slim, and while they had been joking about Dragos's mighty sperm, the truth was both his nature and hers were so uniquely magical that there was no way to know how that might skew the general statistics.

Last time, she had gotten violently sick after they had been together only a few days. After all the brouhaha of finding out that she was indeed pregnant, and then her getting kidnapped, chased and almost killed, Dragos had given her a diamond pendant, infused with an anti-nausea spell, that had become her lifeline through the rest of her pregnancy. Predator and herbivore genes don't play together nicely in the womb.

And what if they were extraordinarily lucky and it did happen again?

After a few moments of hesitation, she pulled out the necklace, tucked it in its own velvet box, and thrust it into her purse. Better safe than sorry, because oh my lord, that nausea would make her one sorry Wyr, and if there was any week she couldn't afford to be sick, it was this one.

Satisfied with her decision, she went downstairs where Dragos was waiting.

They had given Liam options—he could either go to D.C. with them, or he could remain home to stay in school. Excited at joining the football team, he had elected to remain at home, although Dragos had kept him out of school that morning so they could say good-bye to him.

"No unexpected growth spurts," she told him, as

she finger-combed his dark blond hair and straightened his collar. "And no sleepovers, so don't even bother asking. I want to Skype with you every day, so you can tell me how your day went."

"Yeah, okay." Grinning, he ducked away from her ministrations. "Come on, Mom, quit it. I'm all straightened up."

"Fine, I'm stopping. I love you." She grabbed his shoulders and hauled him close for a hug. Despite his complaints, his arms closed around her readily.

"Love you too," he muttered against her shoulder.

Public or open displays of affection had begun to embarrass him, which she thought was so darn adorable, because he still wanted to be hugged, but he had started to act sneaky about seeking out the hugs. She squeezed him tighter before she let him go.

"We're going to talk about a surprise for you when we get back," Dragos told him.

The puppy. She grinned. With everything that had happened, she had forgotten about that.

Liam perked up. "Oh yeah? What is it?"

"If I told you, it wouldn't be a surprise, would it?" Smiling, Dragos hooked a long arm around the boy and hauled him in for another hug. "Be good. And be careful out on the field."

At that, Liam sobered somewhat. He promised, "I will."

Over the summer, Dragos had commissioned an airstrip to be built just a mile away from their estate, so after their good-byes were said, the trip to the jet was short.

The security detail and house staff who would be covering the D.C. trip had already left around ten P.M. the night before, Dragos told her. That included Eva, while Hugh would remain at home to watch over Liam's welfare.

She did a happy little wiggle in her seat. That also meant they would have the cabin of the jet to themselves. More sexy times were a-comin'.

In short order, they boarded the jet. The preflight checks had already been completed, so as soon as Andrew, one of the co-pilots, had tucked the luggage into compartments, closed the door and stepped into the cockpit, the engines began a high, powerful whine.

Pia had tucked her purse into a closet and thrown herself on one of the couches. As the plane started to roll down the runway, Dragos turned to her.

The somewhat terse expression he had worn around other people vaporized. He looked feral again, and clenched.

Her body knew that look. All he had to do was look at her like that, and reach for her with those two big hands, and desire flooded her in a liquid gush of heat.

Either the airplane's acceleration, or Dragos's insistence, pushed her back against the leather cushions. She melted back willingly, while he tore her clothes off. Material ripped—she didn't know what got damaged—she might have to pull out one of her suitcases to get something else she could wear later....

Then all coherent thought vanished. After he finished tearing off her clothes, he stripped rapidly. The slanting light from the windows striped his powerful body. Heavy muscles rippled under dark bronze skin as he came between her legs. The hunger that gripped her was insatiable. She ran her hands over sleek dark hair that covered the wide expanse of his chest.

When he fingered her and found her ready, he entered her without ceremony. Gasping, she threw her head back at the intimate invasion. Thunderous noise vibrated all around her, accompanied by Dragos's low, animalistic growl reverberating against her torso.

Sometimes she didn't know herself when she was with him. She lost that much control. They coupled wildly together. The couch wasn't big enough to contain them.

At one point, Dragos pulled them to the floor so that he could hold her ankles wide as he fucked her. She reached for anything she could grasp to brace herself at the onslaught, while the unbearably intense pleasure shot straight into the stratosphere, higher than the plane, until she shattered with waves of completion.

The rest of the trip disappeared in a passionate haze. He took her again, standing and bracing himself with one hand against the wall, while she wrapped her legs around his waist and hung on for dear life.

Then the air pressure changed slightly, signifying

descent, and the pilot's voice came over the intercom. "Just wanted to check in to let you know we'll be landing in twenty minutes. It's a beautiful day in D.C. and unseasonably warm for October, a balmy 78 degrees and sunny. Looks like you'll have good weather for the week."

Dragos lifted his head from her shoulder. They were both sweaty, and his black hair looked even darker when damp.

She had started out the day by oversleeping, and now she had no strength in any of her limbs. She whimpered, "We have to be presentable in twenty minutes?"

Bending his head, he kissed her swiftly. "They'll remain in the cockpit until I tell them they can come out."

That would mean they would be sitting in the cockpit, knowing full well what she and Dragos had been doing in the cabin.

But who was she trying to fool? Their sex scent drenched the cabin air. Even if she rushed, as soon as the pilots stepped out, they would know what had happened.

She rubbed her face. Her skin felt abraded by his whiskers. "Fine," she muttered. "I get to shower first." If they were anywhere but on the plane, she would suggest that they shower together, but the shower, while luxurious for a jet, was too small to accommodate both of them at once.

He cocked an eyebrow at her. "Are you sure about that? You don't look capable of moving."

He sounded immensely satisfied with that fact. Bah, men. She tried to scowl at him. "Yes, I'm sure. You're faster in the shower than I am. I have more hair to get clean than you do. Besides, if we're not done by the time we land, I would rather they scented you, not me."

His satisfied expression disappeared, and he scowled back. Clearly he didn't like that thought either, even though their pilots were a mated pair of male Wyr ravens and wouldn't be interested in Pia anyway. The dragon was an exceedingly jealous creature.

Standing, he scooped her into his arms and carried her to the back, into the luxurious bathroom. Then he set her on her feet again. He told her, "I'll get your clothes. Hurry up."

She chuckled and stepped into the cubicle for her second shower of the day. Hot water ran soothingly over tired, abused muscles, and while she wanted to stand there and soak it in, she forced herself to lather and rinse quickly, so Dragos could have the shower while she dressed.

The jet's descent steepened as she inspected her clothes. It was her panties that had torn. She didn't have time to dig out a new pair, so she stuffed them in the trash bin and dressed without them, then dug out a travel hairbrush from the stock of toiletries in the bathroom and yanked it through her wet, unruly hair. That was going to have to do. The pilots would still know what happened, of course, but it wouldn't feel as exposing as having them scent it on her skin.

As she sat on the toilet to slip on her sandals, Dragos sluiced off within two minutes, dressed with quick economy and ran long fingers through his wet hair. Then together, they stepped back into the cabin and took their seats just moments before the plane touched ground.

As they braked hard, she felt queasy again, but over the last several hours, she had put out an extraordinary amount of energy. She was sore, achy and tired, and she'd only drunk a cup of coffee for breakfast.

It was far too soon to feel any effects from possibly getting pregnant. The queasiness had to be a touch of motion sickness on an empty stomach.

Still, she couldn't stop herself from placing a hand low on her flat stomach and turning her focus inward to search for a tiny, new precious spark of life.

There was none.

She knew that. She *knew* better, but still a leaden disappointment pulled her down.

Dragos's massive, powerful hand came over hers, warming her. He pressed gently. She opened her eyes. She didn't know what her face revealed, but his expression gentled. He put an arm around her, and she leaned against him, resting her head on his shoulder as the plane taxied to a stop.

The cabin door opened. Dragos's gentle expression faded as both pilots stepped out, but they kept their faces polite and indifferent, and exercised terrific discretion. As his mate pulled pieces of luggage from the bins, Andrew said cheerfully, "Welcome to D.C. I hope you have a great stay."

"Good flight," said Dragos. "For a plane."

"Thanks," Andrew said, with a quick, understanding grin.

When Dragos stood, Pia did too.

Her slight queasiness took a sharp turn for the worst.

"Excuse me," she muttered, bolting for the back of the plane and the bathroom, and slamming the door shut.

She barely made it to the toilet before she vomited violently. Clutching the rim, her eyes streamed as her body heaved.

What. The. Hell.

"Pia." Dragos's sharp voice sounded just outside. The door rattled. "You locked the door. What's wrong?"

He hated locked doors between them. But this time he was going to have to suck it up. There were times when you just needed a moment or two by yourself, damn it.

"Nothing," she gritted out. "I'll be out in a sec."

She grabbed a tissue and mopped her damp face while she waited to see if she was done.

After an uncertain lurch, her stomach seemed to let go of its hissy fit and settled. She climbed to her feet on shaky legs, flushed and compulsively checked again for a life spark.

Nothing. Of course, nothing. Looking grimly at her reflection in the mirror, she shook her head at her own foolishness.

The door rattled again. Dragos said telepathically, *If you don't open this door in the next sixty seconds, I'll come through it.*

She disappeared for TWO SECONDS, and suddenly he was completely determined to break the plane. She rolled her eyes.

No reason to break down the door, she said testily. *I had a touch of tummy trouble and had to use the toilet. I'm just washing up now.*

All of that was true, if a bit ambiguous. She washed her hands and face, and opened a travel packet of mouthwash to rinse out her mouth.

The door rattling stopped.

"Okay," said Dragos. "Do you want your purse?"

Now that she had given him some reassurance, he sounded perfectly mild and sane. Ha. She had gotten to know him all too well, and that perfectly mild and sane voice of his wasn't going to fool her ever again.

She told him, "Yes, please."

Now that the plane was on the tarmac and no longer moving—and her stomach was completely empty—she actually did feel better.

She squared her shoulders and opened the bathroom door. Dragos leaned against one of the seats, waiting for her. He handed the purse to her, while his sharp gaze ran down her body.

She sighed. "It's not a big deal. The only thing I've put in my stomach since lunch yesterday was coffee."

"We'll rectify that as soon as we get to the Wyr residence." Straightening, he nodded to the two pilots waiting near the head of the plane. "Have a good week. I'll be in touch when we finalize a time for our departure."

"Very good, sir," said Andrew.

Putting that rather ignominious arrival firmly behind her, she followed Dragos as he strolled down the aisle, and they deplaned into the sunny day.

EVA WAS WAITING for them in the pickup lane, leaning against an armored black Cadillac Escalade.

Preferring to drive, Dragos took the keys and slid into the driver's seat, while Pia got into the front passenger seat and Eva climbed in the back.

Actually, he would have preferred to avoid the heavy D.C. traffic altogether and fly directly to the Wyr residence, but there were strict no-fly laws over the area where they were headed. His cloaking ability was excellent, but he wasn't altogether sure what the human sensors could detect of his presence.

Prosaic radar technology couldn't detect him when he was cloaking, but he would bet the Cuelebre Enterprises gross profit for the year on humans having more than just mechanical sensors guarding their capital. If he were a human in charge of guarding such an important city, he would have squadrons of witches laying protection spells over the city like gigantic, invisible spiderwebs.

In any case, now was also not the time to break human laws and get everybody riled over something relatively unimportant. Not when humankind had become so nervous at the perceived damages caused by the Elder Races in the last two years.

The Elder Races held a lot of magical Power, the most in the world. But humans held a lot of power of a different sort, in terms of sheer numbers in their population, along with military strength. Over the last few centuries, their numbers had multiplied so that their presence virtually covered the earth.

Continuing to coexist was the very best thing that could happen for everybody concerned. If they couldn't achieve amicable coexistence…

Well, the world would get a lot colder and meaner, if that happened. The possibility troubled him more than he liked to say.

So he throttled back his impatience, put the car in drive and pulled sedately away from the curb and into traffic.

"Tell the house staff to prepare a meal for when we arrive," he said over his shoulder.

"You got it," Eva said.

He glanced in the rearview mirror. Eva's dark head

bent as she texted on her phone. His attention turned to Pia, who watched out her window curiously. She had never been to D.C. before and was hoping to find time to sightsee some of the famous landmarks.

Did she look more pale than usual? She wasn't wearing makeup. Frowning, he asked telepathically, *You okay?*

She turned to smile at him. *Don't fuss. I'm fine.*

Fuss? He wasn't a fusser. Scowling, he accelerated aggressively to cut across traffic to the fast lane. After he finished the maneuver, he told her shortly, *You look pale.*

I always look pale. She placed a slender hand on his thigh. Her light touch managed to dispel his bad temper. She said aloud, "How long do we have until we need to leave for the White House this evening?"

"Couple hours." He glanced at her again, noting the dark shadows underneath her eyes. "There's time to eat, and you can take a nap before we go."

She shook her head at him with a smile filled with feminine pity. "Oh no, I can't. I've never been to the White House before. I'm not going to just throw on clean clothes and run my fingers through my hair, like you do."

One corner of his mouth lifted. "Well, at some point I am going to shave too."

Her eyes danced. "So am I. Plus, there's the makeup, and I'm going to put my hair up, so I need to allow time for hot curlers."

He loved it when she pinned her hair up in big, fat curls, in a style reminiscent of sixties chic. It bared the elegant line of her neck, which he loved to explore with his mouth.

Later, when it was time to take her hair down, he would be the one to do the small chore, letting the curls fall loose one by one as he kissed the nape of her neck and slid down the zipper of her dress.

In an instant, he was hard again and aching for her. It was hard to believe he had just taken her so many times on the plane. The mating frenzy was the only thing that had ever held him in its grip for long.

If it was a prison, it was one he didn't want to leave. He relished its claws digging underneath his skin, driving him to extremes. But they wouldn't have time now to succumb to another bout of lovemaking until after the evening's function.

Forcing the urge back, he exhaled on a long, steady breath.

Pia's fingers tightened on his thigh. Either she could scent the mating pheromones, or she had been eyeing his crotch.

He looked at her. Her gaze was down and directed sidelong. She *was* watching his crotch, and a rose blush stained her pale cheeks. She raised her gaze to look at him, biting her lip. She was as much a prisoner of the mating frenzy as he was, and she looked helpless with desire.

Fuck yeah.

He loved it when she was helpless and begging for his touch.

"Jeebus," muttered Eva. "Gettin' hot in here." She rolled down her window and fresh air swirled into the car. "Thank the gods we're almost there."

In short order, he turned onto Massachusetts Avenue. He glanced at Pia again as they approached the section known as Embassy Row, where embassies, diplomatic missions and other representations were concentrated.

The mansions grew larger, older and grander, and the rows of town houses became more spacious. When he pulled through the front gates of the Wyr mansion, her eyes went round.

She whispered, "This is ours?"

"This is ours," he said. "It's been the Wyr residence in Washington since 1895."

As he parked under the portico, the front doors opened, and two uniformed Wyr came briskly down the steps. Behind them, the gates quietly closed.

She unbuckled her seat belt as she craned to stare up at the roof, as she asked, "How many rooms does it have?

"Eight bedrooms, twelve bathrooms, all modernized," he told her. "Dining room, library, etc."

"Along with a very modern home theater, bowling alley, and a wine cellar in the basement," Eva added. "There's a black, wrought iron railing that runs up both sides of a marble staircase. You should see the house lit up at night. I took a walk through the neighborhood last night. It's all white marble and light. Very elegant."

The property also had tunnels that ran several blocks underground in different directions before leading to innocuous-looking openings—street gutters, the sewage system with manholes and the like.

Nobody would trap the Wyr in this place. In case of emergency, those who couldn't fly could still get out. He always liked to lay contingency plans, especially in places that could be less than friendly.

Once the car had stopped moving, Eva stepped out to direct the guards to the rear of the SUV, where they pulled out luggage and carried it inside.

Pia squinted at Dragos. "You almost never come here. It's got to be a hellacious expense to keep this property maintained."

He inclined his head in agreement. "When I come here, I come as a world-class power. Washington does well to remember that. One of the ways I choose to remind them of that fact is by maintaining this residence."

"I guess keeping one of the town houses wouldn't carry the same impact, even though I'm sure they're just as spectacular in their own way."

"Also, I would never share walls with someone else. It leaves one too vulnerable." He stepped out of the vehicle, his sharp predator's gaze studying the surroundings outside the black iron fence.

He knew watchers were stationed on the residence,

both human and other. He might have carefully cultivated allies among humankind, but he had no true friends here. Humankind was as wary of the dragon as any of the Elder Races. Many of the watchers would be unfriendly, but none of them were visible.

As he surveyed the area, the guards returned to make sure they had carried everything in. One of the guards, a tall, young handsome male, offered his hand to Pia with a smile.

Violent jealousy shot through Dragos's body. Moving fast, he rounded the front of the vehicle and bared his teeth to hiss at the other male before Pia had a chance to grasp the outstretched fingers.

The guard recoiled, turning pale, and Pia's expression stilled as her gaze turned sharp and wary. She paused, one slender, sandaled foot already on the pavement.

Dragos drew in a deep breath and fought for calm. He said quietly to the guard, "Go into the house."

Bowing his head, the guard fled, leaving him and Pia to regard each other.

Finally he said, "You don't have to say anything. I know that was excessive."

"Are you all right?" she asked.

Was he? She had asked the question in all seriousness, so he pondered that. "I think so. Just—be careful not to get too close to any other males right now. I'm too much in touch with the mating frenzy."

"I understand," she said quietly. "Perhaps we

should have considered things more carefully and put off trying to get pregnant until after this week was over."

"We made an emotional decision. There's nothing wrong with that. We'll make it work. I'll talk to Bayne, so he can warn the staff, and I'll be on guard when we're in public." He bent slightly to extend his hand to her. "Welcome to one of your homes, Lady Cuelebre."

The concept that she was part owner of the magnificent mansion clearly startled her, as her eyes widened even further, but she swallowed down whatever she might have said and placed her hand in his.

As he supported Pia's exit out of the Cadillac and straightened, he swept the scene once more.

Then Dragos Cuelebre, Lord of the Wyr, escorted his mate and wife into his Washington abode.

Chapter Four

ONCE INSIDE THE elegant foyer, Pia told Eva, "I want to see everything."

Dragos tightened his hold on her fingers. "You need to eat."

"Ten minutes," she said. "I want the quick tour. I'll be right back."

Her eyes were sparkling and the color was back in her cheeks, so he reluctantly let her go. As the two women jogged up the marble staircase, Bayne appeared, strolling down the hallway.

As the sentinel on duty for the week, Bayne was in charge of all the security details. Instead of wearing his usual jeans, T-shirts and boots, which was the standard attire for all the sentinels at home in New York, the gryphon wore a dark gray suit, with a black shirt and tie. The outfit emphasized his large, tall build and short, tawny hair.

Dragos ran a critical eye down the other man's figure. The excellent cut of the suit hid his weapons well. Bayne would be an acceptable addition at any except the most formal functions, and for those, he had brought a black tux.

As the other man reached him, Bayne gave him a nod in greeting. "One of my guards wanted me to apologize to you on his behalf," the sentinel said, tucking his hands into the pockets of his tailored slacks. "Rather profusely, I might add. So, he's really, really sorry. What'd he do?"

Dragos blew out a breath through his nostrils in an inaudible growl. It was going to be a long damn week. "He almost took Pia's hand to help her out of the car, and I snapped at him."

"I see." Bayne's tone was neutral.

He shot the other man a look from under lowered brows. "Pia can get out of a fucking car by herself. She doesn't need males tripping over themselves to touch her. And in any case, I'll be the one to escort her. At all times. You hear?"

Eyebrows raised, Bayne pursed his lips and nodded. "Yeah, I hear you. I also sense there may be some, ah, underlying tension?"

Dragos strode for the dining room, and the other man fell into step beside him. Telepathically, he said, *Keep this confidential. We're trying to get pregnant, and yes, it's brought back the mating frenzy. So, make sure everyone is warned.*

Bayne began to smile. *And I was worried this week might be boring. I'll prep everybody to take care.*

In the dining room, the long, gleaming antique mahogany table had two place settings at one end.

They lived very informal lives in upstate New York. Even when they stayed in the penthouse in Cuelebre Tower in the city, more often than not, Pia chose to cook. But here in D.C., appearances were everything. He noted in approval the gleaming polished silver, formal bone china, and heavy cream linen napkins.

Two uniformed staff were in the process of bringing dishes of hot food from the kitchen—pasta with sundried tomatoes and garlic in olive oil, a kale and artichoke salad, ham sliced fresh off the bone, roasted potatoes, and green beans garnished with something colorful and red, perhaps peppers.

"Set another place at the table," Dragos told one of the servers. She nodded and headed back into the kitchen. He said to Bayne, "Stay and eat with us. I want to hear about everything you've been doing and what you've heard so far."

"You got it."

"Make that two places," Pia said to the server from the doorway.

She and Eva walked into the room. At first Pia made as if she might go to hug Bayne—something that was perfectly acceptable under normal circumstances, and very like her usual affectionate style with all the sentinels—but Bayne took a nimble step back, and she jerked to a halt and redirected to pick up one of the place settings.

It could have been ridiculously uncomfortable, but dancing around sensitive mating issues was such a way of life for the Wyr, everybody adjusted smoothly, and within a few moments, they were all seated at the table and serving themselves from the silver platters of food.

"Almost all the other demesne leaders have already arrived," Bayne said, as he piled ham onto his plate.

All of the U.S. demesnes had committed to coming—Tatiana, the Light Fae Queen from Los Angeles; Ferion, the new Elven High Lord from Charleston; Dragos, as leader of the Wyr in New York; Isalynn, the head of the witches demesne from Kentucky; Jered, the current head of the Demonkind assembly from Houston; and even Niniane, the Dark Fae Queen from Chicago, had come, despite the fact she spent most of her time in the Dark Fae Other land Adriyel.

Dragos shook his head. All the demesne leaders convening in D.C. at the same time. That had never happened before. To anyone paying attention, that alone said more than anything else about how seriously the demesnes were taking the human unrest.

He asked, "Did Julian come?"

"Well no, not Julian," Bayne replied. "He's still adamant about taking a year off from the political scene, but Xavier is here as Julian's regent and Nightkind representative. From what I heard, Isalynn was arriving sometime this afternoon too. Tric— Niniane and Tiago got in last night. Eva and I had dinner with them."

"We ordered a shit ton of pepperoni pizza," Eva

said with a grin.

Pia's tired face lit with pleasure. "I'm looking forward to seeing them. How are they?"

"Really well," Bayne told her. "All the fresh air and potential assassinations in Adriyel are good for Tiago. And Niniane looks happy. Only it's more than that."

"How so?" Dragos asked curiously.

Bayne frowned. "I guess I want to say she looks settled."

"I'm so glad to hear that." Pia smiled.

Bayne helped himself to another slice of ham. "The not-so-good news—there are thousands of people outside the White House, protesting the summit. It's been all over the news. There's been backlash to that as well on the news, with some idiots on the other side putting down the human protestors for being close-minded bigots." The sentinel looked at Pia. "I know you were looking forward to doing some sightseeing if you could find any time, but I don't recommend it. Not for this trip."

The pleasure died from Pia's expression, and she looked tired and pale again. She said quietly, "Of course, that doesn't matter."

It did matter. Anything that drained the smile from her face mattered. Likely nothing dangerous would happen in any potential sightseeing jaunt, but there could be some unpleasantness.

Dragos told her, "Civil unrest happens all the time. Look at the sixties and the Vietnam War. We'll come back when things have calmed down. I'll take you sightseeing, myself."

"I'd like that," she told him. Abruptly, she set aside her cutlery. "If you'll excuse me, I'm going to go get ready for the evening."

He glanced at her plate. She had eaten perhaps half of her food.

Eva stood too. "I'll check to see if they're done ironing your dress and bring it up if they are."

"Thanks." Pia stepped close to press a kiss to Dragos's forehead. She told him telepathically, *I ate what I wanted. Don't fuss.*

I don't fuss, goddammit, he growled.

She chuckled in his head as she walked away. *Keep telling that to yourself, my love.*

He glowered at her plate but didn't say another word.

BREATHING EVENLY, PIA climbed the magnificent staircase on shaky legs.

She managed to get to the bathroom in the master suite before she began vomiting. Rushing to the bathroom sink instead of the toilet, because it was closer, she made it just in time before her body struggled to rid itself of everything she had just put in her stomach.

When she finished, she hung her head, panting, while she tried to think.

I'm usually healthy as a horse.

(Heh. Horse.)

Why would I start vomiting now, of all times? The timing seems awfully suspicious.

Putting her hand to her abdomen, she sent her awareness into her body again. This time, she wasn't distracted by the jet landing. She didn't do just a cursory scan, but went deeper than she had before.

No life spark. Not even the tiniest, newest hint of a little spark.

Unwelcome tears filled her eyes. It was stupid to feel such disappointment. She needed to find some emotional ballast. They had barely started to try to get pregnant. Realistically, it could take them a very long time before they either got pregnant or eventually gave up.

And she was okay with that, except… why was she shaky and vomiting all of a sudden?

"I can't get sick," she muttered. "Not now of all times. This trip is too important."

Let alone the question of what was making her sick. She didn't get colds. She rarely, if ever, caught the flu, and anyway, flu season had barely started. It was far more likely for her to break a limb than to come down with some kind of illness.

Glancing at the sink had her stomach lurching again. Quickly, she turned on the water to rinse out the basin as footsteps sounded in the bedroom.

Eva called out, "I've got the dress."

"Great," she said, watching the water swirl away the last of the evidence.

"You sound so thrilled," Eva told her dryly. Pia hadn't had a chance to close the bathroom door, so Eva appeared in the open doorway. The other woman frowned. "What's wrong?"

Straightening from the sink, Pia wiped her mouth as she replied, "What makes you think something is wrong?"

Eva's dark gaze narrowed. "Because you look like shit."

Eva was utterly devoted to her, and completely loyal, except, Pia knew, in one instance. If Eva thought something was wrong with Pia, she would tell Dragos in a heartbeat, despite what Pia might have to say about it.

And if Dragos thought for a second that something was wrong, he would overreact.

He would ditch the summit and fly her personally back to New York to a whole herd of Wyr doctors.

But despite what Dragos said about civil unrest, this summit was too important to ditch. People protested any number of things, yet this issue had infiltrated the U.S. government. Lawmakers were unsettled, and that meant the worst kind of trouble if they couldn't repair relations.

Pia wasn't exactly sure what the worst kind of trouble would mean. Her imagination wasn't good enough to create something that seemed dire enough, but she did know the schism would be felt across the entire country and throughout the rest of the world.

What was a bout or two of vomiting in the face of something like that?

So she lied. Well, misdirected, at least.

"I was up all night having crazy monkey sex," she said, turning away from Eva's too-sharp gaze to go back into the bedroom and look for her purse. "Of course I look like shit. That's why I'm going to slap ten pounds of makeup on my face after I take a shower."

Eva shrugged. "Okay. Need anything else?"

"No thanks, you can go get ready now." With Dragos so touchy at the moment, Eva was not just Pia's main bodyguard but probably her only one for the week.

"See you downstairs."

As Eva left, she pulled the door closed behind her, and Pia was finally alone. She located her purse, tucked on a table by a large vase filled with purple irises and yellow roses, and pulled out the jewelry box holding the diamond pendant.

She didn't have time to be sick, but luckily she had something she could do about it for now. If she was still sick later, she would see a doctor next week when she got home.

As soon as she settled the necklace into place around her neck, she felt better, steadier. That'd do.

With a renewed sense of purpose, she turned back to the bathroom. Now it was time to get down to business.

By the time Dragos stepped into the bedroom, she had showered, dried her hair and rolled it up in hot curlers, and she sat at a vanity in a royal blue dressing gown as she applied the requisite ten pounds of makeup.

He walked over to her, hooked a finger into the neckline of the dressing gown and pulled it away so that he could kiss her naked shoulder. At the touch of his warm, firm mouth on her skin, a shiver of pleasure ran down her spine, and she leaned back against his thighs with a throaty murmur. She had to make a conscious effort to remember to hold on to her mascara wand as he cupped her breast.

"We don't have time for that," she told him.

"I know," he murmured, massaging her through the thin silk. "I just couldn't help touching you." He grew still. Then his hand left her breast to touch the diamond pendant as his gold gaze met hers in the mirror.

"No, I'm not," she told him in answer to the question he hadn't asked. "I'm wearing it as a precaution. You know, just in case. I don't want to throw up unexpectedly on anybody important this week. Besides, it's pretty."

His hard mouth pulled into a slow, sexy smile. He touched the diamond where it dangled just above the hollow of her breasts. "It is pretty, isn't it? And it's resting in one of my very favorite places in the world. I look forward to taking it off later this evening."

She looked forward to taking it off later too, but for an entirely different reason. Hopefully by that point the strange bout of sickness would have passed and she would be back to normal.

Careful not to mess either her curling hair or her makeup, she turned her head to press a kiss against his forearm. His hand traveled up to caress the line of her neck. "What are you wearing this evening?"

"I decided to go ultrachic," she said. "So I settled on the black sheath Dior."

"Perfect." He smiled. "I'd better shower and shave, and we'll leave in a half an hour. Is that enough time for you to finish getting ready?"

"Absolutely. All I have to do is take the curlers out, pin up my hair and slip on the dress." She turned her attention back to her reflection and picked up her lipstick. Around the *O* she made with her lips, she said, "Oh, and also do this."

He murmured, "You look good enough to eat."

"Don't you dare," she warned. "You'll mess everything up, and I don't have time to pull this off again."

Laughing, he stripped off his clothes. "Oh, I dare. I'll just eat you later."

Nude, he walked into the bathroom, and she had to pause to admire his powerful, lithe body. His sleek, heavy muscles rippled under dark bronze skin. In his human form or as a dragon, he was the most magnificent male she had ever laid eyes on.

She raised her voice. "I thought you should know. You make me so stinking happy. Especially when you walk around nude."

His laughter sounded. "You make me pretty stinking happy too, lover."

The sound of the shower started, and only then was she able to turn back to what she was doing.

She triple-checked her makeup for any flaws. By the time she had shimmied into the floor length, strapless gown and slipped on her high heeled Pradas, Dragos's electric travel shaver was buzzing in the bathroom. Quickly she pulled out the hot curlers and ran her fingers through her hair. Large shining curls tumbled around her bare shoulders.

The buzz of his razor stopped. She looked over her shoulder and found him frozen in the doorway. Except for a towel slung around his hips, he was still nude, and he stared at her with such naked hunger, it scorched her skin.

"I think I've changed my mind. I'll leave my hair down tonight." Tilting her head, she gave him a small smile. "Our half an hour is almost up. Shouldn't you be hurrying?"

His sharp intake of breath was audible across the room. She laughed. Stepping back, he slammed the bathroom door.

When he stepped out again, five minutes later, he was fully dressed. Fastening the last of her diamond stud earrings into her ear, she turned away from the vanity mirror and lost the ability to breathe.

She could almost get used to the daily reality of how he impacted her—almost—until she saw him like this, his massive, powerful body clothed in a severe, elegant black tux. The formal clothes did nothing to make him appear domesticated. If anything, they highlighted his handsome, brutal features, jet-black hair and piercing gold eyes, while the pristine white shirt brought out the richness of his dark bronze skin.

His soft growl reached her from across the room. "Don't look at me like that, or we really won't get out the door this evening."

She jerked away and scooped up her beaded black clutch. Like a gawky yearling with too much leg, she didn't feel quite in control of all her limbs. "Right," she muttered. "Out the door."

Quiet masculine laughter ghosted through her head. He strode for the door and held it open for her. Somehow she managed to walk out of the bedroom.

They made it downstairs with three minutes to spare of the half hour Dragos had given her. Bayne and Eva were waiting for them in the front hall. Bayne wore a tux too, his evening clothes heightening his rugged good looks, while Eva wore a silk gray Chanel suit.

"I still think you should have worn the red dress," Pia told her. "You look stunning in red."

The other woman shook her head with a grin. "Not

while I'm on duty. The heels that go with that red dress are killer to run in."

"All set?" Bayne asked Dragos.

Dragos nodded, and the four of them stepped outside where two black SUVs and a limousine were waiting. Security rode in the SUVs in front and behind, while Bayne and Eva climbed with Dragos and Pia into the back of the limo.

At first their conversation remained lighthearted. Dragos took her hand, lacing long, dark fingers through hers while Bayne and Eva engaged in good-natured banter.

As Pia listened to them with a smile, she absentmindedly scratched at her right thigh. She hadn't taken the time to smooth lotion on after her shower, and her skin felt dry and itchy.

The banter died away, and Bayne and Eva fell silent as they drew close to the White House.

Protestors lined the street, carrying signs and shouting at the passing cavalcades. Pia watched the faces scroll past. The armored limo blocked the sounds so she couldn't hear what the protestors were shouting, but their expressions were angry and distorted.

Disquieted and scratching at her itchy thigh again, she glanced at Dragos. He was wearing his inscrutable expression, his gold gaze flat and unrevealing as he watched the protestors. It was one of his most dangerous expressions.

What was he thinking when he looked into the

crowd? With a single pass over their heads and a rain of dragon fire, he could so easily destroy all of them.

Of course, that would mean he would also destroy the entire Wyr way of life as well.

She crooned in his head, *Honey, I'm so proud of you for not killing anybody.*

His gaze flashed to hers, and that flat, assessing expression vanished as he laughed. Squeezing her fingers, he told her, *Week's not over yet.*

More seriously, she asked, *What do you think it will take to smooth things over?*

His sexy mouth took on a cynical twist. *Money, business and political agreements, the promise of less violence from the Elder Races, and a lot of charm. Other people, like you, are going to have to supply the charm.*

She nodded, unsurprised by that last bit. *If I'm expected to dance with anybody, you're going to have to suck in your mating crazy. You up for that?*

The laughter left his face, and he gave her a sour look. *I'll make it happen. Thankfully, most human male politicians are old, ugly, lying fuckers. They're not your type at all.*

It was her turn to burst out laughing. *Well, you are old, and you do lie better than anybody I know.*

His eyelids lowered. *That might be so, but you don't think I'm an ugly fucker.*

True. She laughed harder. He might deal with politics out of necessity, but at his core, Dragos was far too rude to make an excellent politician. His real skills lay in cutthroat business.

And war. He was unsettlingly talented at going to war.

That thought sobered her up fast. Still absently rubbing at her thigh, she looked out the window again as they passed through the security gates and approached the White House.

When the limo rolled to a smooth stop, Bayne and Eva exited first, then Dragos.

Camera lights flashed nearby, blinding her as she took Dragos's hand and stepped out of the vehicle. She looked up at the famous, imposing building. At first she had thought she would be very nervous at facing the evening, but to her surprise, a sense of calm anticipation settled over her.

Time to go make nice with the old, ugly, lying fuckers.

Giving Dragos a sidelong, laughing glance, she tucked her arm into the crook of his sleeve and walked with him into the building.

Chapter Five

THE WHITE HOUSE function was a large, lavish affair. Ostensibly, the purpose was to give all the senators and members of Congress a chance to mingle with the seven demesne leaders as a way to break the ice for the week's meetings and help to dissipate interracial tensions.

Dragos had never told anyone what happened in his head when he entered such large gatherings, not even Pia.

The dragon rose up to look out of his human-seeming eyes.

Look at all the fragile humans, dressed in their finery and girded with a sense of their own importance. He took note of the glittering jewels that the women wore, the beat of pulses at soft, vulnerable throats, and the way eyes slid away from meeting his.

The president and first lady greeted them with polite smiles. Silently, Dragos inclined his head when spoken to, while the dragon thought, I play at your games because it suits me to do so.

President Ben Johnson was a hardy, athletic-looking male in his early sixties, and universally acknowledged to be a charming, poised and intelligent man, but when he spoke, all the dragon heard was bleating, like a sheep. His mate responded with a quick reply, and both president and first lady smiled at her.

The pleasantries over, the dragon and his mate moved away to greet other dignitaries. Frailer, self-important prey.

They came face-to-face with an enemy—the vice president of the United States, Sarah Colton—and her husband, Victor. The vice president was much younger than the president. A graduate of the Yale law program, she was a clever, trim brunette in her early forties with a photogenic smile.

Dragos whispered in Pia's head, *Vice President Colton is one of the ones responsible for stirring up much of the anti-Elder Races sentiment in Congress. Along with Senator Jackson, she spearheaded setting up the federal subcommittee that is investigating alleged abuses of power by the Elder Races.*

Pia's smile never wavered. She had grown used to their internal dialogue at such functions. *Senator Jackson—he's the one who lost his son in a boating accident earlier this year, right? I remember when news of his death was splashed all over the news.*

Yes.

This time no pleasantries, no matter how insincere, were exchanged. Neither the vice president nor her husband offered to shake hands. Dragos did not deign to offer his either, and with a quick glance sideways at him, Pia took her cue and remained self-contained and composed.

"Mr. Cuelebre," said the vice president, watching him with cold eyes.

It was clearly meant as an insult. The proper form of address was Lord Cuelebre. The dragon almost smiled at such pettiness, but that might involve showing too many teeth. And if he did that, he did not think he would be able to resist a little snap at the air in front of her.

Instead, he deliberately dropped the vice president's honorific as he replied, "Mrs. Colton."

As he spoke, he took in an instinctive breath to mark the scent of his enemy… but caught no scent from either her or her husband.

No scent at all.

Instead, all he scented was a faint chemical stink.

Realization raged through his veins. Both the vice president and her husband had sprayed themselves with KO Odorless Odor Eliminator.

Deer hunters used the spray to mask their scent. So did Wyr criminals.

This time the dragon did show far too many teeth. He put his hand over Pia's as it rested in the crook of his arm, tightening his grip so hard he felt rather than heard her silent intake of breath.

He told the humans, "I look forward to having you for dinner tomorrow."

"We will be there." The vice president inclined her

head in brusque acknowledgment.

Her manner clearly said they would be present because they had no other choice. As he spun Pia away from the other couple, she wiggled her fingers protestingly under the weight of his iron grip.

You look forward to "having them for dinner"? she asked silently, giving him a rebuking look. *Really, Dragos, you're not even trying.* She paused to search his expression. *What's wrong?*

He said, *Did you catch their scents?*

No, I— She paused thoughtfully and her eyebrows drew together. *No. Not at all.*

That's because they were masking them. He glanced down into her confused face and explained, *Human hunters mask their scents when they're hunting prey. And Wyr criminals mask their scents to avoid detection.*

Her confusion darkened into disquiet. *That's… why would they do that?*

That is a very good question, and one I would like to get answered. He switched mental gears and looked for Bayne. The sentinel stood several feet away, talking to Eva. Dragos said to him, *The vice president and her husband are masking their scents. I want to know why. And I want to know if there's anybody else present who is doing the same.*

Other than a quick flicker in his hard hazel eyes, the sentinel's expression never changed. Calmly, Bayne said, *I'm on it.*

Since the White House was protected by the Secret Service, protocol for the evening's function kept their individual security detail to two, one for each dignitary, which meant Bayne's investigative capabilities were limited.

Take Eva with you, said Dragos. *I'm staying with Pia.*

You got it, said Bayne. The sentinel touched Eva's arm and the pair headed off, disappearing into the crowd.

Pia rubbed her thigh as she looked over the crowd. She said in a quiet voice meant for his ears alone, "Suddenly I don't feel like making nice or dancing with anybody."

Distracted from larger questions, he frowned as he looked down at her leg. "Why do you keep rubbing yourself like that?"

"You don't have to make it sound so dirty." She scowled back at him. "My leg itches. Do you have to take note of every little thing I do? I mean every tiny, little thing, Dragos."

"Yes," he said simply. "When I look at you, even when things are going to hell, somehow everything is all right."

"*Ooh.*" Her grumpy gaze melted into warm affection. She stepped close to slip an arm around his waist and lean against him. A corner of her mouth tugged upward. "Even when you're about to put yourself in the doghouse over something, somehow you manage to say just the right thing and get yourself right out again."

He put an arm around her, hugging her briefly as

he pressed his mouth to her forehead. "That's because you love me, and you hate having me in that doghouse anyway."

"True…" Then she focused behind him, and her expression transformed into such complete delight, he didn't have to turn around to know who was standing behind him. "Niniane!"

Pulling out from underneath his arm, Pia dashed forward. He pivoted on one heel to watch her throw her arms around a petite, curvy Dark Fae woman. Niniane, or "Tricks" as she had been known when she had lived among the Wyr in New York, threw her arms around Pia with an excited squeal.

Before Dragos killed her uncle Urien, who had murdered her family and usurped the Dark Fae throne, Niniane had been a refugee at Wyr Court, living under Dragos's protection.

Back then, she had been prone to very high heels, sparkly sequins, marabou, and other kinds of feminine froufrou, but he saw that her tastes had sobered or matured somewhat since she had assumed the Dark Fae throne, at least in public.

Tonight, she wore richly embroidered Dark Fae traditional attire in subtle hues—a long, high-necked tunic over slim trousers. She had also let her black hair grow longer and wore it in an elegant chignon that bared long, pointed ears and emphasized her large, dark gray eyes. Nestled atop her sleek hairdo, she wore a thin circlet of sparkling sapphires, and she looked every inch a pocket-sized Dark Fae royal.

He was very pleased. Tricks did indeed look like she was thriving. For the first time since entering the White House, Dragos's smile turned real. He looked his attention from the embracing women to the enormous Wyr male who stood just behind them. Tiago also wore traditional Dark Fae attire, although his outfit was entirely black.

Bayne was right, Dragos thought, amused. All the fresh air and prospect of political assassinations did seem to be doing Tiago a lot of good. He looked both relaxed and deadly, his dark skin burnished from good health and sunshine.

Once one of Dragos's seven sentinels, Tiago had mated with Niniane and went with her to live in the Dark Fae Other land of Adriyel.

When the Earth had been formed, time and space had buckled, creating Other lands that were connected to Earth and sometimes to each other by dimensional crossover passageways. They were magic-rich places where combustible technologies didn't work, and where time ran differently.

Sometimes the Other lands were immense, as Adriyel was, and they had several crossover passageways to other places. Sometimes the Other lands were mere pockets of space that led nowhere. Adriyel had significant time slippage from the rest of Earth, so that visits from Niniane and Tiago were rare.

As Tiago had been a Wyr sentinel and she had

become the Dark Fae Queen, according to Dark Fae law, they could never marry, but neither had found that to be an impediment to their happiness. Tiago lived at her court as her chief of security.

In the face of Dragos's friends, the dragon's feral internal voice retreated into the shadows. Stepping forward, he clasped hands with Tiago. "You look good."

"You too," Tiago said, eyeing him with a glance of approval. He turned to survey the large, crowded ballroom. "Good job not killing anybody."

"That's what Pia said," Dragos told him. "Night's not over yet."

"I kinda love it more than I ever thought I could, especially since I have such bad memories from when my family was killed," Niniane was saying to Pia. "But I can't get over missing junk food. I have it shipped all the way to Adriyel. Reese's Peanut Butter Cups. Doritos. Skittles, and oh my gods, Hostess Ho Hos. And you just can't ship fresh-baked pepperoni pizza. I've been gorging on it ever since we arrived."

Dragos met Tiago's black gaze. "You ship Hostess Ho Hos to Adriyel?"

"They're very important," said Tiago impassively. "In fact, they have become quite the court fashion in Dark Fae circles. A single Ho Ho is now worth twenty Dark Fae doubloons. We're making a killing."

A bark of laughter burst out of Dragos, surprising him. Releasing Pia, Niniane turned to fling her arms around him. "Dragos! It's so, so, so good to see you! Come down here, I need to kiss you."

Obligingly, he bent and turned his head so that she could smack him on the cheek. She hugged him tightly again, and as he put his arms around her, he glanced at Pia, who was, after all, in the mating heat as well.

Her face had turned sour, and she sucked a tooth, but she didn't say anything. Still amused, he said in her head, *Okay there, lover?*

If it was anybody else but Niniane, I'm not sure I would be, she told him. *Thankfully, you're not very approachable to most people.*

At that, he cocked a sardonic eyebrow, but as she was right, he let it pass.

He caught sight of Bayne winding his way between clumps of people and told the others, "Excuse me."

Stepping away from the small group, he asked, *What did you find?*

Bayne shook his head. To a casual observer, he might still look relaxed, but Dragos knew him very well and caught the subtle tight compression to his mouth.

Bayne said, *I counted close to seventy people who are masking their scents, mostly congressmen and other officials and their spouses, along with a few interns. I cornered the White House press secretary, since Angela's always been on friendly terms with us. She said it started sometime early last week in a sub-faction of people who are against maintaining warmer relations with the Elder Races. They're calling it a Right to Privacy movement.*

Dragos rubbed the back of his neck. *Seventy fucking people, most of them government officials. That's a sub-faction?*

I know. Bayne met his gaze with a grim look. *Washington is pretty strongly divided on how to deal with the Elder Races right now. Rumor has it,* Angela said, *that the vice president started it. This is the president's last term in office, and she thinks Colton might be cultivating the issue to use it in her platform in a bid for election.*

Fucking hell. If Colton became president, the world for the Elder Races, and the Wyr in particular, would get very cold indeed.

Automatically, he scanned the crowd for Colton. As he was taller than most people, he was able to locate her easily, standing to one side of the large ballroom with a tall, lean man. They looked like they were having a tense conversation, perhaps even an argument.

He strained to hear what they might be saying, but even though he was very good at pinpointing something specific from some distance away, there were too many people, and the orchestra was too loud, for him to catch any of their conversation.

Who is that man standing with Colton? he asked Bayne.

The other man turned to follow his gaze. *I think that's her chief of staff, Aaron Davis.*

If he was Colton's chief of staff, then Davis would be coming to dinner tomorrow evening. Dragos's eyes narrowed. There might be something he could do to increase the tensions between the two. He would make a point of talking with Davis, to see if the other man's loyalties might be less than concretely fixed.

Anything else you need? Bayne asked.

No, not now, thanks. Circulate, and see if you can overhear anything useful.

Will do.

Bayne disappeared into the crowd again.

Deep in thought, Dragos joined Pia, Niniane and Tiago. Waitstaff threaded through the crowd, offering platters of hors d'oeuvres to people as they passed.

While Dragos responded to the conversation, and smiled when the others did, in the back of his mind, he began to lay plans.

If Colton announced a bid for the presidency, he was going to funnel money into every PAC he could find that operated against her candidacy.

Because he was always thinking of contingencies.

He played with budget numbers for a while, but ultimately set it aside as unsatisfactory and considered other options.

There was always assassination, of course. But assassination was tricky to pull off without having it backfire. If Colton announced a bid for the presidency and gained any traction—and even if she didn't—her death could potentially add fuel to her causes, which would eventually make everything worse.

No, assassination wasn't the most preferred course of action, at least not in this case. He could work to discredit her. Hire human spies to dig up dirt on her. That might have some merit, but it still wouldn't dispel the antipathy against the Elder Races and the Wyr that she had whipped up.

He needed to think of something else to address that particular problem. And in case that didn't work… what other contingency plans could he set into place?

Just then, Xavier del Torro, regent of the Nightkind demesne, and Tatiana, the Light Fae Queen, strolled up, and he set aside that train of thought with a mental note to pursue it later.

The evening passed in a grueling haze of forced pleasantries and hidden tensions.

And, occasionally, some not so hidden tensions.

The Light Fae Queen Tatiana apparently refused to talk to the Elven High Lord Ferion, not even in pleasantries, and she cut him dead when he approached. The gods only knew what that was about.

And at one point the head of the Demonkind assembly and the head of the witches demesne broke into a soft-voiced argument.

Jered and Isalynn's dislike for each other was well known. As they smilingly engaged in a quiet spat, Pia poked Dragos in the ribs and said in his head, *People are taking note of this. We'd better break them up.*

He almost rolled his eyes, but as he glanced around, he saw that Pia was right. Others were watching the two, some covertly but others with quite open, and not particularly friendly, interest.

Moving together with Pia, he took hold of Isalynn's arm and walked away with her while Pia distracted

Jered.

Think of it. The dragon was practicing diplomacy.

He chuckled to himself, even as Isalynn hissed under her breath at him, "Let go of my arm, Dragos!"

"Not until you and Jered are far away from each other," he said. He switched to telepathy and said bluntly, *Pull your shit together, Isalynn, and smile at me like you mean it, because if you don't think we're on trial right now, you haven't been paying attention. And you're a lot more stupid than I thought.*

Damn it. You're insufferable at the best of times. I hate it when you're right. She took two short, angry breaths, then turned to show her teeth at him.

His cold gaze ran over her bold, attractive features. He didn't care that her dark gaze still snapped with anger and dislike. All her facial muscles had moved in a close approximation of a smile, and that was all anyone else would see.

He walked her over to a buffet table where they helped themselves to refreshments. As two congressmen approached, he left her to converse with them and circled back around to find Pia.

Pia did end up dancing twice, once with President Johnson, and a second time with Ferion, while both times Dragos held himself in a clench and managed not to bite anybody's head off.

Not even Johnson's relative age helped. Despite being a politician in his sixties, Johnson wasn't an old, ugly fucker. He was still a handsome, fit son of a bitch, and as he whirled Pia around the dance floor, she threw back her head and laughed more than once.

And watching her waltz with Ferion felt like someone just out of eyesight was raking talons down a blackboard. His hands tightened into fists as he imagined grinding the handsome Elf into the polished floor.

"Dragos, is that a flame I see coming out of your nostrils?" Niniane asked.

As he had been obsessing over Pia's dance, the little Queen had maneuvered to stand directly in front of him, her head tilted sideways as she squinted at him.

He sucked in a breath, swallowing down the fire, and growled, "I don't know what you're talking about."

"It was too. *That* was a tiny little flame." She pointed an accusing finger at his nose. "What are you trying to do, create a general panic and destroy everything everybody is trying to achieve here?"

"Of course not," he snapped. "I was holding myself in check, goddammit."

She considered him for a moment then said telepathically, *I actually believe you think you are. Tiago said you and Pia were in a mating phase.*

We are. Goddammit, of course Tiago with his sensitive sense of smell would pick up on that. Dragos might just buy some KO Odorless Odor Eliminator and join the Right to Privacy movement himself.

"Well, just so you know," Niniane said aloud, patting his arm, "I'm pretty sure I overheard Ferion and Pia setting up an assignation for tomorrow at noon, for somewhere called the Paradise Motel."

That snapped his gaze away from the dancing couple. He glowered at Niniane. "What the fuck are you talking about? Pia would never set up an assignation with Ferion."

"I know, right?" Niniane let out a peal of laughter. "Even smart men can be such dumbasses." When he glared at her, she sobered somewhat and told him, "Stuff that mating nonsense down deep somewhere before you do something stupid. I mean, Dragos… Pia and Ferion? Come on."

"You never used to talk to me that way when you lived in New York," he said, his eyes narrowed.

"I never used to do a lot of things before I became Queen," she said matter-of-factly. She gave him a small charming smile. "Besides, you like me, and I'm not telling you anything your brain isn't already telling your hormones. You'll deal with it."

"Dictatorial little shit," he muttered. "I don't see you dancing with anybody."

Her smile faded, and she looked sidelong at Tiago, who stood with his arms crossed, talking with Bayne.

"Yeah, well, I can call out irrational behavior, but I can't necessarily stop it, can I?" she muttered in reply.

That snagged his full attention. Turning away from watching Pia on the dance floor, he studied Niniane as he switched to telepathy. *Everything okay, pipsqueak?*

She gave him a quick smile. *Oh, everything's fine. Don't*

worry. Tiago and I just have a completely different relational dynamic than you and Pia. You and Pia are all out there—rings, public displays of affection, matrimony and a child, etc. But Tiago and I have to be more discreet about our relationship.

He frowned and rubbed his jaw. *Is that a problem?*

She shook her head. *No, not as things stand currently. I'm pretty sure we're a well-known secret in Dark Fae society, but as long as we don't flaunt anything, they're accepting it. They're accepting him.*

That's good, he murmured.

It is, but there's always that slight tension, you know? He has to refrain from making any public statement of claiming me, and in return, I try to act with a little more sensitivity about things, like dancing with other males in public. We're balancing things just fine.

As he listened, his gaze fell on the vice president and her husband, dancing the waltz. He asked, *What if the balance shifts?*

Niniane's mental voice remained firm and strong. *We don't let it shift. Right now, we're both engaged, challenged and satisfied with our status quo. If we decide we want to do something else, or have a different definition of our lives and relationship, I'll abdicate and we'll go somewhere else.*

Go somewhere else.

They would have to, since, much as the Dark Fae had accepted Tiago for what he was, they would never accept a marriage between their Queen and a Wyr ex-sentinel. Curiously, he asked, *You could give up all that power, now that you have it?*

Absolutely, if it was the right thing for either Tiago or me—for us both. She gave him a quick smile. *And anyway, my point is, we're in a different place than you and Pia are. So even though you've got all those mating hormones running around in your dragony head, keep your sights fixed on why you and Pia broke up Jered and Isalynn before they came to blows. There's a lot at stake here.*

Point taken. He crossed his arms. *And, I might add—again—I haven't killed anybody yet. I should get credit for that.*

She patted him on the shoulder and switched to verbal speech. "Let's just keep it that way while we're all in D.C., 'kay?"

He shook his head grimly. "I'm doing my best, pipsqueak."

She snorted. "I'd say we're all probably doing our best to at least appear to get along. Which is pretty pathetic when you think about it. If you really have to eat somebody, at least please wait until Tiago and I leave for home again."

His mind switched gears. "You're not going to attend the Masque in New York?"

Annually, on the winter solstice, the Elder Races celebrated the Masque of the Gods. Dragos always threw a lavish party in the city for the event, and when Niniane lived with them, she used to love attending.

She sighed. "No, I'm afraid not. The solstice is still two months away, and we can't stay that long, not with the time slippage being what it is between Earth and Adriyel. We have things we need to attend to back at home."

"Understood." He crossed his arms. "Pia will be disappointed, but there isn't much that can be done about that."

She grinned up at him. "You'll just have to come visit us in Adriyel someday."

He raised an eyebrow. "That would be an interesting trip."

"I can just see it now," she declared, spreading out both hands. "Everybody would shit themselves to have the dragon come onto Dark Fae land. It would be *glorious*."

He barked out a laugh as the orchestra finally stopped playing that infernal waltz, and Ferion escorted his mate back to him.

She looked beautiful, as always, but underneath the bright vivacity of her makeup, she also looked tired. He put an arm around her. "We're done for the night."

"Are you sure?" she asked. Her gaze darted over the dance floor. "Nobody else has left yet, I don't think."

"Someone has always got to be the first," he replied. "Besides, it's almost eleven. We've put in a respectable enough showing."

"Okay." She leaned against him in relief.

They began the long, tedious process of saying their goodnights, until finally they were able to climb into the back of the limo and relax with big sighs. Eva and Bayne settled in the seats opposite them.

Bayne was the closest to the mini liquor cabinet. Dragos told him, "Pour me a double scotch, would you?"

"Sure." As Bayne handed the drink to him, he asked Pia, "You want anything?"

"Just water," she said. Her words disappeared into a wide yawn. "I guess for a fairly disastrous event, it didn't go too badly?"

Dragos snorted as he swallowed amber liquid and felt a pleasurable fire burn down his throat. "I guess you could say that."

Opening the cold water bottle that Bayne handed to her, she slid off her shoes and curled against Dragos's side. The soft, warm weight of her body resting against his felt soothing, and he let go of the tension that had tightened his muscles all evening.

She asked him telepathically, *What are we going to do if we can't smooth things over?*

I've been thinking of contingency plans all evening, he admitted. Finishing his drink, he held it out to Bayne in a silent request for another. He thought of the conversation he'd just had with Niniane. *We always said that if we needed to walk away from my position we would, but that wouldn't solve the problem for any of the other Wyr.*

No, she sighed. *In fact, it might make things worse for everybody else. If we walked away, I would want to take all of them with us.*

At that, an idea burgeoned in his head, and he went still as he thought it over.

It was sweeping and drastic, but it was also the first idea all evening that made his uneasiness subside.

If worst comes to worst, he promised, *we will take all the Wyr with us. At least, all the Wyr who want to come.*

Chapter Six

P IA LIFTED HER head to stare at him. He looked alert and focused, as he always did when his mind was racing.

She didn't know if she should be amused or maybe even a little frightened. She said uncertainly, *You do realize it's physically impossible to run away with the world's entire population of Wyr. Don't you? I mean, isn't it? Even if we could corral them all together. Oh lordy, that would be like trying to herd thousands of cats all at once.*

Chuckling, he kissed her. *Don't worry, worst is not going to come to worst.*

But if it did, she insisted.

If it did, I think we should take a leaf from the Dark Fae's example, he told her. *They never did invest entirely in integration into human society, which is why they have such a thriving culture in Adriyel.*

You mean leave New York? She felt her eyes widen. *Completely?*

He laced his fingers with hers. *You know our house in the Other land, the one where I like to experiment with what technologies can be brought over from Earth?*

She thought back. *You told me about it… last May, I think, but you haven't mentioned it since.*

I've been too busy to tinker around with that project, he said. *But that land is massive. It's roughly the size of Greenland, only unlike Greenland, there's lots of arable farmland, lots of clean water, and clear, fresh skies, and almost no people. That's one of the reasons why I like it so much. More importantly, at least right now, the main access to the Other land is near our estate in upstate New York.* He met her gaze. *That land is mine, and it has limited entry points which makes it easily defensible, along with plenty of natural resources.*

She sat up straight as she turned the thought over in her mind. Yes, there was tremendous possibility, but there were huge obstacles as well.

She said slowly, *You're talking about transplanting a lot of people who don't know how to live without modern Earth technology. Many of them live in cities, and they buy their groceries along with everything else they need in stores.*

Well, I didn't say it would be easy, or that it should happen quickly, he replied. *Or even if it should happen at all. But if worst came to worst, and we couldn't find a way to continue living peacefully with humankind, we would have a place to go that would be safe and sustainable. I just need to hire a team of civil engineers and maybe some Dark Fae consultants to lay the groundwork, so that we're not caught completely vulnerable and unprepared.*

Oh yay, we get to build a whole new utopian society in our free time? She yawned again.

Potentially, he said, chuckling. *A whole new potential*

utopian society. If worst came to worst.

I'll be honest, she confessed. *I'm too tired to really absorb an idea of this magnitude. I can't imagine the kind of infrastructure you would need to lay down that would support thousands of people, let alone the training programs you would need to help them acclimate to such a different way of life.*

That's okay. He hooked an arm around her and pulled her back against his side. *Because the worst isn't going to come to worst. Things will smooth over.*

She didn't believe him. Perhaps things might smooth over, but Dragos never relied on blind optimism as a viable course of action. She had no doubt that very trait was one of the reasons why he was still alive, and so successful.

Her heavy eyelids refused to remain open any longer and drifted shut. *You're still going to hire that cadre of civil engineers and consultants, though, aren't you?*

Hell, yes.

They might have only been together for eighteen months, but in some ways, they already knew each other so well. She smiled, and the smooth rhythm of the limo's engine lulled her to sleep.

When she woke up again, they had arrived back at the Wyr residence and he was carrying her up the magnificent staircase. He had slipped her high heeled shoes off, and they rested on her stomach.

"Shades of Rhett Butler," she muttered, putting her hand on the shoes to make sure they didn't slip off and fall to the floor.

"What's that?" He bent his head toward her. "I'm sorry I woke you."

"*Mmph*. Don't be sorry." She yawned again. "I have to get ready for bed anyway."

He rested his cheek against the top of her head. "I was going to zip you out of your dress."

Her tired body pulsed at the idea, but overpowering as the mating instinct could be when it held her in its grip, instead of perking up, she felt rather ill. Scratching her thigh, all she could look forward to was shedding the Dior so she could spread some lotion over her itchy skin.

"Much as I would love to," she mumbled, "I'm too exhausted tonight."

"I wasn't suggesting we do anything." He used her feet to push open the bedroom door and carried her inside. "We both need a good night's sleep to face tomorrow and the rest of this week."

He set her gently on the end of the bed, and she braced her body upright with both hands planted on the mattress. "We have all those horrible people coming over here for dinner. Actually, I like several of them individually. It's just that so many of them don't like each other, and when they all get together, all these squabbles break out." She rubbed her forehead as she thought of the Coltons. "Only some of them are just plain horrible."

"Don't think about that right now." He shed his jacket and pulled off his tie with a sigh. "Think about crawling between nice, cool sheets and turning off the light."

As she was thinking of the Coltons anyway, her mind went to what had happened earlier, and she started to snicker.

"What?" He glanced at her curiously as he stripped off his shirt.

She deepened her voice to mimic him. *"I look forward to having you for dinner tomorrow."*

A wicked grin lit his hard face. "The look on their faces was my one pleasure of the evening."

While he strolled into the bathroom to brush his teeth, she went to sit at the vanity to smooth cleansing cream over her face. As she wiped off the cream and makeup with tissues, her true complexion appeared. She looked dead-fish white, with blotchy areas where she had been rubbing her skin and dark circles under her eyes.

She made a face at herself in the mirror. When Dragos got tired, he just looked more rugged and dangerously sexy, with a piratical hint of dark beard shadowing his lean cheeks. When she was exhausted, she looked like something a cat might throw up.

He left the bathroom, totally nude, and climbed into bed, and it was her turn to use the bathroom. She forced herself upright and went to brush her teeth as well, and splash the last of the cream off her face. Her skin was still blotchy from where she had rubbed it with tissues. She frowned at her reflection and shimmied out of her dress.

Then she reached for her body lotion and propped her foot on the rim of the bathtub to rub lotion on her irritated skin.

A large bright, angry red patch covered the expanse of her thigh. Freezing, she stared at her leg. Then she looked over her shoulder again at the reflection of her still blotchy face.

"Oh, God," she sighed. This was the last thing she needed.

She hadn't said it very loudly, but her mate had ears sharper than any other creature she had ever personally met. Dragos said from the bedroom, "What is it?"

"I'm all blotchy," she complained.

He appeared in the doorway, frowning as he took in her appearance. "Did you eat any of the hors d'oeuvres?"

"Yes, but I made sure to ask if they were vegan first. I always do."

His frown deepened as he touched her leg with one forefinger. He motioned for the bottle, and when she handed it to him, he began to spread body lotion gently over her leg. "Recipes can be sneaky. Maybe the servers made a mistake, and something had a trace of meat, fish or dairy in it. Do you feel nauseated at all?"

She was vegan, not only by choice, but by nature too. Her digestive system simply didn't recognize any meat, fish, or dairy products as food.

"No, but I'm still wearing the diamond necklace."

She made a face at him. "I don't want to be blotchy this week, not while the world's going to hell in a handbasket."

He studied her with narrowed eyes. "Take the necklace off."

Sighing, she complied. As soon as the pendant left contact with her skin, her stomach heaved. Tossing it with a clatter onto the nearby counter, she lunged for the toilet.

While she struggled to rid herself of everything in her stomach, strong hands came down on her, one cupping her forehead and the other bracing her back. Feeling too sick to indulge in self-consciousness, after she finished vomiting, she leaned her trembling body against his large, steadier frame.

"That was utterly vile," she muttered.

He stroked the damp hair off her face. "It's better to throw up than have it take the long way through your system. Hopefully after a good night's sleep, you'll feel better by morning."

"True."

After he helped her to her feet, she brushed her teeth again and followed him to bed. He opened his arms to her, and she crawled over to curl around his long, stretched out frame. Comfort sank deep. Nuzzling the bare, warm skin of his shoulder, she closed her eyes.

Just before she fell asleep, the tired fog lifted from her mind and she remembered.

She had been nauseated well before eating the hors d'oeuvres that evening, and her skin had begun to feel irritated too.

Time to make an appointment to see Dr. Medina when they got back home.

Then darkness called, and she was unable to resist its inexorable pull.

WHEN AWARENESS DAWNED next, she discovered that she had curled on her side, and Dragos lay spooning her from behind. The room lay in deep shadow, although a sliver of light at the edge of the curtain indicated it was close to dawn.

His warm mouth traveled across the nape of her neck, while he stroked her torso from breast to hip. His large, hot erection pressed against her buttocks.

"Good morning, lover," he whispered in her ear. "How are you feeling—any better?"

"*Mmm*," she murmured, luxuriating in a long, all-over body stretch that might also have made her brush all along the length of his body as well. She adored the feeling of his body next to hers, dark bronze skin covering sleek, iron hard muscles and sprinkled with black, silken hair. It was beyond a doubt the very best way to wake up in the mornings. Rolling onto her back, she rubbed her face against his chest. "Still tired, but okay."

He cupped her breast and pressed a gentle kiss against the jut of her nipple. "Okay enough for this?"

She took stock. Her muscles ached and her thigh still itched, but none of it could dispel a growing sense of hunger for him. "I want to," she admitted. "But I don't feel very rambunctious."

"We'll go slow and easy this time," he promised. "I can do all the work. You can lie back and count your *pows*."

Delighted, she snickered as she tilted her face up for his kiss. "You offer a bargain so good I can't resist."

He cupped the back of her head, supporting her neck as he slanted his mouth over hers and kissed her gently, deeply. A sense of golden well-being suffused her, physical pleasure mingling with the emotional.

He was so good, so good. He was more fierce and demanding than anyone else she had ever known, but he was also the tenderest of lovers too, and he handled her as if she were a treasure beyond compare.

It was impossible to maintain worry when she was in his arms, impossible to hold on to anything negative or isolating. When they were together, they were all in, utterly immersed in each other, invested completely in this intangible, essential thing they had developed between them. Nothing else existed.

Trailing light kisses along her body, he nipped at her breasts gently and suckled at the stiff, sensitive peaks of her nipples. While he caressed and licked at her, she quested down his body with one hand, running her fingers through the silken tract of hair low on his tight, flat abdomen until she located his erection.

Closing her fingers around his cock, she massaged the long, thick length. His skin felt like silk stretched over iron. Using the ball of her thumb, she rubbed circles along the broad tip of his penis.

In response, he exhaled hard and flexed his hips so that he pushed against the palm of her hand, while his mouth traveled up the line of her neck to caress her lips again.

He wasn't a man filled with soft words or poetry, and it was rare for him to say that he loved her. But he told her in so many different ways, the lack of soft words and poetry never mattered, not in the slightest.

He told her through the touch of his lips, and the depth of emotion expressed in every caress of those callused, powerful hands. He told her in the amount of attention he paid to every detail of her life, and the way his hard face would light up whenever she entered a room.

He told her every time he put his arm around her, or complained at her absence. This, from a male who did not tolerate the presence of others very well in general.

In a thousand different ways, he made her feel cherished and valued, and this bout of lovemaking was no different. He was as good as his word, and even though she could feel his rising heat and hunger, running like lava underneath his skin and hardening his big, tough frame, he never once broke out of the gentle pace he set for himself.

Using just his fingers, he stroked her to climax, and only when she had eased out of the shaking pulse of completion did he come between her legs to settle his hips against hers and push into her entrance easily, carefully.

A hot wave of emotion washed through her as she felt his cock entering her. Both physical and emotional pleasure lit her up entirely. She wound her arms and legs around him, cradling him with her whole body, trying to tell him without words just how important he was to her too.

At this one place, their conversation was unchanging.

Here I am, her cradling body said to him. I'll be your home.

Looking deep into her eyes, he began to move. Here I am, his body said to her. I'll cover you and keep you safe.

At this one place, his normal possessive nature shifted. At any other time, he told her in a dozen ways, you are mine.

But here, in this one place, he told her, I'm yours.

His own climax took him over, and he gave it to her. She watched him without blinking, without hardly breathing, stroking his face as he gave her everything he had.

After staying with her for long moments, he eased away, reached for the tissues on the bedside table, and helped her to clean off her inner thighs. Then he pulled her with him, so that they rested with their legs entwined. Utterly drained and satisfied in the best way possible, she buried her face against his chest and fell deeply asleep again.

When she woke next, she was alone in the bed. Rolling over, she took stock of her immediate surroundings. While the room still remained in deep shadow, a bright yellow band of sunlight along the edges of the curtains told her the day had advanced significantly.

Dragos wasn't anywhere in the room. The open door to the bathroom revealed that it was empty and quiet. He had left her to sleep in.

She *tsked* softly, partly in exasperation but mostly in contentment. There was so much to do that day—so much—but she couldn't deny that it had felt really good to get her sleep out.

As she rolled to her side of the bed, she saw a piece of paper resting on the bedside table. Picking it up, she saw that it was covered with Dragos's bold scrawl.

> *No need to come with me this afternoon. Try to relax today. The staff can take care of everything for tonight. - D*

Try to relax, when the president, the vice president, the speaker of the House, both the majority and minority leaders of the Senate, and all the demesne leaders, along with their spouses and personal security retinues were coming to the Wyr residence for dinner?

"I love you," she told the note. "But sometimes you are a foolish, foolish man. Although undeniably a very handsome, sexy one."

Kissing the paper, she set it aside, called down to the kitchen to request a pot of coffee and a bowl of fresh fruit and then she got out of bed.

As soon as she stood upright, nausea punched her, hard and wicked, and more powerful than ever. She bolted to the bathroom, and her body twisted into wretched spasms.

Finally, she was able to sit back on the floor and take in a deep breath. Instinctively, she scanned her body again. Still no baby.

She didn't have time to mourn the lack of a tiny life spark within her. Damn it. Damnity damn damn it. Her leg itched furiously, and as she scratched it, the itching grew even worse. She looked down at herself.

Her thigh was redder than ever, a dark, angry color, and covered in bumps.

A knock sounded at the door. Pia rolled to her feet. Swirling nausea gripped her by the throat. She grabbed for the diamond pendant, slung it on, and the nausea subsided. She called out, "Who is it?"

"Eva. I've got your breakfast tray."

Her bathrobe hung on a hook on the back of the bathroom door. She snatched it and put it on. "Come in."

The door opened, and Eva carried the tray inside.

As the other woman set it on the bedside table, Pia strode up to her and yanked one flap of the robe aside to bare her thigh. "What is this?" she demanded. "Do you know?"

Eva turned to look at her leg, and her eyebrows rose. After a moment's thought, she replied, "Looks likes hives to me."

"Hives?" Pia was trying to avoid scratching at it, but the itching was driving her crazy. "Isn't that what happens when you're allergic to something?"

"Yeah. What'd you do, eat something you shouldn't have?"

"No." She frowned. She had also never before had such an extreme reaction to eating something she shouldn't. "At least I don't think so."

"Well, if you're allergic to something, you might react within a couple of hours, but it can take up to seventy-two hours for food poisoning to set in, so you could be reacting to something you ate as long as three days ago," Eva said. "It could take you a couple of days to get over it."

Pia tried to think back, but she had no idea what she had eaten three days ago. She hadn't been paying attention… although she was pretty sure she had eaten everything from home that day, so the food should have been safe.

She growled in frustration and dashed back to the bathroom to look at her reflection. Her skin was still pale and blotchy. She threw up her hands. Great, just bloody great.

"Maybe you should see a doctor?" Eva had followed her to the bathroom and was watching her with a troubled expression.

"See a Wyr doctor in D.C.?" Snorting, she turned away from the offending mirror. "Good luck finding one. Humans take over-the-counter medication for allergies. It's called antihistamines. Have you heard of it before?"

Eva rubbed her face. "Yeah."

Her gaze met Eva's. "I'll put in a call to Dr. Medina, but in the meantime, get me some antihistamines. I don't care what brand. I'm going to make it through this day if it kills me."

But first, she was going to take a shower to see if that would calm down the infernal itching, at least until Eva could get back with the medication. Eva took off, while she showered, smothered her leg in lotion and dressed in jeans and a light silk sweater.

Thank the gods, Dragos had taken off some time ago to attend the day's functions without her. She drank a quick cup of coffee, ate a few bites of fruit, and called the doctor's office.

Dr. Medina was busy dealing with an emergency, the office manager told her, but she would be sure to return Pia's call as soon as she could. Pia hung up, went to the vanity and smoothed another ten pounds of makeup on her face to hide her blotchy complexion, until she looked more or less normal.

Then Eva returned with several different packages of antihistamines. Together, they scanned the dosage directions.

"Don't operate any heavy machinery, may cause drowsiness…." Eva read aloud.

Pia popped a dose out of foil wrap and swallowed them. "Or in other words, keep the coffee coming."

"You sure you feel up to this?" Eva pursed her lips in concern.

"I am totally up for this," Pia said grimly. "Let's go."

With that, she plunged into the day's preparations. It seemed that everyone had saved up at least a dozen questions to ask her. There was a mistake on the order of fresh flowers. Would the substitutes do? What about the seating arrangements for dinner?

Thankfully, her leg stopped itching after about a half an hour or so. When the doctor returned her call, a couple of hours later, she was so busy she let the phone call roll to voice mail. She could call Dr. Medina back in the morning.

The afternoon sped by too fast. Dragos arrived back at the residence in a foul mood. He was standing in the middle of the foyer watching staff scurry past, his hands on his hips, when Pia found him.

"How did your day go?" she asked.

"I hate people."

He sounded grumpy, but no more than usual when he had to deal with a lot of people. She held her face up to him. He took his time kissing her and did such a thorough job, she was flushed and laughing when he finally lifted his head again. "How are things going here?"

She looked around. "You might not be able to tell by looking, but it's a controlled kind of panic. It's just as well I didn't go with you today—there was too much to do here, but I think I can let go and get ready for the evening now. Come upstairs with me?"

"I will in a minute. I'm going to get a scotch, and I want to talk to Bayne first."

"Okay." She left him to jog up the stairs to their suite.

Last night, the outfit she wore was classic chic. Tonight, should she go romantic and wear the midnight blue dress? Or perhaps sophisticated with the silk taupe pantsuit?

Upstairs, the bedroom had been cleaned and straightened, and the packages of antihistamines had been stacked on the bedside table. Seeing them reminded her.

She kicked off her jeans to inspect her thigh. It hadn't itched for several hours, but the patch of skin was still red and angry looking. So, the hives had gone down some, but the irritation wasn't gone. She was masking a symptom, not eradicating the problem.

Sighing, she grabbed at the open package. After double-checking the instructions, she swallowed another dose.

There was no way she was going to try to take off the pendant at this point. Later tonight, she could take it off and see how she was really doing then.

Because nothing short of a full-scale natural disaster was going to keep her from getting through the dinner party this evening.

Chapter Seven

OWNSTAIRS, DRAGOS RAN over security plans for the evening with Bayne. Every Wyr would be on duty that night to make sure the perimeter of the property was guarded tightly. All the nearby streets were cordoned off for three blocks in every direction, and guards were mounted on the tops of nearby buildings.

Inside, while the house was too old to have a modern-day security system running through the walls, Bayne had installed tiny hidden wireless cameras in every room, which were monitored in the security room in the basement, behind the wine cellar. The house's Wi-Fi network was a closed system, and it was backed up with an electric generator and a second server. They were as secure as modern technology could make them.

None of it calmed the dragon's uneasiness at staying in an unfriendly city. All the security in the world wouldn't protect the building from a long-range missile strike.

That was an extreme, highly unlikely scenario, but

extreme shit happened. While he knew that the other demesnes, along with the different human police agencies, would also be on high alert throughout the city, he didn't like to trust his safety or that of his mate to other people's efforts.

Compulsively, he went below to make sure the openings to every tunnel had not been accidentally blocked off by all the trunks, boxes and furniture accrued over the last hundred and twenty years.

Yes, he was paranoid, but he had also been hunted before, several times throughout the ages. Being paranoid and untrusting had kept him alive, and he was vitally interested in maintaining that status quo.

Finally, he went upstairs to find the bedroom in chaos.

Pia had thrown different outfits along with matching jewelry sets on the bed. Small cardboard boxes littered one of the tables. As he raised his eyebrows and looked around, he found her crouched in front of the closet. She was wearing her dressing gown, her hair was rolled up in the hot curlers again, and she was busy pulling out shoes.

All her shoes. As far as he could tell, when she stood up, she carried in her arms every pair that she had brought on the trip.

As she caught sight of him, she muttered, "I'm so behind. I thought I was going to wear either the midnight blue dress or the silk pantsuit, but now neither one seems right, and I can't make up my mind!"

She threw her armful of shoes on the floor beside the bed.

He walked up behind her and put his arms around her. Her body vibrated with tension. He tightened his grip on her. The hot curlers hampered his desire to put his mouth in her hair, so instead, he put his mouth to the hollow where her neck met her shoulder.

"You're wound a little tight there, lover," he murmured.

"Yeah, sorry. I've downed a bucket of coffee today." She leaned back against him. "All of them are going to be here, Dragos—all of them under our roof."

"I know." He pressed a kiss against her warm skin.

"Has that ever happened before?"

"No, it hasn't. We've had a majority of leaders at functions and meetings before, but not every head of state in the continental U.S. at once."

She gave a reluctant chuckle. "You could have told me a reassuring lie. I'm sorry I'm being such a flake. I was fine until about fifteen minutes ago, and then I dissolved into this big ball of nerves."

"You're going to be amazing tonight," he told her. Pia didn't have a fancy political science degree, but she had good instincts about people, so he asked curiously, "I meant to ask you earlier but forgot—what did you think of Johnson when you danced together?"

The tension in her body eased somewhat. "You know, I liked him. Of course we didn't talk about anything very important, and I know he's known for being charming, but still he seems to have a core of real decency. He didn't try to disguise his scent, and just the fact that he asked me to dance says that he has a moderate stance to us—not only the Wyr, but also the Elder Races in general, I think."

He nodded slightly, while still maintaining contact on her skin with his mouth. "That's been my impression too. I think he's genuinely concerned about the outbreaks of violence that have occurred over the last two years, and he wants to work together to minimize the risk of further violence in the future. And another positive—neither he, nor his wife, are participating in the Right to Privacy movement."

"It sounds like you had a productive day today," she said, reaching back to stroke his cheek.

"We did, I think." He lifted his head to consider the outfits strewn over the bed. "Wear the midnight blue dress. The blue almost matches your eyes, and I like how you look in it."

She let out a big sigh that sounded relieved. "I should let you pick out all my outfits this week. It'll save me a lot of time."

He grinned. "As long as I get to pick out your lingerie too, you're on."

"Okay, but you'd better hurry," she muttered. "I mean it. I'm going to be downstairs in twenty minutes. Other people can afford to be late, but not the hosts."

Obligingly, he turned to the dresser that held her intimate apparel. As he did so, his gaze fell on the small boxes on the nearby table. He asked, "By the way, what are these boxes?"

She threw a glower at the boxes as she rushed to the vanity table to pull out the hot curlers. "They're antihistamines for my rash."

"So it hasn't disappeared yet?"

"No," she sighed. "Maybe it will be gone by tomorrow."

He pulled out a dark blue bra and matching panties, relishing the feel of the silken material. Later, he would take these off her after she stepped out of that shimmery dress. At the thought, his cock stood at attention, but she was right. He didn't have time to indulge the urge.

Later, he promised himself.

Turning around to offer the lingerie to her, he asked, "Have the antihistamines helped any?"

"Sort of. The itching is a little better, at least so that I can ignore it when I'm busy, but the rash hasn't gone. I called Dr. Medina, but she was in an emergency, so if the rash isn't gone by morning, I'll call her again." She snatched the lingerie from him, pulled off her dressing gown and dressed swiftly.

He had to look away from the luscious sight of her tucking her full, pale breasts into that sexy bra. Focusing on her leg instead, he frowned at how much skin the dark red rash covered. "Call her anyway, even if the rash calms down. I want to know what she has to say."

"Okay." She shimmied into the dress and put her back to him. "Zip me up?"

"With pleasure." He helped her with the zipper and placed a final kiss at the back of her neck. Then he changed into a clean suit, a darker one more suitable for the evening, and as they left the bedroom, the dragon surfaced again in his mind.

He had once been much more feral, but age had taught him how to appreciate the more delicate aspects of warfare conducted over a well-cooked meal.

Because he had no doubt of it—while some of his guests tonight would be more moderate and open-minded, other guests were definitely waging war against him.

Tonight was his best chance to study them in order to discover the best way to defeat them.

If that included destroying them in the process, well then, so be it.

✧   ✧   ✧

AS THE FIRST of the guests arrived in a flurry of greetings, for the dozenth time that day, Pia did another mental head count of everybody attending.

The humans attending were the president, vice president, their respective chiefs of staff, the Senate majority and minority leaders, and the speaker of the House, along with all their spouses or plus ones.

On the Elder Races side—and even though Isalynn LeFevre was human, as head of the witches demesne, she counted personally and politically as one of the Elder Races—all seven of the demesne leaders were present, along with their spouses or plus ones.

Neither the Elder tribunal nor any of the members of the Supreme Court were involved in this week's talks, just those involved in active governance.

So there were fourteen and fourteen. Then there was the security staff, but they didn't count in terms of making sure glasses were refilled and seating arrangements at the dinner table.

Big and stately though the mansion was, it didn't have the sheer space or capacity to hold the high numbers that the White House could, and after some discussion and negotiation, most of everybody's security details awaited them outside, while each couple was allowed one person indoors, which made thirteen extra bodies to account for as a total head count.

Dragos and Pia's security didn't factor into that number, for their security staff was also the waitstaff. They threaded through the guests, offering hors d'oeuvres, wine and mixed drinks with polite smiles and watchful, smiling eyes. No expense had been spared for this evening. Five hundred dollar bottles of wine flowed like water, and only the highest quality liquors were offered to those who chose to partake.

When someone—Pia didn't catch who—suggested they open the large French-style doors and enjoy the unseasonably warm evening outside, Dragos moved to open the doors up and people spilled out onto the wide terrace.

In anticipation of doing just that, earlier that afternoon, when they were sure the weather was going to hold, Pia had worked with the staff to set out tables covered with white cloths, bouquets of fresh flowers and candles. After the doors had been opened, Bayne walked from table to table, lighting candles, until the terrace and the half-acre of manicured gardens were lit with sparks of soft, golden light.

Sipping with moderation at a glass of French Bordeaux, Pia circulated too, joining conversations briefly with small clusters of people before moving on to the next, while her gaze kept roaming constantly to make sure everyone was getting his or her needs met.

Aside from polite smiles and the most basic greeting, she avoided the vice president and her husband altogether—she wouldn't be able to change the Coltons' minds about anything, and she felt no need to engage with them. Thankfully they were Dragos's problem, not hers, and while she was happy to work to support him in what he did, she wouldn't change places with him for the world.

After the first forty-five minutes, the tight knot between her shoulder blades started to ease. Relations between humankind and the Elder Races might not be improved after this week, but that wouldn't be because of any fault in this evening.

At least she devoutly hoped not. Because, as Dragos would say, night's not over yet.

Then Gennita, the head chef, appeared in the open French doors and said discreetly in Pia's head, *My lady? When would you like for us to serve?*

How about in fifteen minutes? she replied.

Very good. I'll put the soufflés in the oven now, and we'll be ready. Gennita slipped away.

Pia could hear a high, constant buzzing in her ears, which was incredibly annoying. She didn't know if it was from nerves or the antihistamines, but she had no time for either. Abruptly, she set her glass of wine aside on one of the small tables, turned and came face-to-face with Tatiana, the immaculate, chic and—at least to her—rather frightening Light Fae Queen.

"I've always envied Dragos this property," Tatiana told Pia, as she sipped a glass of sparkling wine. "Dragos certainly made all the right decisions at the right time when he bought the land and hired the architect. Now, of course, the place would sell for tens of millions of dollars—not that he's in the market to sell it, of course. But if he ever is, do get in touch with me, won't you?"

The Light Fae Queen wore a backless dress the deep, rich color of claret. It emphasized her golden skin, hourglass figure, and the dark curling hair she had pinned high at the back of her head. Secretive shadows seemed to flicker in her lovely, famous eyes, or perhaps that was just the effect of the night breeze on the nearby candles.

There were actually only twelve attendees on the

Elder Races side, as Tatiana's only companion that evening was the captain of her guard, Shane Mac Carthaigh. Or was he her plus one? He was certainly doing double duty that evening, but Pia wasn't sure how to categorize him socially.

The Light Fae Queen showed not a single hint of discomfort at the evening's gathering, either in her beautiful, composed face or in her scent, while Pia felt circles of damp sweat soaking in her dress under her arms.

Envying the other woman her poise, she told Tatiana, "We'll be sure to let you know, if he ever decides to sell. I think I've stuck my head in every room and closet now, at least once, and everything is this beautiful. The attention to detail is everywhere."

"I can imagine." Tatiana studied her. "You interest me, young woman. You have a very interesting story that you've chosen not to share with the world. Dragos must see something very special about an herbivore of unknown nature. I always thought if he were to mate, it would be with one of the long-lived predators."

Pia slid a wary sidelong glance at the other woman. Instead of indulging in polite pleasantries, the Light Fae Queen had zeroed in on one of the Cuelebres' most touchy subjects.

Instead of getting more nervous, however, Pia suddenly relaxed. Both she and Dragos had been dodging questions like that from theWyr for the last eighteen months, and while she used to fumble much more in the beginning, by necessity she'd had to learn to grow a thick skin about the topic.

She gave Tatiana a smile. "You know, I would have thought that too, but it's funny how things work out. Speaking of which, I've been meaning to ask you—is Captain Shane your plus one, or your bodyguard for the evening?"

"Does he have to be one or the other?" Tatiana's smiling gaze met hers over the rim of her champagne flute.

"In reality, of course not," Pia told her. "But for dinner plans, yes, I'm afraid he does. Will he be joining us at the table?"

"He would be welcome to, as far as I'm concerned, but I think he would prefer to stand guard."

She inclined her head in thanks. "That's what I needed to know. If you'll excuse me, I need to go make a slight adjustment to the table."

"Of course," Tatiana replied. "You're on duty too, this evening. Everything is lovely, by the way. I do hope we get a chance to chat further sometime this week."

"That's very kind of you," Pia told her. As she left the other woman on the terrace, she muttered soundlessly to herself, *Not if I have anything to say about it, we won't.*

The Light Fae Queen was too curious about things that didn't concern her, and she didn't appear to have any compunction about pursuing them. Pia had fended her off for now, but she didn't have any doubt that Tatiana would circle back around to the subject if it suited her to do so.

Irritably, Pia went in search of someone to flag down to tell them about the place setting, but either the waitstaff were outside with most of the guests, or the kitchen staff were racing madly about, putting final preparations on the salmon soufflés that would be served as the first course.

Or, in Pia's case, a vegan spinach soufflé. While Pia had no idea how to cook one, apparently there was such a thing.

After a few moments, she gave up. It would be quicker and easier if she just took care of things herself.

In any case, she could use a few minutes alone. She felt tired, strung out from all the coffee she had drunk earlier, and the buzzing in her ears was driving her crazy.

She stepped into the dining room and paused to admire the long table, decorated with runners of fresh white roses, and beautifully set with antique bone china, polished silver and cut crystal Italian glasses. Long white candles would be lit just before guests came in.

After dithering over which place setting to pull, she gently gathered up a setting in the middle of the table on the side nearest the entrance to the kitchen. Everything—crystal, china so thin she could see light through it and the silver—was original to the building of the house, kept in perfect condition, fragile and irreplaceable, so she held the pieces with nervous care.

Instead of spreading the other place settings out and disrupting the balance of the table, maybe they could find something decorative to set in the empty spot. There might be more of the white roses in the kitchen, or maybe a candle.

Hell, at this point, she didn't care. They would throw something in the space.

Standing there, with her hands filled with bone china, silverware and crystal, her impetus ran out, while her thinking grew confused and jumbled.

The… there was a cabinet in the butler's pantry….

No, that butler's pantry was in their home in upstate New York. Not in this house.

She blinked down at the pretty, foreign pieces in her hands. She couldn't remember where anything went.

"This doesn't matter," she muttered grimly, as the wheels in her head ground to a halt and refused to move. "Solve it and move on."

Someone in the kitchen would know what to do with the place setting. They could take care of it after they dealt with the soufflés. For now, she could just shove it in a closet somewhere.

There weren't any closets in the dining room, so she hurried out into the hall. There was a rear closet in the hall, in an area near the kitchen, that held a built-in, hidden secretary desk where historically the house-keeper had kept household records. At least her tired brain remembered that much. It would do for now.

As she came within a few feet of the closet door, she smelled blood.

Fresh blood.

Which made no sense. There were doors opening and shutting all over the house, and in any case the meat dish wasn't going to be served until the third course. Why would the scent of blood linger in this quiet nook of the hallway?

Propping the place setting carefully under her arm, she opened the closet door, and flicked on the light as she stepped inside.

Oh, well, there was the fresh blood. Quite a lot of it, spilled in a massive puddle on the floor.

It came from the lacerated throat of Mr. Colton, the vice president's husband, who sat against the farthest wall in an ungainly sprawl, his head leaning far to one side. His white shirt was soaked in the blood that had pooled on the floor.

She blinked down at the wet, sticky pool of blood she stood in.

Then she set the place setting gently, oh so gently on the narrow secretary desk.

Mr. Colton still looked surprised. She wasn't sure her legs were going to support her for much longer. The buzzing in her ears grew louder.

Dragos, she said telepathically.

Yes? Where are you? His mental voice sounded far away. *I thought you were outside with us.*

I was, she said. *But now….*

How exactly does one break the news to her husband that she's standing in a closet with the dead body of one of their dinner guests?

Something's come up, she told him. *You'd better come inside.*

Chapter Eight

I'M IN THE *middle of something.* He sounded impatient. *Is the house on fire?*

She considered that. Metaphorically, in a way, it was, with one of those sneaky house fires that smoldered in a tucked away corner but would blow their lives apart in, say, the next half hour or so.

The world wobbled, and she grabbed at the back of the chair that was tucked tight against the desk. She could feel Mr. Colton's blood beginning to soak into her shoes.

She didn't want to contaminate the scene any more than she already had. Swallowing hard, she eased one foot out of a shoe and stepped backward, out of the closet. As soon as she felt balanced enough on her bare foot, she stepped out of the other shoe.

Pia?

Yes, she told him. *The house is actually on fire. In a manner of speaking.*

Even as she said it, she heard voices as people approached.

"…you are asking the wrong person to explain

human behavior, Jered," Niniane said. "Out of all of us, Pia's the best to ask—she's the one who lived as a human for so many years. I'm sure I saw her come this way a few minutes ago…"

Oh gods. Conflicting impulses careened inside.

What should she do?

Jump in the closet and hide until they passed? No!

Where are you? Dragos asked. His voice had changed. No longer impatient, he sounded sharp and totally engaged.

Just as Niniane, Jered and Tiago rounded the corner, she slammed the closet door and rushed toward them.

"Hi, sweetie," Niniane said. Her gaze fell to Pia's feet, and her eyebrows went up. "Where are your shoes?"

With the dead man in the closet.

"I h-had an accident." Pia pressed shaking hands against her stomach.

Jered, a tall, blond male Djinn with diamondlike eyes, demanded, "Can you explain why we are all here to talk when some of those humans won't engage in conversation?"

PIA, Dragos thundered in her head, making her jump.

She snapped at him shakily, *Don't yell at me like that!*

Tiago said suddenly, "I smell blood."

Well, of course he did. He had, if anything, a more refined sense of smell for such things than Pia did.

"Blood?!" Niniane exclaimed.

It was pointless to try to assert control over something so outrageous, but Pia tried anyway. She said, "Yes, well, there is a problem. I mean, I found a p-problem. I don't suppose I could convince any of you to go back outside and keep everyone busy while Dragos and I deal with it?"

Niniane grabbed her by the arms. "Are you hurt?"

"It's not her blood," Tiago said.

Pia had tried to position herself in the middle of the hallway to act as a barrier, but he shouldered past her. So much for her attempt to gain a little time.

Closing her eyes, she listened as the closet door opened.

After a moment, Tiago said, "It's his blood."

"What on earth are you talking about?" Niniane's grip fell from Pia's arms.

She turned to watch as Niniane and Jered swept past her. Tiago took a step to one side, and all three of them stared into the closet.

Dragos rounded the corner, wearing a fierce frown. "Why didn't you answer me?" he demanded, dropping a hand onto her shoulder. "Where's the damn fire that won't wait?"

Wordlessly, she pointed back down the hall to where the other three stood. As Dragos looked behind her, Niniane pointed into the closet. After a moment, both Tiago and Jered pointed too.

Pia said between her teeth, "I am really going to

love living in our version of Greenland. I bet it's peaceful there. The murder rate can't be anything like D.C.'s."

Dragos's hand tightened on her before it fell away. He strode forward to join the others and looked in the closet.

Niniane said to Tiago, "Once upon a time, I would have been so much more shaken than I am right now. I thought we were going to get a break from this kind of shit on this trip."

"You know, as your chief of security, I have to advise you that we leave right now," Tiago told her.

"We can't leave!" Niniane exclaimed. "That would make us look like we have something to hide."

"I don't give a damn what it looks like, your argumentativeness." Tiago crossed his arms. "Someone has been killed. It's a safety recommendation."

"Fine." She rolled her eyes. "Duly noted."

Dragos's gaze met Pia's. His expression looked calm but she knew from his incandescent, molten gaze that he was furious.

Suddenly the distance between them seemed too great. She hurried toward him, and when she reached his side, he put his arm around her.

He asked, *Why are your shoes in the closet?*

She shivered. *We had an extra place setting, and I was looking for somewhere to stow it when I stepped inside and-and found him. I didn't want to track b-blood everywhere, or contaminate the scene any more than I already had, so I stepped out of them.*

He rubbed her back. "Okay. Now, I want you to go into the security room in the basement and stay there. Will you do that for me, please?"

She shook her head. "No."

"That's a good idea," Tiago said to Niniane. "You could go too."

Dragos glared at her. "Pia. The vice president's husband was murdered *in our house.*"

She gave him an exasperated look. "Like I don't know that already! I am not going downstairs, so put a guard on me if you have to, but I'm staying up here to help."

Jered snapped, "Enough of this squabbling over who is going to run away. You need to catch the murderer immediately, before all our diplomatic chances are ruined."

Dragos rounded on the Djinn. "*I* need to catch the murderer? This has nothing to do with the Wyr."

The Djinn gave him an incredulous look. "You must be joking. The human male's throat was slashed just as a Wyr might do. And as you said, it happened in your house. This is your responsibility. You're involved whether you like it or not. And others will blame you—again, whether you like it or not. Hell, I don't even know who did it, and I blame you."

A hot burst of anger fired through Pia's veins. She snapped, "That's completely unfair! None of our people would do such a thing!"

The Djinn glanced at her. "Fairness has nothing to do with it. Appearances are everything." He turned back to Dragos. "You need to either find the murderer quickly, or you need to hide it. If you want someone to get rid of the body, I can do it."

"Bullshit," muttered Niniane. "He's *the vice president's husband*, Jered. You can't just whisk away the body!"

"This is a stupid conversation," Tiago said.

Jered rounded on him. "I see that you haven't come up with anything useful."

"*That's enough*," Dragos hissed. As they all fell silent, he said to the others, "Leave. Go back to the others and mingle." As they hesitated, he said between his teeth, "You're wasting valuable time."

Niniane touched Pia's hand and said in her head, *I don't care how much Dragos snarls or tries to order everybody around. If you need me, call and I'll come.*

Thank you. Pia grasped her fingers briefly.

Even still, Niniane lingered until Tiago pulled her away. He told her, "Let's go. And you do not leave my side for anything, faerie. I mean you do not step two feet away from me."

"Oh, pffft," Niniane exclaimed, as she walked away with him.

"I think you're making a mistake not getting rid of the body," Jered said. With that parting shot, he strode after the other couple.

"For being such a bright people, sometimes the Djinn are remarkably clueless," Dragos muttered. He turned his attention to her. "Bayne's on his way. How long do we have until dinner is supposed to be served?"

Calculating rapidly, she said, "Soon. Maybe in five or six minutes. Gennita checked in with me just a little while ago, and I told her fifteen minutes. That was when I went to take the extra place setting off the table, and-and-and—"

Words seemed to stick in her throat as her brain seized up again.

Giving her a sharp, questioning glance, Dragos put one bracing hand on her back again, right over the tense knot between her shoulder blades. Grateful for his silent touch, she managed to stop stuttering.

Bayne rounded the corner and strode toward them, his big body a fluid, fast machine. He didn't waste time asking questions when he reached them. Instead, he swept the scene quickly with those hard, hazel eyes, taking everything in, and then he turned to Dragos.

Pia was used to seeing Bayne smiling in a laid-back stance, usually with hands tucked into his jeans pockets. It always jarred her when the sentinels flipped some internal switch in their heads and went into warrior mode.

Dragos said to him, "Guard Pia. Go where she goes, no matter what."

"You got it," said Bayne.

Before Pia could mention that Eva was a perfectly adequate guard, thank you very much, Dragos added,

"And Bayne? If necessary, you fly her out of D.C., and you don't stop flying until you both get back to the Tower."

So that was why Dragos wanted Bayne guarding her, not Eva. Eva was a highly trained, effective warrior, but her Wyr form was canine. Not only could Bayne fly, but he also had the strength to carry Pia in flight.

"Understood." Bayne turned that hard gaze to Pia, and his expression softened somewhat as he looked down the length of her body at her bare, smudged feet.

Furiously, Pia wanted to snap at both men for thinking they could decide her fate without her input, but she managed to catch herself up before she said anything she might regret later.

She wasn't thinking as rationally as she could be, and she knew Dragos wasn't either. He had seen a dead body and clicked into hyperprotective mode, and nothing was going to ratchet him down again until he felt like he had gained some measure of control over the situation.

There was that concept again – control over the situation. She glanced at dead Mr. Colton again and nearly burst into hysterical laughter. Like her going into hysterics was going to help anybody. She managed to swallow that impulse down too.

Dragos turned an incandescent gold gaze onto her. He said, "Stall dinner for as long as you can. Go."

She nodded. "Got it."

With Bayne on her heels, she ran barefoot to the kitchen, which was awhirl with activity. The kitchen staff was busy preparing the second course to follow the salmon soufflé, delicate grilled endive salads with light shavings of aged parmesan cheese and paper-thin Parma ham arranged in a fan on top.

She didn't try to talk over everybody else. Instead, she said telepathically, *Gennita, we need to stall dinner for at least another half hour. Longer, if possible.*

The chef spun to face her, eyes widening in dismay. *We can't stall dinner! The soufflés are almost done cooking!*

Normally she would be much more gentle with Gennita's wounded feelings, but now she didn't have the emotional or physical time. She told the other woman grimly, *We have much bigger problems right now than the soufflés. Get another round of hors d'oeuvres outside as fast as you can.*

But they're all gone! Gennita quivered visibly.

Pia threw up her hands. *Send out the salads then! Send out anything, along with more alcohol. Lots and lots of alcohol.*

Gennita rounded on her staff and started snapping out orders.

As Pia turned to Bayne, Eva slipped into the kitchen, caught sight of her and walked over. "When are you going to announce it's time to go into dinner?"

"I'm not," she said grimly. "Run upstairs and get me a pair of shoes."

Eva stared at her bare feet. "What happened to the ones you were wearing?"

"Later," she told Eva.

"But you only have one pair with you that matches that outfit. Which ones do you want?"

"I don't care!" she cried. "Shoes, get me shoes. Dark ones, that nobody will notice."

At that, Eva seemed to catch up with the fact that something had gone badly awry, because her expression changed until she looked much as Bayne did, bladelike and focused. She took off running.

"I need alcohol too," Pia told Bayne. She meant it desperately.

He took her at her word, strode over to the counter where the liquor bottles sat, swiped up a bottle of cognac and handed it to her.

She took a long pull, coughed and handed it back to him. He drank from the bottle as well.

Gennita rushed up to her, wide eyes teary. "What should I do with the soufflés?"

Pia's gaze went unfocused. She stared into space a moment. Then she said, "Burn them."

The chef's expression quivered. "They're made with Balik Fillet Tsar Nikolaj smoked salmon. It costs $360 a pound. We can't just burn them."

"Yes, we can." Pushing past the other woman, she rushed over to the ovens and turned them to their highest settings.

Gennita followed behind her. "What are you doing?!"

Pia said between her teeth, "There are too many

guests with sensitive noses. We need the smell of something burning to fill the air. And I need to be able to tell the truth when I go out there and say we've had a slight accident in the kitchen, and dinner's going to be a little later than we thought."

"That would never happen in real life," Gennita muttered. "Not in my kitchen."

"Nobody outside the Wyr knows that," Pia said. "At least I don't think."

Bayne dropped the cognac, and the bottle shattered on the floor. Everybody stopped what they were doing to stare at him.

He said, "Oops. Accident."

Eva loped back into the kitchen, carrying high heeled black pumps. Pia snatched at them and slipped them on her feet. She told Eva, "Find Dragos. Do whatever he needs."

"But…" The other woman paused. Normally Eva guarded Pia, no matter what. Clearly confused, she looked from Pia to Bayne.

"We're switching roles tonight," Bayne told her. "Go."

Eva shot out of the kitchen again.

Pia strode to the liquor counter, grabbed another bottle at random and took a healthy swig from it. The two hits of alcohol seemed to make the buzzing in her ears fade away, until she felt dizzy, with her head stuffed with cotton wool.

The first faint hint of an acrid smell filled the

kitchen.

"Okay," she whispered. "Okay."

She waited another minute until the acrid smell grew stronger, and then, followed by Bayne, she strode outside with a big apologetic smile to face her powerful, intelligent, and not-altogether-friendly guests.

✧ ✧ ✧

DRAGOS DIDN'T KNOW how Pia would stall things, and he didn't care. He just knew she would handle it.

Dismissing the issue from his mind, he concentrated on the problem at hand.

Problem equaling corpse, of course.

Bracing one hand on the doorway, he leaned into the closet without stepping inside, and inspected Colton. It was easier to do, now that he was by himself and not distracted by the others.

The dragon surfaced in his mind again, not at all perturbed by the unexpected dead body. He noted details.

He took note of faint whiffs of old scents, along with the scent of aged wood, and set them aside. The only new scents in the closet were Pia and, of course, Colton's copious blood, along with a faint, underlying hint of chemical stink.

Colton was wearing KO Odorless Odor Eliminator again, as was his wife. Dragos had taken note of it as soon as the Coltons had stepped into his house. He had also noted every other smiling guest who wore it.

All of them were his enemies. They knew it.

He knew it.

And one of them had murdered a man in his house.

Still leaning into the closet, he reached for the pen in his breast pocket. With the tip, he probed at the wounds on Colton's neck. There were five wounds, four on one side, and one on the other. As Jered so obnoxiously pointed out, on the surface at least, it did look like a Wyr kill.

Dragos was very familiar with the general pattern. The style of the wounds was reminiscent of a Wyr ripping out someone's throat with his talons. He had done it himself a number of times over the centuries, but if there was one thing he would stake his life on in that moment, it was that no Wyr present would *ever* betray him in his own house. Everyone on this trip was handpicked, either by Bayne or by himself. Only the highest-qualified Wyr, and the most loyal, had been chosen.

So, not only did someone who was wearing KO Odorless Odor Eliminator kill Colton, but they had somehow made it look like a Wyr had committed the murder. They had planned this very carefully. Bayne had installed the tiny security cameras in every room, but not in the hallways, and certainly not in any of the closets. The killer had murdered Colton in one of the blind spots.

Eyes narrowed, he probed deeper at one of the wounds. The flesh at the two edges of the cut fell apart cleanly. The wounds were almost surgical in their neatness. The blades had been very sharp.

Even still, the blood would have spurted until Colton's heart stopped. How had the murderer kept from getting blood on him—or her?

He looked more closely at the area around the body, at the closet floor and underneath the desk. There, he discovered a cheap pocket rain poncho stuffed behind the chair. He didn't bother to pull it out. If he did, he knew he would find it splattered with blood.

A footstep sounded nearby in the hall.

Sir, Eva said in his head. *I'm supposed to help you with whatever you need.*

Eva was smart to telepathize before trying to approach behind his back. He pulled back from the corpse and straightened to turn to her.

Two things, he said. *First, get security to search the house from top to bottom, and move fast. We're looking for a weapon, some kind of glove with razor blades attached to the tips of the fingers and thumbs. When it's found, let me know. I want photos taken. Nobody should move it or touch it with their bare hands.*

Standing on the balls of her feet, Eva looked sober and sharp, and ready to run as soon as he finished giving orders.

Second thing, he told her. *Get a list of people who disappeared from the security cameras nearest this location, from the time the guests arrived to—*he checked his watch—*about five minutes ago, when Pia walked down this hall. Tell them to* *move very fast. I want a list of possible suspects in the next fifteen minutes.*

Yes, sir. She bolted.

In the distance, his sharp hearing picked up Pia's voice outside, followed by what sounded like good-natured laughter. Almost at the same time, he noticed an acrid scent, like burning food, and he smiled to himself. She had dealt with the problem splendidly.

If he wasn't missed beforehand, Colton would definitely be missed when dinner was announced. Dragos needed to come up with a plan of action, because every moment right now was critical.

Coming to a decision, he closed the door, straightened his cuffs and strode down the hall. *Pia, please quietly ask the president to meet me in the library.*

Okay. Her mental voice sounded tense. *Our time just got shorter. Vice President Colton has started looking for her husband.*

It was bound to happen sooner or later, he told her. *By the way, what kind of fresh meat do we have in the kitchen?*

Don't tell me you're hungry.

She had been acting so shocky earlier, he was glad to hear a hint of dark humor in her voice. *No,* he said. *But I would like to know if there is a very large cut of something, a roast perhaps, or a leg of lamb. Even a turkey would do. Whatever it is can't be frozen. If we do have anything, I need it in the library too.*

I'll check then go talk to the president.

Thank you. He paused for the briefest of moments.

Everything is going to be okay, you know. Even if we can't make this okay, we're going to be fine.

Her voice warmed. *I know we will. I love you.*

I love you too, he told her.

He realized he didn't tell her that enough. She never complained or appeared to take hurt from it, but still, he made a note to tell her more often. He tried to show her how he felt, but she deserved the words too.

Stepping into the library, he poured himself a scotch, took a seat, crossed his legs and waited.

Shortly, one of the kitchen staff walked in briskly, carrying a tray that held a large, irregularly shaped item wrapped in butcher's paper. Following Dragos's orders, he set the tray on a round Chippendale table and left.

Within a few minutes, he heard Pia and Johnson chatting as they came near. They walked into the library, with Bayne and the president's guard following behind.

"You two," Dragos said to Bayne and the president's man. "Wait outside."

The Secret Security guard looked to the president, who gave him a nod. Only then did he move with Bayne to step outside the room.

Dragos added in Bayne's head telepathically, *Cordon off the area of hall where the body is. And nobody comes in this room without my say-so. Do you hear? I mean come hell or high water, nobody comes in here, and I expect things will get very unpleasant out there soon.*

I hear you, said Bayne, as he backed out of the room,

closing the double doors to the hall. *Nobody's coming in, not even this nice, dedicated soldier standing with me right now, although I hope to gods I don't have to shoot him. I'll have George stand guard with us.*

George was part of Bayne's security detail, a massive, easygoing man who was also a rare Wyr elephant. As strong and stubborn as a troll, if George stood guard at the doors with Bayne, nobody would get in unless Dragos said they could.

Very good, Dragos said. Leisurely he stood. "Thank you for coming, Ben. Can I pour you a drink?"

The president laughed. "You've been very generous with the alcohol this evening, Dragos. I think I'd better pass on any more until we have some dinner."

"About that dinner," said Dragos.

As he spoke, he moved to the liquor tray, refreshed his drink and poured a second scotch for the president. With a quick glance at Pia, he raised his eyebrows at her in inquiry. She looked tense again, and very pale. Dark patches of feverish red touched her cheeks. Twisting her fingers together, she shook her head.

Johnson laughed again, only this time he sounded uneasier. He looked back and forth at Dragos and Pia. "Don't tell me there's been another kitchen accident."

"No, there hasn't." Dragos turned to face the president, holding both drinks. "I'm going to ask you for one thing—only one, but it's going to be hard for you for a little while."

"What's that?" President Johnson's intelligent

expression had turned closed and wary.

Walking over to him, Dragos held out a scotch. "We need to have a frank, tough conversation, you and I. And whatever you may think, or however you may react while we're having it, I need for you to hear me out."

Chapter Nine

J OHNSON SEARCHED HIS gaze then turned to study Pia's anxious figure. His gaze fell to her twisted hands. "Okay," he said simply, reaching out to accept the scotch. "I believe we can have a civilized discourse. Now, what's this about?"

Here goes, Dragos thought. He met Pia's gaze as he said, "In the last hour and a half, one of your humans murdered the vice president's husband, and they tried to make it look like a Wyr did it."

Johnson's eyes narrowed, and his frame stiffened. "Murdered—Victor is *dead?*"

"Very dead," Dragos told him bluntly. He swallowed scotch. "His body is in a hall closet. The killer used some kind of glove with either razor blades or knives attached to the end of the fingers and thumb. My staff is looking for the murder weapon now. The motion used was an inward, slashing one, as if the killer went to grab Colton's throat one-handed, only instead of strangling him, he closed his fingers and yanked. The carotid arteries on both sides of Colton's throat were cut. He bled out within ninety seconds, tops."

Outside the library, someone called out. Dragos could hear the vice president's voice in the distance, asking, *Have you seen Victor?*

Dragos tuned her out.

Johnson remained standing where he was, his tall, distinguished figure vibrating with reaction, expression blazing with shock and outrage. "Victor is dead, and you're claiming that a human did it?!"

"It's a fact, Ben," Dragos said. "I can prove it."

Turning, Dragos walked to the desk, set aside his scotch and began to unwrap the large piece of meat on the tray. When he had opened the package, he discovered it was a leg of lamb, nicely covered with a thin layer of white fat. Excellent. The fat would show every mark.

Pia moved to sit with a plop at one end of the sofa. Both she and Johnson watched Dragos, their expressions filled with fascination and repugnance.

"The killer was cunning," Dragos told them. "He put a great deal of planning into the murder. He dodged security cameras and made a murder weapon that would simulate a Wyr's capabilities. But he was stupid too. The murder weapon didn't simulate a Wyr's talons. Wyr handgrips are stronger than humans. Maybe he was concerned his human grip wouldn't be able to strike a killing blow. If I were him, I would have wanted to make sure I could cut the carotid arteries, so I would have been focused on making sure my blades were very sharp. That's what he did. Watch closely now—these are what my talons look like."

As Johnson and Pia stared, he held out one hand and made the slight shift that brought out his talons. Splaying his fingers, he held them up for the others to see.

Johnson said, "I've never seen that in person."

"Most people haven't," Dragos told him.

The president looked at Pia. "Do you have talons like that too?"

She shook her head with a smile that looked strained. "Only predator Wyr have talons like that. I'm an herbivore. I don't have the nature or the personality for it."

"You're perfectly safe, Ben," Dragos told the president. "You can step closer, if you like. Do you see how the talons are shaped?"

Fascination overtook Johnson's shock and outrage, and he took a few steps toward Dragos. "They're curved and angled to a point, from the fingertips to the tip."

"Exactly. They're extremely sharp, but they're also natural. They're made of a hard protein called keratin—which means they aren't exactly uniform either, not like a manufactured blade is. Watch what happens when I make a wound like the ones that killed Colton."

Striking quickly, Dragos grabbed hold of the leg of lamb. He had to pin the meat to the tray with one hand while he tightened his grip and pulled with the other. Flesh tore underneath his talons. Both Johnson and Pia flinched back, but when he was finished, they moved closer to stare at what lay on the tray.

Stepping away from the lamb to give them a little space, Dragos let his talons retract as he pulled out a handkerchief and wiped off his hands. It was getting noisy outside. Questions were being asked, along with demands.

Concentrating on his small task, he said, "This meat was refrigerated, so it's a little stiff, but it will still show you want I want you to see. If you look closely at the marks I just made, you'll see there is a bit of tear to them. The edges are jagged. It's hard to kill someone like this. It's messy. Likely as not, you'll tear out chunks of flesh when you do it." He looked up and met Johnson's sharp gaze. "Colton's wounds are not like this, Ben. They're surgical. The edges of the cuts are sharp. They were made with blades, not talons."

"Why are you telling me this, now?" Johnson asked. His shock and fear had receded, and he studied Dragos with his arms crossed.

"Because this is the single piece of evidence I have that will be the most compelling for you," Dragos told him. "The killer might have been cunning, but aside from being stupid, he was also bigoted and insulting. He believed the first thing anybody would think when they saw Colton would be that a Wyr had killed him. In my house, Ben. With my handpicked staff, my highly trained and reliable security. *With my wife present.* He believed that everybody would think the *Wyr* were that stupid. And he ignored the fact that none of us have any motive to commit this crime."

Only then did Dragos let his rage show. Pia swallowed hard, and Johnson's gaze flickered, but he didn't flinch or back down like he had a few moments ago.

A knock sounded at the door, and a man called out, "Mr. President, are you all right? The first lady is asking after you."

Johnson raised his voice. He sounded strong and steady. "Yes, Brock. We're all safe in here. I'll let you know when I'm done."

"Very good, sir."

Johnson said to Dragos, "So the wounds are the most compelling piece of evidence, you said. What other evidence do you have?"

"Other than Colton's blood and Pia's scent—she was the one who found him, by the way—there were no other scents. The killer was wearing KO Odorless Odor Eliminator. Only deer hunters wear the scent blocker, or Wyr criminals—and of course now anybody who is involved in the Right to Privacy movement is wearing it too." Dragos gave him a cynical smile. "But only the Wyr would know that or be able to make that claim, and nobody would be listening if we were the suspects. And the only people wearing KO Odorless Odor Eliminator here tonight are human. Your killer is one of the humans."

Johnson drew in a sharp breath. "Do you have any

idea who the killer might be?"

Dragos shook his head. "No, and I don't care. At first I trapped myself into thinking I had to find the killer before Colton's murder was discovered, but then I realized—this isn't my problem. I'm insulted that the killer did this in my home, and I'm offended, but this is a human issue. And the fact that it happened during the one week when humans and the Elder Races were making an active effort to maintain good relations is disturbing. Aside from whatever the killer had against Colton, someone doesn't want us to get along, Ben."

"My God, what a bloody mess," Johnson muttered. He rubbed his face and looked at Dragos over the tops of his fingers. "Okay, I believe you."

Dragos relaxed slightly. "Thank you," he said. "I appreciate that. My staff has been looking for the murder weapon, but they have instructions to take photos only and not to disturb anything if they find it. And security has been reviewing recordings of who disappeared from view from the cameras placed in the rooms during the time that the murder took place."

"I need that list," Johnson said. "Along with footage of the recordings to back it up." His somber expression turned sour. "And I would appreciate a list of all the people who came here wearing that scent blocker. Up until now, I've ignored the Right to Privacy movement, as I thought it would blow over once we got things on a better footing, but not anymore."

Johnson might have the luxury of ignoring it up

until now, but Dragos, for one, wouldn't be ignoring anything to do with the Right to Privacy movement. In fact, he planned on investigating it thoroughly and having extensive dossiers created on every prominent person involved.

"Of course," Dragos told him. "You'll get the full list of everyone I noted, so you can compare it with the shortlist compiled from the security footage. Your killer will be one of the humans on the shortlist. And naturally, we'll open our home up to your people for a thorough investigation."

"Thank you." Johnson stepped forward and extended his hand. Dragos shook it. "And thank you for your calm and incisive thinking, and for your help as the authorities resolve this matter."

"You're welcome," Dragos told him. When Johnson made as if to withdraw, he maintained his grip until the other man met his gaze. "It's important to me that we remain allies, Ben, just as it is important to every other demesne leader here, which is why we've all come. But make no mistake—we're not here because we're apologetic. We're here because we're concerned about Elder Races violence, just as we're also concerned about human abuses and violence—the hundreds of people killed in school and theater shootings, and the thousands killed in terrorist attacks. Violence against police, along with police bigotry and brutality, and the tragedy of what happened at Devil's Gate. We're willing to work together with you as partners to lessen these incidents, but none of us are willing to become scapegoats."

The president's expression tightened, but he gave Dragos a short nod. "Understood."

As Dragos released the other man's hand, for the first time in a long time, Pia spoke up telepathically. She said softly in his head, *You're sexy when you're incisive and imperious.*

The dragon in his head hadn't receded and preened at the compliment from his mate. He gave her a sidelong smile as he told her, *I didn't know how the conversation was going to go or how difficult it might get. All I knew was that we needed to walk out of this room allies, but Johnson also needed to know—the Elder Races aren't going to be his bitch, just because some humans decided to throw a hissy.*

That's my dragon politician I know and love so well, she crooned.

He laughed softly. They watched as Johnson squared his shoulders, strode for the double doors and threw them open.

A noisy crowd of guests had gathered outside in the hall. Tumultuous noise blasted into the room, as everyone tried to talk or shout at once. The president stepped forward and raised his voice to address them.

Pia rolled her eyes and said, *I can't even deal with all the drama llama.*

As Dragos cocked an amused eyebrow at her, she collapsed in a dead faint.

✧   ✧   ✧

PIA DREAMED THE dragon coiled around her in a white heat and raged at anybody else who tried to come close. All the protestors with their slogans and placards had to remain outside on the sidewalks.

You're not helping any, she tried to tell him. *We need to get the dinner on the table, or the soufflés will be ruined. We can serve Mr. Colton in the closet. There's already a place setting on the desk.*

But she was wrapped in thick cotton wool that made it impossible for her to move or say the words out loud.

Then the dragon picked her up and raced around with her, as they searched for her spinach soufflé so that she could eat it before it fell flat. *I'm not hungry*, she wanted to tell him, while in the kitchen, Gennita sniffled over the endive salad.

The Djinn Soren appeared in a swirl of Power, but he was a member of the Elder tribunal. He wasn't one of the demesne leaders, and they didn't have a place at the table for him.

"Bring Wyr doctors," the white-faced dragon told him. "And Soren, I swear to all the gods, if you try to bargain with me right now, I'll—"

"I will return as quickly as I can," said the Djinn, his starlike gaze fixed on Pia. His physical form disappeared.

And then there was blood, so much blood. She cried and wrung her hands, because her shoes were ruined, and she didn't have time to wash her feet.

That brought the dragon's attention back to her. Somehow they had arrived in an unfamiliar bedroom. She couldn't figure out whose house she was in. As she lay stretched out on the bed, he bent over her prone figure and placed a hot hand on her forehead.

"Hush, darling," he murmured. "Don't cry so. Everything will be all right."

Suddenly the dragon vanished, and it was Dragos stroking her forehead, Dragos, who looked stark and on the edge of panic.

She didn't think she had ever seen Dragos in a panic before. That frightened her more than anything she could have imagined. *Don't go*, she said, trying to reach through the cotton wool to take his hand. *Don't leave me.*

Strong fingers closed over hers. They were as hot as the hand stroking her hair. "What nonsense are you talking now?" he whispered gently. "I could never leave you. Pia, you're hallucinating."

Rousing, she finally managed to get verbal words out of her mouth. "I am not," she told him in a strong voice. "There is too a dead man in our closet."

Well, in somebody's closet. She was pretty sure they weren't at home. If only she could remember where they were, and why.

"Ssh," he told her. "None of that matters right now."

She huffed. Easy for him to say. He's not the one who raced around like a crazy person all day trying to pull off the most important dinner party of his life.

Dr. Medina appeared in her line of sight, just behind Dragos's shoulder. Okay, maybe she really was hallucinating, because she hadn't even called the doctor back yet.

"Get out of my way, Dragos," the doctor said.

He moved away quickly, and the doctor leaned over to smile at Pia. "Just relax, dear," she said, showing Pia the glove she wore. The one with five blades on the end of the fingers and thumb. "You won't feel a thing."

As she opened her mouth, true darkness rose up to swallow her scream.

Chapter Ten

WHEN SHE NEXT opened her eyes, she found herself in their bedroom in D.C., tucked underneath the covers. She ached everywhere, like she had the flu or someone had beaten her in every major muscle group.

The room was still a mess, clothes strewn everywhere. The curtains were pulled, with no hint of sunlight along the edges, but the bedside lamp on Dragos's side of the bed was on, throwing a circle of warm illumination into the room.

Dragos lay stretched out on his back beside her on top of the covers, fully clothed in black jeans and a black silk sweater. He had the fingers of one hand draped over his eyes, while he held her hand with the other.

She could hear several voices in the distance, along with movement, both inside the house and out. Someone slammed a car door outside.

She squeezed Dragos's fingers, and he erupted upright to bend over her, eyes blazing. He called out, "Medina, she's awake."

Almost immediately, the bedroom door opened, and Dr. Medina stepped inside. "I'm here."

Briefly, Pia considered sitting up, but it seemed like too much effort. "I thought you were a dream," she told the doctor in a rusty voice.

Dr. Medina smiled at her. "You were pretty confused when I arrived."

"You fainted," Dragos told her. Lines of tension scored his face. "Scared centuries off my life when I saw you collapse like a rag doll."

Contritely, she squeezed his fingers as she thought back. "We were with the president in the library. How long ago was that?"

"Last evening. It's almost dawn now. Investigators have been here all night." Dragos touched her face, stroking the curve of her cheek. "How do you feel?"

She admitted, "Achy."

"Do you need anything, perhaps a drink of water?"

"Maybe in a bit," she sighed. His caress was so soothing, it made her want to close her eyes again.

Dragos turned a hard expression to the doctor. "You said you would talk to us both when Pia woke up. Well, she's awake now, so start talking."

The doctor gave him a look of rebuke. "I also told you she was going to be okay." She turned to Pia. "And you *are* going to be okay. Do you feel up to having a conversation right now, or do you need more rest?"

Beside her, Dragos felt so tight, like he was going to explode. Remembering the raging dragon from her dream—hallucination—she nodded. She did need more rest, but she didn't think he could hold off any longer.

"Okay," said Dr. Medina, straightening. "I have some great news and some not very great news for you, and it's all tied together. Remember, the most important thing is—you're going to be okay, and so is your baby."

"*What?*" Pia said, not believing what she had just heard. Was she hallucinating again? She glanced sideways at Dragos, who looked as thunderstruck as her. "I'm not pregnant. I can't be pregnant."

Swiftly, Dragos placed one large hand over her flat stomach. She felt his Power probing deep within her. Placing her hand over his, she sank her awareness deep into her body too.

"I don't sense anything," Dragos said.

Pia muttered, "I don't either."

Dr. Medina folded her arms and regarded them both with a certain wry, sour expression. "You're not really questioning my diagnosis, are you? The last I heard, neither one of you had a medical license."

"But I'm not feeling anything." She felt close to tears. "Does that mean something's wrong?"

"*Wait.*" Dragos leaned closer, his expression arrested. "Fuck me. I've got it."

"I don't feel it! I can't sense anything." Frantically she searched harder, but she couldn't feel a thing, not until Dragos's Power surrounded her awareness and drew her attention to…

A slight something, nestled deep, hardly more than a shadow. Catching her breath, she strained everything she could toward that subtle shadow but couldn't pick up any more details.

She would have missed it entirely if it hadn't been for Dragos pointing it out.

And Dragos had missed it entirely until the doctor told them.

"Can you feel it now?" Dragos asked.

"Yes, but what does it mean?" she whispered anxiously. "Liam didn't feel anything like this."

An incredulous smile lit Dragos's hard features, and his gold gaze flashed up to hers. "I think the little shit's cloaking itself. And its cloaking ability is so damn good, it fooled even me."

Pia's gaze flew to the doctor's, who nodded in confirmation. Wonder coursed through her tired body, along with a tumultuous cascade of joy.

She said to Dragos, "You *do* have mighty sperm. Once we made the decision, we must have gotten pregnant on our very first *pow*."

He kissed her swiftly but sobered as he turned back to face Dr. Medina. "You said there was not so great news."

"Yes, well." The doctor looked down at her feet and pursed her lips. "Remember this, and keep it firmly fixed in your mind—you're going to be okay, and the baby is going to be okay."

Pia's anxiety came back, squashing the incredulous joy. Not wanting to hear what came next while she was lying flat on the bed, she pushed herself upright. "What is it? Why have I felt so sick and had so many symptoms?"

"Sometimes, when a predator and an herbivore are mated, complications can arise," Dr. Medina told them. "Sometimes those complications turn serious. You remember how nauseated you were during your pregnancy with Liam?"

She snorted. "I'll never forget it. I was sick every time I took my necklace off."

"You can roughly compare this situation to when a human mother has a different Rh factor in her blood than her baby." The doctor paused. "Have you heard of that before?"

Dragos shook his head, but Pia nodded. "I've heard of it."

Dr. Medina looked at her. "Often there's no problem with the first child a mother has, but during the pregnancy she develops antibodies to carrying the fetus, so there can be complications with the second child. Those can get severe."

"What are you saying?" Pia asked, gripping Dragos's hand tightly. "Are you saying I've developed antibodies to carrying Dragos's fetuses?"

"That's a simple way to put it, but yes, you have," the doctor replied. "And your symptoms appeared much more quickly and are more extreme."

"But you said they would be all right," Dragos said sharply.

"And they will." Dr. Medina turned to her and said forcefully, "You *will*. We will make sure of it. There is no reason at all to panic over this. You will do everything you did for Liam's pregnancy. You will eat right, exercise when you feel good and whenever possible avoid stress. Last night I treated you with spells to dampen your symptoms. I can also develop a drug protocol specifically targeted to suppress your antibodies, so that your body doesn't reject the baby. We will monitor this pregnancy very closely. That means examinations every two weeks, so that we can make adjustments if necessary."

Pia tried to calm the shaking in her limbs. "Okay," she said unsteadily. She tried to smile at Dragos. "We can do that. It's going to be okay."

"Yes," he said simply. "Nothing else is acceptable."

But Pia could tell—they both felt too much on edge, too close to disaster to really settle, which was why, when Dr. Medina took a deep breath, they turned to her so quickly.

"Now for the not so great news," Dr. Medina said.

Pia felt her stomach bottom out. She whispered, "I thought *that* was the not so great news."

The doctor gave her a kind smile. "That was part of it. The other part is—and there's no easy way to say this—Pia, this has got to be your last pregnancy. I'm very sorry to tell you this, but if you try to get pregnant a third time, as extreme as your reaction has become, the likelihood is, you'll miscarry it almost right away. You would almost certainly miscarry with this pregnancy too over the next month or two, if you hadn't received medical attention—which you *have*, and you and this baby are *just fine*. But if you were to try for a third pregnancy, you'll only put yourself at risk and both you and Dragos through a great deal of heartache. I can help you bring this baby to term, but I can't help you with another one."

Pia held herself still, absorbing the news. After a moment, she said, "Is that all of it?"

"Yes, pretty much."

She bit her lip as she looked from Dr. Medina to Dragos. "I was so sure I wasn't pregnant, I took a couple of doses of antihistamines yesterday. Is that a problem?"

The doctor shook her head. "Not at all. Some human drugs work well for Wyr, and that happens to be one of them. And since you're *not* human, you can enjoy everything that you did when you were pregnant with Liam, including wine and alcohol, since there's no placental transfer of alcohol for expectant Wyr mothers."

She expelled a quick sigh of relief and the stiffness went out of her spine.

Dr. Medina continued, "I want you on bed rest for the next two days, so that your system can recover from the symptoms you've developed while I get your protocol developed. Then you can take your first dose. I've been making arrangements through the night for my other patients, and I've set up temporary privileges at Georgetown Hospital while you remain in D.C. That's where I'm going in a few hours to work on creating your protocol, so I'll be on hand if you need me. If you have any questions or concerns, you've got me on speed dial. Until then, calm down, don't stress, eat lots of lovely good food and enjoy your new pregnancy with that very intriguing mystery you've got baking in your oven." Dr. Medina's gaze slid to Dragos. "And let your husband pamper you."

"I can't thank you enough," Pia told her.

Dr. Medina touched her shoulder. "It's my pleasure, Pia. I'll leave you two alone now."

When the door shut behind her, Pia sat for a moment, absorbing everything the doctor had said.

Then she whirled around to throw her arms around Dragos, her face suffused with glee. "Oh my God, we're really pregnant! Part of me was so convinced it wasn't ever going to happen!"

His arms came around her, crushing her ribs, he held her so tightly. He rasped, "When you fainted like that, you scared the shit out of me."

"I know, I'm so sorry." She stroked the back of his head.

Pulling back, he kissed her hard, several times, then hugged her tightly again and rocked her.

Compulsively, she put her hand on her stomach

and sought once more for that subtle shadow. When she found it, joy thrilled through her again. "You didn't by any chance get a glimpse of what sex it is, did you?"

"No. It's cloaking too tightly." Catching what she did, one corner of his mouth lifted as he said, "He's sneaky."

"Or she's discreet," she told him. "Oh my God, I really didn't think we could do it—and I certainly didn't think we could do it so soon."

Dragos's smile died. He asked, "How do you feel about the rest of what the doctor told us?"

She sobered too as she considered. After a few minutes, she said, "You know, I feel good. I'm still in shock that we actually *got* pregnant, and I'm just relieved to know that the baby and I are fine." She caught a glimpse of his face and added quickly, "And we're going to continue to be fine. As far as the rest of it goes… Dragos, we're lucky that we have one child, let alone that we're going to have two. I think—I'm not going to lie, I think it's going to make me sad sometimes. But if that happens, it will be far in the future, and all I will have to do is look at the two beautiful children we do have and I'll be able to remind myself how lucky we are. Besides, if we get ever desperate to have another baby around, we can always adopt." She sneaked a peek at his frowning expression. "How about you?"

"As long as you're okay, everything is okay even when it's not." Unsmiling, he met her gaze. "When you're not okay, the world is hell."

He had tightened one hand into a fist. She laid her hand over it, remembering the raging dragon in her hallucinations. She said gently, "And I'm okay. I'm more than okay, I'm over the moon."

"Despite feeling achy?" He passed one hand over her hair, tucking it behind her shoulder.

"This is worth feeling achy any day of the week." Somewhere, a door slammed again, reminding her of the outside world and its concerns. "What happened while I was out of it?"

He made a face and gesture that sliced through air. "Drama llamas."

"What?" She laughed.

The stress had begun to lift from his face, which she was glad to see. He cocked an eyebrow at her. "Don't you remember what you said just before you collapsed?"

She thought back then shook her head. "No, I'm afraid not."

"You rolled your eyes and said, 'I can't even deal with the drama llama.'" He chuckled then rubbed his eyes. "It wasn't funny at the time, though, dammit."

"I'm so sorry." She leaned against him, and he shifted to put his back against the headboard while keeping one arm around her. She curled against his side, one leg draped across his hips. "Do they have any idea who did it? Who killed Colton, I mean?"

After a moment, he told her, "After studying the

footage from the cameras, security narrowed the suspects down to three people—Aaron Davis, Janice Wilmington and the speaker's security detail. And a few hours ago, they found the murder weapon. It was exactly what I thought, a gauntlet with curved blades welded to the ends of the fingers and thumbs. The murderer had it custom made."

She shuddered at the thought. "Where was it?"

"The killer had pried up a board and stuffed it under the floor in one of the bathrooms."

"I know we own this house, but I'm so glad this didn't happen in our actual home," she told him. "I would feel so violated if it had."

His hold tightened. "We would never have had any of those assholes in our home."

"True." She had to think a moment to place the names with titles and faces. Aaron Davis was the vice president's chief of staff, Janice Wilmington was the majority leader. She couldn't remember what the speaker of the House's security detail looked like. Curiously, she asked, "Who do you think did it?"

"I'm positive it was one of the two men, Davis or the security guy. Colton was a tall man. Wilmington isn't tall enough to have inflicted the wounds on him, at least not at the angle the cuts at his throat were made. As for why, I really don't give a damn. I just want them all out of my house and gone for good."

He pressed his mouth to her forehead, and they rested for several minutes.

"Bed rest for two days." She sighed. "I didn't bring any books with me. I thought I was going to be too busy to read this week."

"I'll go out and get you something to read tomorrow," he whispered. He began rubbing her back in long, soothing strokes. In no time, she grew sleepy and relaxed.

"Pregnant," she murmured. "I feel so gleeful about that, I could bust. We're pregnant, and we have no idea what it is."

"I could try to scan again, but I don't want to force it," he said quietly.

"No, I don't either. He or she will come out from behind that cloak when they're ready." She smiled sleepily. "Not knowing is kind of fun, kind of like a Masque or Christmas present."

"What an interesting future we're going to have," Dragos said. "I'd like to keep the news to ourselves for a little while, if you don't mind. Let's just enjoy it for a few weeks, then we can tell Liam and our close circle. Is that all right with you?"

"That sounds perfect."

This time she fell asleep peacefully, and she had no more bad dreams.

LATE THE NEXT morning, when she woke up, Dragos was still in bed with her, although he had showered and dressed, she saw, when she rolled over. He was busy reading some kind of typed report, which he set aside as she gave him a sleepy smile.

"What are you doing here?" she asked in a sleep-blurred voice as she stretched. All the muscle aches had eased, allowing her freedom of motion. "Why aren't you at—what was supposed to happen this morning? I can't remember it now."

He raised his eyebrows at her. "You collapsed last night, remember? I get to stay at home today to make sure you're recovering."

"*Hmm.*" She hummed contentedly as she lifted her face for his kiss.

"Are you hungry?"

She nodded, and as he called down to the kitchen to order her some breakfast, she sat up in bed. Across the room, a high pile of wrapped presents sat on the table. "What are those for?"

"Those are for someone who is newly pregnant and can't leave her bed for two days." He lounged back against the headboard, looking sexy and wicked. "They'll be fun to look at until you can go get them, won't they?"

She rounded on him with a look of utter betrayal. "You wouldn't!"

He laughed. "No, I wouldn't."

"Well, okay then," she grumbled, subsiding. "Besides, I can't stay in bed for the entire two days without getting up. I've got to go to the bathroom and brush my teeth."

She did so, and she also washed the remnants of

last night's makeup off her face, while he carried the presents to the bed. She felt shaky while she was on her feet, and when she was done with her toilette, she was glad to crawl back between the covers.

Then she opened presents while Dragos handed them to her, one by one. Sexy lingerie, a half a dozen books, several magazines, and *ooh* look, a beautiful pair of aquamarine earrings, vegan chocolates, a warm chenille robe, and a new tablet.

He had noticed that she had broken the screen of the tablet she had at home.

Warmed again by his attention and thoughtfulness, she turned to kiss him. "Thank you."

"You're welcome. I can buy you a TV too and have a dresser moved in to set it on, if you want."

She looked around the lovely, historical bedroom. "Thanks, but no, I like the bedroom this way. I can always watch things on the tablet if I feel like it."

"Well, let me know if you change your mind." Tilting her face further, he kissed her again. "I hope this all helps with the bed rest."

"It does," she promised.

The next day, he left her to join in the normal meetings and activities for the week. He texted her often, while she slept far more than she thought she would—she was still so tired—and nibbled on chocolates, and read.

The enforced bed rest also gave her a chance to really think about what the doctor had said, but even after a bout of soul-searching, the only real reaction she had was one of deep relief that she had actually fainted, which had gotten her the medical attention she needed before she could miscarry.

"Because you're the most important thing," she whispered to the tiny shadow nestled deep inside her. "The absolutely most important thing."

Also, if she were to be honest in the privacy of her own thoughts, she wasn't sorry at all that she got to miss two days of the week's activities. Only the thought of worrying Dragos would keep her from pretending to be sick so that she could get out of a third day as well.

For now, she was quite content to keep up with the latest happenings through Dragos's texts and by watching news shows on her new tablet, which was how she discovered that the police had made an arrest in the murder case.

It was early in the evening on the second day. Dr. Medina had given her the first shot of the drug protocol and cleared her for normal activities in the morning.

Eva lounged on the bed with her, reading and keeping her company while Dragos attended yet another dinner. Bored, Pia had run a Google search on Victor Colton's death. To avoid disturbing Eva, she popped an earbud into one ear and clicked on the CNN link that promised BREAKING NEWS.

After watching a few minutes of the segment, she sat up straight and said, "Holy shit."

"What is it?" Eva looked up from her mystery.

Her eye glued to the small screen, she muttered, "They arrested Aaron Davis, the vice president's chief of staff…. There's allegations of an affair with the vice president, who's denying it…." She pulled the earbud out of her ear and looked at Eva with round eyes. "This is very bad news for the White House administration, but it might be very good news for us."

Later, when Dragos walked into the bedroom, he was smiling.

Pia stopped her Fruit Ninja game and set her tablet aside. "You look like a cat that got away with something."

He pulled off his tie, shrugged out of his suit jacket and threw them into a chair. Toeing off his shoes, he rolled up his shirt sleeves and crawled up the bed to give her a kiss. And all of that was so damn sexy, she could have climaxed just by watching him.

Delighted to see him, she burrowed back against her pillows, kissing him back. He said against her mouth, "I missed you."

"I missed you too." When he pulled back, she smiled at him. "Did you hear the news about Aaron Davis's arrest?"

"Oh, hell yeah. Things couldn't be going better if I had arranged them, myself."

As well as she thought she knew him, he had quite the capacity for surprising her. She squinted one eye at him. "You didn't, did you?"

"No, but I almost wish I had thought of it. The vice president is now being accused of starting the Right to Privacy movement as a setup for the murder. She's going to have to resign, or Ben will be forced to get rid of her. And nobody was wearing a scent blocker this evening."

She sighed. "That's a huge relief."

"It doesn't solve all our problems." He rubbed his face. "There's still plenty of protestors to the week's summit, and we're facing plenty of guarded government officials in our meetings. Senator Jackson is in clear opposition to mending fences, and public opinion is still on the downturn from the Nightkind massacre. But this latest development has slowed the momentum of the backlash against us, and I don't think we'll need to immigrate to our Other Greenland just yet, although I did talk to Niniane about hiring some consultants. She's going to send some people when she gets back to Adriyel." He slid back down the bed to put his head on her stomach. "How are you two doing?"

"We're great." She threaded her fingers through his black, silky hair. "And I'm excited that I get to go off bed rest in the morning."

"I'm excited too." He tilted his head so that he could look up at her. "Did the doctor clear you for normal activities?"

"I know what you really mean." She tapped his nose with one finger. "And yes, I'm cleared to resume normal activities in the morning."

He grabbed her finger and kissed it. "I can't wait. And you got your shot. How do you feel?"

"I feel tired again, and my arm hurts a bit, but Dr. Medina said that's all normal. She said she can give me the shot every two weeks in the evening, so I can just go to bed afterward." She made a face and shrugged. "It's not a big deal."

"I'm glad to hear it." He didn't let go of her hand. Instead, he rubbed her fingers against his mouth.

Warmth spread through her at the gentle caress. She urged, "Tell me what else is new."

"You've already heard the great news this evening," he said against her fingers. "But there is also some not so great news, too."

"Oh, no." Her heart sank. "What's happened now?"

"Today we were talking about what measures the demesne leaders could take that would lessen the risk of violence instigated by the Elder Races, and some goddamn fool in Ben's administration got the bright idea that we could 'foster good will and peace among the demesnes' by having all seven leaders commit to sending a family member to visit another demesne for a week sometime in the next six months."

"That's ridiculous," she exclaimed. "It sounds exactly like some stupid, useless program the government would come up with. That's like the nobility who used to send their children to live with other nobles as hostages. What do they think, that we're living in the Middle Ages?"

He cocked a sardonic eyebrow. "That's precisely where they said they got the idea. Several of us objected most strenuously, but after a lengthy argument, it was put to a vote. The majority agreed to the measure." He frowned and growled, "I hate decisions by consensus."

"But you only have two family members, me and Liam. Well, you have three now, but the littlest one isn't going anywhere without me for a really long time, and I'm telling you right now, Dragos—Liam is not going to visit any other demesne on his own. I don't care how many bodyguards you put on him."

"Of course he isn't." Dragos's frown hadn't lessened.

"Which leaves me," she said flatly. "Of course."

"That was acknowledged in the meeting." He paused. "Almost everybody at our dinner party saw you faint two nights ago, and know you're on bed rest for some mysterious ailment, so Niniane pushed to extend the time limit on the Wyr visitation, and the others agreed. You now have a year, which does us no good whatsoever, because you'll have the baby then."

"Ugh, this is awful," she stared at him. "Do I at least get to pick where I go, and who I visit? I could go see Niniane in Chicago."

He rolled to his feet and strode over to a small liquor cart tucked into a corner. As he poured himself a scotch, he said, "No such luck. The fuckers drew straws."

The space over her left eye was beginning to throb. She pressed against it with three fingers. "Don't tell me I'm supposed to go visit the Elves again."

"Nope. You're supposed to visit the Light Fae demesne in Los Angeles. Tatiana told me to tell you, she's delighted."

"And I'm supposed to spend an entire week with her?" She threw up her hands. *"Oy vey."*

He tossed back his drink and poured another. "I didn't want to fucking talk about it anymore, so I shut up. But we're not going to comply. *Nobody* tells me where I should send my family."

She flung herself back on her pillows in exasperation and stared at the ceiling. If he did that, an idea that was supposed to *foster good will and peace among the demesnes, HA!* would end up causing more bickering and discord than ever.

"Stop," she said. "If we dig in our heels, it will only create the kind of resentment the whole damn thing is supposed to alleviate. It's not worth it. I'll go."

Angling his head, Dragos turned to look at her. "No, you bloody well won't."

She just looked at him. "Come on, it'll only be for a week. We'll suck it up and get it over with."

But she knew better than to say, what's the worst that could happen? Because they already saw how badly that could go, when she went to visit the Elves earlier that year.

He was wearing that stubborn expression of his that said he wasn't going to budge, no matter what. "You're not going anywhere without me. Period. And I wasn't invited."

She started to laugh. "When has that ever stopped you from doing anything?"

Did his scowl lessen just the tiniest bit? "Well, that's true."

"Let me get this straight—did anybody tell you that you *couldn't* go?"

The fierce scowl disappeared, and he began to smile. "It was implied, but actually, no."

"Well, there you are, then," she said. "We got all wound up over this for nothing."

Although it wasn't easy to sneak a dragon-sized critter across demesne borders, they would manage. Somehow, they always did.

Setting aside the scotch, he strolled back to bed. "Who knew that marrying a sneaky penny thief would come in so handy?"

"Hey," she said. "Discreet."

"That too." He stripped off his clothes, climbed into bed and turned off his light. Pia turned on her side so that he could spoon her from behind. He stroked her hair back and kissed her neck. "Time to get to sleep," he whispered in her ear. "We want to make sure you get all your rest out by morning."

Sleepy glee suffused her. Pretending to be clueless, she whispered back, "What's going to happen in the morning?"

"Oh, you know," he told her. "'You diddle here, I suck there. Or maybe you suck, and I diddle. Or both. Couple of pats, and ten or fifteen thrusts. Oh baby, you're so good, I can't take it, *pow*, et cetera, let's go raid the fridge.'"

Nodding in contentment, she closed her eyes. "That's what I hoped you would say."

Pia Does Hollywood

Thea Harrison

Chapter One

DRAMATIC MUSIC EBBED and swelled on the widescreen TV.

"Here it comes," said Liam, poking Pia in the ribs with an insistent finger. "One of my favorite zombie movie quotes ever. Wait for it...."

For Halloween that year, Liam had set a goal to watch (and in some cases rewatch) all the zombie movies available for rental or purchase. Halloween had since come and gone, and now, in early November, he had fallen behind, but he was still determined to persevere until he had finished all of them.

The young actor came on the screen. Pia couldn't remember the guy's name.

Then Liam said along with the actor, "In those moments where you're not quite sure if the undead are really dead, dead, don't get all stingy with your bullets."

When he finished, he cackled.

She ran her fingers through his honey blond hair, relishing his cheerful mood. "You have the whole movie memorized, don't you?"

His dancing violet-blue gaze slid to hers. "Of

course."

"Why do you like that line more than any of the others?" she asked curiously. "It's a pretty funny movie."

Actually, in truth, she wasn't a big fan of zombie movies, but she also wasn't about to tell Liam that. If this was what he wanted to do, why then, she wanted to do it with him.

Their lives were busy and demanding, and took them away from Liam too much as it was. And childhood was so brief and fleeting at the best of times, but even more so for Liam, as he grew at such a fast rate. As a result, she threw herself into everything he wanted to do with complete enthusiasm. No reservations—she was all in, every time.

"I *do* like all the rest of it," Liam said, his gaze cutting back to the television screen. "I just don't want to quote too much while it's playing, so you can enjoy the movie too."

My good, sweet boy, she thought. Even when he's acting like an adorably normal, obnoxious kid, he tries to be considerate.

They lay on the carpeted floor together, their bodies making a *T*. Pia stretched out parallel to the couch where Dragos lounged, one leg draped off the couch, his foot planted on the floor.

Dragos was working on his laptop and half watching the movie along with them. Pia rested one hand around his ankle, enjoying the simple, tactile contact. Liam lay facing the TV with his head propped on her abdomen as a pillow.

Outside the family room windows, the November weather had turned sharp and cold as a wet, slushy mixture of rain and snow fell, but inside, they were warm and cozy. A fire crackled in the fireplace, filling the place with soft golden light. Pia had a cup of hot cocoa, made with coconut milk, that sat cooling on a coaster on one of the end tables, but she was too comfortable and happy to move.

At least not yet. She would have to move soon enough.

As the Cuelebres' part of the diplomatic deal they had made last month with the other Elder Races demesnes and the human government, later that evening she would be taking the company jet to fly to Los Angeles to visit with the Light Fae Queen, Tatiana, for a week.

The diplomatic deal stated that each of the seven U.S. demesne leaders was supposed to send a family member to another demesne to visit for a week to *foster good will and peace among the demesnes'*. The whole concept came from a Medieval practice of nobles sending their children to live in other nobles' households as hostages.

Supposedly, the diplomatic pact would lessen the likelihood of inter-demesne violence in the modern day United States, but whatever human idiot in the president's administration had thought up the scheme didn't really know jack shit about the Elder Races, their long memories, and their proclivity for holding grudges over centuries.

A week's visit wasn't going to fix anything. In fact, depending on how well or badly that family representative acted, it could very well cause more resentments and bad feelings between the demesnes. Or even outright war.

Also, it couldn't have come at a worse time. They had so much to do to get ready for the massive Masque that Dragos hosted in New York on the winter solstice that preparations always began a few months early, so Pia wasn't going to be forgiving that anonymous fool in a hurry for proposing the idea.

Dragos, in fact, wanted to reject the pact outright. He wasn't a fan of decisions made by consensus. At the best of times, he fought to rein in his autocratic instincts whenever the seven demesne leaders needed to convene over anything, and he had especially opposed this particular arrangement. But in the end, Pia told him, it would be easier to acquiesce on this one issue than to dig in their heels.

She could have waited to go later, after the Masque and sometime early next year. In fact, Tatiana had even emailed her the previous day, suggesting that she come at a later date.

But when Pia thought of the reason why that option wasn't attractive, she lost her crankiness and began to smile.

All things considered, it was better for her to suck

it up, get on the plane that night and get the damn visit over with, despite how much she dreaded spending the week with the Light Fae Queen and her nosy questions. So she emailed Tatiana back, thanked her for the suggestion, and said she would be touching down in L.A. the next morning as originally planned.

Dragos would be traveling to Los Angeles too, under separate cover. He didn't volunteer how he was going to make the trip, and she didn't ask. Probably he would relish the chance to stretch out his massive wings and fly cross-country in the darkness and solitude, but they had agreed—if she didn't know what he was doing, she could say with perfect sincerity that she had traveled alone to the Light Fae demesne.

After all, the best way to lie to someone with a highly developed truthsense was to, well, tell the truth. Pia believed wholeheartedly in plausible deniability, at least as much as possible.

After her exchange with Liam, she met Dragos's amused gaze, gave him a small nod, and squeezed his ankle. In answer, he closed his laptop as she said to Liam, "Hey sport, could you put the movie on pause for a few minutes?"

Instantly, Liam's sparkling smile vanished, and he scowled. "You said you could watch the whole movie with me before you left."

"I know I did, and I will watch the whole movie with you," she told him. "But first, your dad and I have something important we want to tell you."

Heaving a sigh, he held up the remote and hit pause. "What is it now?"

"Don't be pissy," Dragos told him. "And while you're readjusting your attitude, sit up and turn around."

Pia could feel Liam sigh again, but so far, he had been unwilling to challenge Dragos's authority when Dragos used that particular tone with him. (And lordy, wouldn't life get interesting whenever Liam did decide to challenge Dragos and rebel.)

As the boy pushed to a sitting position and swiveled to face the couch, Pia sat too and leaned back against Dragos's legs.

As Dragos dropped a large, warm hand onto her shoulder, he asked her telepathically, *Do you want to be the one to tell him?*

She drew up her knees and wrapped her arms around them, hugging herself with glee. *It's okay with me either way. You can tell him if you want.*

Okay. Dragos switched to verbal speech. "Liam, we're pregnant. You're going to have a new sibling."

For the space of a moment, Liam's expression went blank with surprise.

He held still just long enough that Pia had time to rethink their decision. She and Dragos had kept the news to themselves for a few weeks, which was easy to do since the new little peanut appeared to be determined to keep his—or her—presence a secret. Only Pia's doctor and Eva knew the truth, and only because Pia had collapsed last month during their trip to Washington for the Elder Races/human summit meetings.

But what if Liam reacted poorly, for some reason? What if he wasn't happy with the news? They were dropping a big bombshell on him then leaving for a week, so they wouldn't be around to help him work through any of his emotions.

Anxiously, she twisted her hands together and came to a fast decision. If he reacted poorly, she was going to override his decision to stay home and in school. She would make him come to L.A. with her. Somehow, she would juggle things so that she would get some time alone with him.

Then Liam's expression changed into one of pure joy. "Oh wow, really? Are you kidding me?" he exclaimed. "You mean I'm not going to be the only one anymore? That's fantastic!"

Thank the gods. Her face broke into a beam as she nodded. "Yes, we're pregnant. Really, truly!"

He dove forward to sprawl on his stomach and put his hand on her abdomen. "When did it happen? Is it going to be a brother or a sister? Can I feel it?"

"Be careful," she said quickly. When he tilted his head to look up at her, she told him, "Yes, you can try to sense it, but you have to be super gentle so you don't scare it. He—or she—is cloaking pretty hard. That could just be part of its nature, or maybe I frightened it. We got pregnant when we went to D.C., and I was pretty stressed that week."

She tried not to obsess over what had happened last month when they had traveled to Washington to participate in a summit between the leaders of the Elder Races and the human government, but the thought that she might have frightened that new, tiny spark bothered her quite a bit. Between the anti-Elder Races sentiment, the occasional outright hostility, the vice president's husband being murdered at their house during a very important dinner party and Pia's subsequent collapse, it had been one of the roughest weeks she had ever lived through.

Liam frowned. "I don't remember being frightened, and from all the stories you've told me, you were pretty stressed when you got pregnant with me too."

"You have a point." She wanted to believe him badly and bit her lip. "I know you've said before that you didn't pay attention to much of what happened outside your own experience, except the time that Urien shot me."

The time she—they—had almost died. Then, Liam, who had been nothing more than a peanut himself, had flared up to try to heal her, until Dragos laid his Power over the bright, new little spark and gentled him down.

A good thing, too, Dragos murmured in her head. *Considering all the rampant sex we had.*

Laughter flared, and she looked over her shoulder at him with dancing eyes. *And continue to have.*

"Yeah, that's right," Liam said, resting his cheek on

her leg. "I remember sleeping a lot. Man, those were the best naps. I just sorted of drifted, weightless. And I remember feeling like you were so big, you were my entire universe. Which I guess you were."

She ran her fingers through his hair again. "And you felt safe?"

"Totally safe, except that once." His smile faded only briefly then returned. "Then I remember Dad being there, and I was safe again."

Relief coursed through her. Dragos's fingers tightened gently on her shoulder. She reached up to stroke his long, warm fingers as she said, "Okay, if this peanut is anything like you were, then what was happening in my reality won't really impinge on his—or her—awareness. Agh, these pronouns are going to be hard to juggle until we know the sex of the baby. Anyway, it must be cloaking itself out of instinct, so that's part of its nature."

"Can you sense it now?" Liam asked.

"I can, but your dad had to show me how at first. And he only knew because Dr. Medina told us I was pregnant," she replied. "Want me to show you?"

He nodded, and when he sank his bright, familiar Power into her body—gods, Liam was every bit as strong as Dragos—she brushed her awareness against his and told him telepathically, *Ease up a little there. You're feeling pretty intense.*

Sorry! he said. *I'm just excited.*

I know. I am too. When his presence lightened, she

guided him to the subtle, tiny shadow, and together they hovered to observe it.

After a few moments, it occurred to her that Liam had unique capabilities that were quite different from anything she, Dragos or Dr. Medina had.

She asked him curiously, *This little shadow is all any of us can pick up. Can you sense anything?*

Once again, he took his time in responding, and she held her breath as she waited for his reply.

Finally, he said, *I'm not sure. As I watch it, I keep getting impressions of fire.*

Fire? she repeated. *I guess that would make sense. Both you and your dad are pretty fiery.*

She felt rather than saw, Liam shake his head. *No, I'm not quite the same as Dad. I don't think I'm as hot as this one is. This one feels as hot as Dad does, to me.*

Oh wow, was she going to have another dragon baby? The suspense was going to kill her!

Hugging herself tighter, she told herself she wasn't going to ask it, but then immediately she caved and asked it anyway. *Can you sense if it's a boy or a girl?*

This time, he answered her quickly. *No, I'm not picking anything else up. Just heat and fire.*

Well, that's more than your dad and I have been able to sense so far. How exciting! As Liam's presence pulled away, she surfaced with him. They grinned at each other.

"You both look like a pair of Cheshire cats," Dragos told them. He was smiling as well.

"Tell him what you saw." She poked Liam in the

stomach. "Tell him!"

He was very ticklish, and his lanky body folded around her prodding finger as he laughed. "I'm not sure I saw anything!"

"You did too," she insisted. Twisting to look at Dragos, she told him, "He did too."

"You've got good instincts," Dragos told Liam. "Trust them. What was it?"

"I just kept getting impressions of fire," Liam said to his father. "That's all. It felt hotter than I do, more like you."

"Ah," said Dragos, with intense male satisfaction. "That sounds like it could be another dragon."

"You don't know that." Pia waved a cautioning finger in the air. "It could mean a fiery nature."

"True." He captured her finger, pulled her hand to him and kissed the finger. "But I doubt Liam would just sense a hothead. My guess is, whether the baby is a dragon or not, Liam is somehow reading the new one's Power."

Laughing, Liam held up both hands. "I don't know anything for sure! Maybe I imagined it. I just think it's so cool I'm going to have a baby brother or sister. Maybe it'll be like me in some ways!"

Did that statement carry a hint of loneliness in it? Always hypersensitive to the possibility, Pia's heart clutched at the thought.

So many things served to isolate him. He had so little in common with other children. He was growing up so fast, he couldn't make lasting friends, and he was the prince of his people, with both unusual dangers and unusual privilege. And as he said, his nature was not like his father's; Dragos was, at heart, a solitary creature. Liam loved people.

In the next instant, the feeling melted into another warm glow of happiness. If Liam had felt any kind of loneliness at being an only child with such a unique nature, this new little one had already eased it.

Dragos said quietly, "I think you need to leave. Right now, the temps haven't dropped below freezing, but I want you safely in the air and well away from here before ice develops on the runway. There's more than an hour left to the movie—you'll have to watch the rest of it after the trip after all."

Even though Liam had responded to the news so much better than she had feared that he might, she still felt reluctant to let go of the moment.

Turning back to Liam to search his dark blue gaze, she said, "You can always change your mind and come too, you know. You sure you want to stay here? It'll be sunny and warm in L.A. And while I can't promise, we might be able to sneak away for an afternoon at Disneyland, if you want."

"No," he said. "I'd like to go to Disneyland someday, but I'd like to go some time when you know you can make the trip. This week, I really want to stay in school. We have a football game on Friday night. I want to play in it, and besides, you said this is the last trip you're gonna be making for a while. And you'll be back by next Monday, right?"

"That's right," she replied. "I'll be home on Monday by the time school lets out."

He shrugged. "Okay. Do you want to watch the rest of the movie with me when you get back?"

"Of course I do." She leaned over to poke him in the ribs again. "Unless you want to go ahead and finish it tonight, which is okay too. If you watch the rest of it, we can start a new movie when I get back."

"Okay." He laughed and squirmed away from her finger. "And hey, maybe by the time you get back, this peanut won't be hiding anymore."

"You never know." She grinned. "Peanuts do tend to have a mind of their own. But you were 'Peanut' when you were little. Do you think we need to come up with another nickname to call this one?"

"Nah," Liam said. "I outgrew that a long time ago, so we can call this one Peanut too."

She looked sideways away from him, adopting a shifty expression. "Does that mean I get to have your bunny now?"

"No way!" he exclaimed. "Keep your paws off my stuffed animal!"

Laughing, she told him, "I'll keep my hands off him for now. That's all I'm going to promise. If you ever feel the need to get rid of him, you know he's got a home with me."

"Yeah, I know." He grinned.

Behind her, Dragos shifted. "Time to get this trip started. The sooner you leave, the sooner we can put this week behind us and move on with our lives."

Taking his cue, she rolled onto her knees and stood. Liam stood as well.

Pia called out, "Eva!"

After a few moments, Eva appeared in the doorway. "You bellowed?"

"Pia's ready to leave for the airstrip," Dragos told her. "Is the Escalade loaded up?"

"It sure is." Eva bounced on the balls of her feet. "We're ready to roll as soon as you are."

He nodded. "Get the car warmed up and wait for us outside, will you? We'll be out soon."

"Sure thing." Eva disappeared down the hall.

Pia turned to Liam. Good gods, he was almost as tall as she was. She said, "Remember …"

He ducked his head with a self-conscious grin. "I know, I know. No unexpected growth spurts while you're gone."

She waited a moment when he stopped speaking, then prompted, "And?"

"We'll Skype every day after school." He added quickly, "Except for Friday, because there's the game. And Hugh's going to tape it, so you can watch it when you get back."

"That's what we're going to do, first thing after school on Monday," Dragos told him. "We'll watch it together."

"Okay!"

Pia watched as Liam hugged Dragos. When he turned to her, she was ready. She threw her arms around him and kissed his cheek. He whispered to her, "I'm so glad I get to have a Peanut too."

"Me too, darling." She kissed him again. "I just know he—or she—is going to look up to you and adore you, and want to play with you all the time."

"I can't wait. I'll even learn how to change diapers!" His brows twitched together, and he added, "As long as they're not poopy."

She burst out laughing. "Wow, that is excessively good of you."

He kissed her cheek quickly and stood back. "Have a good trip!"

"We will," she told him. Liam threw his thin, lanky body onto the empty couch and turned the movie back on as they walked out of the room.

Then, as Pia followed Dragos to the front of the shadowed house, she said to him, "Unless, of course, we don't. Because I swear to you, Dragos, I'm beginning to feel like we're travel cursed. Something always happens when we go away."

"Like I told you once, we're lightning rods. We don't have to go away for things to happen," he said sardonically. At the front hall closet, he pulled out Pia's coat. "Things happen when we stay right here at home too."

She would not look at the thin white scar on his

forehead. She had obsessed over that wound more than enough already. A few months ago, when Dragos had been seriously injured, that wound had ruled her life and haunted her nights.

Now, he still suffered partial memory loss, but he had remembered everything that mattered to her, everything that was vital to their lives and happiness. More importantly, he had healed until he was as strong and healthy as he had ever been.

And they were going to have a new, mysterious, fiery little peanut.

So she patted him on the cheek as she told him, "I'm too stinking happy to care. The universe can bring it. We'll deal with whatever may happen next. We always do."

He bent his head to kiss her. "Damn straight, and we always will."

The kiss quickly turned scorching as he slanted his mouth over hers and deepened it, cupping the back of her head and plunging between her lips with his tongue. She stroked his hair, savoring the feeling of the silken strands flowing through her fingers and the sensation of his warm, firm lips caressing hers.

He had been drinking coffee while watching the movie, and the dark, smoky flavor lingered pleasantly on his tongue. Murmuring in pleasure, she kissed him back hungrily.

The mating frenzy between them had flared when they began to try to get pregnant. Now, only a few short weeks later, it had eased back somewhat but it hadn't gone to sleep entirely.

Pia was beginning to think it never would. She could never get enough of him, never, and now, if they weren't able to steal away for a few private hours, it was likely they wouldn't be able to be together for a whole damn week, which was another reason to hold a grudge against that unnamed idiot in Washington.

Dragos lifted his head, and in the shadows of the front hall, his gold eyes flared incandescent. He looked hungry, and angry. It was all the warning she got.

Grabbing her by the waist, he lifted her into his arms. Laughing and trying to muffle the sound, she managed to hook an arm around his neck as he strode the short distance to his office.

"What are you doing?!" she whispered, breathless from trying to hold back her giggles.

"I'm taking my wife." Slamming the door with one booted foot, he carried her to the massive desk and swept everything out of the way as he set her on the polished surface.

Her body knew what was coming next. Her pulse rate ratcheted up, until she felt she had a fever, and a hungry ache throbbed in the private place between her legs. "I thought we didn't have time for this."

"Screw it," he growled. "We'll make time."

Chapter Two

DRAGOS KNEW HE was throwing off heat as if he were on fire. He felt like he was burning up. He loved the fact that she never minded his heat. When they were in bed, she cuddled close, even in the warmest weather.

She spread slender hands across his chest. Her plump, inviting lips were unsteady as she whispered, "What about the roads?"

"They won't freeze in the next ten minutes." Undoing the fastening of her jeans, he hauled them and her panties off, taking her slip-on shoes with them. Then he yanked her legs apart.

She burst out laughing again. "Eva's outside in the car!"

"She knows her job," he muttered. "She'll wait."

Dragos knew when he got like this, there was no reasoning with him.

But fortunately, when he got like this, there was no reasoning with her either.

She didn't waste any more precious time arguing, not when he could tell she wanted this as much as he did. Arousal perfumed her scent. He took in deep breaths, gripping her shoulders as she worked to get his jeans open too.

When she did, and his stiff, aching erection spilled into her waiting hands, they both sucked in a breath.

It was a terrible thing to grow to need someone the way that he had grown to need her. For so many millennia, he had been content to be a solitary creature. The dragon in him was baffled by the unrelenting drive he felt to be with her, and stupefied at the experience of being in love.

Because he did, he loved her. He didn't love often, or very many people, and he was content to have it that way, but she consumed his life. She burned him up, until there was nothing left but his essence, taken out of his massive body and flying weightless again in the endless, unmeasured spill of profligate golden sunlight, just as he had once flown in the earliest days of his very long life.

Their lack of time lent urgency to their actions. She pumped his cock once, twice, three times, spiking sensation along his nerve endings until he could have spilled right then and there into her welcoming hands, but he didn't want to climax that way. He wanted to bury himself into her velvety soft, tight sheath.

As he yanked her soft sweater up, she obligingly raised her arms. Shimmering pale blonde hair tumbled over her laughing, sensual expression. He tossed the sweater to the floor and greedily filled his palms with her round, soft breasts, framed prettily by a cream lacy bra. Bending his head, he licked and bit lightly at the luscious swell of flesh. When he put his mouth over one nipple and sucked at her teasingly, through the material of the bra, she moaned and hooked her legs around his waist, trying to pull him close.

It was impossible—he couldn't suckle at her breasts and still come up to nestle against her pelvis. After a last hard pull and nip at her breast, he gave up, straightened and put an arm around her hips to pull her to the edge of the desk.

As she wriggled eagerly into position, he put a hand between her legs, fingering her soft, delicate folds. She was wet for him, but he already knew that from the arousal in her scent. Relishing the liquid glide of velvet flesh against his callused fingertips, he probed until he found the tight, stiff little pearl he was looking for.

She sucked in an unsteady breath as he caressed her, tightening her fists in the material of his shirt. He could feel the muscles in her inner thighs shaking against his hips. For a few moments, she thrust her pelvis against his hand, mimicking the rhythm they found when they were joined together, until his blood caught the rhythm, pulsing urgently through his veins.

Then she pushed his hand away, hissing, "Stop being so damn considerate and get inside me already, will you?"

Laughter welled up. Gods, he loved how frankly sensual she was with him, and her unabashed enthusiasm for sex.

She took hold of his cock again, rubbing her thumb along the broad sensitive head until moisture came out of the tip. Then she positioned him at her entrance, and gripping her hips, he pushed inside.

It never got old, never. Each time, he caught fire like it was the first time. When he planted himself deep inside her, she let her head fall back. Her gaze was unfocused, and her breathing came in short, quick pants.

Bending over her arched torso, one arm wrapped around her hips, he fucked her in short, hard jabs. The friction was excruciating, delicious. *She* was delicious. He bit at her neck, sucking at the delicate skin.

She raked her fingernails down his back, leaving trails of fire. Relishing the small pain, he growled and accelerated his pace. His erection felt huge, impossibly hard and thick. If he didn't spill soon, he was going to go crazy.

Slipping a hand between their torsos, he searched for her clitoris again—and as he connected with the tiny peak of flesh, she sucked in a breath, whined and climaxed. The ripples took her over. He could feel her pulsing around him, and that sent him over the edge.

Groaning, he pumped into her, jetting with each thrust. She bit and licked at him, until he lifted his head to take her mouth with his. They fused together, kissing wildly, muscles clenched as the last of the pleasure spiked and then eased on a slow ebb.

When it had passed, she wrapped her arms around his neck. He hugged her tightly, and they rested against each other for a moment until he felt her racing heart begin to slow.

"Okay," he said, as he rested his mouth in her tousled hair. "Now you can go."

Bursting out laughing, she smacked his arm. "After you completely destroy me, mess up all my clothes and tangle my hair, you're going to boot me out?"

He grinned. "Well, I lost track, but I suspect our ten minutes might be up."

"Ugh, men!" Her hold on his neck loosened, and her thighs eased away from his hips.

Before he let her go, he had to take her chin and tilt her face up for one last hot kiss. Damn, he hated to let her go. "All right," he said reluctantly against her soft lips. "The half bath is right across the hall, and nobody's in the front of the house—you make a run for it while I straighten up your clothes. I'll bring them to you."

"Okay," she whispered. She stroked his face. In the shadowed room, her eyes looked dark as midnight and impossibly deep. She smiled at him. "I love you."

He kissed her again, hard. "Love you too. Get going, before I change my mind and keep you here."

She lingered to search his face. "You wouldn't."

"Damn straight, I would."

"But all the demesne leaders, and the human administration, agreed on this."

"Fuck them. Fuck the agreement." He angled out his jaw. "Nobody tells me what to do, or where to send my family."

✦   ✦   ✦

OH LORD, HE was serious.

Only a few moments ago, while they were making love, he had looked so intense, he almost set the air around him on fire, his eyes glowing like gold coins in the darkened office.

Now he looked intense for an entirely different reason, and just as sexy. His dark brows had lowered, and his face had hardened into his most stubborn expression.

Shaking her head, she hopped off the desk. "I don't have time to argue with you about this," she told him. "We already decided—it's not worth antagonizing all the other people we have to live with on this continent over this one thing. You need to save all that obstinacy for times when you really do need to dig in your heels. If you're going to pick your battles, Dragos, this one isn't worth fighting."

He said between his teeth, "I *hate* decisions by consensus."

"I know," she crooned. "You handle it so much better when you can be an absolute dictator, don't you, honey? It's been very hard on you since the planet has become so populated, and we've all had to learn to get along together sometimes."

"Well," he said, his tone truculent. "It has."

Her shoulders shook. Gods, she adored every inch of his growly, autocratic self. "We've put it off long enough. Now I've really got to go."

Reluctance clear in every line of his body, he stepped aside, and she made that dash for the half bath across the hall.

Once inside, she cleaned up, washed her face and hands, and ran her fingers through her tousled hair. A quick rap sounded on the door, then Dragos opened it to slip her clothes inside, and she dressed quickly. She hopped out of the bathroom again in two minutes flat.

He was waiting for her, still glowering, holding her coat in one hand. As she shrugged into it, his arms closed around her tightly in one last hug. For that one moment, she felt entirely enfolded and utterly safe.

Then he let her go, and together they stepped outside.

The rainy snow splattered them as Dragos opened the front passenger door of the Escalade that waited idling at the curb. Inside, Eva lounged in the driver's seat, looking lazily amused and not at all surprised.

Pia turned to Dragos. Wet drops sprinkled his ink black hair.

"Do you have your next dose of medication?" he asked.

She nodded. "I've got it in my purse. I triple-checked."

"And I have the backup dose, just in case."

When she had collapsed in D.C., they had found out that she was pregnant. They had also discovered that this would be their last child.

It had to be, as Pia's body had developed lethal antibodies to fight off carrying Dragos's children. Sometimes it happened, when two very different kinds of Wyr mated.

Dr. Medina had likened it somewhat to the human Rhesus factor, only unlike humans, who could prevent dangerous sensitization with an injection of Rh immunoglobulin, there was no way to prevent what had happened to Pia.

Once her body had turned that corner, nothing in modern medicine could turn the clock back again. Not even her own magical nature could save her. While she had extraordinary healing Powers, her body had grown to recognize the fetus as an intruder and was fighting to protect itself. She would miscarry any future pregnancies.

She would be able to carry this new, precious peanut to term, but only with the help of the drug protocol that Dr. Medina had developed for her, in the form of a shot she had to take every two weeks.

Uneasy at being so vulnerable and dependent, after the first two doses, both Pia and Dragos had insisted they learn to give her the shot in case Dr. Medina wasn't available to administer it. Pia was due to have her next shot in two evenings.

Dragos touched her cheek gently with the callused

tips of his fingers, lingering over the kiss. Then he pulled back and told her, "Have a good flight. I'll see you soon. I'll get in touch with you in the morning, after you've landed."

She nodded and gave him a smile. "Sounds good. Talk to you in the morning."

Eva put the car in gear while Dragos slammed the door.

As they drove away, Pia glanced back. Dragos never moved to go back inside. Instead, he stood watching her leave.

The next time they talked, it would be in secret in southern California. She watched him too, until his tall, dark figure and their glowing, inviting home faded into the darkness.

Only then did she turn to face the direction in which she was going. Belatedly, she realized she hadn't put on her seat belt, and with a muttered curse, she yanked the belt around her body and jammed it into the buckle.

"Good job being all reasonable with his lordship, dumbass," she muttered to herself. "If you'd only let him dig in his heels, you wouldn't be making this trip right now."

And to hell with the rest of the world.

"Anybody would think you really weren't going to see each other for a week," Eva said with a chuckle.

All her good mood from that evening vanished. Scowling, she crossed her arms and sank down in her seat. "You never know. The Light Fae demesne doesn't have an edict forbidding him to cross their borders like the Elven demesne did when we went to South Carolina, but he's still not supposed to be along for this trip. Even though he'll be in L.A. too and I'll be able to talk to him, I might not actually get a chance to see him for the whole week."

Eva shook her head. "I don't believe it. That man's too sneaky, and I mean that as a total compliment. If he wants to see you, he'll find a way to make it happen, whether he's supposed to or not. Only question is how he does it. I can't wait to see how he pulls it off."

Pia's scowl lifted and she began to smile. "You do have a point."

Chapter Three

PIA'S SECURITY TEAM had already boarded the plane.

She heard the familiar arguing voices as she and Eva stepped into the cabin. Her astonished gaze took in Quentin and Aryal's presence as they sprawled on one of the couches.

The two sentinels looked lethal and relaxed, even as they sniped at each other. Quentin's sexy, scarred face wore a subtle amused expression, while Aryal scowled as she scratched a long-fingered hand through her tangled black hair.

Pia laughed out loud. "He never told me he was going to assign you two to the trip."

Quentin stood and stepped forward to press a kiss to her cheek. "He didn't want to say anything, in case you thought it might be a bad idea."

Aryal remained in her slouched position, one leg thrown over the arm of the couch, although she raised a few fingers in nonchalant greeting when Pia looked at her.

"No offense," Pia said, "but I do think it's a bad

idea. While I love you two—yes, I've grown to love even you, Aryal—neither of you are known for your skills in diplomacy."

"That's not our job, cupcake," Aryal told her as she kicked one booted foot. "Diplomacy is your job. Our job is to make sure nobody kills you."

Within the space of five words, Aryal had already managed to get her irritated. No matter how many times Pia told her not to call her cupcake, the harpy persisted.

She threw up her hands. "Stop it. Nobody else but Graydon uses that nickname. Why do you keep calling me that?!"

Aryal's face went blank for a moment. Then, with a slightly baffled expression, she said, "It's—it's just so fitting. With your frothy blond hair, cute painted toenails and bright, pretty outfits, you *are* a cupcake."

Pia dropped her hands, lowered her chin and glowered at the harpy for a long moment. She said, "You're not even trying to be offensive right now, are you?"

Mutely, Aryal looked sidelong at Quentin as she shook her head. Eva had moved to the back of the cabin. As the other woman caught Pia's attention, Eva rolled her eyes.

Eva and Aryal couldn't stand each other. Pia had once said to Dragos that they were worse than oil and water. Eva was oil, and Aryal was a naked flame.

This wasn't just a bad idea. It was terrible.

Behind Pia, the door to the cockpit opened, and Alex, one of the two mated Wyr-ravens that worked as co-pilots, stepped into the cabin. "We're ready to take off when you are," he said, smiling at Pia. "The sooner the better, of course. The temperature outside is dropping fast."

Oh, for God's sake.

Pia turned her back to everyone else and looked at Alex. "You answer to me on this trip, correct?"

To his credit, Alex didn't look at the others either. "Yes, ma'am. You're the ranking Wyr official on board."

"Then we don't take off until I tell you to," Pia told him. She swiveled back to look at the other three. At the back of the cabin, Eva contemplated the ceiling with her generous lips pursed. Aryal had turned to inspecting her fingers, while Quentin's handsome expression grew more amused.

"My husband is an idiot," Pia declared.

Hey, Dragos said telepathically.

That meant he had followed the car to the airstrip. Dragos's hearing was very good, but even so, he had to be quite close to hear her through the plane's closed exterior. She imagined him in his dragon form, cloaking his presence as he paced impatiently around the jet, waiting for the engines to rev in preparation for taking off, and she had to suppress a smile.

If he was indeed in his dragon form and pacing around the plane, that meant he could look in through the windows and see her. She would not let him see that she was amused.

"Ma'am," said Alex. "We certainly won't take off until you say we can, but the weather has turned."

"Yes, I know it has," she said. She looked from Eva to Aryal and back again. "But I'm not going anywhere until I hear you all swear that you will get along on this trip and not cause me any headaches. Because guys, I don't need any of you with me in order to make the trip to L.A. I could kick you all off the plane and go to the Light Fae demesne by myself. In fact, that idea sounds pretty good to me. We're not at war with Tatiana. She'd look after me just fine."

In her head, the dragon gave a warning growl, while Quentin lost his smile. Aryal straightened and stood.

Quentin told her, "Pia, you can't go by yourself. That's ridiculous."

Crossing her arms, she retorted, "It's not as ridiculous as the alternative could be."

Because oil couldn't help but be oil. And a flame burned where it would. At some point, it was inevitable that the two would connect and explode. She gave both Eva and Aryal glances filled in equal parts with exasperation and affection.

"What's it going to be?" she asked. "Are you all going to get along on this trip and not give me any grief, or do I kick you all off the plane and go by myself.

You're not going by yourself, and that's final, Dragos

growled.

Well, I know you're coming too, honey, she crooned.

That's not what I meant, Pia, he snapped. *I might be in L.A. too, but you need to have someone with you inside Tatiana's household as well.*

While Dragos thundered in her head, Quentin, Aryal and Eva all started to speak at once.

She clapped her hands over her ears and exclaimed, "Do you *see* what I'm talking about?! Arguing is exactly what I asked you not to do!"

"I'm only trying to point out that some of us might promise, but what if not everybody does?" Aryal snapped in reply. "Do you kick them off the plane, and keep the others? It's a legitimate question!"

As Eva glared at Aryal, Pia realized she was hearing more than Dragos growling in her head. Eva was growling too.

Because oil was oil. And flame couldn't help but be flame.

She would not laugh. She wouldn't. Instead, she rubbed the bridge of her nose and said pathetically to Dragos, *I'm supposed to avoid stress, you know.*

The dragon's growling stopped as abruptly as if she had turned it off like a faucet. When he next spoke, his voice was quiet and nonconfrontational. *I'm sorry, baby.*

That solved the issue of his growling. She turned her attention to Eva, and met the other woman's gaze silently. After a moment, Eva's low growl wavered and stopped. Eva said apologetically, *She makes me crazy.*

And I don't want to go visit the Light Fae demesne, Pia told her. *Deal with it like an adult or get off the plane. If you make this trip harder on me than it needs to be, I won't take you with me anywhere.*

Eva glared. *I wouldn't make it harder!*

Pia raised her eyebrows. *And so?*

Heaving an aggrieved sigh, Eva said out loud, "I promise to get along for the duration of this trip and not cause you any headaches."

"Thank you, Eva." She turned to Quentin and Aryal.

The amusement had crept back into Quentin's blue gaze. Pia could tell that he had figured out that while she was certainly serious, she wasn't really upset. He laid a hand over his heart and said, "Well, *I* promise, so that means I get to come too, right? I was looking forward to a sojourn in sunny SoCal, and Eva and I would be fine pair of bodyguards for the week."

At that, everyone on the plane looked at Aryal, who had crossed her arms and wore a truculent expression. She angled her head to look at them all.

"So that's it," she said. "The whole trip is going to come down to this moment, isn't it? Agh, people make me crazy. If anything happens, everybody's going to say, 'oh, Aryal, you were the last one to promise. We all knew you were going to be a hassle. You always are.' Okay, okay! Of course I promise!"

Smiling, Quentin said to Pia, "She is the best, most perfect example of what a self-fulfilling prophecy is, isn't she? I just marvel at her every day."

Pia said to Dragos, *I am not going to forgive you for this in a hurry.*

It was a tactical decision, he told her. Did the dragon sound apologetic? Now, that was unusual. Pia was winning points all over the place. *I wanted you to have the strongest defense with the least number of bodies, and Quentin and Aryal work very well as a team.*

Uh huh. Pia walked over to Aryal and stuck a finger under her nose. Her finger was getting a lot of exercise that evening. She told the harpy aloud, "Do not make me regret taking you along. Because I can send you home from L.A. too, you know."

Aryal's mouth took on a sour tilt. With a quick sidelong glance at her mate, she muttered, "Got it."

She nodded to herself and turned away, muttering to Dragos, *I still think this is a bad idea.* Aloud, she said, "Okay, Alex. Sorry for the holdup. Let's go."

"Yes, ma'am," Alex said cheerfully, and with evident relief.

THE NORMAL FLIGHT time from New York City to LAX was a smidgeon over six hours, but they were traveling from upstate New York to another private airstrip just outside of L.A., so their trip would be over seven hours.

Since she had the luxury of choosing, Pia had decided to deal with the long flight and subsequent jet lag by staying up a little later then traveling through the night, so that they would touch down at eight the next morning. With all the amenities that the jet provided, including good food, a comfortable place to nap, and the chance to shower, she expected to arrive alert and hopefully ready to face spending the week with the formidable Light Fae Queen.

After they had taken off, Alex's mate and co-pilot Daniel served them a late supper. Pia bolted her food down. So far this pregnancy was affecting her appetite as much as her last one had, and she was massively hungry all the time.

Thankfully, because the flight wasn't commercial and Cuelebre Enterprises owned the jet, the supper was outstanding and catered to her needs and personal tastes. After an excellent meal of a savory sweet potato casserole, sautéed Brussel sprouts, a green salad, and lemon cake with raspberries for dessert, she stretched out on one of the couches with a blanket, slipped a black travel mask over her eyes and sank her awareness deep into her body where a small, subtle shadow rested.

I love you, she said to the shadow. *No matter who or what you are, I'll always love you. Precious little Peanut.*

Then, because probably the shadow didn't understand words, she tried to send all the love she had at it, as gently as she could. While she was doing that, she fell into a deep sleep.

The next thing she knew, she was climbing along her favorite trail in the Adirondacks, admiring the glorious fall colors as the trees turned brilliant red, orange and yellow.

She had been raised a city girl, because her mother believed that the best place for them to hide was in the middle of a dense, busy population. But part of Pia had always been wild, and one of the things she relished about moving to upstate New York was being able to sink into the outdoors without worrying about her safety. It soothed a part of her nature that had never before gotten the chance to stretch out her legs and roam.

Something rustled in the underbrush, and part of her attention turned to it, but she kept walking.

The slight rustle followed.

Pausing, she bent to pretend to tie her shoe. As she did so, she studied either side of the trail carefully.

Deep in the shadows of nearby brush, gold eyes watched her.

Small gold eyes, close to the ground. She raised her eyebrows. There was no way that could be Dragos.

She started to smile. "It's okay if you want to come out. Wouldn't you like a hug?"

The gold eyes blinked, but nothing emerged from the brush.

"Okay," she said with a shrug. "Suit yourself."

Straightening, she began to walk again.

The small rustling followed her.

She paused again. This time, without looking, she said, "Are you sure you wouldn't like to come out for a hug?"

Nothing happened. No rustle or movement of any kind. She listened to the wind and watched the clouds while she waited.

Then amusement got the better of her. She muttered, "We've got this all wrong, haven't we? You're not another Peanut. You're a little Stinkpot."

Giving up, she looked around and located the stinkpot. The small gold eyes had found another deep shadow from which to watch her.

"It's okay, darling," she said gently to it. "You can hide for as long as you want to…. I'll be waiting whenever you want to come out. I'll always be here for you."

Turning back to her path, she continued on the trail, while the shadow followed close behind.

The air around her shifted, and she woke up to the sound of the jet's engines changing. They had begun their descent.

Hugging herself, she went over every detail of her dream.

Gold eyes! Like Dragos's! Sure, it had only been a dream, but everything she had ever dreamed about Liam had turned out to be true in some way. God, she couldn't wait for the little stinkpot to make up his—or her—mind to come out of hiding!

Sitting up, she looked around. Outside, faint streaks of light spanned the edge of the horizon. Alex had lowered the cabin lights after supper, and in the shadows, she saw that Eva had settled deep into her seat, engrossed in the contents of her e-reader.

Quentin and Aryal occupied the other couch, opposite Pia. They had curled up together, Quentin spooning Aryal from behind, his arm around the harpy's waist.

They looked so peaceful when they were asleep. Almost, dare one say, normal.

Muffling a snort, Pia indulged in a full body stretch. She had managed to sleep several hours, which was very good news. While she wasn't as rested as she would be if she had slept in her bed at home, she felt like she had gotten enough rest to get through the day with plenty of energy.

Her thigh itched, and absently she scratched it. She had panicked when she had begun to itch after her first shot of the protocol, but Dr. Medina had assured her it was just the drug beginning to wear off. As long as she could tolerate the irritation for the twenty-four hours or so, she was still good, still on track.

She put a hand over her stomach and whispered, "Because you're staying right where you belong, no matter what. Little Stinkpot."

With that, she stood, collected her overnight bag and went to the back of the plane to shower and prepare for her day. She dressed casually, in a long, dark blue maxi dress, sandals, and a sheer, lightweight sweater, and took time with her makeup. While this was supposed to be an informal visit, from what she knew about the Light Fae Queen, Tatiana was relentlessly elegant, so she wanted to look nice.

When she stepped out, Eva was ready and waiting to shower too. Then Quentin and Aryal stirred and took their turns, and then Daniel stepped out of the cockpit to serve them a quick continental breakfast. After that, there was nothing left for Pia to do but watch out of a plane window and get more nervous about the upcoming week.

Tatiana was not just relentlessly elegant. She was relentlessly inquisitive as well, and in D.C. she had asked uncomfortable questions about Pia's real nature. Pia wasn't looking forward to the next week, which was all the more reason to rip that Band-Aid off and get it over with. Otherwise the trip would have been hanging over her head, perhaps for months. Now, at least, they could get on with their lives soon enough.

On Monday, to be precise.

So while she was unenthusiastic, she was certainly composed enough when the plane touched down.

Hey, baby, Dragos said in her head.

When she heard his dark, Powerful mental voice, surprised pleasure flowed through her. *Hey yourself. How did you get here so quickly? No wait, never mind—I'm not supposed to know that.*

She could hear the smile in his voice as he asked, *Did you get any sleep?*

I sure did. Covering her mouth, she yawned. *I missed you, though. How did your night go?*

I went fishing and flew up around Big Sur, he said. *It was good, but I missed you too.*

She confessed, *I dreamed about the little stinkpot.*

The little stinkpot? He laughed. *How did it manage to get that nickname?*

In my dream, I was hiking, and Stinkpot was hiding in some underbrush. Sharing the small story with Dragos had her grinning all over again. *In the dream, it had gold eyes like yours, but that's all I could see. I tried to coax it out for a hug, but it still doesn't want to come out and say hi yet.*

It will when it's ready.

Yes, I know it will.

As they talked, the plane taxied down the runaway to an eventual stop. *Okay*, Dragos said. *I don't want to distract you. I just wanted to let you know I was in town.*

I'm glad you did, she said. *Talk to you later?*

Absolutely. Just call whenever you have any time to yourself, and I'll hear.

Without ceremony, the jet's built-in airstairs were deployed. Quentin and Aryal descended first, and Pia followed, with Eva staying guard at her back.

As she stepped out of the hull of the plane, she paused at the top of the stairs to take in the scene.

The morning was cloudless, bright and already warm. On the east lay the San Gabriel Mountains, and at the edge of the western horizon, blue water sparkled in the sun. As they had chosen a private airstrip for landing, there was a minimum of bustle around the edges of the wide, open area.

Several Porsche SUVs waited nearby, and ten armed Light Fae guard spread out in a semicircle nearby, broadly circling a tall blond woman with short, curly hair. All eleven wore the signature tan and blue uniforms, and the woman was also armed.

Quentin said in her head, *That's a lot of guards for an informal meetup, especially when they knew you would have your own security with you.*

Is that why you and Aryal are hesitating? Pia replied. *Look how they're watching the surrounding area. They're guarding the woman—is that one of Tatiana's daughters?*

Yes, that's the younger daughter. Bailey, I think her name is.

As they hesitated, the blond woman strode forward to the bottom of the airstairs, looking up at Pia.

She said to Quentin, *Let's go.*

After a moment, Quentin said, *Okay. But I want to know why they think they need to have so many guards—either to meet us or to guard Bailey—in the heart of their own demesne.*

Oy vey. With so many watching her, she would not roll her eyes.

She muttered in Quentin's head, *If you're going to poke your nose around and ask questions, fine, just be sure to be discreet about it.*

Of course, he said, giving her a quick glance over one broad shoulder. *I am nothing like my mate. Well, at least about discretion.*

She laughed. That was true enough. She had known Quentin for several years. He was one of the most secretive people she knew, and he had been long before he had become a sentinel and Pia had worked for him at his bar, Elfie's.

With that, she stepped down the stairs, toward the tall blond woman, who held out a hand. "Good morning, Lady Cuelebre," the woman said with a smile. "We haven't met yet, but my name is Bailey—I'm Tatiana's youngest daughter. Welcome to the Light Fae demesne."

"Thank you," Pia said, taking her hand.

While Bailey's smile had vanished quickly, she looked friendly enough. Like her older twin, the Light Fae heir and actress Melisande Aindris, Baily had thick, tawny curling hair, but unlike her famous sister, she wore hers short and tousled. Her eyes were more hazel than green, but her gaze was clear and direct, and she had a strong, firm handshake.

Then Pia almost stumbled with a lie, but she managed to catch herself before she said, *It's nice to be here.* Instead, she said, "It's nice to meet you."

"And you as well." Bailey nodded a greeting to Pia's guards, tucked her hands behind her back and inclined her head toward the waiting motorcade. "If you'd like to come this way, please."

"Certainly." Pia accompanied her to the appropriate Porsche, climbed inside with Eva, and with that, her week's visit officially began.

Chapter Four

ONCE THE JET had taken off safely, Dragos had turned his attention to making his own journey.

As fast as he might be able to fly, he couldn't beat the jet to California. If he chose to stay in dragon form for the trip, he wouldn't arrive until the evening of the next day.

There wasn't a thing wrong with that decision, and he almost chose to do it. The long, solitary flight did sound appealing. Having to relate to so many different creatures on a daily basis was wearing, and if he didn't get regular time to fly alone, he grew short-tempered and snappish. Well, more snappish than usual.

On a whim, more than anything else, he decided on a different mode of travel and called the Djinn Soren to give him a quick trip. Traveling Djinn style meant that he could get to California hours before Pia. He could still enjoy a long flight and plenty of solitude, and also be ready and waiting when her plane landed.

Sometimes it was very handy to have a Djinn owe you a favor. A few weeks previously, Soren had asked Dragos if he had any information about an upcoming commercial venture between the Nightkind and the witches' demesne. It just so happened that Dragos had developed an extensive file on the subject, and he had given a copy of the file to Soren in return for a favor. All he had to do was request the trip.

Dragos's face and form were too distinctive, so instead of booking a stay at a luxury hotel in the city, he chose a modest, remote motel bordering the nearby Angeles National Forest. After Soren had dropped Dragos and his luggage off, he checked in quickly, threw his travel bag on the bed and left again to shapeshift and take to the night sky.

Dragos didn't care for L.A.—although he had laid claim to New York long ago for tactical, political and business reasons, he wasn't fond of any city and only tolerated them at best—but he did appreciate southern California's balmy climate. The salty breeze off the ocean was the perfect combination of warm and refreshing.

By the light of a half moon, the dragon stretched out his wings and coasted on the thermals. He wore his cloaking spell to prevent detection, and after a few hours, he felt relaxed and tension free. He flew offshore some distance and dove into the water, fishing until he had eaten his fill. Then he gained altitude again and winged north to watch the ocean waves break against the cliffs of Big Sur, relishing the solitude and the clear, brilliant starlit night.

He had circled back around in a leisurely fashion,

arriving at the airstrip in plenty of time to watch the arrival of the Light Fae motorcade.

Tatiana had a few formidable magic users in her court. One of them was the captain of her guard, Shane Mac Cartheigh, so Dragos made sure to be circling very high in the air over the site and cloaking his presence tightly, as the troops poured out of the vehicles.

The dragon's sharp gaze could pick up small prey from two miles away. He had no trouble picking out the individual soldiers. He saw Tatiana's daughter Bailey direct the troops with a wide sweep of her arm. They jogged to every end of the airstrip and studied the surrounding countryside, weapons ready.

He approved of their security measures, but why was Bailey directing Light Fae troops instead of Shane? Last he heard, she didn't live in California but resided somewhere rather remote. Puerto Rico, or maybe Jamaica. She and Sebastian Hale ran a security company. Hale was Wyr and an excellent fighter, and Dragos made sure to track excellent Wyr fighters who weren't his own.

No wait, Hale had mated and retired. Bailey ran the security company alone now. So why was she here?

After thoroughly searching the perimeter, the troops down below converged again around Bailey. A few moments later, the Cuelebre jet came into view. Watching approvingly as the jet touched down in a textbook perfect landing, Dragos chatted with Pia until the jet's airstairs were deployed. Then Quentin and

Aryal appeared, began to descend and froze halfway down the stairs.

They sensed something too. What did they sense?

He said in Aryal's head, *What is it?*

The harpy didn't evidence any surprise at his presence. She said tersely, *Quentin and I think it seems like a lot of troops for a simple pickup.*

It is. He told her about watching them spread out and search the area around the airstrip. *A group of that size was able to establish a secure perimeter very quickly.*

From the distance, he saw the harpy shrug. *That's probably it. Private airstrips don't have the kind of security that airports do. They were being thorough and efficient before we arrived.*

Probably, he agreed. *We do tend to be paranoid.*

Just because you're paranoid, blah blah blah, etc., Aryal told him sourly.

I wondered where Shane was, and why Bailey is here, he said. *She usually lives in Jamaica. Or Puerto Rico. Whichever one it is.*

You're so nitpicky, Aryal told him. *Now I'm wondering that too. Maybe he's on vacation. Does Tatiana's captain take vacations?*

The dragon snorted. *I have no damn idea.*

Aryal said to him, *Pia says to go ahead. What say you?*

We are *being nitpicky,* he told her. *So go ahead, but keep a watchful eye out. Report back to me if you notice anything unusual.*

You got it.

The foursome continued to the tarmac, merged with the Light Fae troops, and was swallowed up by the motorcade.

Dragos followed the motorcade until it reached the outskirts of Bel Air, the affluent neighborhood where the Light Fae Queen's residence was located. When the car carrying Pia turned onto Tatiana's street, his eyes narrowed at the barricade that waiting troops moved into place across the street. After putting the barrier into place, the troops stood at attention behind it, facing outward.

The Light Fae Queen's residence was in the same neighborhood as those of celebrities, musicians and movie stars. Ronald Reagan had once lived in Bel Air, and so had Alfred Hitchcock. Tour buses traveling through the neighborhood were a normal way of life.

As far as he knew, blocking the neighborhood off was something new. It looked as though Tatiana was taking no chances with the Lord of the Wyr's mate, an attitude that he approved most heartily.

He had watched and waited, and touched base with Pia, and indulged in paranoia. Now, there was nothing more for him to do but bide his time until he could talk to her again.

He had packed his laptop. He could go back to the motel to work. Or he could just take time off. It was rare for him to have free time on his hands. He could go fishing again, and fly over the coast and spend the week avoiding other people, and while he liked the sound of that quite a bit, his nitpicking, paranoid discussion with Aryal left him restless and uneasy.

He contacted Aryal again. *Have you arrived yet?*

Yes, we're here, the harpy told him. *Nobody's gone insane and stabbed all of us yet. Pia's in the guest suite unpacking, and we've got the suite next to hers. Tatiana is in a meeting, but she's supposed to have breakfast with Pia soon.*

What happened to the Light Fae troops in the motorcade?

They went wherever Light Fae troops go when they fly back to the home hive. They sort of dissipated and soaked into the woodwork, no doubt on the Queen Bee's orders. Aryal sounded cheerful. *But maybe they'll still swarm back and stab us all to death, before any of us can yell to you for help. You never know.*

He snorted. *Your sense of humor can be damn odd at times.*

All I'm really saying is, maybe this time, our paranoia really was just paranoia. Of all his sentinels, Aryal was the most prone to impatience, but she didn't sound impatient now. She sounded kind. *For now, everything seems fine.*

He told her, *Good enough. Report back later.*

Will do.

He had drifted south and east while they talked, over the Bel Air Country Club. Abruptly, he made up his mind, chose a direction and flew for it. While the distance would take a half an hour or so to drive by car, or even twice that, depending on traffic, he covered his trajectory within a few minutes.

When he came to Rodeo Drive, he waited for a lull in the traffic. He didn't have to wait long—traffic was unusually sparse for such a popular area. Then he dropped down and shapeshifted as he landed. Still cloaking tightly, he strolled down one of the most luxurious shopping districts in the world until he reached Van Cleef & Arpels. After admiring the jewels in the showcase, he strolled down the street to the next jewelry store.

He stopped at a few other jewelry stores, admired Cartier's display, then he came to a uniquely Elder Races jewelry store named Songs of Fire.

He had only intended to window-shop, until he laid eyes on the firebird.

It was a necklace, very high-end jewelry, the kind of showpiece that would sell very rarely and only to a relatively select clientele. After just a brief glance, he knew the cost must be in the high six figures, if not seven.

The body of the bird rested at the hollow of the mannequin's throat. Made of fiery diamonds and rubies, it was easily as long as his thumb. The bird's eye was an emerald the size of his thumbnail. The wings swept up on either side of the mannequin's neck, tapering off gracefully so that the tips came together at the nape.

He loved having Pia as his mate for many reasons. She was sexy, and funny, and smart and wise, and far kinder than he. She curbed his worst impulses, as much as he would let her, and having sex with her was so smoking hot, they burned up the air around them when they coupled.

And one of the things the dragon loved best was to buy his mate jewelry.

Because she was his.

So when he gave her jewels to wear, they were his as well. All his, forever.

He loved to fuck her when she was wearing diamonds and nothing else. She was jaw-droppingly gorgeous when she wore jewels, all lush and naked, delicately pink in all the most private places, and sparkling bright. Pia was the crown jewel in the dragon's hoard.

He struggled with his impulses, briefly, while part of him knew it had been a foregone conclusion as soon as he had laid eyes on the firebird.

After a moment, glancing left and right, he waited until passersby on the street were either walking or looking away. Then he let his cloaking fall away, opened the door and walked inside.

It was barely after ten o'clock, so the store had just opened for the day, and he was the only customer.

Good. He liked it that way.

As a tall, model-slim woman hurried into the store from the back, he said, "I would like for you to lock your doors while I'm here. As I plan on making at least one significant purchase, it will be worth your while."

The woman was Light Fae and beautiful, with long, thoroughbred bones, skillful makeup and designer clothes. She also looked tense and unhappy. "I'm sorry, it's against company policy to lock the doors during store hours."

Dragos paused. It was highly unusual for people to tell him no, and it was never an experience he appreciated. Cocking his head, he drew his brows together and asked, "Do you realize who I am?"

The woman looked at him, "Should I? Oh … oh, wait. Are you Lord Cuelebre?"

"Yes, I am, and I'm here *in private* shopping for my wife." He narrowed his eyes on her. "I expect you to be discreet about my presence here."

"Sure, of course," she said, waving a hand in dismissal of the subject. "We're always discreet."

Again, he had to pause. He was a jewelry store's wet dream. Managers bolted out of hiding to fawn over him. They had involved and passionate discussions about clarity and cut, quality grades and light.

This woman's preoccupied attitude was not normal.

He persisted. "And you'll lock the door while I'm here?"

"Oh yes, of course." She stepped around the end of one counter to walk toward the door and lock it. As she did so, she sighed. "What is it you would like to see?"

His short amount of patience was evaporating rapidly.

"I wanted to examine the firebird necklace you have on display," he told her, his tone short. "Along with the accessory pieces, but is this a bad time?"

"Excuse me?"

For the first time since he had entered the shop, she looked at him directly. He noted the shadows under her eyes. The whites of her eyes were bloodshot. His attention snagged by the small details, he took a step forward and caught a whiff of her scent.

She was not merely preoccupied and unhappy. She was quite distressed.

He sighed. The dragon didn't care if the woman was having a bad day. All he wanted to do was ignore her, examine the necklace more closely and make a buy decision.

Actually, what he would have liked to do was just steal the damn thing and be done with it, but he had started out in a leisurely, aboveboard fashion, and now the store's security system would have a record of his presence. And security recordings in jewelry stores were never stored on site, not with so many potential and extremely talented thieves scattered throughout the Elder Races.

In social situations like this, he had taken to asking himself WWPD? (What Would Pia Do?)

They had such different reactions to most things, and she was so much better at interacting and relating to people than he was, that he had learned asking himself WWPD helped avoid unpleasantness from time to time when he was in pursuit of something that he wanted.

The small exercise helped. Often, he wasn't able to

achieve what Pia would *actually* do, because it was just too foreign to his nature. But more often than not, he was able to approximate something between what she would do and what was his natural inclination to do.

As a result, a rumor had started in his corporation that marriage and mating might be softening him up. Curious and coldly amused, he tracked the rumor down to its source, and the whispers died a quick and decisive death.

He was a contented dragon, not a tame one.

In this instance, if Pia were here, she would ask after the woman's well-being. He didn't want to go that far, but perhaps he might talk to a manager and have a normal discussion about jewelry after all.

He said, "You're clearly not focused on your work. No doubt you have some personal matter that needs your attention. Just get your manager for me, then you can take care of whatever it is you need to take care of."

The woman burst into tears.

Oh fuck. He almost threw up his hands and walked out. Only the memory of the firebird's sparkle anchored him in place.

"I'm s-sorry, there's no one else here," she said. "Two other people, including my m-manager, were supposed to show up for work, but they haven't yet. And I'm so sorry and embarrassed to burst into tears at you like this, Lord Cuelebre."

He closed his eyes briefly then told her, "Clearly

this isn't the best time for you to be dealing with customers. I'll leave now and come back when your manager is available." Pausing, he stared at her. She was busy wringing her hands, while tears streamed down her face. Gritting his teeth, he demanded, "Are you paying attention to anything that I'm saying to you right now?"

"I know, I'm sorry. I a-p-p-pologize, but I've had a sleepless night. I was looking for my mother everywhere, and nobody's around, and nobody showed up for work either, even when I tried to call in and take a sick day, and …"

His short amount of patience snapped.

Staring into her brimming gaze, he said in a quiet, compelling voice, "Stop this meltdown immediately. You're calming down now. You're growing quite calm, do you understand? And lucid. You are definitely growing more lucid."

"But you don't understand," she sobbed. *There's nobody around.*"

Hm. Sometimes, when the subject was overwrought like this, it took his beguilement a little while to take effect. Plus, there was always the possibility that she was delusional. It was very difficult to beguile a delusional person until he actually understood what they were delusional about.

"What do you mean, there's nobody around?" he asked. Beguilement also didn't work very well when he let his own impatience get in the way and upset people, so he tried to curb the sharpness of his tone. "Of course there are people around. There are cars and people in the street right now. You're growing calm and lucid now, remember? In fact, you're feeling so calm, you're quite capable of using your keys to go get that necklace for me to examine."

Abruptly, she did calm down. Her sobbing stopped as if a switch had been thrown, and her twisting hands loosened.

"There aren't any people in my neighborhood," she whispered. "My mom lives on the next block. She's gone too. We always have breakfast together, but she wasn't there when I let myself in. When I called the police and told them my mother was missing, they said they would drive by her house to check into it, and get back to me. I haven't heard from them either."

Okay. He had tried his hardest not to engage, but that snagged him. He repeated, "There are no people at all in your neighborhood."

Mutely she shook her head.

Perhaps this was the delusion he needed to understand to make his beguilement effective. Crossing his arms, he frowned. "How do you know this?"

"Because I live there!" the woman cried. "I know!"

Abruptly, he decided he'd had more than enough of talking to her. He snapped, "What's your address?"

Jumping at the sharp command in his voice, she blurted out an address.

He held out one hand. "Give me the keys."

The woman hesitated, then started shaking her head. "I-I don't think I c-can do tha—"

Oh for the love of all the gods. Injecting all his strength into his voice, he told her, "SHUT UP AND GIVE ME THE GODDAMN KEYS."

Her hand jerked out, offering the set to him. Taking the ring, he rifled through them until he found the right key to unlock the display case. Scooping up the firebird necklace, a matching bracelet and dangling earrings, he gave them a brief, very thorough look.

The workmanship was top-notch. He was looking forward to examining the pieces in greater depth, but for now, he shoved the jewelry into the front pocket of his jeans. He told the woman, "Tell your boss to bill me."

She stood frozen and mute, staring at him with huge eyes.

Because he had, in fact, told her to shut up. Well, that would wear off soon enough, but thank the gods, not while he was around.

Slapping her keys on the counter, he let himself out of Crazy Town and into the welcome fresh, sunlit air. Rotating first one shoulder, then the other, he angled his head and looked up and down the street.

Yes, there were people around, both shoppers walking down the sidewalks and people driving by in cars.

He was just about to dismiss the woman forever as a mental case, when one small detail caught his attention.

Everyone walking down the street was human. There weren't any of the Elder Races in sight.

That happened quite often, actually. There were far more humans than people of the Elder Races. … But he was standing in front of a popular Elder Races shop, which strengthened the likelihood that he would see a member of the Elder Races—any of the Elder Races— quite a bit.

Frowning again, he turned his attention to the cars passing by. The next five vehicles were filled with humans too.

It was probably just a huge, boring coincidence. But Tatiana had guards barricading her street. And it *had* seemed like she had sent a large number of troops to meet Pia's flight.

Fuck it. He would go check out Basket Case's address and determine for himself whether or not there was anybody around.

When he consulted Google Maps briefly on his smartphone, he found Basket Case lived in a neighborhood north and to the west. Pulling his cloaking tightly around him, he shapeshifted and took to the air. By car, he guessed it would take Basket Case a good forty-five minutes to drive into work. Sometimes he pitied wingless creatures.

As he flew the distance, he turned over various thoughts in his mind like searching for the spark of jewels in a mound of earth.

People, any kind of people, tended to congregate in enclaves and cluster in clumps. Sure, there were crossovers, but overall, families liked to flock to family-oriented amusements and neighborhoods. Hipsters flocked to whatever hipsters liked to do. Dragos was acres and miles and continents away from being a hipster, so he had no real understanding of that new subset of society, but he thought it involved drinking lots of artisanal coffee and organic wines.

Those who were religious behaved in the same way. They went to church, or synagogues, or temples, and enjoyed social outings together. The Elder Races also followed the same behavioral trend. They tended to shop at Elder Races stores and live in neighborhoods filled with Elder Races creatures.

The Light Fae were no exception. As a people, they tended to be clannish anyway, and Basket Case had said her mother lived on the next block over from her. It stood to reason that Basket Case probably lived in a neighborhood filled with Light Fae.

Her mother was missing. Her co-workers and manager, who were in all probability Light Fae as well, had not come in to work.

Locating the street on which Basket Case lived, he coasted down the length of it until he reached her block. Then he landed, shapeshifted and walked down the middle of the tree-lined street until he came up to her address.

It looked like a modest, smart neighborhood, with a

mix of single-family homes and other houses that appeared to be divided into apartments. Along with oaks and other varieties of trees, palm trees dotted either side of the streets. Fences were painted; lawns were well kept. While modest, this was not a neighborhood in decline.

No cars traveled down the street to disrupt the direction of Dragos's stroll.

Nobody mowed their lawn.

He began to listen closely for any signs of movement in the houses he passed. There were none. A couple of houses stood with their front doors open. Silence beat down on his head, along with the strength of the southern California sun.

Basket Case had not been delusional, after all. There were no people in her neighborhood.

Some people might think that meant he owed her an apology. In fact, if he considered WWPD, she would definitely say that he did, but as far as he was concerned, it was a moot point, as he had no intention of ever speaking to or seeing Basket Case again. There was just so much of the rest of his life to live, which took a far greater urgency.

Wait, there was a sound. It came from some distance away, perhaps a couple of blocks over to the right. It sounded metallic, like a trash can had been knocked over.

He broke into an easy jog, reached the end of the block and turned right. The small sound of his own footsteps overrode what he had heard, so he had to stop once or twice to listen again before moving forward.

There—more sounds came from down this street. It was virtually a replica of the street he had just left. This was all part of the same neighborhood.

On his left, a house stood with its front door open. He passed several more houses with open doors.

Who leaves their door open when they leave their house? People evacuating, or in a panic, except how could Basket Case live in this neighborhood and not be aware of an evacuation or a panic? Had she gone out the evening before, so she wasn't home to notice this general air of abandonment?

His mind shot to the unpleasant heart of the matter. Was he really going to have to talk to her again, after all?

There. He stopped.

The noises came from behind that stucco house. Now that he was closer, it sounded louder, like there were several creatures making it. A pack of dogs, perhaps, rooting through an alleyway. If people had left in a hurry, some of them might have abandoned their pets.

He walked around the side of the house. A six-foot-high privacy fence surrounded the backyard, so in the last several feet, he gathered up speed and leaped over it.

The backyard was charming and as well kept as the

rest of the neighborhood. He jogged to the back fence, gathered himself and leaped again.

As he landed in the alley, he startled a group of people.

Quite a large group of people, all Light Fae, in various modes of dress. To a one, they were streaked with blood and open wounds.

Staring, he straightened from his landing crouch as the group whipped around to glare at him. Their eyes were all black. No whites.

Some had only half their faces, the remaining flesh looking as though it had been chewed by wild beasts.

People tend to flock, and these were no exception either. Moving as one, they hurtled at him. They were incredibly, impossibly fast. There wasn't enough room in the alley for him to shapeshift and launch. Then he thought to turn and leap back over the fence.

As he crouched to spring, the foremost of the group gathered into a huge leap and landed on his back, knocking him off balance. It was followed by two more. Then the entire group was upon him. Pain flared as one of them bit him on his arm, tearing through the skin.

Like the snick of a trigger on a gun, Dragos's mind clicked over to Plan B:

Fight savagely and throw lots and lots of fire.

He cut loose.

Chapter Five

ATIANA'S RESIDENCE REMINDED Pia of classic old Hollywood grandeur. The white mansion had Corinthian-style columns in the front, large receiving rooms and a large pool in the backyard surrounded by an immaculately kept garden.

The furnishings inside were classic old-world Hollywood too. Pia's suite had a massive four-poster bed in the bedroom with a peach coverlet and sheer drapes tied back, and antique Chippendale furniture. She had a sitting room all to herself, with a wood fireplace and two divans, and her bathroom had a walk-in, marble bathtub with gold furnishings.

After unpacking and admiring the view out her windows, she texted Eva. `I'm ready to go downstairs.`

Within the next breath, a rap sounded on her door. Eva didn't wait for a reply but opened it and stuck her head in. "I'm ready too."

Unless they encountered a situation that warranted a change in plans, for now, while Pia was in the Light Fae Queen's residence, she would have one guard with her at all times, so that Quentin, Aryal, and Eva could rotate shifts around the clock.

Pia hoped that would help to generate a relaxed atmosphere among everyone, and besides, the other two were close by if anything happened.

She stepped out in the hall and took the stairs with Eva by her side. Just like earlier at the airstrip, Bailey had evidently been waiting for them, and she moved smoothly to the bottom of the stairs to meet them.

At least Bailey wasn't flanked by ten more guards inside the house, Pia thought wryly. Because that would be awkward.

"Are you all settled in?" Bailey asked.

"Yes, thanks," Pia replied cheerfully. "The place is magnificent. Is it all right if we look around?"

"Sure," Bailey told her. "I'll come with you."

"Are you my babysitter?" Pia asked, smiling.

The Light Fae woman returned her smile, but like before, on the tarmac, it was brief and faded again quickly. "It's my pleasure to spend time with you."

So she is *my babysitter,* Pia said to Eva. *I don't mind. I suspected there would be somebody, but I did at least expect some kind of greeting from Tatiana when I arrived.*

Guess a Queen's gotta do what a Queen's gotta do. Eva's mental voice sounded dubious.

Pia, who had been on the receiving end of many events that needed immediate attention, didn't feel nearly as dubious about Tatiana's absence. Things happened, and when you were a demesne leader (or his mate), sometimes you had to react quickly.

Bailey turned to indicate the direction of the rear of the house, and as they fell into step beside her, she said, "My mother asked me to apologize for her. She had planned to be free to greet you personally, but in the last two days she's been dealing with an unexpected situation. I'm sure you know how it goes."

"I do, actually," Pia replied. "We're often disturbed in the middle of the night for one reason or another. Demesne business never seems to stop."

"I get it," said Bailey. They reached double French doors, which she opened. She led them onto a wide verandah. "You and Dragos are one of those places where the buck stops, aren't you?"

"Yes, we are."

"My mom is too. It's one of the reasons why I mostly live somewhere else. I love my family, but I don't want to eat, drink and sleep all things Light Fae. And I *really* didn't want to go into the family business. I have about as much acting ability as a tin can."

"What do you do, at your home?" Pia asked her curiously.

Her first impression of Bailey had been one of tough competence, but the other woman hadn't seemed all that friendly during the motorcade ride to Bel Air.

Now, she received a different impression. Once they stepped inside the Queen's home, Bailey seemed to have relaxed, and as a result, she had grown more talkative.

"I run a security company out of Jamaica," Bailey said.

"What does a security company do?" Pia asked.

"It can involve anything from supplying bodyguards for specific events to either running expeditions or providing security for them. One of the most interesting expeditions we recently undertook was to retrieve a magical library from a deserted island."

"You're talking about Carling Severan's library, aren't you?" Pia said, her attention snagged by the scenario. "I heard about that. It must have been a fascinating trip."

"Yeah, it was. That was the trip my business partner Sebastian found the love of his life, mated and retired." Bailey gave her a sidelong grin. "But usually things aren't quite so eventful. On a daily basis, my job mostly involves a lot of drinking and suntanning. When we take on jobs to pay the bills, it can often involve a lot of fighting too, so by and large that makes me happy. Only thing I don't like is the paperwork. Sebastian, my former partner, used to take care of most of that, but now that he's retired, I've been drowning in it."

Out of the corner of her eye, Pia saw Eva smile. Pia told Bailey, "My husband hates paperwork too, which is why he has several assistants."

"Yeah, assistants." Bailey heaved a sigh. "If you don't do it yourself, you have to be a manager for somebody else who does. Or even a couple of somebody elses. I'm just not sure running a business by myself is going to work out. It takes away from the drinking and the suntanning."

Pia laughed. "Bummer."

As they talked, they stepped outside to walk the grounds. In the growing heat of the sunny morning, Bailey unbuttoned the jacket of her uniform, shrugged out of it and slung it over one shoulder. Underneath she wore a shoulder harness and gun over a plain white, short-sleeved shirt. The shirt hugged her lean torso and supple, muscled biceps.

Pia had gotten used to the sight of armed people as a daily occurrence a long time ago, but she couldn't help but wonder—if Bailey was comfortable enough in her role to shed the uniform, why did she still feel the need to go armed?

After all, Bailey was essentially in her own home, and there were other guards around. When sentinels or other military personnel visited Pia and Dragos's house for any length of time, they disarmed, left their weapons in a safe place—usually Dragos's office—and relaxed. It was only when they were making a brief stop that they didn't bother.

Did Bailey stay armed because Pia and her three guards were here? Or was it some other kind of Light Fae protocol? If Bailey was supposed to be on duty, perhaps she was required to be armed at all times.

And if she ran a security company in Jamaica, what

was she doing here in southern California?

Pia filed those questions away to pursue another time. Hopefully, everybody would relax during her visit, and she might find a time to ask some of them at a later date.

The grounds were beautifully landscaped. They weren't as glorious as the former Elven High Lord's consort Beluvial's grounds were, but Beluvial had a special gift for growing things.

Still, the Light Fae Queen's gardens were beautifully kept and worthy of being featured in *Home & Garden*. When Pia thought of the sturdy, no-nonsense landscaping of grass, mulch and trees that they had decided to do around their home in upstate New York, a pang of homesickness washed over her.

Thrusting that aside, she focused on the present. "The weather is gorgeous," she said, taking a deep breath and turning in a circle to admire the cloudless blue sky. "When I left home last night, we were getting a combination of rain and snow, with a forecast of more snow through today."

"Did you bring your swimsuit?" Bailey asked. "L.A.'s forecast for the next week is more weather like today's."

"I didn't think to pack it," she confessed.

"No problem. Mom keeps a variety of swimsuits for guests, or if you want, we can always send out for one." Bailey had taken them on a big circle around the property, and as they turned to stroll back in the direction they had come, she added, "Sorry, I'm not as good at hostessing as my sister Melly or my mom. I should have asked you if you've eaten breakfast already."

"How is your sister doing?" she asked. Earlier that year, Melly had been kidnapped and held hostage by a ruthless Vampyre elder. In the process of being rescued, Melly and the Nightkind King, Julian, had rekindled an old love affair.

For some reason, Pia's question made Bailey's expression darken. "We don't talk like we used to, but she seems well, and she sounds happy."

Bailey didn't appear to appreciate her sister's rekindled relationship. It was time to move the conversation on to something else.

Pia told her, "I'm glad to hear it. It was a terrible thing that happened to her. And thank you for bringing up breakfast. We had a light breakfast on the plane, but I wouldn't turn away a second chance to eat."

The shadow passed from Bailey's expression, and she gave Pia a quick grin. "We'll be like Hobbits then, and eat second breakfast. And elevenses too, if you'd like."

Pia laughed. She liked Bailey. "That sounds good."

As they neared the house, a tall, elegant Light Fae woman stepped outside and strode toward them.

Tatiana, the Light Fae Queen, had finally freed herself of other obligations and was coming to greet Pia.

Pia took in the other woman's appearance. When she had seen Tatiana at political functions, the Light Fae Queen had worn haute couture. She had the height, the beauty and the poise to carry off outstanding creations.

Now, the other woman wore black clothes and boots. The shirt was tailored, and the cut of the pants elegant, and if those boots cost under $5,000, Pia would eat her own sandals, but still, the outfit was much more plain than any she had previously seen Tatiana wear.

Instead of sporting a mop of curling dark blond hair like her daughters, which was typical for the Light Fae, Tatiana must have had her hair straightened, for it fell like a sleek waterfall to below her shoulder blades.

Her expression was poised and serious, and in the full, bright light of the sun, faint shadows darkened the skin underneath her eyes. The last time Pia had talked with her, Tatiana had been smilingly inquisitive, poking at Pia delicately like a cat batting her with a paw. Tatiana's claws had been sheathed at the time, but you knew she had them.

Something's wrong, Pia thought. She let the observation sit in the back of her mind, while internally, she braced herself.

"Good morning," Tatiana said as they came up to each other. "Bailey tells me that you had a good flight."

"Yes, we did," Pia said. Then, because she sometimes had claws of her own, she batted gently at the Light Fae Queen. "Thank you for sending such a robust greeting party."

Was that a flicker of response in those famous, beautiful green eyes?

"You're welcome," Tatiana replied. "We take the issue of your safety while you visit here very seriously. Please, come sit with me on the verandah. Bailey, would you see that refreshments are served?"

"Certainly. Pia and I were discussing doing just that."

Pia told Eva, "Why don't you go with Bailey?"

"Sure," Eva said. Telepathically, she asked, *You've got your phone?*

Yes, in my pocket. I can text if I need you.

Bailey inclined her head to Pia, and she and Eva strode into the house.

Pia followed Tatiana to a white painted, wrought iron table and chairs that were tucked well into the shade of the porch roof. As they seated themselves, she told the older woman, "Your home is lovely."

"Thank you," Tatiana replied. "I've lived here since the early twentieth century, when moving pictures were just becoming all the rage. Perhaps sometime you might be interested in touring the Northern Lights Studios. We've kept a great deal of memorabilia, and it can be amusing to take the tour."

At last, something that Pia could answer with complete honesty. "I would love that," she said, even while she noted Tatiana's use of words.

"Sometime," the Queen had said, not "this week." Was she beginning to let Quentin and Aryal's paranoia infect her?

"In the meantime," Tatiana said with a smile, "Bailey and I have been talking about possibilities for your visit. We wondered if you would enjoy staying at Melly's beach house in Malibu. The beach is quite lovely, and the swimming and surfing is very nice at this time of year. The house is located in a gated community, and after what happened to Melly earlier this year, the security has been increased until the area is all but airtight. It's a wonderful vacation spot. I've stayed there myself from time to time."

But I'm not on vacation, Pia thought.

She watched Tatiana closely, but the other woman had many years of experience with being in the limelight, and her poise remained flawless.

Still, the suggestion said everything. Something *was* wrong.

It was oh, so tempting to accept the invitation. She could soak up some sun, get in some pleasure reading, and swim to her heart's content, and probably even sneak in a few conjugal visits with Dragos.

But if word got out that this was how she spent much of her week with the Light Fae, what would the other demesne leaders think? How would the human government react?

She chose her response with care. "What a wonderful suggestion. Thank you for thinking of it, but I thought the point of this week was that you and I interact and get to know each other a little better? If I stayed at the Malibu beach house, I'm concerned that the other demesnes and the White House administration will not look on that choice with favor. And I have too many commitments over the next several months to consider committing to another week's visit."

The Queen was not pleased. Pia watched the subtle tightening of Tatiana's mouth. "Yes, I know." Tatiana snapped off the ends of the words with a delicate bite. "You made that clear when I emailed you and suggested that you visit at a later date."

Despite the diversity among the Elder Races, there was one thing demesne leaders had in common that Pia had noticed over the course of the last eighteen months—absolutely none of them liked being crossed or denied in any way.

Well, Tatiana was just going to have to suck it. Pia didn't like the situation any more than the other woman did, and her time and needs were just as important as anybody else's.

Still, if something was indeed wrong, she didn't want to make a bad situation worse. Again, she chose her words with care.

In a quiet, nonconfrontational voice, she said, "I know the terms of the diplomatic pact are difficult, and not just for all the demesne leaders but for their families as well. The last thing I want to do is disrupt your life as much as mine has been disrupted by this. If there's anything I can do to help ease the situation for you, please let me know. I'm happy to help you in any way I can."

The Queen stared at her with hard, glittering eyes just long enough to make Pia nervous. After all, she didn't know Tatiana well, but from everything she had heard, the other woman was formidable in every way. This exchange wasn't going to lead to some sort of royal tantrum, was it?

Then Tatiana let out an explosive sigh and rubbed her eyes. "Just tell me this much," she said. Her words were still clipped and short, but there seemed to be slightly less bite to them than before. "Did Dragos follow you here?"

Pia froze. In retrospect, she should have expected something like this, but she hadn't and the bald question caught her completely flat-footed. Like a frightened rabbit, for a moment she didn't even breathe.

Trying to stall for time, so she could think of a good way to lie, she asked cautiously, "Why would you ask such a thing?"

Tatiana barked out an unamused laugh. "Pia, everybody in the entire world has heard in great detail what happened when you went to visit the Elves in South Carolina."

"Yes, but the Wyr and the Light Fae aren't enemies, like we were with the Elves when that happened," Pia said cagily, while telepathically, she said to Dragos, *Uh-oh, I think we've been made.*

I'm busy dealing with an unexpected issue, he said tersely. *I'll be in touch soon.*

What on earth was he busy with?

She had just time to turn grouchy at his response when Tatiana snapped, "Stop prevaricating. I've asked you a straight question, and I expect an honest answer. Is Dragos here in Los Angeles or not?"

Great, numbskull. Just bloody great. You've already managed to piss off the Queen. What's next on your agenda, setting fire to Disneyland?

"He might be," Pia muttered. Nerves had taken her over. She scratched at her itchy thigh then smoothed the fabric of her dress over her thighs with tense fingers. "Nobody said he couldn't take a vacation in southern California during my visit."

Inexplicably, Tatiana relaxed. Sitting back in her chair, she said, "This visit of yours might turn out to be useful after all. Why don't you get in touch with him and ask him to come here, will you?"

She felt her eyebrows shoot up. "You—*want* him to come here?"

The other woman snorted. "You probably don't hear that all too often."

"No, frankly, I don't. I love my husband very much, but I'm under no illusion about how stressful his presence can sometimes be to others." She hesitated.

The strength and range of Dragos's telepathy was a

closely guarded secret. Not only that, but he had sounded pretty terse when she had telepathized to him earlier, so under Tatiana's watchful gaze, she pulled out her phone to text him.

Tatiana knows you're in L.A., and she's asked you to come here to her residence. After a moment's thought, she added, I think there's something wrong.

Just then Bailey stepped outside again, along with Eva. Behind them, a Light Fae servant wheeled out a cart filled with a variety of food and drink.

Tatiana said to Bailey, "Stay and join us."

With a quick questioning glance at Pia, Bailey replied readily enough, "Sure."

As she pulled out a chair and sat, Pia glanced at Eva uncertainly. As Tatiana's daughter, Bailey had many liberties that others wouldn't necessarily be expected to share.

If they were at home, Pia would invite Eva to sit down with them too, but while the Wyr had many complexities that other cultures did not—such as the intricacies and dangers in mating, and the tensions that lay between herbivores and predators—in many ways they had a less formal society than other demesnes. To the Light Fae Queen, Eva was a servant and a guard, but to Pia, Eva was also a friend.

Oh, screw it.

She looked at Tatiana. "Eva is a friend of mine. If I were at home, I would invite her to join us too. Would that be acceptable to you?"

The other woman's eyebrows rose, but despite the tensions just a few moments ago, she replied easily enough, "I have relationships like that as well. As you might remember from your aborted dinner party, my Captain Shane is one of them. As long as you count her in your inner circle and you give her access to privileged information, she can join us."

That was better. Feeling more comfortable, she smiled and nodded to Eva, who pulled out a chair opposite Bailey and sat.

"Thank you," Pia said to Tatiana, while she glanced down with a frown at her phone. It was unlike Dragos to take this long to text her back. What was his unexpected issue? It didn't have anything to do with Liam, did it?

The server set place settings and food on the table. Bailey said, "Eva and I double-checked all the recipes to make sure everything was vegan."

That brought Pia's attention up from her phone. She glanced again at all the dishes. There were scones, fresh strawberries, a pot of something that looked like cream but Pia's nose told her was coconut cream, not dairy, little round containers that looked like avocado mousse with pretty flecks of orange zest, some kind of berry crumble, and a complex savory salad with tossed greens, olives, and other vegetables.

Usually Pia could eat one or two dishes out of an entire meal's spread, but the Light Fae had ensured that she could eat everything on this table. It was a kindness she hadn't expected.

"This was really thoughtful of you," she told them. "Thank you."

"It was no trouble," Tatiana replied. "I often choose to eat vegan meals." As they helped themselves from each dish family-style, the Queen added, "I'm afraid I don't have much time I can spare for you. That was one of the reasons why I suggested the Malibu beach house. Over the last few days, a situation has developed that is consuming a great deal of my attention and resources."

Pia and Eva exchanged a glance. Pia asked, "You said that was one of the reasons behind the invitation to enjoy the beach house. What were the other reasons?"

This time, it was Tatiana and Bailey's turn to exchange glances. She had time to note that Bailey's expression had turned closed and unrevealing. Then Tatiana gave her a direct look. The Queen's gaze had turned grim.

Tatiana said, "Your safety. If you insist on being here this week, the Malibu house is the best place for your protection."

Carefully, Eva put down her fork. Her demeanor changed from relaxed to sharp and poised. She asked, "Are you saying that you don't feel safe in your own home?"

"That is a possibility, yes," Tatiana replied. The

Queen looked perfectly calm and composed as she scooped a tiny spoonful of avocado mousse out of a cup. "Naturally we're doing everything we can to counteract that."

Oh Lord, Pia muttered in Eva's head. *It looks like my travel curse is alive and working fine. I can't wait to hear what Dragos has to say about it.*

Just then, her phone coughed out a polite-sounding *ping*. Murmuring an apology, she checked the screen.

It was a text from Dragos. `Damn right something's wrong. I'll be there as fast as I can.`

Whatever his situation had been, it seemed to be over with. Telepathically, she accused, *How do you know something's wrong? You haven't been relaxing or fishing at all, have you?*

He didn't respond.

She was getting practiced at refraining from rolling her eyes in public. Setting her phone aside, she said, "Again, my apologies for letting the phone interrupt us. Dragos is on his way. He says he'll be here as soon as he can."

"In that case, there is no point in going over everything twice," Tatiana said. "We should finish our meals while we can."

With that ominous-sounding statement, the Queen calmly speared an olive on her fork and ate it.

Chapter Six

A FTER A SECOND'S hesitation, Pia followed suit.
Between her new life as Dragos's mate and
having a small child, at least for several months, in the
household, she had learned to eat heartily when she
could.

The quality of the food was excellent, of course,
and her constant appetite ensured that she cleaned her
plate.

The conversation could have turned stilted, but it
didn't. Tatiana plied her with questions about her daily
life and asked after Liam. Part of Pia found the chitchat
rather bizarre. Clearly something was wrong enough to
require Tatiana's attention, but the Queen behaved as
though there was nothing more urgent than discussing
school choices for children.

"Your son sounds remarkable," Tatiana said. "And
how unusual that he has grown so much, so fast."

"Yes, he's remarkable in every way," Pia replied.
"And while his magical nature has made him unique,
the important thing is, he's a really good person. I don't
just love him, I respect him."

When Tatiana met her gaze, her expression had turned warm and sympathetic. "I understand. I have always felt that way about my daughters too."

For the first time since arriving, Pia felt like she had made a real connection with the Queen. Any sense of achievement she might have felt at that was overshadowed by concern for Dragos.

When the dragon took to flight, he could eat away miles like chomping through popcorn, but it had been over half an hour since he had last texted her. Shouldn't he have arrived by now?

She resisted fiddling with her phone. It hadn't pinged with a new message, and obsessing over a phone while in someone else's company was rude. Older members of the Elder Races, for whom new technology was intrusive anyway, were especially offended by such things.

While she wasn't sure how old Tatiana was, she knew the other woman had to be quite old. The *Sebille* had been an exploratory voyage sent out by Tatiana to find new lands for her people to settle in, and that ship had wrecked off the coast of Bermuda in the fifteenth century.

When Pia saw that Eva's plate was clear, she murmured to her, "Please go update Quentin and Aryal, and let them know Dragos will be here any minute."

"Sure thing. I'll be right back." Eva stood, gave Tatiana a slight bow and left.

One moment trickled after the other, excruciatingly slow. Tatiana sipped coffee and remarked how well the daffodils bordering the verandah were doing, while Pia wanted to do nothing more than jump to her feet and pace. Bailey, clearly not immune to the slow-building tension either, rubbed her face with both hands.

Eva returned, and this time, she took a position behind Pia's chair, while she said telepathically, *They're coming down ASAP.*

Good, Pia said.

New footsteps sounded at the doorway, and a tense-looking Light Fae guard appeared. "Ma'am," he said to Tatiana, while he flicked a nervous gaze to Pia. "Lord Cuelebre has arrived and is outside."

"Don't make him wait," Tatiana said impatiently. "For the gods' sake, let him in."

The guard grew more nervous. "My apologies, ma'am, but we can't."

"What do you mean?" the Light Fae Queen snapped.

As Pia pushed to her feet, she reached out telepathically, *Dragos? What's going on?*

There was no response.

No response, yet Dragos was here.

The wrongness of that pounded in her head. Abruptly, she abandoned civility. Quickly she strode into the house, leaving the others to exclaim and scramble after her.

As she moved toward the front of the house, she

picked up her pace until she was running. The double front doors stood open, framing a sunlit lawn. Two guards stood in the doorway, facing outward.

There was just enough space between the two guards. As Pia wriggled between them, she realized they both had their weapons drawn.

Had the world gone crazy?

She almost made it through to outside. Exclaiming, both of the guards grabbed for her, and one of them managed to catch hold of her by the arm.

"Are you insane?" she hissed furiously. "Put up your weapons. We're invited guests!"

"Lady, you don't understand," the guard said. "You can't go out there."

"Like hell I can't," she said between her teeth.

She caught what happened next in snatches.

Dragos stood on the lawn, his clothing torn and bloody. He had his hands on his hips, his hard expression grim. One of his forearms had cloth tied around it.

Then Pia was knocked sidelong, as Eva tackled the guard who held on to her arm. Stumbling, she fell to the ground, scraping her elbows on the concrete pavement while Eva and the guard grappled with each other.

Bailey ordered, "Stand down! *Everybody stand down!*"

Then Quentin and Aryal shot onto the scene like dark, deadly arrows. Pia didn't catch what happened next, but as she rolled to her feet, suddenly weapons were drawn everywhere, Light Fae guards and Wyr pointing guns at each other.

Dragos roared, "WYR—LOWER YOUR GODDAMN WEAPONS *NOW!*"

Immediately, Quentin and Aryal stepped back, guns lowered. As Quentin edged around the group to approach Pia, Eva jerked out of the grasp of the Light Fae guard she was grappling with and threw a roundhouse punch at him that made him stagger.

"Don't you *ever* put your hands on her again, asshole," Eva snarled at the guard. Then she skipped back a couple of steps, hands raised.

Quentin threaded between people to reach Pia, his blue eyes hard. He asked telepathically, *You okay?*

Yes. She turned and started toward Dragos again.

This time Bailey lunged forward to grab her by the arms.

"What the hell?" Pia snapped. "Will you people stop grabbing me?!"

"I'm sorry, I'm sorry, I'm sorry," Bailey said. "Pia, you can't."

Quentin rounded on Bailey and slammed a flattened hand against her chest, physically knocking her back from Pia, while Eva growled, and the whole fiasco might have escalated again, except that this time, Dragos said sharply, "Stop. *Everybody stop.* Pia, do what they say and stay back."

Exasperated now, and still badly unsettled, she wheeled around to stare at him. "I don't understand.

Why can't I come close? How the hell did you get hurt?"

"I got curious and started poking around." When he met her gaze, she saw that his gold eyes had darkened. Compared to their normal brilliance, they looked almost dull.

Immaculate and as coolly poised as if she were still drinking coffee on the verandah, Tatiana stepped around the clump of angry, unsettled people on her doorstep.

The Light Fae Queen and the Lord of the Wyr regarded each other for a moment.

Dragos growled, "Your people have a discipline problem under pressure, Tatiana. Tell them to put their goddamn weapons up."

Unhurriedly, she studied him while making no move to do so. "You're infected."

"Apparently, yes," he said between his teeth. "With whatever the fuck this is."

Infected.

The word bounced around in Pia's head. This time, instead of struggling to get to him, she met Quentin's grim gaze. Her breathing sounded harsh to her own ears.

"Did you get bitten?" Tatiana asked.

"On my arm," he said tersely.

"What happened to the one who bit you?"

"It was with a group of thirty or so others. I burned them." Dragos's gaze switched to Pia. He told her,

"Whatever this is, it's affecting my Power. I can't telepathize, and I can't shapeshift either. I had to hot-wire a car and drive here."

Struggling to sound calm and rational, Pia said, "What the fuck is happening?" She rounded on Tatiana. "What do you mean, he's infected?"

Regret filled Tatiana's expression, along with resolve. The Queen said to Bailey, "Call Shane back to the house. Tell him to hurry." Then she turned to her guards. "As long as Dragos remains lucid, don't shoot him."

DESPITE DRAGOS'S WARNING to stay away from him, Pia plunged across the lawn. Eva, the sentinels, and Bailey followed her immediately. Uneasily, Dragos took several steps back as they neared.

"You guys have to stop," Bailey insisted. "He could turn rabid at any time."

Dragos felt the urge to bare his teeth at her, but he was mindful of the guns still trained in his—and now Pia's—direction and refrained. Tatiana's guards were spooked enough. If he showed how he was really feeling, the gods only knew who they might accidentally shoot.

"I'm not turning rabid right at the moment," he snapped.

Tatiana's guards weren't the only ones who were spooked. Bailey gave him a leery glance. She asked,

"How long has it been since you got bitten?"

"Over forty minutes ago." He turned his attention to Pia, who was pacing around him in a wide circle, wearing a fierce scowl.

"We're not in California five minutes." She flung up a hand, fingers and thumb splayed. "Five minutes, Dragos, and you managed to get bitten by… by …" She stopped pacing. "What bit you?"

"An infected Light Fae."

She studied him worriedly. "Show me the wound."

In answer, he unwrapped the cloth from his forearm and showed it to her. They both regarded the bite mark, which was clearly visible, the tears in his skin dark red.

"It's negligible," he said. "Barely more a nuisance. It should have healed within ten minutes. Instead, it's not healing at all. After I burned the pack, I discovered I wasn't able to telepathize or shapeshift."

As he spoke, he was aware that the others were listening as well. Aryal swore softly and raked her hands through her hair, while Quentin pinched the bridge of his nose.

Bailey's eyes had widened at his story. She said, "Your constitution is very strong. The people we know who were bitten turned within fifteen or twenty minutes. This is very bad news. So far as we knew, only the Light Fae have been affected. We had no idea until now that others of the Elder Races could be infected too."

He had no intention of mentioning it to anyone, but he could feel the infection from the bite, coursing through his veins like poison, and his Power had roused to combat it. It felt strange and tiring. He was almost never too hot, but now he had broken into a light sweat and felt both hot and cold at once. Was this what a fever felt like?

Pia stood facing him with her feet planted apart, hands fisted at her sides. She looked grim and determined, and ready to do battle. "I want to telepathize with you so badly right now," she muttered.

He glanced at the others and said to her, "I want to telepathize with you too."

"It's going to have to wait," Bailey told them. "We think the contagion is passed through blood and saliva. Dragos, you're a walking hazard—you've got blood smeared all over you. We have to burn your clothes and get you as disinfected as we can."

"Privacy is the least of anybody's concerns right now," he said. "Let's do this. Somebody get me something clean to wear. How are you disinfecting people?"

"We've been using propyl alcohol, along with an antiseptic detergent." She turned away. "Follow me."

He did so, and the others trailed after him several feet behind.

Bailey led them around the far corner of the house, to an area where they had constructed a large structure draped with plastic.

"I see the tour of the grounds you gave me earlier didn't lead over in this direction," Pia said to Bailey, her voice bitter.

The other woman looked chagrined. She said to Dragos, "It's a decontamination chamber. It's pretty makeshift but it will get the job done. When you step in, leave your clothes and shoes by the outer flap. We'll get you something else to wear. You'll find the alcohol and detergent in the shower area. I'm sorry, the shower's cold—for now, we're just running water from the sprinkler system."

"A cold shower is the least of my concerns right now," he snarled. He stalked into the plastic-draped area and stripped to the skin.

Bailey was right, the construction was crude but effective. After he had stripped and left his clothes in a crumpled pile where she had indicated—saving the jewelry, which he kept in one hand—he stepped into the makeshift disinfectant chamber. He scrubbed his whole body for at least ten minutes with the sharp-smelling detergent then doused himself with the propyl alcohol, making sure to scrub and douse the jewelry as well.

Both the alcohol and detergent should have stung in the bite, but they didn't. The skin around the bite had turned numb, and he still wasn't healing. As he prodded the wound and inspected it, dark streaks had begun to shoot out from the puncture wounds. His Power might be slowing down the progress of the poison from the bite, but it wasn't stopping it.

Once he had finished showering, they had collected other medical supplies, and he securely taped a bandage over the bite mark. He even wiped off his phone thoroughly with disinfectant.

He dressed quickly in the jeans and shirt they had found for him. The gods only knew where they had found an outfit big enough for him, because typically the Light Fae were nowhere near his massive size. The clothes were snug, but they would do. Stuffing the cleaned necklace, earrings and bracelet into the pocket of his new jeans, he stepped out of the plastic area.

Pia stood nearby with the other Wyr waiting in a close, tense huddle, while the Light Fae had retreated to give them some semblance of privacy.

After sweeping the scene, Dragos kept his eyes on Pia. She was biting her nails and tapping one foot nervously. He strode over only to stop several feet away, clenching his fists in frustration. The urge to take her into his arms was almost overwhelming. He hated he couldn't act on it.

Her gaze went immediately to the white bandage on his arm. "How is it?"

"Still there," he replied. He looked at the others. "Give us some space, will you?"

Reluctantly they stepped away, Aryal scowling over her shoulder at them.

Pia burst out, "This is so wrong. I can't even touch you."

"I know," he said, very low.

They stared at each other. The morning had evaporated into a hot afternoon. Indirect sunlight gilded the ends of her hair, and sent shafts of illumination into her dark gaze. She said between her teeth, "Everybody on the property has supersharp hearing, and I want to telepathize with you *so badly*."

He pulled out his phone. "Let's text it."

She snatched hers out of the pocket of her maxi dress, and her slender fingers flew over the tiny keyboard. When she was finished, she did one final, emphatic stab.

His phone pinged, and he looked down at the screen.

She had written: I don't have time for a meltdown. Let's pretend I just spat out a lot of AGH and UGH and OMG HOLY FUCK!!! and get it out of the way, shall we?

A hint of laughter ghosted through him. He texted back, I'm almost sorry I missed that.

She gave him a brief glare and turned her attention back to her phone. We need to get enough privacy so that I can try to heal you.

Agreed, he replied. But you might not be able to. You're taking a drug protocol that suppresses your own abilities.

For a moment she stood frozen, staring at him with wide eyes, her phone dangling from her lax hand. Then she set to typing again furiously. The dose is wearing off. I'm supposed to take the next round this evening.

"I just want you to be braced," he told her aloud, quietly. He texted the rest. `You're supposed to take the dose before the effects of the protocol have fully worn off. If you wait and take it late, you could endanger both yourself and the baby.`

That was assuming he could stave off the effects from the bite long enough, but he didn't text that thought. A look of sheer terror flashed across her face, and he had to clench down again on the need to take her into his arms.

Then her jaw firmed, and she said, "Let's not get trapped into thinking it's an either/or scenario. None of this may be necessary. Wait here."

"Pia—" he began.

The glare she threw at him had sufficient strength to stop him in his tracks. "I know what you're going to say, but don't even bother, because we don't have time for that either. Let's pretend we had an entire argument about it—you just said we can't, and I just said we have to. You said what about the secret, and I'm telling you right now *I don't give a fuck about the fucking secret!*"

"Calm down and think about what you're saying," he rasped.

"Well, I can't calm down, and I am thinking about it. Think about how many people already know, Dragos. The sentinels. Eva and Hugh. Liam, Dr. Medina and Dr. Shaw, and you know Stinkpot's going to know as soon as he—or she—gets big enough. And probably there are other people I'm forgetting right now. No, wait! That's right!" She threw out both hands. "Beluvial and some of the Elves know. The list keeps getting larger and larger, and chances are, we won't be able to keep a lid on this forever."

"We've got a lid on it for now," he snapped.

"Yes, but it's a train crash in slow motion. It might take months or it might take years, but sooner or later, that lid is gonna blow. In fact, the way I feel right now, I could just shout the fucking secret to the whole fucking world. So just wait there a fucking minute."

Belatedly he caught up with everything that she had said.

Stinkpot?

She had sworn more in the last three minutes than she had in the last six months, but he had gone well past the point of any desire to laugh. Crossing his arms, he glared back at her but complied. He watched as she strode over to the other Wyr. After a silent exchange with them, Quentin reached into his pocket to pull out something and hand it to her.

She swiveled and jogged back, but instead of stopping in front of him, she continued past. "Come on," she said over her shoulder as she headed back around the corner toward the decontamination chamber.

He threw a wary glance at the Light Fae by the front door. They were watching him closely. As he spun to follow Pia, he noted security cameras mounted high along the corners of the walls. He would bet all the jewelry in his pocket that he was being watched right now.

Rounding the corner of the building, he came upon Pia, who had opened up a pocketknife. Her face tight with determination, she gestured to him. "Come on. Pull the bandage back."

"Damn it, Pia," he growled. "This isn't private either. We're being watched."

She blinked. "What do you mean?"

He jerked his head up, toward the direction of the security camera, and she rolled her eyes. She looked beyond fed up. In fact, she looked like she had joined Basket Case and driven straight to Crazy Town, and he knew if she wasn't stopped, she really would shout the fucking secret to the whole fucking world.

He needed to derail that meltdown, if he could. Glancing around, he eyed the decontamination chamber.

"Take a breath," he told her. "The camera won't be able to see anything we do behind a few layers of plastic. Come on."

It was her turn to follow him as he led the way through the thick plastic flap. Ignoring the sharp, acrid smell inside, he turned to face her.

Still wearing an expression that told him she was close to the edge of panic, she rotated her wrist at him. "Hurry up. Pull back the bandage."

"Lower your voice," he whispered. "The plastic will

stop the camera from seeing what we're doing, and it might muffle our voices somewhat, but there are still a lot of people around with very sharp hearing."

"I don't care," she muttered. She gripped the knife like she meant to stab herself with it.

He roared, "I care! I mean it, Pia. Get a fucking grip."

Freezing, she stared at him. For a moment, her mouth wobbled precariously, then she firmed up. The strain was evident in her voice as she said, "I apologize. It's just—Dragos, when I weigh the secret against the thought of possibly losing you, there's no contest."

At that, he wanted even more desperately to put his arms around her. Instead, he whispered fiercely, "One way or another, it's going to be okay. But we've got to think our way out of this. We're not going to get there if either one of us is in a panic. Understood?"

Jerkily, she nodded. "Yeah."

"Okay. Get braced. This isn't pretty." He pulled back the bandage and showed the bite wound with the slowly expanding dark streaks to her.

He watched as the sight hit her like a blow. She swallowed and blinked rapidly. "Does it hurt?"

"No," he said tersely. "It should, but it doesn't."

Giving him another terror-filled glance, she took the knife and held her hand over his forearm.

Uneasy at exposing the open wound so close to her, he muttered, "Careful, don't touch me."

"I'm not touching you!" she flared. Then, giving

him an apologetic look, she said more temperately, "Just hold still."

He did, clenching his fist as she drew the pocketknife across the end of one forefinger quickly. Bright blood beaded in the cut. She squeezed her finger, forcing the blood to flow more freely until a few precious drops fell onto the open wound.

He had said they had to think their way out of this, but he couldn't help but feel they were fast running out of options. If this didn't work … well, they would cross that bridge when they came to it.

If it did, the gods only knew how they were going to explain their odd behavior or his unexpected healing in such a way to keep the fucking secret.

Chapter Seven

T OGETHER, THEY STARED at the bite mark while Dragos waited for the signature wave of her Power to wash through him. Her healing Power was an amazing, unstoppable sensation, unlike anything he had ever experienced. When Pia healed him, he felt like he was bathed in light.

Nothing happened.

The moment dragged on, weighing down both their shoulders. Pia rubbed her forehead, and her mouth shook again. "It didn't work."

"Well, now we know," he said. He slapped the bandage back into place over the wound. "So now we've got to think about alternatives. Let's go talk to Tatiana. I want to know how this outbreak happened, why the fuck they didn't warn us, and what measures they're taking to contain it. Maybe they're close to finding some kind of effective antidote."

Straightening, she nodded. "While you were showering, Tatiana's captain arrived and went inside."

"Let's go see what they have to say for themselves."

They pushed their way out of the plastic-draped chamber and walked to the front lawn again, where Quentin, Aryal and Eva, along with the Light Fae, were waiting.

The other Wyr joined them, questions in their eyes. Aryal's gaze dropped to the bandage Dragos still wore, and she swore, while Eva's face tightened and Quentin blew out a breath.

Together, the group of Wyr strode toward the front entrance of the house, where several guards stood. As they drew near, the guards swung around to stand in formation, and all of them had their guns trained on Dragos.

Bailey was with them. She stepped forward, her expression regretful. "I'm so sorry, Dragos," she said. "But we can't let you in the house."

"That's preposterous." Pia gestured angrily. "Look at him—he's in perfect control of himself."

"Yes, he is, for now," Bailey agreed. The Light Fae woman gave them an apologetic glance. "But that could change quickly, and if it does, we won't be able to reason with him. And even without his ability to shapeshift, your husband is still very powerful. He could do a lot of damage, and infect a lot of people, before we could stop him." She turned her attention to Quentin, Aryal and Eva. "None of us want to hurt any of you, but we may not have any choice. You may not have a choice either, and you all need to be prepared to face that fact."

Pia whitened, while Aryal rubbed her face and swore.

"She's right," Dragos said, interrupting whatever Pia might have said next. He asked Bailey, "Where are we going to meet?"

"My mother is willing to let you into the back garden," Bailey told them. "Shane will be there, and she'll be surrounded by guards, but it's a compromise of sorts, and it would allow us to discuss possible next steps."

"Fine. Let's go," Dragos said. As they strode around the house to the back, he asked, "What about the neighbors? These houses and yards are large, but that's no real protection, either for them, or for any sensitive discussions we might have."

"That's not an issue," Bailey told them. "Bel Air has already been evacuated."

Unexpected anger burned, hot and bright. He demanded, "Since when?"

"We evacuated for several blocks around 10 P.M. last evening," Bailey replied, giving him a hassled glance. "We thought at the time we were just erring on the safe side, but as it turns out, it's good we did."

"This morning, you brought my wife, and my people into this mess," he snarled. "You got me involved in this."

"Look, in the last forty-eight hours, this outbreak has grown exponentially," Bailey shot back, her eyes sparkling with quick anger. "As soon as my mother got the first hint that something might be wrong, she sent for me and tried to cancel Pia's visit, but you guys insisted. This morning we tried to remove Pia to a safe location in Malibu. And *you* aren't supposed to be anywhere near here, Lord Cuelebre, let alone wandering around and sticking your nose into things, so let's try to stop with blame throwing and work on finding some solutions, all right?"

As she spoke, she opened a gate in a stuccoed wall and strode through.

Dragos met Pia's burning gaze. Behind them, Aryal whispered, "If I start slapping people, I might not be able to stop."

"Everybody's stressed right now," Quentin muttered. "Rein it in, harpy. Don't add to it."

"Much as it pains me to say this," Dragos growled, "Bailey is right again. Arguing about what happened and who might be to blame is useless. In any case, this is no longer just a Light Fae problem, because it sure as hell has become a problem for the Wyr." He looked at Pia and said more quietly, "Come on."

At that, he reached out to put a hand at the small of her back, but then he caught himself up.

Reaction glittered overbright in Pia's eyes. Tightening her mouth, she stepped through the open gate, and he followed.

PIA'S NERVES WERE jumping all over her body. She felt

as if she might leap out of her own skin like a scalded cat, if given the slightest provocation.

Avoid stress, the doctor had said. Eat lots of good food and enjoy this little mysterious bun cooking in the oven. Ha!

Dragos stalked by her side, a dark lowering shadow, his hard face cut with severe lines. Even in his human form, he moved with a lethal fluidity that spoke of the fact that he was an apex predator. He was faster and stronger than anybody she knew. It was no wonder the Light Fae were still terrified of him, despite the fact that he couldn't shapeshift into the dragon.

From the short time he had disappeared to shower, his eyes had grown darker, and the dark lines shooting from the bite wound was one of the most terrifying things she had ever seen. He never got sick, never. It was as if germs vaporized whenever he became exposed to them. The fact that he wasn't healing from the bite might force her to consider a terrible choice— her mate or her child.

No. Her mind went into a frenzy, and she tore that idea to shreds. There had to be other alternatives, ways to think outside of this box that they didn't know about yet. If the Light Fae were writing off others who had been infected as a lost cause, it might be in part because they had turned so quickly. Dragos hadn't, yet. They needed to gather as much information as fast as they possibly could.

"Fight it," she said to him a low voice. "Fight as

hard as you can."

Just as low, he replied, "I am."

Bailey had paused to lock the gate behind them, and as they rounded the rear corner of the house, she took the opportunity to send Dr. Medina a quick text. `Urgent - How long can I safely go without taking the protocol?`

When Pia had collapsed in D.C., they had put the doctor on retainer. The doctor would continue to see other patients only for minor things during the length of Pia's pregnancy, so that meant she was able to answer almost immediately. `Don't tell me you lost your dose?`

`Not relevant,` Pia replied. `Too busy to explain. How long can I hold off taking the protocol without endangering the baby?`

Dragos had moved close to read over her shoulder. As she glanced up at him, he gave her an approving nod.

"They're waiting for us," Bailey said.

Dragos gave her a sharp look from under lowered brows. "We'll be there in a moment. This is urgent."

Bailey's baffled expression clearly indicated she couldn't imagine what could be more urgent than their current situation, but she subsided, while Quentin and Aryal exchanged a frowning glance. Things were too complicated to give them a quick, telepathic explanation, so Pia took the short route.

She said in Eva's head, *Please fill Quentin and Aryal in about the pregnancy and drug protocol. The protocol is suppressing my healing abilities, which we think might be why it didn't work when I tried to heal Dragos. We're trying to find out how long I can go off the protocol, without endangering the baby.*

Oh shit, Eva muttered. The glance she gave Pia brimmed with compassion. Then her expression changed. She looked like she did when she was thinking fast and hard. *Pia, what about Liam? He has some of your healing ability, right? Do you think he might be able to help Dragos?*

She recoiled, and her response came straight from her gut. *No! We would never bring him into something dangerous like this. Honestly, the thought never occurred to either of us.*

Okay, honey. It was just a thought. Eva gave her a troubled glance. Then she turned to the sentinels.

Dr. Medina's reply to Pia's question was slower in coming. Pia could almost see the doctor's cautious, thoughtful expression. As short an answer as I can give—I don't know. There are lots of factors to take into consideration. Any delay will cause a risk, and the risk will escalate the longer you go without. I wouldn't want to see you go more than two days at most, and only that long if you have no other choice. Right now, your doses overlap. As the last one wears off, you're taking the next, because the protocol takes at least eight hours to work through your system. Let me know when you're able to talk. I'll be on standby.

After typing out a quick thanks, she met Dragos's gaze. Two days, and from the sound of it, Dr. Medina didn't feel good about pushing it that far.

And that was assuming that Dragos could even hold strong against the contagion for that long. They still didn't have enough answers yet.

All Pia knew was that she wasn't letting go of anybody—not Dragos, and not the baby either. They needed to see what they could do to increase their odds.

She gave him a nod, and he said to Bailey, "We're ready now."

As they continued around the rear corner of the house, Eva slid up to Pia's side and dropped a hand onto her shoulder. Grateful for the support, she reached up to squeeze the other woman's fingers. Then Eva's hand fell away, and they reached the verandah.

The Light Fae had not been idle. Tatiana and Shane were bent over maps that had been spread out on the wrought iron table. Several watchful guards were stationed around them.

Roughly ten feet in front of the verandah, a long line had been created with masking tape on the lawn. Shane and Tatiana straightened as Bailey and the Wyr drew near the line.

"Stop," Shane said.

Pia had met Shane for the first time at the summit in Washington. His reputation tended to precede him, as he was known as one of the Elder Races' most Powerful magic users. The Queen's captain was a tall, handsome man, with a square jaw and a ready smile, and the athletic build of a football player or a jouster. He wore his curly hair trimmed short, and carried an aura of deep, old Power that she had found appealing in D.C.

Now, that Power was roused and pointed at them like a sharpened sword.

Watching him warily, along with the several guns that the other guards pointed at them, the Wyr came to a halt. Bailey, Pia noted, stayed with them. It was a reassurance, of sorts.

Dragos put his hands on his hips. "I have to tell you, Shane. The guns are getting old. Note that my sentinels are not pointing weapons at you."

"I'm sorry," Shane said. "But none of my people are infected, either. This is very unfortunate. Right now, your people are in a hell of a lot more danger from you than they are from us."

Tatiana spoke up. "You must understand. This isn't personal, Dragos. We are taking a significant risk by allowing you to come this close. All your people are welcome to join us." The Queen looked around the group. "In fact, we strongly urge them to. Please, come up onto the verandah. He'll slaughter all of you if and when he turns."

"We'll stay right here," Aryal said. The harpy stood with her arms crossed.

"Have it your way," Shane said briefly. "Just know you're welcome. Dragos, we need to come to an agreement. As long as you stay on the other side of that line, I'll know you're still lucid. If you cross that line, it means you no longer remember what I've just said, and I'll have no choice but to take you down. Anybody who remains on the other side of that line is going to be collateral damage."

"Understood." Dragos turned to Pia. "Go."

Did he feel the contagion growing stronger? Dread made her stomach bottom out. Fighting back panic, she said in quiet, anguished protest, "No."

He raised one hand toward her then let it fall back to his side. His darkened gaze was intent, and his hard expression had gentled. "Listen to me," he said quietly. "They're right. If I turn, then I might kill you all before they stop me. Those things I came across—they were incredibly fast. You need to get some distance from me while you can."

"Is it worse?" she whispered, searching his gaze. "Can you tell?"

His expression turned inward. "Not yet. And I am fighting it as hard as I can. But if we separate, you can keep searching for a cure even after I've turned. If you stay by my side, it might doom us both."

"That's right." She whirled back to face Tatiana and Shane. "He might turn, but that doesn't necessarily mean he'll be lost to us if he does. We need more than a line made of masking tape. We need chains, and something to anchor them to."

Shane's eyebrows rose. He asked Dragos, "You will allow us to chain you?"

"I'll put the chain on myself," Dragos said.

Tatiana and Shane looked at each other. Shane said, "So far, I've had to destroy every infected one that I've found—they've been too dangerous and frenzied to capture. Dragos might be our best opportunity to find a cure for everybody."

"Get an SUV back here, and the heaviest chains you can find," Tatiana rapped out. With an assessing glance at Dragos, she added, "You'd better make it two SUVs."

"Ma'am," said one of the guards. "The gate to the back isn't wide enough for vehicles that big to fit through."

"I don't give a shit," she snapped. "Knock down a wall, if you have to. Move fast!"

They leaped to obey. Within short order, Pia heard an engine gunned, and a Hummer slammed through the gate opening, tearing down a good chunk of the wall with it. Roaring around the corner, it stopped between the house and the swimming pool. It was joined immediately by another Hummer.

A few minutes later, a couple of guards brought thick ropes of chains. Pia didn't want to think about where they might have had the chains stored, or for what purpose. Working quickly, and with Dragos's active cooperation, they soon had him chained to both vehicles, a Hummer on either side of him.

Watching him test the give on one of the chains, Pia rubbed her arms and shivered. Even though it was for everybody's protection, and it might possibly save his life, the sight of him trapped between the two vehicles was terrible.

Tatiana walked up beside her, watching Dragos with a calculating expression. The Queen asked, "Do you think it will hold him if he turns?"

If Dragos had been able to shapeshift, she would have snorted a derisive laugh. As it was, she shook her head and answered honestly, "I don't know."

Tatiana sighed. "Well, we had to try. At the very least, it might slow him down."

Shane had helped with chaining Dragos, and now he moved up beside the two women. "We need to move on to business."

Dragos shook his arms to settle the chains into place. "Tell us everything you know."

Shane crossed his arms, watching him. "When we got word of the first sightings, two nights ago, we moved in fast and hard, and I thought we had eradicated the problem, but then more infected people popped up just north of here. Until you, we thought this was a purely Light Fae affliction—virtually every infected person we found was Light Fae."

"No humans?" Pia asked.

He shook his head. "Not at first. Not until today. A few hours ago, we discovered a couple of magic users who lived at the edge of a Light Fae community had turned. Most humans appear to be unaffected."

"The contagion might be sorcerous in nature,"

Dragos said. "I can feel it attacking my Power."

Shane paused, studying him. "That would make sense. And if it's true, most humans won't be affected at all, but all of the Elder Races, along with any humans that have sensitivity to magic, will be susceptible to it."

The other Wyr stood nearby, listening intently. Quentin interrupted. "What do you mean, that makes sense? What makes sense about it?"

Shane sighed. He looked at Tatiana. "I haven't had the chance to tell you this bit yet. When you called me in, we had just finished engaging in a skirmish with several of Isabeau's Hounds."

Who was Isabeau, and why had they killed her dogs?

As Pia looked questioningly at Tatiana, the Queen said in brief aside to her, "My twin sister. The Hounds are her attack force."

Ah. The twin sister who was also a demesne ruler, the Light Fae Queen with the Seelie Court in Great Britain, from whom Tatiana and her followers had fled in the fifteenth century. What kind of history lay between the two sisters that was so bad that, centuries later, Isabeau would send an attack force to Tatiana's demesne? Or perhaps the attack force was in response to some new antagonism?

Glancing at Dragos, she gave Tatiana a silent nod of acknowledgment as she chewed on a thumbnail.

Shane continued, "We killed several of them, but a few escaped." He paused and took a deep breath.

"Tatiana, I think one of them was Morgan. I didn't get a good look at him, so I can't say for sure. If it was Morgan, he was one of the ones who got away."

For the first time since Pia had arrived, Tatiana showed a visible reaction at the news. She flinched, and the skin around her mouth whitened, while fear flashed across Bailey's face. Quentin pursed his lips and somehow managed to look both intrigued and pained at once.

Dragos asked, "Who's Morgan?"

Yeah, good question, Pia thought.

Then, in the next moment, she realized it wasn't a good question at all, as both Shane and Tatiana turned to stare at Dragos.

"What do you mean, 'Who's Morgan'?" Tatiana asked. "Isabeau's Chief Hound. He's been in her Seelie Court for centuries, remember?"

Dragos's expression tightened and briefly he closed his eyes, which was when Pia realized what a major misstep he had just made.

Slowly, his gaze as sharp as swords, Shane added, "You must have met him several times before, Dragos. You did frequent the Seelie Court decades before the rift between Tatiana and Isabeau occurred, and Morgan wasn't with her then, but at the very least you must have heard of him. Morgan of the Fae is one of the oldest, most famous sorcerers in the British Isles. Surely, you haven't forgotten—or have you?"

Dragos looked at Pia, and the frustration and self-recrimination in his darkened gaze made her want to put her arms around him so badly, she almost went and did it despite the danger of contamination. Biting her lip until it bled, she wrapped her arms around her torso and forced her feet to remain planted where she stood.

"Actually, I had forgotten," he bit out.

Tatiana took a few steps toward him. Her gaze had turned fascinated, speculative. "That's unlike you, dragon. You have always had a remarkable mind for minutiae, even centuries later, and the time you spent at the Seelie Court is no piece of minutiae."

Of all the things they had worried about—the baby's safety, Pia's fucking secret—they had forgotten to be on guard for pitfalls that might stem from Dragos's memory loss.

And of all their secrets that could have been betrayed, she thought this one would cause the least amount of damage, but still, Dragos would hate it. He hated the thought of exposing anything that might be seen as a weakness.

As he had said to her before, the dragon was one of the oldest of the Elder Races, and he was not a peaceful-minded creature. He had made enemies. Dangerous, old enemies.

Pia didn't pause to think. Instead, she leaped into the conversation. "It *is* unlike him," she said nervously. "Do you think the infection could be affecting his cognitive abilities?" Turning to face Dragos, she asked, "Dragos, do you remember anything at all about

Morgan?"

Dragos's eyelids had lowered when she'd started speaking, and his expression had turned guarded and closed. Walking to the rear bumper of one of the Hummers, he leaned back against the car. The pose should have suggested relaxation. Instead, he looked as coiled as a king cobra about to strike out. Despite the heavy chains shackling his wrists and ankles, if it came down to a free-for-all melee against all the others, she would bet everything she had on him.

Much as she hated to admit it, the Light Fae were right to keep their guns trained on him, even now.

He said, "Now that you've mentioned him, of course I do. I don't recall my time at Isabeau's Court, though. And as Tatiana said, it's unlike me to forget."

Tatiana tapped a manicured finger against her bottom lip. "Maybe this is what happens to every victim before they turn. They forget who they are and become like rabid beasts. Only for them it happens quickly, within fifteen minutes or so. But Dragos is changing much more slowly. I wonder what else you might have forgotten."

Dragos's shuttered gaze met Pia's again, and then he looked away. "Once I've been healed, it won't matter, will it?"

"One hopes," Tatiana murmured. She had not lost that dangerous, speculative expression. "It would be most unfortunate if you suffer permanent memory loss from this. As long-lived as we are, it does not do to lose track of memories of dangerous things."

In retrospect, it had been rather miraculous that Aryal had been silent to date, but now she snapped, "Which is all the more reason for us to step up the pace of this conversation, don't you think? I'm growing gray hair over here. Goddamn, let's stop the useless speculation about whether or not Dragos has forgotten anything, and move along already, before he does actually have time to turn. So, Morgan might be one of the Hounds in L.A. So what?"

For once, Pia felt overwhelmed with gratitude for Aryal's abrasive, impatient nature.

Thank you, she said in Aryal's head.

You're welcome, the harpy said shortly. She hitched a shoulder. *Also, I was just being honest.*

That, Pia believed. But she still could have kissed her.

"So," Shane said, "if Morgan and others of the Queen's Hounds are here, and the contagion is sorcerous in nature, I don't think this outbreak is some terrible random act of fate. I think it's a planned attack on the Light Fae."

Bailey said suddenly, "That would explain why the outbreaks keep popping up in different places. When someone is infected, they don't really have time to travel around before they turn. This hasn't behaved in the way other diseases do. With some things, like the flu, the incubation period is long enough that someone who has been infected can travel across the world before they realize they're sick. Whereas here, if someone gets bitten, they change almost immediately. The infected haven't had time to travel to other areas."

"At least not yet," Pia said.

Silence fell over the group as everyone stared at her, absorbing the implications of that statement. Reluctantly, she continued, "This might have started with the Light Fae, but it's now jumped to both humans and to the Wyr. What if other races react to the contagion more slowly, like Dragos has?"

Quentin rubbed his scarred, handsome face with one hand and muttered, "If that happens, then this could go global very quickly."

Shane said crisply, "We can't let it go global. That's all there is to it."

"Then we need two things, as fast as we can get them," Tatiana said. "We need to stop the Hounds from spreading this further, and we need a cure."

"Actually, we need three things," Bailey said. "We not only need some kind of cure. We need an inoculation, so that further outbreaks can't happen. That's the only way to completely neutralize whatever this is."

"I know which part is my fight," Shane said. "I need to go."

"Quentin and Aryal will go with you," Dragos told him. "Because this is now our fight too."

Pia burst out, "Before they leave, I need to talk to all of you. Quentin, Aryal, Eva—come over here to

Dragos." She looked at Tatiana. "I'm sorry, but this is confidential. Can you and your guards give us some space?"

The speculative expression flashed through Tatiana's gaze again, but the Queen replied, "Of course. Everyone, fall back to the verandah."

"Don't take long," Shane told them. He had turned grim, his ready smile nowhere in evidence. "We need to stop the Hounds before they can do more damage."

Pia stepped directly in front of Dragos, her back to the verandah. As Eva, Quentin and Aryal gathered around her, she gestured wordlessly to Dragos to step around the end of the Hummer.

Eyes narrowed, he tried, but the chains wouldn't let him move all the way to the far side of the vehicle.

So be it. She whispered to the others, "Cover what I'm doing."

With a smooth, liquid glide, Quentin stepped into place behind her, and Eva and Aryal crowded close. When she pulled out the pocketknife, Dragos covered his mouth with one hand and growled softly, "There are at least half a dozen guards watching us right now."

She whispered furiously, "We're going to keep trying this every hour on the hour if we have to, until we find some other alternative that works. Every hour that passes means I have that much less of the drug in my system." She looked sidelong at Aryal. "Are you guys blocking their cameras?"

Aryal studied the area, eyes narrowed. "Yeah. I

really think we are."

Pia told Dragos, "Now stick your damn arm out."

Running his sharp gaze over the tableau, he complied, and peeled back the bandage. Pia stared at the bite wound worriedly.

Had the dark streaks grown? Did it look the same as it had before? Honestly, she just couldn't tell.

With a quick slice, she cut the end of her thumb and let the blood drip over the torn skin. Collectively, the five of them stared at the wound for several moments. It was such a small wound to mean so much. As Dragos said, it should have been negligible at most.

It couldn't take everything away from her.

Pia wouldn't let it.

Chapter Eight

EVA AND ARYAL'S eyes had gone wide—neither one of them had witnessed Pia heal anyone firsthand. Behind her, Quentin had stopped breathing.

Nothing happened. The bite mark remained, the puncture wounds raw.

Without a word, Dragos smoothed the bandage back into place.

"Damn," Aryal breathed.

Snapping the knife closed, Pia jammed it back into her pocket. She told Dragos, "This is our life now. Every hour, on the hour. I'm not even scheduled to take the injection until this evening. And we'll count every hour past then."

He nodded. "We'll figure out a way to hide it. Until we have another alternative."

"That's our cue to get out of here," Aryal said to Quentin. She paused "Just how worried should I be about coming up against this old, famous Morgan of the Fae?"

Quentin said without hesitation, "He's going to kick our asses."

The harpy barked out a short laugh. She had switched over to fighting mode, Pia saw, and looked fierce and eager. "So be it."

The pair strode for the verandah where Shane waited. When they left, Bailey went with them.

"You go on too," Pia said to Eva. "Give us a minute."

Eva paused with a frown. Telepathically, she said, *Okay, but for the record, I don't like leaving you so close to him right now.*

Duly noted, Pia told her. *And, for the record, if he changes, I'm faster than you are.*

Yeah. Okay, you have a point, Eva said. *Just—Pia, you might be faster than I am, but that doesn't mean you're going to react fast if Dragos changes.*

Pia reached for patience. Eva was only trying to protect her. *I appreciate your point, but I'm still asking you to go.*

Emitting a soft growl, the other woman complied.

Pia turned back to Dragos, cupping her elbows so that she didn't forget and reach out to him. "We touch each other a lot," she muttered. "I'm always just about to reach out to you, and then I have to catch myself up."

"I know," he said. "I'm doing the same. It's driving me insane." With a quick, impatient flick, he snapped the heavy chain that shackled one wrist. "I'm also beginning to realize how much I pace."

"We'll get you free." She tightened her fingers,

gripping herself hard. "Dragos, Eva brought up Liam. She wondered if he might be able to help you."

His darkened gaze flared. "No! We're not going to bring him into this mess."

She jerked her head in a nod. "I had the same reaction. I could never knowingly put him in danger." She searched his expression. "But what if we're wrong? Your life could be at stake. Hell, mine and Stinkpot's could be too."

He shook his head, stubborn determination stamped on his rugged features. "We're not there yet. Did you notice? The wound hasn't gotten worse."

Her breath left her, and she sagged. "I wasn't sure. I didn't dare to hope."

"I noted before—the ends of the streaks were just beginning to show at the edges of the bandage." He held out his muscled forearm for her to inspect. "Look. They haven't gotten worse. We're holding our own."

She sagged. "That's the best news I've gotten all day."

"Chin up." Dragos's voice had gentled. "Look at me."

She lifted her gaze to his. He looked so wrong, with his fierce gold eyes darkened. It was like the sky going dark in the middle of the day. The sight made the tiny hairs on the back of her neck raise.

But his expression was all his, fierce and tender at once. Giving her a slight smile, he whispered, "I'm putting my hand to your cheek right now."

The stubborn strength that had kept her knees locked threatened to give way. Closing her eyes, she whispered back, "I'm putting my arms around you, and leaning my head on your shoulder."

"And I'm stroking your hair, and kissing you." He took a deep breath. "And I am always, always going to hold on to you with all of my strength. Always, Pia."

The adamant surety in his voice steadied her like nothing else could have. Following his lead, she breathed deeply, taking in the reality of him. Then she looked up at him again. "We'll deal with whatever may happen next."

His smile deepened, and she knew that he had gone back to the first time she had said it. "We always do," he agreed. "Now, since I'm chained up here, and Quentin and Aryal have left, why don't you go take a look at those maps and see how many areas this contagion has spread to?"

"Okay." She nodded. "We need to know that. If it spreads too much further, they're going to have to go public about this. I guess I can understand why they haven't yet, but this might have grown into something they can't control anymore."

"If they continue to be reluctant to go public," Dragos said, "then we will. I hate as much as anybody the fact that this appears to be yet another catastrophe instigated by the Elder Races, but people need to be aware of the danger. Too many lives are at stake. If there's any political fallout from this, we'll just have to deal with it later."

"Understood," she said. She searched his expression. "Do you need anything—anything to drink or eat?"

"I'm good."

"I'll be back soon." She smiled and whispered, "I'm kissing you right now."

He swore softly, frustration evident in the snap of his voice. "I'm kissing you too."

With that she had to be content enough to walk away.

WWPD WAS NOT the only question Dragos asked himself. Sometimes he asked, What Would Pia Think? (WWPT?)

That question never failed to entertain him, because as smart as he was, and as good as he was at playing chess, he could never guess her thoughts with 100 percent accuracy. He imagined he could play the small mental game throughout the endless centuries like puzzling over an eternal Rubik's Cube. He knew there had to be a magical combination that would unlock the entire puzzle, but he suspected he would always be doomed to failure.

Because they were polar opposites in so many ways. He was a predator; she was an herbivore. He was intensely male, and she was all woman. Often they didn't laugh at the same jokes. Really, it was amazing they got along as well as they did. Sexual attraction helped, but it couldn't be the entire glue for the relationship.

Somehow, magically, they clicked. She gave when he couldn't—and he was honest enough to admit that she did it more often than he did. And when she couldn't, he found a way to reach for her.

As he watched her walk away, he knew they had just experienced another point in time where their views divided, and he wasn't even sure if she had been aware of it.

What he had said was true: too many lives were potentially at risk from this contagion. When she had agreed, he knew she had leaped to concern for all those who might be in danger, but he hadn't.

People died all the time. They always had, and he cared about almost none of them. The dragon was not generous with squandering his emotions.

No, his concern about the increasing number of lives that might be endangered was strictly limited to two things. One was, how much danger did it mean for those few people the dragon did care about?

The second was, the more people who died from this, the worse the political fallout would be. Last month, the human world had put the Elder Races on notice—they were watching, and they were disturbed by what they saw.

In fifty short years, the spring massacre in the Nightkind demesne, along with all the other issues that had arisen over the last eighteen months, would become nothing more than minor footnotes in history. But right now, the massacre was too soon, too raw in people's memories.

This problem in the Light Fae demesne might not be Tatiana's fault, but the humans wouldn't see it that way. Non-magical humans might not be susceptible to catching the contagion, but they could be caught and killed by hordes of those who had turned. This was everybody's problem, and it appeared to have been caused by the Elder Races. It wouldn't matter to the human government that the Elder Races demesne responsible lay in Great Britain. When reacting with racial bias, people tended to get very simplistic in their thinking.

So aside from the personal considerations, the calculator in Dragos's head clicked on, and he looked at this whole fiasco as a numbers thing. The more people who died or were victimized, the larger the fallout would be, and right now, he couldn't finish that equation, because they hadn't succeeded in containing the hazard yet.

He needed to step up the preliminary work with the Dark Fae engineers he had hired from Niniane, just in case. The Other land under his control from upstate New York was a massive, protected place, but it was also almost completely pristine and undeveloped. The political and social tensions from the summit in Washington D.C. had shown that co-existence might not remain a safe option for the Wyr, and he was determined that they would have a safe place to retreat to, if it ever became necessary.

Retrieving his phone from one pocket, he sent a few texts. As he hit send on the last one, out of the corner of his eye, he watched Tatiana walk toward him.

It was a maneuver he did not appreciate, as the Light Fae guards with their guns perpetually trained on him grew tense.

Crossing his arms, he leaned back against the Hummer's bumper and tried to appear relaxed. As Tatiana drew near, he said, "I'm still not thrilled with how trigger-happy your guards look, Tatiana. If you need to have a conversation, are you sure you wouldn't rather call me on my cell?"

Tatiana did not look over her shoulder at her guards. "They won't shoot unless you present a clear danger to me."

Then they were stupid for not shooting him right away, because the dragon always presented some kind of danger.

But so often it didn't do to educate people out of their stupid.

He crossed one booted foot over the other, basking in the hot sunlight, while he waited for the Light Fae Queen to get around to whatever it was she wanted to talk to him about.

"How are you holding up?" she asked.

That wasn't what she wanted to talk about. He said

in a brief, flat reply, "I'm fine. How are you, Tatiana?"

He could tell by the flicker in her eyes and the tightening of her mouth that she hadn't liked the sarcasm in that. But she chose to answer him honestly. "I'm pretty much as you might expect. My people are being decimated, so I'm enraged and worried." She hesitated. "Would you consent to letting my doctors draw some of your blood? We need to find out everything we can about the contagion in order to stop it."

He didn't like that, and his knee-jerk reaction was to refuse the request. You could learn a lot by studying someone's blood, and it was never a good idea to give anybody information about himself.

As she watched his face, she urged quietly, "Please, Dragos. You're the only person we have so far who might provide clues about how to build a resistance against the contagion. Everyone else has succumbed in less than half an hour."

Goddammit. He rubbed his forehead, struggling with conflicting impulses. Finally, he said, "The only way I'll let you have samples of my blood is if we get a doctor that I trust into your labs to monitor what you do with it. And I want the samples destroyed afterward."

"Damn it, Dragos, this isn't the time—" she began.

Impatiently, he interrupted her, "I mean it, Tatiana. Like the guns you have trained on me right now—my decision isn't personal. But you know as well as I do that Powerful spells can be built on someone's blood. I'm not letting go of something that could be that valuable and dangerous to me without putting some guarantees and protections in place beforehand."

Biting her lip, she nodded after a moment. "Okay, you have a point. It's a deal. But what I was going to say is, the problem is how long it might take for you to get one of your doctors here. We need your blood samples now, not tomorrow. We actually needed them yesterday."

He had already squandered the trip he had bargained for from Soren, so he told her. "That isn't my problem. That's yours. You're resourceful. I know you can make it happen, if you put your mind to it."

Her expression darkened. They both knew that in order to make it happen, she herself would have to strike a bargain with a Djinn. But damned if he would incur a Djinn debt just so that he could safely give her some of his blood.

As her silence grew prolonged, he remarked, "You know, I would much rather prefer to have my own doctors study my blood and give any synthesized results or antidote to the Light Fae, anyway. If you would prefer."

"Fine," she snapped. "Which doctor do you want present?"

The two doctors he trusted the most were Dr. Shaw and Dr. Medina. Both were privy to sensitive information. Dr. Shaw was the sentinels' surgeon, and she had also consulted with him over his head injury, so she would keep any findings confidential.

But Dr. Medina was Pia's doctor, and there was no better time or opportunity to send for her than this. She could be close at hand, if they needed to prolong Pia's next injection. This could work to their advantage.

He glanced over to the verandah, where Pia and Bailey talked as they looked over the maps. He told Tatiana, "Collect Dr. Medina, along with my sentinel Grym. Grym can watch over Medina and your doctors, to make sure the lab stays secure. He'll also see that the samples are destroyed when they should be. I'll call them now to make sure they're ready."

Tatiana gestured an abrupt assent and strode back to her house, while Dragos quickly called Dr. Medina and Grym to tell them to prepare for an unexpected trip and assignment. The sentinel picked up on the second ring.

He told Grym, "A Djinn will be arriving momentarily to pick you and Dr. Medina up and bring you to the Light Fae demesne. When you get here, be sure to talk to Pia and Eva to get fully briefed on what's happening."

"What about you?" Grym asked.

"I'm not available for private conversations at the moment."

"Okay. You got it."

He hung up and punched Dr. Medina's number.

"How's Pia doing?" the doctor asked, when he

spoke to her.

He glanced at the nearby Light Fae on the verandah. "I'm not able to talk freely right now. You'll find out when you get here."

"Okay." The doctor sounded uneasy. "Just tell me this much. Do I need to bring an extra dose of the protocol?"

"No," he said, and hung up.

Curious about which Djinn Tatiana would call to bargain with, he watched as a tornado of Power whirled into the yard and coalesced into a tall, feminine form. The Djinn had vaguely familiar, regal features, white skin, bloodred hair that fell past her shoulders, and the signature starlike Djinn eyes.

After the Light Fae Queen and the Djinn had a brief, private conversation in silence, the woman whirled away to return a few moments later with Grym and Dr. Medina. Both of them looked around as they got their bearings and stared at Dragos, chained to the Hummers. They converged upon Pia. Eva joined them, and the four Wyr engaged in an intense, silent conversation, glancing in Dragos's direction often.

He composed himself to patience by closing his eyes and pretending to lie in wait in the warm sunshine during a hunt. He could wait for hours or even days for the right moment to strike at a particular prey, and had done so before, many times.

He was perfectly aware when Grym and Medina approached, but even so, Medina cleared her throat when they drew near. As he opened his eyes again, they both sucked in a breath. Medina looked frightened, while Grym looked … well, grim.

"We need to collect vials of your blood," Medina told him. She carried two bags, a medical bag and another white one with a biohazard sign on the side, which she set on the ground in front of her. "None of the Light Fae want to come close enough to do it."

"Bastards," he said without heat. His bandaged arm itched, and he rubbed at it.

Wait. His attention snapped to high alert.

His bandaged arm itched. It had gone numb before.

He wore off the bandage to stare at the wound. The dark streaks were still present, and so was the bite mark itself, but … he compared the dark streaks to the size of the bandage.

The streaks were smaller. They were definitely smaller.

He raised his voice. "Pia!"

From the verandah, her head snapped up and she bounded toward him, moving across the lawn like a bright shooting star, with Eva in fast pursuit.

Pia skidded to a halt beside the others, followed a scant moment later by Eva. Pia's gaze had gone wide with dread. "What happened?"

"My arm itched," he told her. "Look—the wound is still there, but the streaks have shrunk."

Fierce joy flashed across her face, and eagerly she

reached out to hug him.

Eva grabbed Pia's arm, and he jerked back. He said, "No, not yet. The punctures haven't closed over. It's still an open wound."

"Sorry," Pia muttered, looking crestfallen. "I forgot again."

"Hold still," Dr. Medina told him, as she opened up the medical bag at her feet, snapped on a pair of surgical gloves and prepared a needle along with several empty vials. She drew six vials of blood, stacking them carefully in the biohazard bag. "Okay, we're done."

"Don't let those vials out of your sight," he told Medina and Grym. They both nodded and hurried back toward the waiting Light Fae.

As he started to smooth the bandage back into place, Pia told him, "Keep that arm out. We're not quite done. Another hour's gone by, or near enough to it that it doesn't matter."

He watched her dig out the pocketknife, glance around and nick her finger quickly. He muttered, "You're getting a little too blasé about doing that while we're under such high scrutiny."

"Not blasé," she whispered. "I've made my choice about the risk, and now it's time to live with it."

In some ways, she could be as ruthless as any predator. Eva shadowed her actions, keeping a wary eye on the others as Pia let a few drops of her blood fall on the bite mark. As they waited, nothing appeared to happen.

Finally, Pia whispered, "We just don't know if it's working or not. It could be working very slowly, or you might be fighting off the contagion all on your own."

He smoothed the bandage back into place. "Let's agree on something right now. As long as I'm doing better, you're going to take the protocol this evening."

She scowled at him. "Dragos, we don't know why you're doing better. What if you appear to be healing, but you're not, and you get worse again? If I take that injection, my system will be suppressed for another two weeks. There's no way around that. Meanwhile, you could worsen and turn, and there wouldn't be a damn thing I could do to stop it."

She was right, but that didn't mean he had to like it. Frowning fiercely, he snapped, "Pia, we're going to have to take some steps on our best information at the time."

"I know we are!" She hunched her shoulders. "I'm just not ready to roll those dice yet. Anyway, it's not yet evening—"

"What on earth are you two arguing about?" Tatiana asked.

Dragos's head came up. Pia snapped the knife shut and jammed it into the pocket of her dress, while chagrin flared on Eva's face as she whipped around. The three of them had been so engrossed in what they were doing, they forgot to watch for anyone approaching.

They had too many dangerous secrets, but of all the

secrets they carried, there was one they could throw out to appease the nosy Queen's curiosity. Without a second's hesitation, Dragos sacrificed it as a deflecting tactic.

He told Tatiana bluntly, "Pia's pregnant. We haven't decided when we're going to go public about that yet—all we knew was that we were going to wait until sometime after she got back from this trip."

Tatiana's eyes widened. Her expression, as she glanced at Pia, was filled with both wonder and compassion. "Congratulations," she said. "That's amazing news. You must be thrilled."

"Mostly, yes. We are." Pia rubbed her face. "Except now this has happened."

"You mustn't give up hope," Tatiana told her. "Dragos has made it this far without turning. That's not just significant. It's unique. If we can figure out how and replicate it, it could save a lot of people's lives."

"Yes." Pia's gaze met his. She smiled. "I have a lot of hope."

"Come into the house with me," Tatiana said. "It's been hours since you last ate something. And it's been just as long, if not longer since Dragos ate something." She told him directly, "You may not feel hungry, but you should try to eat anyway. I'll have someone bring out a tray for you."

He blew out a sharp sigh. "Fine. Thank you." Then, as Pia lingered, he told her, "Go. I'll feel better if you eat something."

She gave him a look that said she knew very well he was managing her, but when Tatiana put a hand on her shoulder, she acquiesced.

He watched until the three women stepped into the house.

Just for shits and giggles, he tried to reach out telepathically to Aryal. *How is the search for the Hounds going?*

No response. But then he hadn't really expected one. While he might be healing, he wasn't healed yet.

Sometimes when Wyr were injured, they healed faster when they were able to shapeshift, so he reached as hard as he could for his Wyr form. He knew it was there, like he knew his own shadow, but no matter how he strained, he couldn't quite reach it.

Not yet, at any rate, but he would keep trying. The receding streaks on his arm were all the incentive he needed.

He settled back against the Hummer, closed his eyes and reached for more patience. It came more easily as he thought of Morgan of the Fae, and the predator in him realized, it might not be time for him personally to hunt, but it would be again, someday soon.

Chapter Nine

THE INTERIOR OF the house was noticeably cooler than outside, where the heat of the afternoon had taken over. Pia lifted the bodice of her dress up to let the cooler air lick against her overheated skin.

"Is there anything in particular that you would like to eat?" Tatiana asked. "Or is there anything special that you need?"

Suddenly, she was ravenous again. "I feel like I could plant my face in a plate full of carbohydrates."

"Certainly." She flagged down an attendant and ordered food for them, and more for Dragos. Then she led Pia into a large, comfortable family room, where French doors looked out over the backyard.

When Eva hesitated at the door, Pia said to her, "Please wait here."

Eva nodded and eased the doors shut behind them, giving Pia and Tatiana some privacy.

Now that Pia could see Dragos again, she was able to relax.

Tatiana looked out at Dragos too, with a dubious expression. "Is he all right out there in the sun? I can have guards put up a pavilion for him."

"He's quite comfortable. Unlike me, he could bask all day in the sun." Pia chose a comfortable armchair where she could easily keep Dragos in sight and settled into it. She was too unsettled and distracted to search for the small, subtle shadow deep inside, but that didn't stop her from resting her hand protectively against the flat of her stomach.

Evening was still a few hours away. They were still within their safe zone, and she had at least three more times, maybe four, when she could try without risk to heal Dragos.

Time to take a breath. Time to try to relax. She had been in several tense situations before where a safety margin of four hours would have felt miraculous.

How would Liam and the Stinkpot get along? The thought almost made her smile.

As Tatiana settled on the nearby couch, Pia said, "I can't imagine how you must feel, knowing your sister might be trying to kill you."

In the softer interior light, the Queen's composed expression seemed to sag. "There is no 'might' to it," Tatiana said softly. "Isabeau has already tried many times in the past."

Pia bit her lip, pressing her fingers harder against her abdomen. Please gods, both her children would love each other. "She's your twin, isn't she? Did you ever get along?"

"We had a more cordial relationship once, long ago

when we were children," the other woman replied. She pinched the bridge of her nose. "Although we always had something of an edge that lay between us, and we were prone to quarreling. She was jealous of privileges that I got. I'm younger than her by just a few minutes, you see, but those few minutes dictated the course of our lives. She was the heir, and I was not. I had more freedoms, and she did not. She has an aptitude for magic, and while I have force of will, I have very little else."

The space of a few years between siblings was not quite a few minutes. Already Liam seemed so much older than little Stinkpot, but that gap would close rapidly after Stinkpot was born. The gap in their ages would certainly seem negligible in forty or fifty years, very like a few minutes.

Make note to self, Pia thought. Don't play favorites with privileges.

Tatiana continued, "As we grew older, both our parents were killed in a fire. Isabeau became Queen of the Seelie Court, and that's when her jealous side took over. Eventually she changed so much, she acted like she hated me. Court became a place I avoided as much as possible, but since I was then the heir, I couldn't avoid it entirely. I never really felt threatened, though, until we both fell in love with the same man."

"Uh-oh," Pia whispered, completely drawn into the recounting of the other woman's memories. "What happened?"

"He chose me." Tatiana gave her a wry, bittersweet smile. "We tried to keep it secret for a while, but ultimately that didn't work out very well for us. I became pregnant with Bailey and Melisande, and I reached that inevitable place where I was having difficulty hiding the pregnancy. Dain—that was his name, Dain—and I had started to discuss whether or not we should leave the Court, but we hadn't made any final decision, when he was killed."

Pia sucked in a breath. She had known that, clearly, something had happened to Tatiana's lover, either a quarrel or a tragedy, because to her knowledge, the Light Fae Queen had never been married. Hearing the details seemed to bring the long-ago tragedy much closer.

She murmured, "He died when you were pregnant."

The wry, distant expression in Tatiana's gaze iced over. "Dain was murdered while I was pregnant," she corrected. "He was struck by an arrow while out hunting with his men. At the time, I was very much younger and a lot more foolish. And of course, I was also heartbroken and beside myself. I remember feeling like I had somehow left my body. I confronted Isabeau, and I didn't wait to do it until we were alone. I confronted her in front of others. It was a foolhardy thing to do, but ultimately, that probably ended up saving my life. That was the first time—at least I think it was the first time—that Isabeau tried to kill me."

"How horrible," Pia whispered.

A soft tap came at the door, and a servant poked his head into the room. "Ma'am, your meal is ready to be served," he told her.

"We'll take it in here, Evan," Tatiana replied. "It's quiet and private in here." She said to Pia, "I assume that is all right with you?"

Outside, a Light Fae guard carried a laden tray to Dragos. She turned her attention away from the window, nodding quickly. "Yes, thank you."

Tatiana didn't resume her story again until their food had been set on the tables near their seats. The Queen had a simple sandwich, while Pia had a fragrant bowl of pasta with spinach and what smelled like pieces of vegan sausage in a creamy coconut milk base. A cocktail of sparkling water and fresh juice accompanied the meal. She fell on the food like she hadn't eaten in a week.

Tatiana watched her eat with a small smile. "As long ago as my own pregnancy has been, I still remember those days of being utterly ravenous."

"Sometimes my stomach feels so empty, I feel like it's fused to my backbone," Pia muttered. She sipped at the delicious cocktail. It tasted of apricots, oranges and mint. "Please, do go on."

With a shrug, the other woman picked at her sandwich, shredding bits of lettuce around the edges. "There isn't too much more to tell, I'm afraid. The scene was like something out of a Greek tragedy, or a modern soap opera. There was even a dramatic thunderstorm that evening. Isabeau completely lost it. We screamed terrible things at each other. She accused me of stealing away her man, which was frankly delusional, because Dain was completely faithful to me. She accused me of other things as well, trying to steal her throne, and her people, and she said traitors who acted against her deserved to be killed. By being with me, Dain had sealed his own fate."

Pia stared. "So she actually admitted she killed him."

"Yes. If Shane had not been present, the spell she threw at me would have killed me instantly. As it was, he acted very quickly and deflected it."

"He has quite a reputation as a magic user," Pia remarked.

Tatiana smiled. "He did then too, and Dain had been one of his closest friends. Between Shane and Isabeau, magic flew everywhere. They literally brought the halls down around our ears. This all happened before Isabeau acquired Morgan and her other Hounds, or Shane very well might have been over-powered and we all would have died that night. I remember being shocked at the magical battle, because she had grown unbelievably strong—much stronger than I or anybody else had realized." After shredding the lettuce, Tatiana began to crumble bread between her fingers. "That night caused a schism between our people. Some stayed loyal to her, and others followed me and Shane. We were refugees for several months, traveling across Britain and building a temporary encampment along the shore until we finally decided upon sailing as far west as we could. We ended up settling here in southern California." The Queen gave her a sidelong smile. "Of course, I compressed several years into a few sentences. The actual living of the tale took much longer."

"You sent out the *Sebille* before you set sail yourself," Pia said.

"Yes, I did," Tatiana replied. "Good friends were on that ship. We were heartbroken when it disappeared without a trace."

"Do you think Isabeau had anything to do with it sinking?"

"Sometimes I wonder if she did, although that's mere speculation. Storms happen. Ships sink. At any rate, as I said, the night of the confrontation was, I think, the first time Isabeau tried to kill me, but it wasn't the last. Every so often, an assassin shows up here, or someone tries to plant a bomb. Apparently, my sister is not just delusional, but she's unable to forgive or move on with her life. To be honest, I've grown used to it." Tatiana sighed. "Out of sheer exasperation, I've tried to have her assassinated too, but she's grown too strong and wary for me to get anyone close enough to do it. And somehow, she has gathered her Hounds. They are utterly loyal to her."

Pia finished her meal and set the pasta bowl aside.

Then, because she couldn't resist, she asked, "When was Dragos at Isabeau's Court?"

"Some time before I got pregnant, but now that I think about it, not too much earlier." Frowning, Tatiana set her uneaten meal aside as well and wiped her fingers with her napkin, as fastidious as a cat. She said, "Dragos didn't lose his memory from the contagion, did he?"

Pia stopped moving. For a moment, she didn't breathe, as her mind raced frantically around, searching for a way to deflect or misdirect.

But now that the Queen had flat out said the truth, her options had turned slim to none. The thing about shadows and misdirection was, once someone started to disbelieve the magic, their power dissipated like so much smoke.

She had almost begun to believe that they had tap-danced well enough that they were going to be able to keep all their secrets.

As her hesitation went on a bit too long, the Queen asked gently, "Was it the head injury? The news downplayed his accident this summer, but of course the scar on his forehead is quite visible."

God, she hoped Dragos would forgive her for this. Pia met the other woman's gaze and said directly, "Yes."

Tatiana blinked. Clearly she hadn't expected such a straightforward response. "I see."

"He's going to hate that I told you that," she said

dryly.

Long eyelashes fell, obscuring the expression in the other woman's eyes. "You don't need to let him know that you told me."

Pia wasn't about to play that game. "Oh, yes, I do. We have no secrets between us. Ever."

Tatiana acknowledged that by lifting one shoulder. "That's always the wisest course in a marriage. It's an especially wise course of action to take as Dragos's mate."

"Well, it isn't a tactical maneuver," she replied, glancing out the window. Dragos had eaten some of the food on the tray and pushed the rest aside. Now he lay on his back, eyes closed, hands folded across his flat, lean stomach. Despite the thick chains circling his wrists and ankles, he looked quite comfortable. She smiled to herself. "We trust each other. So, he'll be annoyed with me, but he'll get over it."

Envy flashed across the other woman's face, or at least she thought it did. It had vanished in the next instant, so she couldn't tell. Tatiana asked, "Do you know how much memory he's lost?"

"At first, his memory loss was total. But, thank God, that didn't last more than a few days. Now, almost all of it has returned. Everything that matters to me, at least. He has a few pockets of long-term memory loss, but mostly, those are historical events. It's really just a fluke that the whole thing has come up. If we hadn't been so preoccupied with—with other things, I don't think there would have even been a misstep." She smoothed her fingers along the edges of the chair cushion. "Can you tell me what Dragos was doing at the Seelie Court?"

"To be honest, I don't really know," Tatiana replied. "He was a recurring guest for several seasons. He and Isabeau seemed to have this ongoing thing."

Utterly flummoxed, Pia stared at the other woman.

Thing? What did Tatiana mean by *thing*?

One thought after the other tumbled through her mind. Had they been enemies? *Lovers?* Dragos was older than sin. She had known for a fact that he'd had sex before, and probably quite a lot of it at some point or other, because he knew how to do such wise, wickedly inventive things that made her eyes pop out of her head, and she was quite sure they hadn't exhausted all of his repertoire of tricks yet.

But knowing something had happened and coming up against the reality of it were two different things entirely.

She wasn't jealous at the thought. Not exactly. Dragos was hers, totally, but she did feel sour and unsettled.

The only way to get more information was to pump Tatiana for it, because Dragos wouldn't be able to tell her anything, even if he wanted to. She asked, "What do you mean, they had an ongoing *thing*? Do you mean they had an affair?"

"I don't know," Tatiana replied. "They might have,

but I never knew anything for sure. Even then, I was marginalized at her Court, and I was certainly not privy to any confidences. I remember they sort of smilingly poked at each other verbally, and she seemed to be fascinated by him. And I had no idea how to read him. It had something of a flirtatious hint to it, but there was also this edge, like maybe they hadn't yet decided whether or not they were enemies. She once called him 'that damn inquisitive dragon.' I always wondered if he was either trying to get information from her, or perhaps he was searching for something. Maybe he'll remember in time."

"Maybe," Pia said. Inwardly, she doubted it. He had recovered most of his lost memories within a few days after the accident, and now, the more time passed, the less likely it was that he would remember.

"Well, if you have anything to do with Isabeau, be careful. I cannot say if she and Dragos parted on friendly terms or not, and as you have seen for yourself, she is a vicious and relentless enemy."

"I appreciate the warning." Rubbing her forehead, she wondered how Aryal, Quentin and Shane were doing. No news might be good news. Of course, it might not too. Quentin had seemed pretty certain that Morgan would kick their asses. She muttered, "Why is Isabeau's Chief Hound called Morgan of the Fae?"

"Because Morgan lives at Isabeau's Court, but he isn't actually Light Fae himself. Neither Shane nor I are quite sure what he is, although I make a point of not getting close enough to him to find out. He seems human, but he's also hundreds of years old, which of course no normal human could achieve." Tatiana had tensed while she talked. Now she looked unsettled as well. "If he has human blood in him, he also has something else—either Elder Races blood, or perhaps some kind of magical Power—that has prolonged his life. Not much frightens me, but he does."

A trickle of real fear for Quentin and Aryal ran down Pia's spine. She wished they would get in touch somehow, but of course they would be too busy to call, and Dragos's telepathy was down.

While they talked, she kept part of her attention on the quiet, sunny afternoon outside, which was how she saw what happened next.

The quiet scene erupted. In place of the large, black-haired man lying prone on the lawn, an immense bronze dragon appeared, with the bronze coloring darkening to black at the tips of his long talons, tail and gigantic wings. His sudden appearance knocked the two Hummers sidelong. Looking down at his body, the dragon shook himself like a dog, and his chains fell away.

Fierce joy shot through Pia, as strong as a sunburst.

Guards shouted in both surprise and alarm, causing Tatiana to spin in her seat and stare wide-eyed out the window.

The dragon mantled his massive wings, looked at the guards and said, "If you shoot at me now, you're only going to piss me off."

Surging to her feet, Tatiana strode to the French doors and yanked them open. She shouted, "Any fool that shoots at him will face disciplinary action!"

The dragon strode to the verandah. It took him three steps.

Grinning, Pia pushed to her feet and poked her head around Tatiana. "Hi, baby," she said. "Good to see you."

"Good to be here," Dragos said. He folded his wings into place and cocked his head to look under the verandah roof at her with one golden eye. "I'm going hunting. Okay with you?"

"Everything's great with me," she told him, beaming.

He told her, "Take your medicine."

"I will." Telepathically, she said, *I love you.*

Love you too. Be back later.

With that, he wheeled, crouched and launched into the air.

DRAGOS HAD TRIED to shapeshift every ten or fifteen minutes. When he finally did connect with his Wyr form and shift, he felt the last of the contagion burn away.

Now, he tore through the air, fierce eagerness fueling his flight. He said telepathically to Aryal, *Where are you?*

Whoa, she exclaimed. *You're telepathizing!*

While I appreciate your gift for the obvious, he drawled. *I would rather know your location.*

South Harbor Boulevard, she said briefly. *Near the waterfront. There's a large herd of zombies here, Dragos. The Hounds are here too, behind them, driving them forward at us. They're using them as shields while throwing attack spells at us.*

Zombies?

He coughed out an unamused laugh. That was as good a word for them as any.

He told her, *I'm coming in hot. Tell the others to get out.*

Hells yes! As far as I'm concerned, you can torch them all. Most of them are half eaten—they couldn't survive any kind of antidote or reversion anyway.

That's what I saw in the group that attacked me. He flew west, as hard as he could. *Shoreline's in sight now.*

Quentin and Shane's forces are retreating. They're in an SUV, headed south.

Got it.

The sun hung lower in the sky since he had been chained, reigning over the western horizon and sparkling on the vast water. As he neared the waterfront area, he felt blasts of magic from the battle.

A winged figure shot into the air and swooped. It was Aryal. She held an automatic weapon and sprayed the area below her with gunfire. He caught a glimpse of flying black hair, piercing gray eyes, and her angular, hawkish face.

A deadly spell burst upward like a firework at her,

but dipping one wing, she rolled to the side and let herself fall through the air, and the spell shot past her harmlessly.

The dragon smiled to himself. As usual, she was utterly fearless.

Compared to his size, though, she was like a two-seater aircraft. He told her, *Stay out of my way.*

Flipping, she righted herself and flew south after the SUV.

In the next moment, he was on the scene.

The infected herd was large, and its members as fast as the ones who had attacked him earlier. But they weren't fast enough to outrun him.

As the dragon dove, he opened his jaws and let all of his anger boil out. Fire spewed onto the scene. In just a pass or two of his wings, he had shot past. Wheeling, he turned and dove again, laying fire over four industrial blocks.

Only when he felt sure that he had covered the area thoroughly did he pull up to land in the middle of the hot blaze. The dangerous, pathetic figures of the infected collapsed almost immediately.

From the ground, it looked as though the world was on fire. It suited the dragon's apocalyptic mood. He strolled down the street. The flames were so hot, the asphalt underneath his talons grew soft and sticky, then caught fire. At times like this, when he was enraged and civilization had fallen completely away, he thought he could burn down the world and never miss it.

When that happened, he could hear a quiet voice at the back of his mind.

You could do it, brother, Death whispered. *We could do it together.*

These days, however, when he heard that quiet, far-off voice, he shook away the lure that Death held for him. There was too much buoyant life that surrounded him, and love. His mate. His son. His new, unknown child, as mysterious as an unexplored land.

Maybe we could, the dragon said to the quiet voice. *But we won't today.*

Up ahead, the figure of a man walked toward him, through the flames.

Dragos stilled, and his eyes narrowed. Dragon fire burned hotter than almost any other blaze, save the sun's, but the figure did not appear to be affected.

As the man neared, his features and form became distinguishable. He wore tailored black clothes, leather gloves and a leather suit jacket that could, Dragos noted, hide any number of weapons. He was tall and wide-shouldered, and moved with the kind of liquid athleticism that Dragos associated with his Wyr soldiers, but this was no Wyr.

He looked like a human man in his midthirties, deeply tanned, with chestnut hair and clear hazel eyes, and a strong, contemplative, even sad, face. And he carried so much Power, he felt like a walking, talking nuclear bomb.

The dragon's hackles rose.

"Lord Cuelebre," the man greeted him in a calm voice that Dragos could hear perfectly well over the roar of the flames around them. He spoke with a Welsh accent. "Unfortunately, you managed to kill all my compatriots before I could reach them in time. You are not supposed to be here."

Dragos didn't recognize the male. Perhaps he would have, once upon a time, before his head injury. Falling so unexpectedly into that hole in his memory made him rage even more.

So he took an educated guess.

"Morgan," the dragon growled. The man did not deny the name. "You are not supposed to be here either. You started the contagion." The dragon stalked closer. "And when the Light Fae came close to eradicating it, you worked to spread it."

"My Queen commands, and I am compelled to obey," Morgan said, inclining his head and offering a slight, courteous bow.

"Did your Queen compel you to destroy all the Elder Races?" Dragos barked.

As the dragon drew nearer, the other male turned slightly to walk at an angle, until they were circling each other like adversaries, while everything around them burned. At Dragos's accusation, Morgan tilted his head. "Her quarrel is with this Light Fae demesne. It does not involve you, or the rest of the Elder Races."

"Quite the contrary," the dragon hissed. Lunging

forward, he snapped at the other male, who leaped back, faster and more fluid than Dragos had believed possible. Morgan gestured, and a wall of Power slammed between them, shimmering from the fire. "It involves me. My mate. And it involves any race that carries a hint of Power. Both human and different Elder Races can be infected by the contagion. Your creatures attacked me. One of them broke my skin. I started to turn."

The other male frowned, his clear hazel gaze sharp. "You were susceptible?"

"For a brief time, I was." Dragos pushed at the wall of Power, seeking a way to get through. "And I am not susceptible to any illness. Magically inclined humans have caught it and turned. This contagion is utter *madness*. It will destroy all of us if it is allowed to spread."

Morgan closed his eyes, and his face tightened. "She swore it would only kill the Light Fae in this demesne."

Only kill the Light Fae? He spoke of eradicating hundreds, if not thousands of people.

"Well, the bitch was wrong," Dragos snarled. He clawed at the wall of Power, and the tips of his talons screeched down the shimmering barrier like nails on a chalkboard. As he tried to stalk around it, the wall shifted, keeping pace with him. "You have something that creates this hell. A magic item, or a vial of something. Where is it? *Give it to me!*"

To the dragon's astonishment, Morgan reached inside his leather suit jacket and pulled out an amulet.

Even through the dragonfire and the sorcerous Power that Morgan exuded, the amulet seemed to radiate an aura of blackness.

It wasn't as strong as a Deus Machina, or God Machine. There were only seven Machines in the world, and they could not be destroyed. Back at the beginning of the world, the seven gods of the Elder Races had thrown something of themselves into the world to enact their will through the ages.

Dragos had encountered God Machines before. He knew how to identify them, and while this amulet was no Machine, still, it was imbued with a touch of Death's Power. Dragos might not be susceptible to any illness, but Death's Power could still touch him. Theoretically, he could die, and the fact that he had been susceptible to the contagion reinforced that theory.

Dragos stilled. "Where did you get that?"

"My Queen gave it to me and ordered me to use it," Morgan told him. "But it does more harm than she promised."

He tossed it high in the air, and the amulet fell to the ground on Dragos's side of the barrier. Dragos bared his teeth. "What happened to the 'my Queen commands, and I am compelled to obey' shit?"

Morgan raised his eyebrows. "She did command, and I have obeyed. But now I am done."

With that, he turned and walked away. Within a few steps, the fire appeared to swallow him whole. At the same moment, the barrier melted away.

Scooping up the amulet in one giant claw, Dragos lunged after the other man, but Morgan had disappeared completely from his sight and his senses.

After stalking around the area for several moments, eventually he gave up the hunt. Instead, he turned his attention to the deadly amulet he clutched in one claw. The amulet was made of a large, faceted onyx stone that reflected the dying fire.

Normally, onyx didn't work well for holding magic. The harder jewels, like diamonds and rubies, worked the best for containing magic. Whoever had created the amulet had had a particular flare for Death magic.

As partial as the dragon was to items of jewelry, there were some things too dangerous to hoard.

He concentrated his Power on the amulet, working to crush the magic even as he squeezed his claw to crush the stone.

At first both magic and stone resisted. It was incredibly strong. Drawing on more Power, and all of his strength, he gritted massive teeth and strained until he felt an invisible *snap*, and the onyx broke. He crushed it until there was nothing left but dust.

Chapter Ten

AFTER HE DESTROYED the amulet, he turned his concentration to the fire that still blazed in places. Pulling hard, he drew the flames back into him. For a brief time he was immersed in fire. Closing his eyes and breathing deeply, he let his consciousness be immersed in the brilliant heat.

When it subsided, he contacted Aryal telepathically. *The herd of infected here are all incinerated. I killed a couple of Hounds, but I didn't manage to kill Morgan. He's gone.*

Too bad, the harpy said. Vindictiveness tinged her voice, like the sharp edge of her claws. *You okay?*

Yes. Morgan gave me the source of the contagion. It was magical in nature. I've destroyed it. As he talked, he launched into the air. *I'm going back to Tatiana's. Work with Shane until you're sure the rest of the infected are burned. I might have destroyed the source, but they can still spread the contagion through their bites. Report back when you are all confident the job is done.*

Understood.

There was no way Dragos was going to show up at Tatiana's without making sure he had gotten rid of any lingering traces of the amulet. Flying due west for a half a mile or so, he dove into the ocean until he reached the sandy floor. Scooping up clawfuls of sand, he surfaced again and scrubbed at himself until he felt certain that he was entirely clean.

Only then did he head back to Bel Air, winging through the distance at a tired, leisurely pace.

This time, he landed a couple of blocks down the street and shapeshifted back into a man so that he could walk the rest of the way toward the large, sprawling mansion. The sun had not yet set, but it was low enough in the sky that it had gone down below the silhouette of the surrounding houses, throwing deep shadows across the lawns and the street.

As he walked, he admired the ultra-landscaped lawns in front of the other Bel Air properties. He said in Pia's head, *I'm so glad we don't have a lot of flowers and other plant froufrou around our house. I'd never feel comfortable about shapeshifting, in case I accidentally knocked shit over with my tail, or trampled a rose garden.*

Which is exactly why we don't have all that. There was a smile in Pia's voice as she replied. *Between you, Liam, all of the sentinels and various other Wyr, if we had any kind of fancy garden, it would get trampled to dirt inside of a month. If you can chitchat lawn care, should I take it to mean that whatever situation was out there is taken care of?*

Yes, you should. I'm walking up to Tatiana's house right now. I'll tell you about it later. He paused. He hadn't had anything to do with either the interior design or landscaping of the house. Pia had done all of that, and she had thought everything through very thoroughly. He told her, *You are a wise woman.*

Pleasure warmed her voice. *I do have my moments, don't I? But then … I have other moments too. Dragos, I have to confess something. Tatiana nailed me down about your memory loss, and I couldn't find a way to wiggle out of admitting the truth.*

Oh, for fuck's sake, he sighed. He felt a brief impulse to strangle the Light Fae Queen. *How much does she know?*

Well … pretty much an abbreviated version of everything. I never would have volunteered to tell her anything, but she had already guessed that the contagion hadn't really messed with your thinking. She told me quite a story, both how she and Isabeau became estranged, and also something of your time at the Seelie Court.

Briefly, he wrestled with his pride, and pragmatism won. *Did she give you any indication what I was doing at Isabeau's Court?*

Not really. She indulged in some speculation, but she didn't know anything for sure. She said you and Isabeau sort of flirted, but sort of acted edgy around each other. She didn't know if you were ever lovers, or even if you had parted on friendly terms.

As Pia talked, he grew close enough that Tatiana's mansion came into view.

He told her, *I don't remember any other lover but you.*

I don't believe you.

I don't. I know the facts of other lovers, but all the real, visceral memory, or any emotion has burned away. Those lovers happened to someone else, the man I was before I met you.

She had stepped out onto the lawn. Eva and a couple of vigilant Light Fae guards stood with her, but as the Light Fae guards were actually guarding her, he didn't mind them so much. When they saw him, they didn't draw their weapons. Another win for the day.

Pia saw him at the same time. He started walking faster, and she gathered her skirt up in one hand and broke into a run. She flew down the driveway, and the eager light on her face was simply everything.

She hit him in the chest with her full weight, flinging her arms around his neck. Laughing, he spread his feet wide to absorb the impact and snatched her close. She held him so tightly, she damn near strangled him, and he knew he all but crushed her ribs.

Burying his face into her neck, he growled, "I *hated* not being able to touch you."

"I know. I felt the same." Greedily, she stroked the back of his head, and his shoulders. "You're okay? Quentin and Aryal—they're okay?"

"They're fine. From the way Aryal talked, I believe Shane is fine too, but I don't know anything about Shane's men." He rubbed his face in her hair, tightened his arms until she squeaked, then eased his hold on her. "Come on, let's go inside. That way I can tell this story just once."

Together, they turned and walked to the house. He kept his arm around her shoulders, and she slipped an arm around his waist. She told him telepathically, *I gave myself the injection.*

He had no longer been worried, but still, the confirmation lightened his spirits. *Good. That means you're going to feel tired and achy—or do you feel that way already?*

I'm pretty tired, she admitted.

She never complained about it. Not once. Everything she said about the pregnancy was filled with a positive attitude and eagerness for the new arrival. He replied, *I take it that means you do feel achy too.*

She shrugged. *It's okay.*

He tightened his arm around her shoulders and said aloud, "And that means you need to go to bed soon. See, I'm figuring out your encoded messages."

She gave him a brief, laughing glance.

Tatiana herself came to the front door, meeting them as they were about to step in. She smiled at him. "I just heard from Bailey. They have a few areas they need to scour, but she thinks the tide has turned now."

"It has," Dragos said.

"Come back to the family room and tell me what happened." Turning, she led the way to the back of the house.

Settling on one of the couches, with Pia curled at his side, he told Tatiana and Pia about the encounter with Morgan, and the amulet, which he had destroyed.

"I don't know how she could let something like that loose in the world," Tatiana murmured, looking ill.

"We skirted so close to catastrophe. As it is, I've lost hundreds of my people."

Something teased at the back of his mind, and he paused, waiting to see what came of the sensation. It felt like memory ... or almost a memory. Then, in the next instance, the feeling was gone. Frustrated, he shook his head.

"Isabeau needs to die," he said crisply. Pia rested her head on his shoulder, and he pressed a brief kiss to her forehead. "But then, so many people do. And the reality of it is, she's very well guarded. She has full control over her Other land, and her Hounds appear to be completely loyal to her. And Morgan is—formidable. I'll never understand how obsessive people can command such fanatic loyalty."

"Well, she has more than her fair share of the Light Fae charisma, which would help." Tatiana's gaze fell to Pia. Suddenly her face softened, and she smiled. Looking back up at Dragos, she put a finger to her lips.

He raised his eyebrows. Then he tilted his head to look into Pia's face. She had fallen deeply asleep. Her lashes cast long shadows on the curve of her cheeks, and her soft, full mouth had gone lax.

She whispered, "I remember those days too, when I was pregnant."

"Tatiana," he said in a soft, gentle voice, so as not to disturb his sleeping wife, "if you try to kick me out tonight, I'll make it my personal mission to tear Bel Air down around your ears."

"I wouldn't dream of it," Tatiana said quietly. "You have helped us tremendously today, and I am very grateful. We still need to adhere to the terms of the diplomatic pact, but I think we can get away with you staying one night. And frankly, what you choose to do with the rest of your week is none of my business. I'm certainly not going to be spying on you, should you and Pia meet up somewhere while she is out and about this week."

"Thank you," he said, relaxing.

"For tonight, I'll have one of my guards show you where her suite is."

The Queen stood, and he gathered Pia's warm, soft weight into his arms and stood also. Then he paused. *One other thing,* he said telepathically.

Tatiana paused as well, and looked at him inquiringly.

Don't poke at my wife about her Wyr form, he said. He gave her one of his hardest warning looks. *I mean it, Tatiana. Leave her alone about it. She told me you had questioned her in D.C. Her Wyr form is shy by nature, and in the early days of our mating, it was a real strain for her to contemplate being with me. She gave up a lot to be my mate. She's had to adapt to the limelight, and I won't have her bullied or pressured over it.*

The Light Fae Queen pursed her lips in a disappointed moue. *Oh, very well.* She paused. *By the way, I've heard a preliminary report from my doctors who are studying your blood samples. They're quite electrified at what they're finding. They think they've isolated the contagion and might be able to develop something from it, which will be hugely useful if there are any more outbreaks. Also, apparently your blood is intensely magical in nature, but then nobody is surprised by that. And there's something else—something truly unique, and they don't know quite what to make of it.*

Pia had already tried to heal him before his blood had been drawn. Was it something from her, or was it something inherent to him? Had she healed him after all?

Maybe the protocol had suppressed her nature but had not entirely negated it. Her blood might have worked, but very slowly. Or perhaps he had thrown off the effects of the contagion, himself.

They would never know for sure.

For now, he injected scorn into his mental voice. *Tell me, have any of your doctors ever studied dragon's blood before?*

Her brows twitched together. *You know they have not.*

He snorted. *Then of course it's truly unique.*

Cocking her head, she smiled wryly. *You do have a point.*

He reached out for Grym. *I hear they've isolated the contagion.*

They sure have, and in record time, Grym said. *There's a celebratory air right now in this lab.*

Time to destroy all the blood samples. Make sure they're incinerated, so that not a single cell is left.

You got it. Oh, the weeping and gnashing of teeth that will shortly commence.

Dragos smiled to himself. They hadn't preserved every one of their secrets. But they had managed to preserve the most important one.

Then Tatiana stepped to the door, opened it, and he carried Pia through to the hallway, and up to the suite.

✧   ✧   ✧

PIA WALKED ALONG her favorite trail, enjoying the fall colors.

Wait a minute. She had already done this before. Remembering jolted her so that she realized she was dreaming.

Tilting her head, she walked slowly and listened for a small, stealthy rustle. Sure enough, she heard it, behind her and a little to the left.

She didn't turn around or do anything to spook her small shadow. Instead, pretending to ignore it, she walked along slowly, thinking.

Soon, she came to an area where the trail opened up and the land flattened to form a high, grassy meadow atop a bluff that overlooked the land's long decline. Eventually that decline would lead to their house, which was half hidden by the surrounding trees. Beyond the house lay the flat blue shimmer of the nearby lake.

Strolling through the small meadow, she picked a spot and settled cross-legged on the ground, looking over the countryside. The scene was beautiful, with rolling hills covered with the brilliant gold, yellow and vermillion of the fall foliage. She loved everything about upstate New York in the autumn.

A small rustle might be approaching. Happiness filled her. Cocking her head, she listened to the slight, cautious sounds behind her and fought not to laugh. What would her shadow decide to do now?

Something sharp poked her in the lower back, over her left kidney. She swept a hand behind her to move the stick, or weed, or whatever it was, but her hand encountered nothing but air.

Hm.

The sharp something poked her again.

Moving gently, so as to not frighten the wary shadow away, she twisted to look over her shoulder.

Underneath the slender spire of a horn, fierce gold eyes looked back at her.

Oh, holy gods. She froze. She didn't even dare to breathe.

The small creature standing just behind her shoulder was … was …

It was small like a newborn foal, all gangly legs and overlarge head, with a narrow, racy body. And it was dark bronze all over, almost exactly the same shade that Dragos was in his dragon form, with the colors darkening to black at the legs, nose and tail.

And it had that slender horn at the middle of its forehead. The horn would lengthen and sharpen as it grew to adulthood, but for now, it was short and well suited for a baby's developing neck muscles.

"Oh, Stinkpot," she whispered. "You're so beautiful."

And so frightening.

This was the creature that carried the fiery Power that Liam had sensed. Those eyes, that coloring, were so like Dragos. If its personality was as fiery as its Power, it would have a royal temper. A temper that might even override all the instincts of its Wyr nature, instincts that would urge it to run and hide, or take the less obvious path to avoid detection and danger.

Swishing its tail, Stinkpot bent its head to nibble at the yellowing grass. While it acted like it was distracted, Pia carefully, carefully tightened her stomach muscles and leaned back to see if she could catch a glimpse between its slender, gangly legs.

Oh my God. Stinkpot was male. Delight, wonder and sheer terror clanged through her head like a three-bell alarm.

She whispered, "Are you okay if I pick you up now, darling?"

At the sound of her voice, Stinkpot flicked an ear but didn't appear to be otherwise concerned. Moving slowly and gently, she twisted around to stroke his neck. His body was that of a newborn foal, but he carried the promise of power in the regal arch of his neck, and in the deep width of his chest.

He would be fast, she knew. Faster than almost

anybody else, and he would be able to run for miles without tiring. She could see it all too well in her mind's eye. He would be talented at running all right, but instead of running away from danger, he would run straight toward it.

Stinkpot shifted and reached, as if to nibble at another blade of grass. It also happened to bring his neck closer underneath her hand, so that she could scratch more skin.

"I see what you're about now, young man," she crooned gently. "And I already know that you're going to like keeping your secrets. Are you going to be sneaky too like your daddy?"

He let out a *whuffle*, as if agreeing, and she couldn't hold back any longer. Reaching around him, she picked him up and gathered him close. He didn't protest or struggle. As she settled him in her lap, he folded those ridiculous, overlong legs and tucked his head in the crook of her arm. Bending over him, she buried her face in the thick, coarse hair of his mane.

Funny how love works. Peanut had stolen her heart, and she adored Liam with all of her being. Now Stinkpot stole her heart all over again.

Both her sons were thieves, yet somehow she felt her heart still in her chest, beating hard from wonder, and it was full to bursting.

A large hand cupped her hip, traveled up the curve of her torso and flattened against the middle of her chest. Dragos murmured in her ear, "Pia, it's all right.

You're just having a nightmare. Wake up."

As she startled, the dream vanished.

"*Ssh*, calm down." Dragos's voice was slow, deep and easy. He kissed the back of her neck. "Your heart is racing ninety miles an hour."

"Mm," she croaked, her voice rusty from sleep. Lifting her head off the pillow and squinting, she looked around to get her bearings.

They were in bed together, in her suite at Tatiana's residence. The room lay in deep shadows, so it was some time in the middle of the night. Somehow she had lost her clothing, and Dragos had too. She knew who the culprit was for that. He spooned her from behind, under the bedcovers, his larger, harder body providing a protective shell around her.

Their position was so familiar, so necessary, that even though they were still in southern California, a sense of well-being flowed through her, along with a feeling of being home.

Stretching, she yawned and twisted around to cuddle closer against him. As she rested her cheek against his warm, bare skin, she let her fingers follow the pattern of dark, silky hair that fanned across his wide, bare chest.

He cupped the side of her face, cradling her, and she felt warm, relaxed, completely protected and surrounded.

"Does Tatiana know you're here?" she mumbled.

"Yes." His deep voice was a quiet rumble in his

chest. "We both agreed the circumstances of the day had been unusual enough that nobody would have a problem if I stayed for tonight. Are you still up for visiting the rest of the week with her? We can call this whole thing quits and go home in the morning, if you'd rather."

"And have to possibly come back again? Not on your life." Yawning again, she rubbed the sleep out of her eyes. "There's only six more days to go, and then the whole damn thing is over. Although I shudder to think what tomorrow will hold. What do you think—flood, fire or act of the gods?"

He snorted and pressed his mouth to her forehead. "What were you dreaming about?"

Remembering, she smiled with a small wordless croon. "It wasn't a nightmare. I was dreaming about Stinkpot."

"Really?" A smile entered his voice. "I'm sorry I woke you, then. Your heart was racing so hard, it woke me up."

"S'okay." Rubbing her face against his skin, she murmured in his head, *Do you want to know what I dreamed, or do you want to be surprised?*

You can surprise me right now. Easing her gently back on the bed, he kissed her lightly.

Telepathizing in bed was one of her very favorite things to do. They could have entire conversations while kissing like horny teenagers. The only problem with it was she lost control of her train of thought.

That, and often her verbal skills degenerated to things like: *Holy shit, do that again. My God! Ah, so good ... please—please—*

Smiling at the thought, she inserted the palm of one hand between their lips so that he couldn't distract her into incoherency. She told him, *Stinkpot is a gorgeous, wary, sneaky little boy. He's got your coloring and my Wyr form. And from what Liam was picking up, possibly your Power and temper.*

Dragos froze. She could just about feel the wheels turning in his head. After a moment, he said, *Good gods.*

Terrified glee suffused her. Sticking her tongue between her teeth, she fizzed like uncorked champagne. *Raising that kid is going to kill us both dead.*

Goddamn, Dragos muttered. *Just thinking about it might kill me dead. I can't wait to meet the little booger. He sounds amazing.*

He is, and I can't wait for you to meet him too. Sobering, she threw her arms around his neck. *I'm so happy you didn't turn. I think I might have gone a little crazy today. I had all these manic ideas about converting our basement into a big jail cell and keeping you chained up down there until I gave birth to Stinkpot, so that I could try to heal you then.*

It's okay. Everything is okay now. His arms closed around her tightly. *What do you remember of what I was telling Tatiana?*

Not much. Burying her face against him, she inhaled his healthy, clean scent. *I fell asleep a few minutes after we sat on the couch.*

With a few quick, concise sentences, he filled her in on the conversation. *The lab has the contagion isolated, and Grym let me know about forty-five minutes ago that he personally destroyed all the blood samples. Quentin and Aryal are still out with Shane. They're combing through neighborhoods street by street, but they haven't found any more infected for a few hours now. Right now, they just want to err on the side of caution before calling an end to the search.*

She lay still, absorbing the news. *And you're sure Morgan has gone?*

I'm certain he has, after giving me the amulet. He said he had done what he was commanded to do. Dragos paused. His voice turned darker and edged. *I should have known who he was. I should have remembered him. He's very dangerous, Pia. He walked through my dragonfire unscathed, and he blocked every attempt I made to get at him.*

If he's not Light Fae, then what is he? Could you tell?

He shook his head. *There was too much fire burning all around us, so I couldn't get his scent. Just from looking at him, I think he has some human blood. But he's clearly not fully human. He was faster and could jump much farther than a human could.*

She shivered. *Now I understand why you've been so obsessive about trying to recover those lost memories.*

You never know. Something may still come back to me.

He didn't sound convinced of that, and neither was she. The longer he went without recovering those memories, the less likely it was that he would ever recall them. Dr. Shaw had made it very clear. They would have to live with the consequences of that fact and be grateful that he had recovered as many memories as he had.

Shrugging it off, Dragos leaned over her again. *Enough about him. We have the rest of tonight before your week resumes, and I intend on taking full advantage of it.*

Gladly, she surrendered to the change in focus. *Ooh,* she crooned, running her fingers lightly along the powerful bulk of his shoulders. The silhouette of his body was darker than the rest of the room, as he eclipsed the night. From the darkest part of the shadow, she caught a glint of his intent gold eyes. *What do you have in mind?*

It was too dark for her to see his smile, but she could hear it in his voice. *Probably too many things for the amount of time that we've got, but you never know. I'm an ambitious man.*

Settling back against her pillow, she whispered, "Let's take everything on your list one at a time and see where we get."

"Item one," he growled quietly. The intense shadow moved, and suddenly his mouth was on hers, hard, hot and demanding.

Desire surged through her veins, burning away logic and common sense. In that moment, he could have asked her for anything, and she would have agreed gladly.

Thrusting his tongue into her mouth, he ran a greedy hand down the curves of her body, pinching and flicking at her nipple with a thumbnail and kneading the soft, full flesh of her breast, while the hard length of his erection pressed against her hip.

It could never be boring between them. All their lovemaking over the last eighteen months had conditioned her to associate his touch with such extreme pleasures that all he had to do was touch her hand and give her that keen, hard smile of his, and she melted into liquid heat. Her body was greedy for it, for him, and the thought of what they would do—what he would do to her—made the muscles in her thighs start to shake.

I can smell it on you, he muttered in her head. *Your arousal. It makes me so damn hungry. You're already wet, aren't you?*

Uh huh, she whimpered.

Wiggling under the heavy weight of his large body, she ran her own hand along the long length of his torso. His hot skin felt like silk wrapped over iron muscles. When her questing fingers found the tip of his cock, they both groaned. His own mounting arousal had caused moisture to bead at the slit. Using the ball of her thumb, she took the moisture and rubbed it along the broad, mushroom head, until he hissed and grabbed at her wrist.

Sometimes he could let her tease him, and then other times, like now, his dominant side took over. She was more than happy to go with either scenario. Pinning her wrists on either side of her head, he growled telepathically, *Open your legs.*

Hunger pulsed. God, she loved it when he got growly and autocratic. Arching in a stretch that rubbed her torso against his, she put her mouth lightly against his and whispered, "Make me."

He stilled. Then it was as if she had thrown a lit match on a lake of gasoline. Everything went up in flames.

Yanking her legs apart, he settled into place at the intimate bowl of her pelvis. When she would have reached to help guide his erection into place, he snatched at her wrists again. This time he pinned them over her head with one massive hand.

Testing the strength of his hold, she struggled to get free, although not that seriously. He liked it when she struggled. It struck at some deep predatory part of him that they both recognized and embraced as part of their extensive repertoire of love play.

As she twisted underneath his weight, the growl that came out of his throat was so low and aggressive, the tiny hairs at the back of her neck raised. God, that sound made her wetter than ever. She wanted to take his cock into her mouth and pump him dry. She wanted him to thrust inside her, and thrust, and thrust....

Restlessly she tried to wrap her legs around his hips, but with his free hand, he thrust her back down on the bed. Then, keeping her pinned, he bent to suckle at her breasts, first one then the other, flicking and teasing the stiff peaks of her nipples with his tongue in between drawing hard so that sensations sizzled down the length of her body.

The hunger for his touch grew harder to control, throbbing in time with the pull of his mouth. Physically aching for his touch, she whimpered and started to struggle in earnest, but he wouldn't release her.

"*Dragos*," she hissed urgently.

In response, he lifted his hand from her pelvis.

Only to lay the broad, hard palm over her mouth.

Of course he wasn't gagging her, not really, since they could telepathize, but the move was so dark and primitive, she almost came right then and there, without him ever touching her clitoris.

Shaken at her own response to the maneuver, she groaned. The sound was small and muffled against the palm of his hand. Her breathing came hard and fast, the expelled air from her nostrils hitting his skin in short, hard puffs.

He paused. He was breathing hard too. She could hear the rasp of it, a tiny, raw sound that told her how close he was to losing control. He asked her telepathically, *Okay?*

I almost came just now without you touching me! she exclaimed. *How okay do you think I am?*

The grip he had on her mouth softened. *Does it ache?*

Yes! She struggled against the hold he kept on her wrists.

Bending down, he whispered in her ear, "How badly do you want me?"

She sobbed, *So much! Dragos—please …*

And there it happened again. The heat between them became so intense, her verbal skills flew out the window.

The hard hand at her mouth moved away, and he released her wrists. Sliding down the bed, he murmured, *I'll make it better.*

She knew what he intended to do, and if she let him put his mouth on her, he would work at her until she screamed and flailed endlessly before he finally took his pleasure. While she loved those moments, this time she felt too impatient, too needy.

Before he could settle between her legs, she scrambled onto her hands and knees and told him, *I want you inside me—now.*

He could see better in the dark than she could. As she said the words, she arched in invitation. For a moment, the cool air-conditioning licked along her overheated bare skin. She could feel his gaze like a touch as he watched her. Then the darkest shadow in the room moved behind her to cover her with heat and hardness.

He positioned his cock at her entrance, rubbing himself on the passion soaked petals of her private flesh. As he did so, she hugged a pillow to herself and, bracing her weight on one elbow, reached between her legs to stroke his stiff length. As she touched him, his penis jerked.

Muttering a soft swear under his breath, he found her entrance and pushed in. No matter how many times they made love or just coupled together in wild, no-holds-barred monkey sex, she never grew tired of the sensation of his hard, thick cock entering her.

He gripped her by the hips and didn't stop pushing until he had seated himself to the root. Their ragged breathing played in counterpart as he gave her a moment to adjust. When he began to move, she buried her face in the pillow to muffle the needy sounds she made.

As he fucked her, he reached around to rub her aching clitoris, and her climax came with such abrupt savagery it tore her breath away. Sometimes the pleasure he gave her was almost too great, too sharp. It wrung her body out and destroyed her thinking.

As she shook from the force of the pleasure that rocked through her, he bit the back of her neck. Still pistoning inside her, still massaging the center of her pleasure. She didn't even have a chance to come down from the first peak before the second one slammed into her. Gripping his wrist as he worked her, she bucked and squealed.

Her thinking was destroyed. All she could do was hang on to him, while erotic images and impressions ran through her mind.

All the times they'd had sex. Rutted like the animals they were. Made love with gentleness and emotion. She knew the look in his eyes when she came, the combination of tenderness and intense male satisfaction. She knew how he looked when he came, feral and often inhuman, transported out of his own self-containment. There in the darkness, she saw all of his faces in her mind's eye, and they were all the face of the man she loved.

He bit her harder, fucked her harder. She could feel his teeth pressing on her skin and knew he would leave marks. The small pain combined with the pleasure, and drove her forward into yet another climax. This time she had no breath. All she could do was whine softly, a shaky, raw sound.

Then he paused, buried to the root inside her. She felt him begin to pulse and knew her own moment of intense female satisfaction. Whomever he had taken as lovers before in his very long life, now he was hers, entirely.

She had to say it to him. Licking swollen lips, she whispered, "You're mine. Mine."

He wrapped one arm around her, gently encircling her throat with his hand, taking total ownership of her with the gesture. Rocking against her pelvis, he murmured into the nape of her neck, "Until I take my last breath, and beyond."

Usually he was the one who descended into declarations of possessiveness, and she relished it every time. But whenever she felt the need to claim him as she had just now, he always gave himself to her, unreservedly.

Full of emotion, she reached up and behind her to cup the back of his head. He turned and pressed a kiss to her fingers.

"I don't want you to go in the morning," she complained softly.

Pulling away, he stretched out on the bed and pulled her into his arms. Her muscles felt like jelly, and she went down to him gladly.

As she settled against him, he wrapped his arms around her. "It's only six more days now, and I'll be nearby. And our night's not over yet. We're just going to take a little breather for a few moments."

"Sounds good," she said, face planted into his shoulder so that her words came out muffled. She didn't think she could sit up straight, let alone do something as sophisticated as walk to the bathroom. Light flooded the room, and she flinched with a gasp. He had turned on the bedside lamp. "Why did you do that? The dark was cozy."

"I have a present for you," he said.

She lifted her head to squint at him. "When on earth did you find time to get me a present?"

One corner of his hard mouth lifted. "I have my ways." He reached one long, bare arm to a pile of red and white that lay in a jumble by his cell phone. As he shook out the first piece, she realized it was a necklace. And oh lord, what a necklace! Fiery ruby red and sparks of light flowed over his long fingers.

Turned out, she did have the strength to sit up after all. "Oh my God," she breathed. As she held out her hands, he let the necklace settle into her grip. She examined the firebird. "This is breathtaking. Where did you get it?"

"A shop on Rodeo Drive," he said, his gaze resting on the brilliance lying in her cupped hands. "There are earrings too, and a bracelet."

"It's stunning." At first, when he gave her such extravagant gifts, she had felt uncomfortable, but he got such transparent pleasure out of it, she had set her own discomfort aside a long time ago. Now she simply reveled in the beauty of the necklace. Leaning forward, she kissed him. "I love it so much. Thank you!"

"My pleasure. Here, put it on." Sitting up, he helped her fasten the necklace. The firebird rested at the base of her throat. When she turned to face him, a smile creased his face. "You're as beautiful as I knew you would be, wearing it."

She knew his penchant for making love to her when she wore jewels and she gave him a grin. "Is this on your list of things you wanted to get to, before morning?"

His smile widened. "You know me so well. I've been looking forward to it this whole hellish day."

At the mention of what had happened earlier, her expression darkened, but only for a moment. Reaching for his hand, she twined her fingers through his. "We dealt with it."

He squeezed her fingers. "And we'll continue to do so. The universe can bring it. We'll deal with whatever may happen together."

Something deeper than happiness took her over. Fulfillment, perhaps, along with a rush of love so deep for him, it made her eyes shimmer. "We always do."

With a tug, he pulled her down to him and kissed her. In the middle of the kiss, he rolled so that she lay on her back, and he sprawled across her. Lifting his head, he looked down at the firebird sparking against her skin, and his expression turned purposeful.

He said, "And now to get to the next item on my list."

"Ooh, goody." Eagerly, she surrendered to his kiss, and then she surrendered to a great many other things as well. Pleasure was foremost among them, along with laughter, and more love.

Among his many other qualities, her mate was a very thorough man.

Liam Takes Manhattan

Thea Harrison

Chapter One

L IAM STOOD AT the edge of the rooftop of Cuelebre Tower, looking down at the city streets.

It was the darkest time of the year, after winter solstice and the annual Masque of the Gods, and right before Christmas. Below, the streets were decorated with Christmas lights, the ribbons of brilliant color piercing the frigid darkness.

Dense, icy snowflakes swirled on a wind so cold, it stabbed at the skin like tiny, invisible needles and whipped through his shaggy hair. He ran his fingers through it, but it tangled again immediately after. He needed a haircut, but when had there been time?

It was not just the darkest time of the year. It was also one of the darkest times for the Wyr. For the first time in history, a sentinel had fallen. Constantine was dead, killed in a battle with a first-generation Djinn.

Just a few days ago, they had burned his body on a funeral pyre. Shocked by a loss too deep for tears, the Wyr in the Tower went about their business like automatons, going through the motions. Dragos had decreed that the Masque would still be held, and so they'd done their jobs. Amidst the lavish festival, condolences poured in from all the other demesnes, while the Wyr endured.

Behind Liam, the rooftop door opened twenty feet away, and a soft footstep sounded. Recognizing the footstep, along with the hint of scent carried to him by the knifelike wind, Liam didn't turn around.

His mother stepped beside him, wrapped against the winter night in an ankle-length woolen coat, gloves and a cashmere scarf. As a gust of wind hit her, she shivered and lifted her collar to protect her neck as she looked out over the city.

"I don't know how you or your father can stand being out in this kind of weather without a coat," Pia muttered. "Just looking at you standing there in your T-shirt and jeans makes me feel cold."

Both he and his father carried so much fire inside, no winter chill could affect them.

"It feels good," he said, lifting his face to the wind. The light sting of snow on his skin broke through the distance between himself and the world.

Out of the corner of his eye, he saw his mother nod. Pia Cuelebre was a beautiful woman, tall and slender, with pale skin, light gold hair and dark violet eyes. She shone gently like a candle in the night.

After a few moments, she said, "Supper's ready."

"I'm not hungry." He turned his gaze back to the illuminated streets below. The dragon that lived inside him watched the small, fragile creatures with sharp interest.

"Liam," she said gently. "Please come downstairs and eat something. I don't think I've seen you take a bite since Con's funeral."

While that might be true, it wasn't exactly accurate. His mom had been overwhelmed with funeral preparations and her duties as hostess for the Masque, so the family hadn't shared very many meals like they normally did. Whenever she had checked on him, he hadn't been hungry.

But that didn't mean he hadn't eaten. Driven by instinct and need over the last week, he had shapeshifted into his dragon form and flown over the ocean repeatedly, hunting for massive amounts of food and gorging until he couldn't swallow another bite.

Now, her concern pressed against him like a cage, and he had to fight a small, fierce battle with himself to keep from lashing out at her. The events of the last week had brought his feral side too close to the surface, and he realized that he had become more dangerous.

Battle, his dragon whispered to him, as it had ever since he had learned of Con's death. *Fight. Death.*

Family, he told it. *Home. Love.*

The battle was over, and they had won. But at such a price.

His mom loved him and only wanted the best for him. And he loved her too. He would not give his feral side free rein and hurt her unnecessarily.

He told her, "I've eaten."

The tense line of her shoulders eased. "Well, that makes me feel a little better, but you haven't eaten with us, so I'd like to see some of that action with my own eyes. You're … you're growing so rapidly right now, you must need a lot of fuel."

For the first time since she had joined him, he turned fully to look down at her. Pia stood five-foot-ten, and he had passed that height yesterday.

Because in the darkest part of this particularly dark year, he had lost part of the battle with his dragon.

He had always been prone to growth spurts during times of crisis, and sometimes he'd had to fight to keep his dragon form under control as it strained to become fully grown.

All predator Wyr grew faster and stronger than other Wyr, and the dragon was the apex of the predators. Fueled by the unique magics he had inherited from both his parents, he had grown in massive bursts since his birth, lunging into life.

As he faced her, Pia drew in a breath. Tilting her head up to him, she whispered, "You're nearly as tall as your father."

One corner of his mouth lifted in a wry tilt. "I know."

"Do you … can you tell if you're going to grow any taller?"

He hesitated and flexed his shoulders, considering. "I'm not sure, but I think I'm almost done."

Her violet gaze had turned wide with fascination. "I

can only imagine what your dragon form must look like now."

"It's pretty big," he admitted.

"You'll have to show him to me soon." She tucked her hand into the crook of his arm and turned with him toward the stairwell. "In the meantime, let's get inside where it's warm. Your father and I want to talk to you."

Reluctantly he gave up the wild solitude of the night and went with her downstairs to the penthouse.

Huge though the penthouse was, the walls and warmth felt as confining as his parents' concern, but he endured being inside for her sake. The living room lay mostly in shadows, except for the brilliant multicolored lights glowing on the Christmas tree in the corner.

Pia had been half human before she had accessed her Wyr nature and successfully changed into her Wyr form. As a child, she had celebrated both the Masque and Christmas with her mother, and she had continued that tradition when she became Dragos's mate.

As a result, Christmas decorations filled both the penthouse and their home in upstate New York. Dragos had been content to indulge her, and had joined in the preparations. Stacks of colorfully wrapped presents lay underneath the tree.

Once inside, Pia pulled away and hurried down the hall toward the brightly lit kitchen and dining room. Liam paused momentarily, his dragon's eyes appreciating the lavish decorations and bright jewel-like colors adorning the tree before he strolled to catch up with her.

He knew his father was in the dining room before he rounded the corner. Whenever they were in close proximity, Liam always knew where Dragos was. He could sense Dragos's Power in his mind's eye, like a burning sun. He wondered if his father could sense him in the same way.

Dragos stood at the head of the dining table, his attention focused on the large beef roast on the platter in front of him as he carved it into thin slices. Light from the overhead chandelier gleamed off his black hair and outlined his tall, broad-shouldered figure against the plate glass window behind him.

Porcelain clinked in the kitchen as Pia prepared other dishes. A brief surge of revulsion hit Liam at the sight and smell of the roast. He had eaten so much raw prey lately, the cooked meat looked vaguely revolting.

His dragon focused on the sharp knife his father wielded with such competent, lethal dexterity. Carefully, Liam throttled the beast back. He and his father loved each other too.

Dragos never lifted his head from his task. He said in a quiet voice, "Tell me you're in control, and I will believe you."

He hesitated. Of course his father would sense how close to the surface his dragon was. Dragos had been Lord of the Wyr for a very long time. No doubt he had dealt with many Wyr struggling with the feral side of their natures.

Straightening his shoulders, Liam replied steadily, "I'm in control."

Dragos's piercing gold gaze stabbed at him. Then his father turned his attention back to carving the roast. "Good enough. Go help your mom."

At the order, rebellion surged through him like a flash fire.

He thought, I'm not a child anymore. I won't do everything you tell me to do just because you tell me to do it.

As quickly as it hit, the rebellion subsided again, leaving him rueful and wary. Perhaps he wasn't quite as in control as he thought he was, or wanted to be.

Silently, he obeyed, walking into the kitchen to wash his hands. Afterward, he picked up serving platters filled with roasted sweet and white potatoes, Brussels sprouts sautéed in garlic and olive oil, and gravy.

Pia was just putting the finishing touches on her own meal, a vegan roast with vegan gravy. As he carried the food to the dining room, she gave him a grateful look.

With the quick ease of familiarity, they were soon seated. Dragos and Pia had wine. They didn't offer him any, and why would they? He was less than a year old. To them, he was a gigantic, dangerous child.

But he wasn't a child. Not any longer. He was young, very young and inexperienced, but no longer a child. Bitterness whipped through him at the thought.

He throttled that back too. He was fast growing tired of this constant battle with himself.

After passing the food around, he took note when his mom and dad exchanged a look.

Here it is, he thought as he toyed with his food with a fork. Whatever it is they want to say to me.

Dragos turned to him. "Your mom and I want to apologize."

Taken aback, he blinked. "Apologize for what?"

Pia said, "We swore we wouldn't let this happen, but we got too busy and time slipped away from us. We had come to a decision a few months ago, but with the new pregnancy, and the trips to Washington DC and Los Angeles, and then getting ready for the Masque, and—and Con's death—" Her voice wobbled then firmed again. "Well, the last few months have been really hectic."

"I know," he replied, eyeing both of them cautiously. He had no idea where this conversation was going. "You've been more busy than usual. I get it. What's wrong?"

At that, Dragos and Pia exchanged another, longer look, their expressions too complex for him to read. Pia turned to him and said in a quiet voice, "Nothing new is wrong, my love. A few months ago we decided to let you have a dog, but we haven't had time to do anything about it. We want to get you a puppy for Christmas. Would you enjoy that?"

Carefully he set down his fork and repeated, "You

want to get me a puppy."

"You've wanted a dog so badly," Pia said. While her face and voice remained mild, he noticed she hadn't touched her food either. "But your dad thinks it's best if you start with a puppy, so that it can get acclimated to the predator Wyr it would be living with. I compiled a list of breeders that we could visit next week, if you like."

Liam put his flattened hands on the table, on either side of his plate, and considered them. They were broad across the palm and long-fingered, like his father's. Then he pushed to his feet, strode into the kitchen and retrieved a wineglass. When he walked back into the dining room, his parents hadn't moved, but the atmosphere in the room had grown tense.

They watched in silence as he took the bottle of wine and poured himself a glass. Dragos's gaze flared into incandescence.

The wine was dark red, densely rich like rubies. Experimentally, he sipped it. It was dry, with the merest hint of blackberry and cherries. Gods, it was delicious. He took a deep swallow and returned to his seat.

"When you said you wanted to talk to me, do you know what I was expecting?" he said in a conversational tone. He looked at Dragos. "I was expecting either or both of you to try to talk me out of the pact you and I made when Con was killed."

His father lounged back in his seat, appearing to

relax, but Liam knew he could move faster than almost any other Wyr, except for maybe his mom.

And him.

Dragos said, "I told you I would give you a year to prepare for a trial. Even if it goes against my better judgment, I won't back out of that."

"All I can think about is that a few days of that year are already gone," Liam said. "And you want to give me a puppy."

While his mom continued to look composed, her shoulders slumped, and he knew he had struck some kind of blow. It made his stomach hurt, but he couldn't take the words back. There was an eight-hundred-pound elephant in the room, and his name was Liam. They had to confront it.

He picked up his glass of wine and drank again, noting how both Pia and Dragos tracked his movements and the wariness in their expressions.

"How did you feel when I got myself a glass of wine?" he asked. After waiting a beat for them to respond, he continued. "It felt wrong to you, didn't it? You wanted to stop me."

Pia pushed her plate away and leaned her elbows on the table. "I can't deny it looked odd," she replied. As she met his eyes, her own gaze was steady and unwavering. "It's also odd for me to look up into your face when we're standing side by side. This last growth spurt you've had is the most significant one yet, and we're going to have to go through another period of adjustment. Be patient with us—we'll get there."

But that was just it—time was trickling away, and he didn't think he could afford to be very patient.

His father had given him a year to prepare for the trial to become a sentinel. His dragon had flared to meet the challenge, but he needed both education and raw experience. And everywhere around him were shackles made of love and expectation.

He felt like he was living in a trap. The urge to fly away as fast and as hard as he could swept over him again.

"Thank you for supper," he said, as he pushed his chair back and stood. "But I'm afraid I'm not very hungry again."

"Sit down," Dragos said. "We're not done talking."

He gave his father a long, level look. Whatever Dragos saw in his expression made him stand too, until they stared at each other eye to eye. Dragos's hard cut features were shuttered, but his eyes blazed with light. Liam wondered if his own gaze blazed with the same fierce light.

Neither one backed down. The air between them boiled with heat.

Liam said in a soft, courteous voice, "I'm done talking for now. I'll let you know when I'm ready to talk again."

With that, he pivoted on one heel and walked out. He took the distance to the living room in long strides, but behind him, he could still hear Pia whisper,

"Dragos, let him go."

That was all he had time to hear before he pushed out the door, ran up the stairs to the roof, exploded into his Wyr form and took to the sky.

AS SOON AS she heard the penthouse door settle behind Liam, Pia slumped and put her face in her hands.

"I wondered what life would be like when he reached a rebellious stage," she muttered. "So now I know."

She just hadn't expected him to exercise such control. She had thought he would go through a teenage phase of shouting and slamming doors, and if anything that she and Dragos would laugh about it when they were alone.

This was something entirely different. Almost overnight, it seemed, he'd shot up in height and his shoulders expanded, while his youthful rounded features grew lean and chiseled. Always a handsome boy, he was now indisputably a handsome young man.

They only wanted the best for him. They tried to do whatever they could that would make him feel loved and happy, but tonight the appearance of maturity, along with his quiet voice, and the clenched effort in his demeanor had turned the whole encounter dark with a sense of desperation.

"This is a mistake," Dragos growled. "I'm going to withdraw my decision."

The tension in the room hadn't dissipated with Liam's departure. Dragos's energy was boiling furiously. It felt to Pia like a raw blast of heat.

She lifted her head to look at him. Now that they were alone, he looked tired, exasperated and more than a little angry.

The events of the last week had been brutal on everyone. Bereavement was hard at any time, but Con's death had been hardest on Dragos and the sentinels, who had lost a brother and a comrade-in-arms. Her heart ached for the tired slump in Dragos's shoulders and the shadows under his eyes.

But as long as he was Lord of the Wyr, it was his job to handle it. And because he had such broad, strong shoulders, she knew that he could.

So she didn't say anything to make it easier on him. Instead, she said, "Hold on. You made him a promise, and you have to keep it. No matter how hard it might be, we don't break promises we make to our children. You just told him so, yourself."

He shook his head. "Normally I would agree with you, but Liam can't be a rebellious son and expect to be a sentinel at the same time. I won't allow it. Sentinels obey orders. They have to, Pia."

Of course he was right. Sentinels were responsible for carrying out Dragos's orders, and they were responsible for the safety of the Wyr demesne. It was essential for them to be able to balance following orders with taking independent initiative when necessary.

But Dragos was only right up to a point.

"Well, he isn't a sentinel," she said dryly. She wasn't quite sure how to finish that sentence—Yet? Ever?—so she left it hanging awkwardly in the silence. "I guess that means he gets to be a rebellious son right now."

He looked at her, gold eyes blazing. "Point taken. Should I go after him?"

Dropping her head back into her hands, she scrubbed at her scalp with her fingers as she tried to think.

One of the things that made her so happy was the love she witnessed between father and son. But no matter how much love lay between them, Dragos was very much the autocrat, and Liam had already demonstrated he wasn't responding very well to that at the moment.

Finally she replied, "I think we need to let him be. And trust him. He's our good, sweet boy, and I know he will become a good, sweet man. Let's not make that transition harder on him than it has to be." Pressing her fingertips to her temples, she added, "I think."

Dragos dropped a hand onto her shoulder and squeezed lightly. His touch steadied her as it always did, and she reached behind her to cover his fingers with her own.

Then he sat down at the dining table, rubbed his face and said, "So I guess we eat dinner."

She nodded. "I guess we do."

She thought she had lost her appetite, but they had a new son growing inside her, and the demands he made on her body had her rethinking that almost immediately. As Dragos picked up his knife and fork, she drew her plate back to her, and they ate their meal in thoughtful, worried silence.

Chapter Two

MOST PEOPLE HAD no idea who Liam was.

Most of the public, if they had heard of Liam Cuelebre, prince of the Wyr, would think of him as the new addition to the Cuelebre family. They might remember the baby photos that his mom and dad had released to the media not a year ago. If anything, they would expect him to be approaching toddlerhood.

Even most of the Wyr who lived in Cuelebre Tower didn't know the tall, broad-shouldered Liam who had emerged over the last two days. After flying all night and turning over the puzzle pieces of his trap, he found an odd sort of comfort standing unrecognized in line at the Starbucks on the ground floor of the Tower.

The dark-haired girl standing in line in front of him was cute. Really cute. She wore a tunic and leggings, and her gazelle long legs were sheathed in narrow black boots.

Evidently, she thought he was pretty cute too, as she looked over her shoulder and gave him a shy smile. Male interest sparked in his tired mind. As he took a step closer and opened his mouth, someone tapped his shoulder.

When he turned, he found Hugh standing behind him. Instantly, the small pleasure of sharing a smile with a pretty girl evaporated, and the invisible trap sprang around him again.

"What's up, sport?" Hugh asked, his plain, bony face creased in a smile.

Hugh had been his babysitter and bodyguard for several months now. Retired from active duty in the Wyr military service, Hugh had a long rangy body, lethal combat skills and a mild, soft-spoken manner, and while Liam loved the gargoyle, the last thing he ever wanted to ask a girl he'd been about to invite out on a date was if she had met his nanny yet.

He snapped, "What are you doing here? Did Mom or Dad send you?"

Hugh's smile faded and his hand fell away. "No, I havna talked to them this morning." His Scottish accent was usually faint, but it sounded more pronounced when he was upset. "I was just getting in line to grab a cup of coffee and saw you standing here."

Remorse prickled Liam's conscience. Giving up on the idea of flirting with the girl in front of him, he rubbed the back of his neck and muttered, "Sorry. I didn't get any sleep, and I'm short-tempered right now."

"Don't worry about it," Hugh said. "It's been a tough week for everybody."

"Yeah, no kidding." Whenever Liam thought of

Constantine's still face on the funeral pyre, he wanted to cry or fly into a rage. He had cried, in the dark of the night when he had been alone.

Con had been family too. He did not want to see the other male's death as an opportunity. He did not.

The line moved, and the girl walked away with her drink. Liam placed his order for a cup of black coffee and Hugh did too.

As they collected their drinks, Hugh walked over to the nearby stand to stir three packets of sugar into his coffee. Liam followed and hovered near Hugh's elbow, his thoughts and emotions as unsettled as they had been when he had left the penthouse the night before.

Without looking at him, Hugh asked quietly, "Feel like talking? Or do you have some place you've got to be?"

He knew his mom would be fretting about him, and probably his dad too, if Dragos fretted about anything. He needed to check in upstairs, but he wasn't ready to face them yet. Not until he managed to put himself in some kind of order and had at least some idea of what he needed to say, if not what the end result of the conversation might be.

Blowing out a breath, he replied, "Sure. I mean, if you've got the time. You're supposed to be off this week."

Hugh's rare smile appeared again, lighting up his face. "I always have time for you, sport. Come on."

Walking out of the Starbucks, Hugh led the way to

the large open food court area by an indoor fountain. Several tables were available. As they settled into chairs, Liam gulped at his coffee and looked around. He recognized several of the people at other tables, but nobody glanced at them or appeared to recognize him. By virtue of the acoustics and the noise of the fountain, the area was as good a place as any to have a private conversation.

Hugh removed the lid from his coffee and blew on it. "What's going on?"

"My life is all knotted up," Liam muttered. "And I don't know how to untangle it."

The gargoyle gave a slow, calm nod. "Why don't you start with one piece and let's see what happens."

The cute girl walked by. Slouching in his seat, Liam watched her until she was out of sight. He said, "I feel so damn guilty."

"What on earth do you have to feel guilty about?"

The surprised kindness in Hugh's expression brought unexpected tears springing to his eyes. Shoving his fingers through his overlong hair, he blinked rapidly until they disappeared.

Sometimes things felt so raw that they were almost impossible to say out loud, no matter how much privacy one had. He forced the words out through gritted teeth. "I feel sick that Constantine is dead, but I feel even sicker about the fact that he was barely cremated before I took advantage of it."

Hugh's gray eyes sharpened, and his expression

turned very serious. "Liam," he said with quiet firmness. "There is no way on earth anybody believes that you took advantage of Con's death."

Hunching his shoulders, Liam wrapped his hands around his hot coffee cup and stared down at it. His hands seemed like they belonged to a stranger now, large and powerful. He clenched them into fists.

"As soon as he was cremated, I started pushing my dad to let me fight for the empty sentinel position," he muttered. "And I didn't stop until he said yes. It was all I could think about. It's almost all I can think about right now too."

Hugh took a small, thoughtful sip from his coffee before he replied. "The way I heard it told, the sentinels asked Dragos what he was going to do to fill the position. You joined in the conversation. Nothing wrong with that, Liam. And there was nothing wrong with getting your dad to take you seriously enough to promise to at least give you a chance."

Every careful word Hugh said stung. But then everything stung these days. Liam rubbed his tired eyes and replied flatly, "You don't think I can do it, do you?"

He shouldn't be surprised. Nobody thought he could. Hell, even he wasn't sure if he could.

Dragos's seven sentinels were among the most deadly Wyr fighters in the world. They combined strength, cunning, ruthlessness and experience, and when they went after something, they did it with complete, unswerving dedication.

Liam had one huge asset in his favor—his dragon form. Because of it, he was faster and more powerful than any of the other sentinels, but that didn't give him the experience he needed to win the empty position in a trial by combat. It didn't give him investigative skills, honed by years of work, or tactical battle experience.

He had virtually nothing he could take to the position except for raw magical skills and brute strength. And if there was one thing he would bet on, it was that his father would not pull any punches when it came down to a trial by combat to fill the vacancy.

If anything, Dragos would probably be more ruthless than ever, because he had made it crystal clear: he would not give Liam the position. He would give Liam almost anything else Liam asked for, but not that. Liam would have to earn it, like every other sentinel had earned their place, or he would be out.

And if he was out, he truly had no idea what he would do with his life. He was too Powerful, too unique. There was no place for him in the Wyr demesne that felt genuine.

Dragos had offered him a starter position in one of his companies, but that felt fake and unsatisfying. He didn't want to work for his father. As much as he loved him, he was very much aware that Dragos's age, reputation and Power meant he cast a very long shadow, and Liam didn't want to live under that. He wanted to fight, to claw his way to his own place in the world, and own it.

Searching his gaze, Hugh asked, "Do you even want the position? Because you should think long and hard about that. The sentinels live a hard life. Their lives are dangerous, and they're always on call, always. Getting hurt would be a way of life. Loneliness might well be a way of life too. There's a reason why none of them have mated until recently. It's a rare person who can genuinely, wholeheartedly commit to having a Wyr sentinel as their mate."

Liam's gaze went to the fountain. He said, "I think so. I mean, I think I want it. Fighting for the position, and winning it, and facing those daily challenges sounds … satisfying. But how can I know for sure? The possibility didn't even come up until this week. All I really know for sure is that I want the chance to try for it, even if it seems unlikely that I'll get it." The bitterness crept back into his voice. "Besides, what else am I going to do?"

"First," Hugh said, "feeling at a loss as to what to do with your life is something every young person goes through, Liam, so take heart. As unique as some of your challenges might be, you're also going through something verra normal. Second—you can't become a sentinel just because you don't know what else to do with your life."

He closed his eyes. "I know."

"You've got a lot to think about."

"Yeah. And somehow I've got to find the right

kind of training. The training that you and the sentinels have given me has been great, but—it's not enough. You guys love me. I need the kind of experience where somebody's not going to give a shit if they knock my teeth in. I need to go through real life, live with real danger."

Hugh pursed his lips. "That's not going to be the easiest thing to come by. You also need space to think, and while you might not want to admit this, Liam, you still need some schooling. You're so talented and book bright, and you have a lot of facts crammed into that extremely capacious head of yours, but you don't have real-life application."

"I know," he muttered again. His shoulders slumped. The challenges he faced felt all but insurmountable. "I have no idea how to get any of that. I just…" He took a deep breath and forced himself to say what had haunted him all through the sleepless night. "I don't think I can get any of that at home."

The older man studied him in long silence. Then he leaned forward, bracing his elbows on the table, and said softly, "I'm going to tell you something that, well, nobody told me *not* to tell you. But at the same time, I dinna think your mom and dad would take too kindly that I *do* tell you, so I would appreciate it if you and I can keep this between ourselves. Can you do that?"

Liam's attention sharpened. He replied, "Sure. Whatever you say stays between the two of us."

"Okay." Hugh rubbed his face with one large raw-boned hand. "Have you ever heard of Glenhaven?"

Liam frowned, searching his memory, and came up with a vague reference he had heard at some point. "Isn't that a Scottish college?"

"Yes, it is. More accurately, Glenhaven is *the* college for the Elder Races. It's not actually in Scotland, but in an Other land, with the crossover passageway located just outside of Edinburgh. While the college is run by the gargoyle clans, it's not affiliated with any one demesne or race. When you were very small, yet still clearly showing what a prodigy you were, Dragos and Pia had a brief discussion about whether or not they should send you to Glenhaven."

He frowned, the vague memory teasing him. Was that where he had heard the name? Had he overheard his mom and dad discussing it? "They never said anything about it to me."

"That's because they quickly ruled it out as an option. At the start of each term, Glenhaven closes the crossover passageway. Nobody gets in or out until the term is over. The school claims that blocking access to the outside allows them to maintain their impartiality and high academic standards. It's also supposed to create an atmosphere where students develop their own relationships with each other, with a minimum of influence from outside politics. I think the real truth is that people take their political biases with them into the college, but that's neither here nor there, I guess."

As Liam listened, his mind began to race. "If the college is in an Other land, time doesn't pass there like it does for us. What's the time slippage like?"

Hugh shrugged. "I've heard time passes faster for the college than it does on Earth, but I don't know any actual numbers."

"If time passes faster there, I could possibly get more time to prepare," Liam said, beginning to feel the first stirrings of excitement. "It would be pushing at the terms of Dad's promise, but it's worth considering."

"I think it is," Hugh replied, giving him a sidelong smile. "There are disadvantages too, though. It's a long way away. If you went to Glenhaven, you would be completely cut off from everything and everyone you've known in your life. There's no phone calls home. No email, no Internet, no microwave popcorn, cars or movies. No changing your mind, at least until the end of a term. For those reasons alone, I don't think Pia and Dragos did more than discuss it once or twice and ask me a few questions about it. Also, you might squander a significant portion of your year on something that you find doesn't meet all your needs the way you had hoped, or help you get ready to face the sentinel trial."

Absorbing the information, he nodded. Going to Glenhaven would be a risk. But it might be his best shot to figure out what the hell he needed to do with his life.

Liam asked, "Have you been to Glenhaven before?"

The older man shook his head. "No, I haven't. I'm not from any of the clans that run the college. I have seen drawings and paintings, though, and they look quite beautiful. They have some images posted on their website, if you want to take a look."

"I do," he said absently, as his mind raced through possibilities. Then he caught up with what Hugh had said, and laughed. "They're based in an Other land, yet they have a website?"

The gargoyle chuckled. "Yeah, it's not an extensive website like academic institutions here have, with web portals, online databases and class curriculums. But it does offer some general descriptions. Tuition fees are pretty astronomical, or so I've heard, but I think they also have scholarship programs for intellectually and magically gifted individuals. It's not just the wealthy and privileged of the Elder Races that attend."

"I need to get to a laptop." Tossing back the last of his coffee, Liam stood, and Hugh did as well. He paused to give the other man an earnest look. "Thank you. Seriously. I really needed this conversation."

Hugh's smile creased his lean cheeks. Hooking an arm around Liam's neck, Hugh pulled him into a brief, tight hug. "You're most welcome, sport. I'm glad it helped. I'm going to get some breakfast. Want to join me?"

He shook his head as he returned Hugh's hug with enthusiasm. "Can't. I've got too much to do."

Along with a conversation he needed to have with his parents.

"Call if you need anything else."

"I will," Liam promised. "Talk to you later?"

"Any time."

As they parted, Hugh strolled back to the Starbucks line. Liam strode toward the nearby bank of elevators. Then he paused. While his dad probably had too much to do in the aftermath of Constantine's passing, he would bet money that his mother was spending time in the penthouse, keeping watch for his return.

He still wasn't ready to talk. Not quite yet.

Digging out his phone, he typed out a text. `Hi Mom. I love you.`

Almost immediately, his phone pinged in reply. `I love you too. How are you doing?`

`Pretty good.` His thumbs moved rapidly across the small screen. `I've been getting my head sorted out. I have a few things I need to do, but can we talk at noon?`

`Of course. Do you need anything?`

He smiled. `No. But thank you.`

`You're welcome. You know I'd do anything for you, right? Just say the word.`

`Yeah. I do know. Talk to you soon.`

Once he hit send on the final message, he tucked his phone back into the pocket of his jeans, swiveled and headed out the wide glass doors. The public library would be opening soon. He could use one of their computers to find out more about Glenhaven.

And, just for the hell of it, he might do a little Internet searching on dogs while he was at it.

Chapter Three

S EVERAL HOURS LATER, right at noon, Liam walked into the penthouse to find his mother and father waiting in the living room.

Dragos sat in an armchair nearest the Christmas tree, reading a book on ancient Egyptian treasure, one ankle hooked over his knee and a cup of aromatic coffee on the nearby table. Pia curled up at one end of the couch, flipping through a magazine. The scene looked peaceful and inviting, and they looked quite calm.

Calm was good. Calm was super good.

Dragos was also present in the middle of a workday, during a highly stressed time, so Liam knew just what a priority his parents had placed on talking to him.

As Liam entered, Dragos laid his book on the table, and Pia straightened to set her magazine aside.

Tucking his hands in his pockets, Liam strolled over to throw himself down on the couch beside Pia.

He said, "Hi."

"Hi, sweetheart." She gave him a wry smile. "You

know I have to ask it—are you hungry?"

"No, thanks. I picked up a sandwich when I was out." He returned her smile with a crooked one of his own before he said to Dragos, "I'm sorry to interrupt your workday."

"It's no trouble." Dragos reached for his coffee cup. "You are always going to be one of my highest priorities."

Yeah, he knew that. Once he could get his dragon side to calm down, he could even feel it. Liam was uneasy with how his dragon bristled when his father got too commanding. Dragos was not just a powerful personality. He was a ruler. Rulers tended to get commanding and dictatorial from time to time.

He said, "I have some things to say."

Pia laid a hand on his knee. "You can tell us anything. You know that."

"Yeah, I do." He squeezed her hand and took a deep breath. "First, I wanted to say thank you, and it's my turn to apologize. Things haven't been easy on anybody, but even through that, you guys have been super patient with me, and you've given me space when I needed it. I really appreciate it, and I'm sorry if I've added to your stress this week."

Dragos waved that aside. "Don't concern yourself with that."

Even though Dragos meant nothing but good, and Liam's dragon had calmed considerably, it still bristled at his father's autocratic way of wording things. He choked his reaction down.

Now that he was nearing maturity, would it always feel that way between them? They were two male dragons, both territorial, both possessive.

As much as he'd had to wrestle with himself lately, it would have been handy if he could have split himself in two, because sometimes he simply wanted to put his hands around the neck of his dragon and throttle it.

Pia asked, "The important question is, are you feeling better?"

He nodded. "I flew around all night and did a lot of thinking. Then I talked to a few people and researched some stuff."

"Who did you talk to?" Dragos asked.

Now it was his turn to wave that away. "That's not important. The main thing is, it helped."

"Good." Dragos said, "What else?"

Here we go.

"Thank you for offering to get me a puppy." He looked at both of them in turn. "It was really thoughtful of you. I did some thinking about that too, and I'd like to turn your gift into something bigger, if that's okay."

Pia's gaze went wide with interest. "What did you have in mind?"

"I want lots and lots of dogs. Sort of." He gave them a crooked grin. "I'd like for you to buy West River Animal Shelter."

Dragos's eyes narrowed. "You want us to buy an

animal shelter? Your mom already donates to several already."

Liam turned to Pia. "Yes, I know, but you only donate to no-kill shelters, right?"

"Of course," she said.

"West River doesn't have a no-kill policy," he told her. "I want us to buy it and turn it into a no-kill shelter so that one way or another, every dog that goes there gets a home."

Pia started to smile, and her eyes shone. She whirled to Dragos, who inclined his head and made an acquiescing gesture.

Dragos said, "As long as you two take care of all the details, I have no objections."

Liam grinned. "Thanks for the Christmas present."

"You are the most outstanding son anybody could ever wish for," Pia said as she threw her arms around him. "I love that idea so much, and I have no idea how to go about doing it."

"Are you kidding?" Dragos said dryly. "They will be ecstatic to get this offer. You do realize it will probably mean ongoing donations just to keep the shelter afloat."

"That's okay, I'll add it to my list," Pia said. She said to Liam, "You'll help me with things, won't you?"

"I'll help you as much as I can," Liam told her. "But that kinda leads me to the last thing I need to tell you." Dragos raised his eyebrows, and Pia looked at him expectantly. He braced himself. "This morning I applied to Glenhaven College."

Pia's face went blank with surprise. She said, "You did what?"

Dragos's expression darkened. He sat forward. "You applied to Glenhaven without talking to us?"

It was harder than he had expected to meet his father's blazing gaze, but he couldn't back down now. He said steadily, "Yes, I did."

"Absolutely not," Dragos snapped. "You're not going to Glenhaven. I forbid it."

Whoops, there was no throttling back his dragon at that one.

Liam snapped in reply, "You can't forbid me to go!"

Anger burned in his father's eyes. He snarled, "I can sure as hell refuse to pay for it!"

What the hell? "I didn't ask you to pay for anything!"

"Stop it," Pia said.

"You just asked me to pay for an animal shelter," Dragos shot back.

"What, are you going to refuse to do that now?" Liam felt his fists clenching. "So I guess I only get Christmas presents or college when I do what you say?"

Pia leaped to her feet and shouted, *"Stop it, both of you!"*

There was so much passion and forcefulness in her voice, both Liam and Dragos stopped to stare at her.

Her face was clenched, and tears stood in her eyes.

She pointed at Dragos. "You are saying things in the heat of anger, and you're going to regret them." Then she turned to Liam and told him fiercely, "Of course you get Christmas presents and college. But both of you need to take care right now. Remember that you love each other and act that way."

Unable to sit still any longer, Liam threw himself to his feet and started to pace. "I don't understand why you're trying to forbid me to go. It's the only option open to me that makes any sense."

"You'll have to pick another college," Dragos snapped. "Somewhere more accessible—maybe Harvard, or Yale. Glenhaven is far too remote and too secluded. If something were to happen, you wouldn't be able to get in touch with us. We wouldn't be able to get in contact with you, or help you."

Right now that sounded like heaven to him.

Liam forced himself to breathe evenly and managed not to say it. Instead, he said, "Harvard and Yale aren't appropriate, so if something were to happen, you'll just have to trust me to handle it."

Dragos shook his head. "You're too young."

"If you can't trust me to go away to college by myself," he said through gritted teeth, "then you sure as hell can't trust me to become a sentinel. But you're not expecting me to become a sentinel anyway—are you?"

His father said nothing. But then he didn't have to. His silence said it all.

Tired tears sprang to Liam's eyes, and he spun away to hide it.

"Look," Pia said, her voice sounding a little ragged. "College is a good idea for anybody, and so is finding independence. But Liam, there are a lot of reasons why your dad and I are not reacting well to this, especially after our trip to the Light Fae demesne last month."

He turned slightly at that. "What do you mean?"

"Before Tatiana split from the Seelie Court to form her demesne in Los Angeles, her twin sister Isabeau, the Light Fae Queen of the Seelie Court, and Dragos shared some kind of past together, and your father can't remember anything about it."

That brought him all the way around again. Frowning, he met Dragos's gaze. "Is that part of your memory loss from the construction accident a few months ago?"

"Yes," Dragos said, his voice edged. "Apparently I spent some time at the Seelie Court, and I don't know if Isabeau and I parted as friends or not. All we really know is that Isabeau is very dangerous, and so is her private army. After watching her attack on her sister's demesne, it's clear that she's not inclined to be a forgiving sort of woman. The United Kingdom isn't the safest place for a Cuelebre to be, Liam."

Exasperated, Liam flung up both hands. "The United Kingdom is a big place, Dad. Not only that, but Glenhaven closes their passageway during every term."

Dragos folded his arms. "The United Kingdom

might be a big place, but in many ways, the Elder Races world is a small one. Being my son will attract a lot of attention wherever you go."

Quickly, Liam crossed the living room. He said eagerly, "But that's the beauty of this—I don't want to go to college as a Cuelebre."

Pia stared at him. "Why not?"

He couldn't keep his fists from clenching again, as he said, "For the exact reason Dad just brought up. Please don't take this the wrong way, but you are a really hard act to follow. Your reputation is—well, it's just everywhere. There's no place I can go to escape it if I go as Liam Cuelebre."

Dragos's expression didn't change, but he blinked. He said roughly, "I didn't know you were having a problem with being my son, or that you felt the need to escape."

Agh. Now he had managed to hurt both his parents. Way to go, asshole.

Forcing his way past his own frustration, he reached for gentleness. "That's not what I meant. I love you, and I am proud to be your son. I'm just finding it difficult to live in your shadow. I have to figure out my own way to go in life." He looked at Pia. "I used your maiden name. I set up a new email address, rented a P.O. box, and I filled out the Glenhaven application as Liam Giovanni. I'm pretty sure that guy doesn't have a reputation anywhere that he needs to watch out for." He paused, and then in as neutral a tone as he could manage, he added, "Not only that, but he would probably qualify for either an academic or magical scholarship."

With that, he put everything out there. He knew he was gifted intellectually and magically. While he didn't come right out and say it, the information made it clear—he didn't need his parents' money to go to college. He didn't need their approval.

And he could see in their expressions that they knew it too. Pia blinked rapidly as she absorbed everything he said, while Dragos rubbed his forehead.

Liam's chest felt funny, heavy and dull. He walked over to the couch to sit beside his mom again and put his arm around her. As she leaned against his side, he hugged her and whispered, "I've really thought this through, and I want you to be happy for me."

"Okay," Dragos said suddenly. Both Pia and Liam turned to him in surprise.

"Okay?" Liam asked, hardly daring to hope. "You mean, it's okay if I go?"

"I've listened to your argument, and I've changed my mind. I think you're right." Dragos leaned forward, his elbows on his knees, and his hard-edged face looked alert. He looked at Pia. "This idea will work. We've always protected Liam's privacy, and we've kept a tight lid on his growth spurts. Even those who do know wouldn't necessarily recognize him after this latest one. Look at him. He looks more like you than he does me."

Nodding, Pia wiped her face. She said to Liam, "You would have to keep your Wyr form a secret. Sometimes that takes some tap dancing so you would have to stay on your guard, but you can do it."

"And I won't hear another word about you taking a scholarship," Dragos added. "You're my son. I will pay for your college, and living expenses, and anything else you need while you're in school."

This time, his father's autocratic way of speaking didn't bother him in the slightest. The heavy dull feeling eased, to be replaced by a rush of emotion so intense, tears sprang to his eyes again.

He muttered around a lump in his throat, "Thanks."

"Of course"—Dragos met his gaze—"I have stipulations."

Stipulations were fine. They were good—they weren't an outright refusal. "Oh yeah?" he replied. "Like what?"

"I want an undercover presence in Glenhaven, and another one in Edinburgh to protect the entrance to the crossover passageway. And you don't linger or go on a UK walkabout between terms. There's no sense in taking unnecessary chances. You go in, and when you come out, you leave Scotland entirely."

That all sounded reasonable. He nodded. "I can do that."

Pia said, "If you're sure that this is what's best for you, we'll help you any way we can. And we'll be here waiting when you're ready to come home."

Relief had him leaning sideways so that his head and shoulders fell into her lap. He muttered telepathically in her head, *I hate arguing with you.*

Well, technically, you argued with your dad, she told him, while she ran her fingers through his hair. *But I get your point. And I hated it too. Are we all better now?*

Comfort stole through him at her gentle touch, and he nodded again.

I'm proud of you, she told him.

Twisting onto his back, he looked up into her face. *You are?*

You thought things through, you used your best judgment and took independent action as the situation needed, and you didn't take no for an answer. She smiled down at him. *And who knows what the future will bring. After going to school, you might decide that you don't want to try for the sentinel position after all. But if you still want to—you know, all of those things that you just did are good qualities for a sentinel to have.*

They are?

Yes, they are.

For the first time in a week, he didn't feel the compulsion to fly away. Things had started to feel right again, and that allowed tiredness to take over. A huge yawn cracked his face.

Nearby, chair springs creaked as Dragos stood. He said, "I have to get back to work. Don't hold dinner for me. I think it's going to be a late night."

Pia nodded and said, "Okay. I'll have something

waiting for you in the fridge."

Dragos stepped forward to bend over Liam and kiss his forehead. Liam looked up into his father's fierce gold gaze.

Dragos said, "You are unexpectedly stubborn and resourceful. You're also a good boy, and I'm sorry I lost my temper. And I'm sorry you had to push to get us to recognize what you needed and wanted from us."

"It's all good," Liam said. "I mean, it's not like you guys were experts on what to do with a magically growing kid."

"Well, we're the only experts there are," Dragos told him wryly.

Liam grinned up at him, so happy not to be arguing with his dad anymore. Just plain stinking happy. "And I'm going to college!"

"Yes," his father said, returning his smile. "It appears that you are."

Chapter Four

W HEN EXHAUSTION SET in, it was sudden and fierce. Liam went to bed early and slept in late. The only reason he woke up at all was because Pia knocked on his door and then walked into his room.

"Get up, sleepyhead!" she said.

"*Mmph*," he grunted, and pulled his pillow over his head.

She dragged the bedcovers off his body. "I mean it—get up!"

"Mooooom, it's too early," he complained. "You sound disgustingly cheerful, and I don't need those covers anyway."

"It's not early—it's almost ten o'clock, Liam. Here, I brought you a cup of coffee."

He could smell the coffee from underneath his pillow, dark, rich and alluring. "Get thee behind me, Satan," he said experimentally.

She burst out laughing. "Where on earth did you hear that?"

"Some woman muttered it yesterday when she was looking at the pastries at Starbucks." Light fingers tickled his bare feet, and he jackknifed to a sitting position. "*Hey!* You cheated!"

"There's your beautiful face," she said cheerfully. She had set the coffee mug on his bedside table. "If you get up and shower right now, you'll have enough time to eat breakfast before we go to the West River Animal Shelter to meet with the executive director, Eileen Riley."

"What?" He stared at her then grabbed up the coffee cup. "But it's Christmas Eve!"

She opened her eyes wide. "I know, right? I emailed them a basic inquiry yesterday afternoon, but I wasn't expecting to hear back from them until after the holidays. Eileen just called me, and she would love to talk. Apparently they're having some serious financial difficulties, and she's willing to consider almost anything to keep the doors open. She said my email was the Christmas miracle they'd been hoping for." Pia paused and tilted her head. "You didn't by any chance know anything about that somehow, did you?"

"No," he said. He gulped coffee and stood up. "I just did some quick searches on Yelp and a reference librarian helped me compile a list of shelters. Then I checked addresses, and West River was close enough that I could stop by from time to time to see how things are going."

"Well, hurry up," she told him. "We leave in forty-five minutes. And we have to get you a haircut sometime today. You're starting to look like a sulky rock star."

"Well, I *am* a rock star," he said, deadpan.

She laughed. "That you are."

Galvanized into action, he showered in record time and dressed in jeans, lumberjack-style boots and a navy blue, ribbed pullover sweater. When he strode into the kitchen Pia had another cup of coffee waiting for him, along with a huge sandwich. He leaned back against the counter, took a large bite and said around his mouthful, "Where's Dad?"

"Working." A shadow fell over Pia's face.

He paused with the sandwich halfway to his mouth. "Is it stuff about Con?"

"Probably," she said. The shadow passed, and she smiled at him. "He said if he can get away for an hour, he would join us in a bit. Not to look at the animals, of course. The poor things would be terrified of him."

"I won't go look at them either," he muttered, as he finished his breakfast in record time. "They'll be terrified of me too."

Pia dumped his dishes into the sink. "You never know, they might have some puppies and kittens that you can visit with. Let's go."

He grabbed his leather jacket, she slipped into her coat, and together, they went downstairs where Pia's guard and friend Eva waited with a warm car. Pia climbed into the front passenger seat while Liam took the backseat. He watched the snowy city streets scroll past while the two women chatted.

Hopefully soon, someone from Glenhaven would read his application and get in touch with him. The college had three terms a year, and the next term started directly after New Year's. His stomach knotted with equal parts fear and excitement.

I might be leaving home in a few weeks, he thought. That is, if Glenhaven has any room for new students. What if there's a waitlist? What if I can't get in for a year?

It was the first time he had considered the possibility, and the thought was unwelcome. He knew he was privileged and lucky in so many ways. For the most part, things happened the way he needed them to, and if for some reason they didn't, his parents moved heaven and earth to make sure they did.

But Liam Giovanni didn't have that kind of support. He couldn't, not and still keep his identity a secret.

He blurted out, "What if I don't get in?"

Pia and Eva fell silent for a moment. Eva asked, "Get in where?"

"I'll fill you in on everything later," Pia told her. Twisting in her seat to look at him, Pia said, "Honey, all any admissions counselor has to do is see how you can run fire up and down your hands and arms, while not getting burned. Believe me, they'll let you in. They'll probably try to shove a scholarship at you too, no matter what your father says."

His panic subsided a bit. He muttered, "I sure hope

so."

"Try not to worry." Pia reached back to pat his knee. "Everything is going to be okay."

Her reassurance helped, but only a little. Because what if it wasn't? Sometimes things weren't okay. People died, and bad things happened.

A shiver ran down his spine, but he slid into silence again, crossing his arms and hunching in his seat as much as his seat belt would let him as he stared out the window.

West River Animal Shelter was located in a rundown industrial area in the southeast section of Midtown West, just north of the Lincoln Tunnel and close to the Hudson River. There wasn't a parking lot, so as Eva looked for a place to park, Pia turned around to Liam again.

"If you're going to college as Liam Giovanni, we have to start working now to keep your identity a secret. We can't tell anybody at the shelter about you." Pia's gaze was serious as she searched his expression. "We can't explain that my magical son wanted us to buy the organization. As far as most of the world knows, you're still a baby."

"Yeah, I get it," he said. "I'm cool with that."

"And besides, I don't even know if you can buy a nonprofit. We'll probably have to make a large enough donation so that we can get a seat on the board and change policy from there."

"I'm cool with that too," he said. "I just want to

change it so that it has a no-kill policy."

"Well, one way or another, we'll get that done." She smiled at him. "And in the meantime, you need to be one of my guards for this trip. Okay?"

He shrugged. "Sure."

Finally, Eva located a spot and backed into it, and Liam opened his door to step out on the snow-packed street. He followed Pia and Eva into the utilitarian-looking building, while he noted how Eva's restless dark gaze never seemed to stop roaming.

Eva had been an excellent soldier. She had commanded the unit that Hugh had been in, and now she made just as excellent a bodyguard. But she would never make a sentinel. What was the difference?

Eva was a canine Wyr, and her lifespan was nowhere near that of one of the immortals, but that wasn't the difference. Dragos didn't make a distinction between the immortal Wyr and the others—Eva was just as welcome as anybody else to try for a sentinel position if she wanted it, and if she won the position, it would be hers for as long as she could do her job.

No, it was something else. Perhaps it was fire.

Eva didn't have the drive to become a sentinel. While she had alpha tendencies, she had been content to be a unit commander, and she liked being Pia's bodyguard. But Liam couldn't imagine any of the sentinels being content with such a position for long, even though they liked to wear a laid-back demeanor.

So aside from ability, experience and ruthlessness,

did a sentinel need to be driven as well? And if so, did Liam have that kind of fire in him for the position?

All he knew for certain was that he was going to be asking himself a lot of questions during the upcoming year.

Inside, the large lobby was utilitarian as well. Somebody had tried to make up for it by painting the concrete block walls with bright colors, and a large fake Christmas tree stood in one corner, decorated with pet toys and leashes.

They walked to the front reception desk where Pia gave her name. The elderly receptionist spoke on the phone and then told them that the executive director would be out in just a moment.

Smells assaulted Liam's sensitive nose—disinfectant, along with the scents of stressed animals. A man and two young girls walked past them with a border collie mix on leash. As it neared Liam, the dog shrieked and tried to pull out of its collar.

His heart sinking, he quickly retreated until the family could calm the dog enough to walk it out the front door. Out of the corner of his eye, he saw his mom give him a sad look before Pia turned to the front receptionist and asked, "Do you have a section with puppies?"

"We sure do," the receptionist told her. "All the puppies that are up for adoption are through that glass door. You'll be able to see it in a moment. I'm sure Eileen will want to give you a tour."

"Certainly," Pia said. She looked at Liam and told him telepathically, *Go visit with the puppies if you want.*

He hesitated. *You don't mind?*

Of course not. She smiled at him. *We'll just be talking about annual budgets and policy changes anyway. Go—enjoy yourself. I've got this.*

Thanks. As a brisk gray-haired woman strode up to Pia and Eva, Liam stuck his hands in the pockets of his jeans and strolled over to the glass door that led to the area where the adoptable puppies were kept.

On the other side of the door, a long room held a series of pens with waist-high gates. High squeaks and yaps sounded as he approached.

He peered over the first gate, but that kennel was empty. The next held three sleeping Chihuahua puppies, curled in a pile on a folded blanket. He smiled as he looked at their small, round bellies.

The third kennel held two Rottweiler mix puppies that rolled along the floor and play-fought with each other. He clicked his tongue at them and snapped his fingers, but they ignored him.

Indifference was a lot better than outright panic. Shrugging, he moved on.

The fourth kennel was the largest and it held the most. Seven puppies gamboled about. It was hard to tell what kind of breed mix they were. There seemed to be some German shepherd, along with maybe a splash of golden retriever, or something else he couldn't identify. The result was that the puppies looked somewhat wolfish, with narrow noses, yellow-gold eyes, and brown and tan markings on their soft, shaggy pelts.

As he watched, one puppy chewed its hind leg while one of its litter mates stalked up to it and pounced. Liam laughed as the pair fell over, growling at each other.

Bending over the gate, he reached down to pet one of the largest of the puppies. It promptly turned to gnaw on his fingers with needle-sharp teeth. Another, smaller puppy fixed on him and bounded to the gate. It scrabbled at the barrier.

The thing was, his parents hadn't been wrong. He really would have loved to have a puppy. But now he was going away to school, or at least he hoped he was.

If everything went well, he would be leaving behind everyone he knew. His mother and father. His new baby brother. He would be gambling everything to take a shot at a big unknown.

If everything didn't go well, and he didn't get into Glenhaven in time for the next term, he truly had no idea what he was going to do with himself.

He wished he had friends, because he could sure use a friend to talk to right now. But there was nobody. His last bunch of friends were years behind him in age and development. He had left them far behind with this latest growth spurt, and they wouldn't be looking at going to college for years.

He'd had a good talk with Hugh, but Hugh was like

an uncle. Hugh could offer good advice, but he couldn't empathize with where Liam was at. Because nobody was where Liam was at. He was surrounded by people who loved him, yet he had never felt lonelier.

Everything felt at once too big and yet too restrictive. His chest constricted, and he couldn't breathe as the wide, wild world crushed down on him.

A woman bent over the gate beside him and held a long-fingered, tawny hand out to one of the puppies. She asked, "Which one are you going to pick?"

Liam paused, puzzled. He hadn't heard anyone come in through the glass door. He must have been more preoccupied with the puppies than he had realized.

"I'm just visiting with them," he said in a choked voice. "I can't actually have one."

"Of course you can have one." The woman scratched the puppy behind its ear, and it sat down, lifted its head to her and closed its eyes in bliss.

It was an odd thing to say to a total stranger. Liam gave her a sidelong, wary glance. The woman was dressed in a long black and gold tunic and black trousers, and thick gold bangles dangled at her wrists. As they both were leaning over the gate, he couldn't see much of her face, just a strong, high cheekbone and the graceful curve of her jaw.

It was hard to tell from such a position, but her body was long and muscled, and she looked as though she might be as tall as he was. Tawny hair curled down her back, as wild and untamed as a lion's mane.

"No, I really can't," he told her, leaning his elbows on the gate. "I might be going away to college soon."

"And you can't have a puppy while you're in college?"

Taken aback, he muttered, "Well, I—I guess I don't know. I hadn't really thought about it. I was sort of expecting that I might be staying in a dorm. If I get to go at all. Right now, my whole life feels like a blank page."

The woman picked up the puppy she had been petting. It wriggled happily in her hands, and she kissed its nose. "If your life is a blank page, that only means you have room to write your story. You have the power to tell that story the way you want to. I agree, staying in a dorm wouldn't be possible with a puppy. But if you stayed in an apartment, you could have one—that is, if you really wanted one. After all, young Cuelebre, it isn't as though your family can't afford to put you up in an apartment."

The walls seemed to reverberate with her words.

Young Cuelebre, she had said. Somehow this strange woman knew who he was. His hackles rose. Compulsively he scanned her for magic, or any other hint of Power.

There was nothing. Sucking in a breath, he tried to catch her scent.

All he could smell was the overwhelming, earthy smell of puppies that were too young to be housebroken.

Staring at the stranger's profile, he whispered, "How do you know to say that name?"

Chapter Five

THE WOMAN DIDN'T turn to face him. He watched the corner of her full mouth lift into a smile as the puppy in her cradling hands curled into a ball and fell asleep. "Everyone knows that name, young Cuelebre. Isn't that why you are willing to travel halfway across the world to get away from it?"

He hissed, *"Who are you?"*

"That doesn't matter," she said, dismissing his question with a shrug. "All that really matters is that everything does depend on what you want. If you want a puppy badly enough, you'll do whatever it takes to have one, and you'll fight to keep it."

As she spoke, he looked around wildly for any clues as to her identity. His gaze fell to the border of her tunic. Lions were embroidered along the bottom.

His pulse pounded in his ears. Slowly, he said, "You're wearing lions. Inanna, the goddess of Love, always has lions."

"Fitting, don't you think?" She stroked the puppy's forehead with a long, tapered forefinger. "So many people think love is an emotion. I love you, they say, and that is supposed to excuse all their bad behaviors and elevate them to a higher level just because they happen to feel something. That isn't love; it's an excuse. Love is like a lion. It's fierce and strong. It conquers fear and uncertainties, and it knows how to fight. Love fights to win and keep its mate, to do the right thing, to give to others in service, no matter what the cost. 'Greater love has no one than this: to lay down one's life for one's friends.'"

The scene blurred as tears filled Liam's eyes. He swiped at his nose. "That sounds like a quote."

"It is a quote," said the woman. "It's attributed to the man whose birthday is celebrated all over the world every December. Your sentinel Constantine knew of it. That man might have been a mess, but he knew how to love."

He whispered, "It also leaves a hole behind when they go."

"Yes, it does, and that is when you know you had something worth having." The woman turned to him. "If you really want a puppy, I think you should pick this one. She isn't the biggest in the litter, but she'll grow to be a strong, fine dog. Her life will be much too short, and you'll grieve when she's gone, but while she lives that life, she will stand by you through all your uncertainties. She'll comfort you when you are alone, even when you journey to a distant, strange place, and she'll guard your back when you need protection. And she will love you with all of her loyal, fierce heart. That, young Cuelebre, is a worthy companion to have."

"But what if I take her, and the college won't let me keep her?" he asked.

Anxiously, he thought, what if the college won't take me in time?

Through the blur of his tears, he saw the woman smile.

"This is where you have a little faith that things will work out all right," she said. She offered the sleeping puppy to him, and without thinking, he reached out to receive it. The small, delicate body filled his hands.

The puppy stirred at the disruption, and it tried to open its eyes, but it was too sleepy. Showing its tongue in a wide, pink-tipped yawn, it sniffed at the air then snuggled into his palms.

As he looked down at the soft, warm body he cradled, the constriction around his chest finally began to ease. Warmth stole in, and comfort.

Look at her little puppy head. And those little puppy ears. Gently, he rubbed one of her paws. She stretched out her short, stubby puppy legs with a sigh, and he lost his heart.

Blinking hard to clear his gaze, he lifted his head to get a better look at the woman.

She was gone. There wasn't anybody in the large room, except for him.

He trembled. "Okay, that was pretty weird," he whispered to the puppy as he cradled her against his chest. "She was probably just another oddball New

Yorker, right? Goddesses don't talk to guys just because they're having some kind of internal meltdown. Right?"

The glass door swung open, and he spun around to face it.

Pia and the older woman walked into the room, and both were smiling.

"How did it go?" he asked his mom.

"For a first meeting, it went really well," she said. She turned to the other woman. "Eileen, thank you for taking the time to meet with me on Christmas Eve."

"It was entirely my pleasure, Lady Cuelebre," Eileen said as she held out her hand to shake. "Again, on behalf of the shelter, I can't thank you enough. I'll set up a time for the board to meet as soon after the New Year as I can."

"And in the meantime," Pia said with a pointed glance at Liam, "there will be no more animals euthanized unless medically you have no other option."

"Absolutely. We're still overcrowded, but with your very generous donation, we'll be able to hire new staff and buy enough supplies to care for all the animals we do have."

"Very good." Pia smiled.

The other woman gave Liam a curious glance, but other than that, she didn't comment on his presence. "Well, if you'll excuse me, I have a lot to attend to before we close this evening."

"Please, go do what you need to do," Pia told her.

"I can see myself out."

"Merry Christmas," Eileen said, smiling at both of them.

"Merry Christmas," Pia and Liam replied together.

As soon as the other woman walked out of the room, Pia turned to look at Liam and the puppy.

"Your father texted to say he couldn't get free, but he's definitely going to be done by this evening, and he's taking tomorrow off so that we can travel back home. We've got to get ready for Isalynn Lefevre's niece to visit from the witches demesne in mid January. Then our part in that damn diplomatic pact made in DC two months ago will be done." Her smile turned indulgent. "That puppy is so darn cute, I can hardly stand it. She looks like a baby wolf, but I can't imagine the shelter would have let wolf mixed breeds be available for general adoption."

Liam listened with only half his attention. 'Have a little faith', the strange woman who was probably not a goddess had said. Still, it was good advice.

He bent his head over the sleeping puppy. "I want her."

"Aw." Pia's voice softened sympathetically. "It's hard to let go when puppy lust takes hold, isn't it?"

"No, you don't understand," Liam said, looking up at his mom. "I really want her."

Pia's expression changed. "But honey—you're going to college. Aren't you? You were so adamant about Glenhaven yesterday."

"Oh, I'm still going if they'll have me." Smiling down at the dog, he stroked her small back. "I want to take the puppy with me. It will mean I can't stay in any dorms.… But you know, after thinking about it, I don't think I want to stay in a dorm anyway. I'm going to have to be on guard all the time about who I am and what my Wyr form is, and I think I really need to have a space where I can have some privacy to unwind." He added, "That is, if I can get in for the next term."

He was trying to have a little faith, but at the moment, that didn't take away any of his uncertainty.

Shifting her weight back onto one foot, Pia tilted her jaw as she thought about it. "You make a really good point about needing privacy," she said slowly. "I don't think any of us had gotten that far in our thinking yesterday. And I like the idea of you having a pet with you. It's really hard for me to think about you being off at school alone and cut off from us."

"There, you see," he crooned at his puppy.

"But Liam, she's going to be a lot of work. You'll have to potty train her, make sure she gets all her shots, and she will restrict your social life. You'll always be running home to let her out at lunchtime, and you might not get a full night's sleep for a couple of months. And there's other training to consider. By the size of those paws, she's going to grow up to be a big dog. You'll need to make sure she's well behaved."

"I don't need a lot of sleep," he told her. Bending farther, he pressed a kiss to the puppy's soft, furry head. "And I'll potty train her, and train her to be good, and I'll spend lunchtimes with her too. I want her badly enough, I'll do whatever I have to in order to keep her. Okay?"

His mom took a deep breath. "Well," she said. "I think that's all any of us could ask you to do. As long as you're sure."

"I'm sure." He grinned at her.

She grinned back at him. "Holy smokes, my son is going off to college, and I'm only twenty six years old."

"Well, we *think* so," he stressed. "I *hope* so."

"*Pfft!*" She waved that aside. "And you're getting a dog too! Oh my God, we have so much stuff we need to buy. And we need to buy it right now, before the stores close for the night. What does a baby dog need? I have no idea."

"A bed, and a crate, and chew toys, and a collar and leash," he said. "Really good dog food. The best."

She stared at him. "She's going to piddle everywhere, and the penthouse is seventy-nine floors away from ground level. How do people have puppies in high-rise apartments? Somehow, they do."

While she spoke, the glass door opened again, and Eva strolled through. The other woman took one look at the puppy snoring in Liam's arms and started to laugh.

"You know what to do for living with a puppy in a high-rise apartment, don't you?" Liam asked her, giving his best coaxing smile.

Eva snorted. "Are you joking? You're not, are you? You're really going to adopt that dog? Okay, well, as long as you're staying in the penthouse, you're going to want pee pads and a grass litter box that you can set up on the balcony. There's plenty of room out there, so you can even tuck it out of sight if you want."

"A grass litter box?" Pia said cautiously.

"It's a square of real turf or artificial turf in a big fancy box with a sprinkler system and a drainage option," Eva told her. She paused. "Since it's the dead of winter right now, you'll obviously want to get the artificial turf."

Liam turned to his mom. "Do we need to get that if we're going home tomorrow anyway?"

"Yes," she said firmly. "You never know when we might need to come back to the city, and as long as you have that puppy, it will be good to have on hand."

"Perfect," Liam said with satisfaction. Happiness buoyed his spirits so that he laughed with joy.

"What are you going to name her?" Eva asked with a grin.

"I haven't decided yet." The puppy lay like a dead weight in his arms, her body lax in complete trust. "I was thinking of naming her Marika, or maybe Rika for short."

Pia raised her eyebrows. "After that little Dark Fae girl you went to school with in first grade?"

"Yup." He rubbed the puppy's round belly. "I have a feeling she's going to be just as fierce as Marika was."

"I like it," Pia declared. "It's a good name. Come on, we've got a lot to do. Let's get you through the adoption process, so we can pick up everything we need."

Liam reminded her, "You'll have to adopt her. Officially, I mean. Liam's too young, remember?"

Pia threw up her hands. *"Oy vey."*

LATER THAT EVENING, everything was done. All the supplies had been bought and delivered, and Liam had even set up the fancy grass litter box out on the balcony.

Eva had been right. There was plenty of room for Liam to tuck the large litter box out of sight, at least from the living room, and also against one of the concrete support pylons so that it was somewhat sheltered from the winter wind.

He was sprawled on the floor, playing tug of war with Rika while Pia cooked dinner, when his dad strode into the penthouse.

When Dragos laid eyes on Liam and the puppy, he stopped dead. His entrance got Rika's attention. The puppy turned to consider him, head cocked.

Then with a playful bark, she bounced across the room to attack one of Dragos's shoes.

Dragos cocked his head and gave Liam such an expressive look, he burst out laughing. "Mom!" he shouted. "Did you by any chance forget to tell Dad that we were bringing a puppy home?"

Something clattered in the kitchen. Pia said, "Damn it. Yes."

"Stop it," Dragos told the dog.

Growling, Rika tugged at his shoelace then sat to chew on one end. Bending, Dragos picked her up by the scruff of the neck and lifted her until she was at eye level. He told the puppy, "I said stop."

In answer, she yipped and wriggled, and tried to bite at his fingers.

Dragos carried her over to Liam and deposited her in his lap. "I'm sure there is a perfectly reasonable story attached to this."

"Absolutely," Liam said.

"And what about Glenhaven?" Dragos asked, one eyebrow up.

"I'm going to take her with me—if I get in. I guess we'll know one way or another, soon enough." He stroked Rika then set her on the floor. She promptly ran over to Dragos to bite at his shoelace again. Laughing, Liam lunged after her to scoop her up. "Sorry. I'll take her out."

"I'll just go make sure all the closet doors are closed." Dragos strode down the hall.

Liam carried Rika out onto the balcony and set her on the fake turf in the litter box. With a gigantic effort, she jumped off the box and raced around the balcony. He went after her and set her on the litter box. Happily she jumped off again. She loved the litter box game.

Somehow, it would all work out, he told himself for

the thousandth time.

If he got into Glenhaven.

Realistically, it might take weeks before he knew anything. Waiting to hear one way or another was going to kill him.

His phone rang in his jeans pocket. Digging it out while he set Rika on the litter box again, he checked the number. The call wasn't from any number he recognized. He thumbed the answer button and said, "Hello?"

"Good evening, is this Liam Giovanni?" a pleasant male voice asked.

In a Scottish accent.

Surprise pounded in his ears. Clearing his throat, he replied, "Yes, it is. Who's calling?"

"My name is Ian Killian. I'm a representative of Glenhaven College. Is this a good time to talk?"

"Sure," he said. "I wasn't expecting to hear from you. At least, I mean, not so quickly, and it's Christmas Eve."

"Ach, Christmas Eve," Killian said in a tone that clearly dismissed such human things. "I had traveled to New York for the Masque, and I was about to leave for home again when I received an email from the dean with your application attached. I know this is short notice, but my flight leaves for Edinburgh tomorrow evening—would you by any chance have time to meet in person in the morning?"

"A-absolutely," he stuttered, while he fist pumped

and leaped into the air, making Rika fall over from surprise. She bounded to her feet and barked at him.

"When and where would you like to meet?" Killian asked briskly.

Cupping his phone to shield the microphone from the puppy's barking, he tried to think. "Since tomorrow's Christmas, there's actually not going to be much open," he said slowly. Dare he suggest it? "How about the Starbucks in Cuelebre Tower? The Tower is centrally located, and that Starbucks never closes."

"A sensible suggestion," Killian told him. "Let's say nine o'clock? It shouldna take long, just a half an hour or so."

"Sure," he said. "That would be great. Thank you."

"All right, I'll see you then."

Quickly, before the older male could hang up, Liam said, "Wait—Do you mind me asking what to expect tomorrow?"

"Not at all," Killian replied. "Your application looks quite impressive, young man. I'll just be wanting to verify some of the details. Perhaps you can show me a touch of your talents. If everything looks to be in order, I'll be submitting your request for a scholarship to the finance committee."

That sounded like it could be a lengthy process. He frowned. "How long will that take?"

"Scholarship students are fully funded, which is an expensive process, so the committee might not approve your application for another six months to a year."

His lips tightened. Rika was starting to shiver, so he scooped her up and tucked her inside his sweater, where she snuggled against his chest and promptly fell asleep.

He said, "What if I told you I've come up with financing on my own, so I won't be needing a scholarship after all?"

"Ach, well, that changes things completely," Killian said.

"Do you think my application might be approved in time for me to start the next term? I mean, if there's room for Glenhaven to take me."

"Young man, I can approve your application when I meet you tomorrow. As long as everything is in order, of course. And yes, there's room for you to start this next term, if you can be ready by then, and you don't mind being flexible on what kind of housing you get. If your financing is enough to allow you to get your own apartment, you should be fine. The new term begins on January fifteenth, so that isn't much time for you to prepare. But we can talk all about that tomorrow morning, so be sure to come with a list of your questions."

Excitement pounded through his body. He could hardly believe it, but it sounded like everything really would fall into place. "Yes—yes, I will. Thank you so much, Mr. Killian!"

"You're welcome, Mr. Giovanni. See you in the

morning."

As Killian disconnected, Liam let out a loud whoop. Rika was sound asleep by that point and never stirred, but Dragos and Pia strode quickly into the living room, drawn by the noise.

He rushed inside and waved his phone at them. "That was a representative from Glenhaven College! He wants to meet me tomorrow morning!"

"You're kidding," Pia said faintly. "Already?"

"He said he came to New York for the Masque, so he's already here. The dean forwarded my application to him, and his flight leaves tomorrow evening, so we're meeting in the morning! The next term starts January fifteenth, so it's not quite as soon as I was afraid it would be. And if I can afford an apartment, he said there would be space for me!"

His dad and mom gave each other a long look. It was complicated, that look, filled with a lot of things Liam didn't know how to categorize. Wryness was there, and a touch of sadness, along with pride and acceptance.

"Kids these days," Dragos said quietly. "They grow up so fast."

"Supersonic fast," Pia said just as quietly. She laid a hand on her flat abdomen. "I guess we need to fasten our seat belts, because we're about to go through it all again."

It touched Liam's heart, how much they loved him. "Come on," he said gently. "Be happy for me."

Immediately, Pia strode over to throw her arms around him and hug him, puppy and all. "I am so happy for you," she told him. "And so proud of you, I don't know what to do with myself. I'm not going to lie to you, Liam—I just hate the thought of Glenhaven closing its doors for an entire term. But I understand why you need this, and I'm behind you every step of the way."

Dragos strode over and clapped him on the shoulder. "Good job. I'm proud of you too."

"Well," he felt compelled to say, "I'm not in quite yet."

"Oh, for heaven's sake, *pfft*," Pia said, brushing his caution aside with a wave of her hand. "You're in."

"I think this calls for a toast," Dragos said. He looked into Liam's eyes with a smile. "How about a glass of champagne?"

Liam perked up. He wondered if he would like champagne. He knew he would like finding that out. "Hell yeah."

Pia's eyes sparkled. "Dinner's in the oven, so while we drink champagne and the puppy sleeps, I think we should open a few presents."

Liam nodded. "I second that idea."

While Dragos and Pia left to collect a chilled bottle of champagne and three flutes, Liam pulled Rika out from underneath his sweater and carefully settled her on her new dog bed. She was so sound asleep, she never noticed a thing.

"You need to crate her tonight," Pia said as she came back into the room carrying the champagne flutes. "She needs to get used to sleeping in her own bed, even if she cries a bit at first."

He nodded. Probably so. But he had a feeling he would let her out of the crate and let her sleep with him.

Dragos strolled back into the room, a bottle of champagne in one hand. Pia and Liam watched as he opened it and poured the frothing golden drink into the flutes. When he was done, Pia handed the flutes around, and then she raised hers in the air.

"To family," she said. "We can get through anything together. Even arguments and really weird stuff. Merry Christmas, guys. I love you with all my heart."

They clinked glasses, and Liam tasted champagne for the first time. He said, "Oh God. Oh damn."

Dragos and Pia laughed, and Dragos asked, "Is that good or bad?"

"It's very, very good." He took another sip and savored the flavor. He said fervently, "I love taste buds."

Dragos held his flute up for another toast. As Pia and Liam joined him, he looked at Liam and smiled.

Dragos said, "To your future, son. May it always be bright, and may you find your way home again when you're ready."

They clinked glasses again. Thinking of the golden

woman, Liam asked, "Even if it is filled with really weird stuff?"

His parents laughed.

"Even then," Dragos replied.

Pia had the final word on that toast, as she added, "Especially then."

Thank you!

Dear Readers,

Thank you for reading *A Dragon's Famly Album II*! This is a collection of two previously published novellas and a short story—Dragos Goes to Washington, Pia Does Hollywood, and Liam Takes Manhattan.

While each of my Elder Races novellas can be read on their own, all of them expand on the world-building in the Elder Races universe. Many of them are a series of linked stories that are best enjoyed when read together. For example, the first Elder Races novella is True Colors, which is the beginning of four linked Tarot novellas, including Natural Evil, Devil's Gate, and Hunter's Season. If you enjoyed *A Dragon's Family Album II* and you haven't yet read the previous stories, check them out!

Would you like to stay in touch and hear about new releases? You can:

- Sign up for my monthly email at: www.theaharrison.com
- Follow me on Twitter at @TheaHarrison
- Like my Facebook page at facebook.com/TheaHarrison

Reviews help other readers find the books they like to read. I appreciate each and every review, whether positive or negative.

Happy reading!
Thea

Look for these titles from Thea Harrison